THE WALLS OF WUCHANG

FANG FANG

Translated by
Olivia Milburn

SINOIST

ACA Publishing Ltd
University House
11-13 Lower Grosvenor Place,
London SW1W 0EX, UK
Tel: +44 20 3289 3885
E-mail: info@alaincharlesasia.com
Web: www.alaincharlesasia.com

Beijing Office
Tel: +86(0)10 8472 1250

Author: Fang Fang (Wang Fang)
Translator: Olivia Milburn

Published by Sinoist Books (an imprint of ACA Publishing Ltd) in association with the People's Literature Publishing House

Original Chinese Text © 武昌城 (Wǔ Chāng Chéng) 2011, People's Literature Publishing House, Beijing, China

English Translation text © 2020 ACA Publishing Ltd, London, UK

ALL RIGHTS RESERVED. NO PART OF THIS PUBLICATION MAY BE REPRODUCED IN MATERIAL FORM, BY ANY MEANS, WHETHER GRAPHIC, ELECTRONIC, MECHANICAL OR OTHER, INCLUDING PHOTOCOPYING OR INFORMATION STORAGE, IN WHOLE OR IN PART, AND MAY NOT BE USED TO PREPARE OTHER PUBLICATIONS WITHOUT WRITTEN PERMISSION FROM THE PUBLISHER.

This novel is entirely a work of fiction. The names, characters and incidents portrayed in it are the work of the author's imagination. Any resemblance to actual persons, living or dead, events or localities is entirely coincidental.

Paperback ISBN: 978-1-83890-511-8
eBook ISBN: 978-1-83890-500-2

A catalogue record for Walls of Wuchang is available from the National Bibliographic Service of the British Library.

THE WALLS OF WUCHANG

FANG FANG

Translated by
OLIVIA MILBURN

SINOIST BOOKS

PART I

ATTACKING THE WALLS

1

AT THAT MOMENT, the evening sky was very dark, and the black clouds looked so heavy it seemed as though they might fall and crush you.

Luo Yinan felt even more depressed. As he jumped into a boat at Hankou to cross the Yangtze River, he shouted: "Hurry! Faster!"

The boatman looked across to the opposite bank and muttered: "It's a big river. You have to row across it, one stroke at a time, and shouting won't make the blindest bit of difference."

The vast Yangtze River rolled on in silence, ceaselessly. Although it was the very height of summer, there was a refreshing coolth out there on the waters. However, Luo Yinan was in no fit state to enjoy it. The phone call had been interrupted by annoying static, but the bad news still came across loud and clear: Chen Dingyi had been beheaded![1] His head was hanging over Government Gate!

Luo Yinan's hand that was holding the phone shook violently. Why did I make this call? he asked himself. Why?

His uncle was hard at work out in the courtyard, using a bow to fluff up cotton for a quilt. Even from his position on the far side of the flower-patterned lattice window, his uncle could see that something was very wrong, and he called out: "What on earth is the matter?" Luo Yinan was leaning against the tall table under the window. The inlaid silver bird stretched its wings across the tabletop as if it were just about to fly off, shimmering in the bright light. Luo Yinan looked petrified; he did not answer. The bowstring his uncle was using to fluff up the cotton was dancing about in the sun as layer after layer of grey batting turned white, but to him the world had suddenly gone dim.

It was the summer of 1926.

His uncle made a living by fluffing cotton for the people of Hankou, and normally he had Luo Yinan's cousin to help him. But just the last couple of days, his cousin had bad blisters on his feet, which made walking extremely painful. Luo Yinan had come to visit his aunt and ended up staying with them. His cousin had begged him: "You have to help me out here!" He had always been close to his cousin, so he was happy to agree. The owner of all this cotton batting was a rich businessman, surnamed Bai. Year after year, he would ask Luo Yinan's uncle to come and make freshly fluffed cotton for the family's bedding, so what with one thing and another they ended up knowing each other quite well.

The Bai family had put in a telephone; their young master was a middle-school student, and when he heard that Luo Yinan was studying in Wuchang (maybe this was him being kind, or maybe he was just showing off), he said: "Would you like to speak to one of the other students at Wuchang? You can use our telephone!" Luo Yinan was curious, and he was missing his ex-girlfriend Shuya, so he picked up the phone. Shuya had dumped him a couple of months earlier, and none of the reasons she had given made any sense to him. He had been really angry and upset about it all, though he tried to look calm as he said that he accepted her decision. He knew that Shuya came from a rich family, but he himself was poor. In the world they lived in, such an unequal background would make it very difficult no matter how much they loved each other. But even though several months had now passed, he was still suffering over it all. He didn't blame Shuya, but he was angry that people could be so heartless. Suddenly, he felt a powerful urge to hear her voice again, so he tried to phone her a number of times, and in the end he was put through. He could hear Shuya speaking, but what she was telling him through the crackling of static was horrifying: Chen Dingyi had been beheaded.

Luo Yinan could not believe he was dead; he had to go and see this with his own eyes. He told his uncle what had happened and ran towards the river. Young Master Bai ran after him and asked: "The man who had his head cut off was a member of the Revolutionary Party, wasn't he? Why are you in such a hurry? Are you one of them too?" Luo Yinan paid no attention to him.

The steam launch that ran a regular service across the river had not arrived yet, so there were only rowing boats waiting by the bank. The boatman wanted to go to Wuchang anyway, so he jumped straight in. The river kept on flowing past: no matter how much the world around it changes, it is always the same. Looking down at the waters, Luo Yinan felt an inexpressible anger and pain, or perhaps he was simply terrified. When the boat got close to the bank, without waiting for it to dock properly, he hurled himself out. The boatman was not happy about this and shouted: "Don't be in such a hurry! You won't escape death that way!"

Luo Yinan ran down the road as fast as he could, with the voice of the boatman following on behind him like a shadow. He ran as quickly as if he really were trying to escape death. Hanyang Gate was already crammed with traumatised people, and his mad rush frightened them even more.

Luo Yinan ran all the way to Huo Alley, by Government Gate. He stopped and caught his breath under the shuttered windows of an old house by the entrance to the alleyway. He might have been trying to pluck up courage, or he might have been trying to prepare himself for what he was about to see. He paused for a moment and then raised his head.

There was a head hanging up there.

The head had its eyes half-closed, and the calm expression on its face was one that Luo Yinan was very familiar with. It had always been a long face, but now it was even longer than ever. Of course it was Chen Dingyi. Luo Yinan felt his legs buckling under him; he wanted to sit down, but he also wanted to howl. When he first came to Wuchang to study, standing on the bank of the Yangtze River, seeing such a vast body of water, he started to feel excited. Without even bothering to take off his clothes, he jumped into the river for a swim. He had no idea how dangerous the Yangtze River could be and almost drowned himself. It happened that Chen

Dingyi was rowing across in a small boat and jumped into the river to save him, dragging him up onto the bank. His classmate Liang Wenqi had been travelling in the same boat as Chen Dingyi. Liang Wenqi was shocked and exclaimed: "That's Luo Yinan! Dingyi, you've just saved one of my classmates!" That was the first time they met.

Chen Dingyi was absolutely obsessed with the revolution and regularly came to school looking for Liang Wenqi. Liang Wenqi was a lively young man and often went out and about. So when Chen Dingyi couldn't find him, he would go and look for Luo Yinan. If it got too late, he would stay overnight at his place. That was how they became friends. Chen Dingyi often said that he was sent by heaven to save China. Thanks to his grandmother, Luo Yinan had been brought up as a Buddhist, besides which he had just discovered the works of Su Manshu and didn't have much time for anything else: he really wasn't interested in any revolution.

Liang Wenqi often expressed his surprise at their friendship, saying: "You two are so different – how can you be friends?"

Chen Dingyi would smile and say nothing, but Luo Yinan told him: "It is because he saved my life."

But now he was still alive and his friend was dead. Luo Yinan desperately tried to remember everything that had happened a few days ago when they crossed the Yangtze River together. At that time they stood by the iron railings on the little steamer that plied its way across the river, looking out at the waters rolling towards the east.

Chen Dingyi said: "Look at the Yangtze River – no one can stop it. It is just like the marching footsteps of the Northern Expeditionary Army!"

Luo Yinan almost laughed out loud: "These aren't any marching footsteps. This is just a river."

Chen Dingyi also smiled: "You are quite right – this is just water. Water can float a boat, but it can also sink it. You wait and see – the banner of victory will soon be raised on both sides of the Yangtze River!"

It was too much; Luo Yinan refused to believe it. "How many years will your 'soon' take?"

Chen Dingyi told him: "You will be able to hear the footsteps of the Northern Expeditionary Army within a few days' time, the liberation of Wuhan will take place within a couple of months, and the whole country will be at peace within the next couple of years."

"Man, are you dreaming?" asked Luo Yinan.

"This has been my dream for many years," Chen Dingyi said, "and it is going to come true any day now."

Luo Yinan had no idea how to deal with such a mad-keen revolutionary as Chen Dingyi had proved to be. He laughed heartily but did not believe a word he said.

Now Chen Dingyi was dead, and his dream was finished. His head had been hacked from his body and was hanging in mid-air. Above it, the sky was covered with a thick layer of lowering black clouds. It was a horrifying spectacle for the whole city of Wuchang. What peace? What liberation? What footsteps?

It was all too late.

Luo Yinan could not stop crying.

The shutters on the window of the old house swung open, followed by the window itself, and one corner hit Luo Yinan on the back of his head, but he didn't feel a thing. A puff of damp, stale air came out from the room; and just as if someone had put a wet cloth over his nose, Luo Yinan felt suffocated. His heart was hammering, and it ached... not like when you have been stabbed by a needle, but more like having been hit by an axe. Luo Yinan could never have imagined that his last sighting of the friend who had saved his life would be like this! The circumstances of his death were not just appalling, they were terrifying. Looking up, Luo Yinan did not know what was breaking: perhaps it was his heart. He had always been soft-hearted, and now he felt his heart had been shattered by his very first glimpse of Chen Dingyi's head. The debris of the impact and his blood had mingled and scattered into countless broken fragments, just like beads of mercury spilt across the ground, finding their way into every nook and cranny, never to be brought together again.

Luo Yinan spent the night sitting at the top of the pagoda at Baotong Temple, outside the walls of Wuchang, at Hong Mountain. The seven-storey pagoda rose high into the sky. He just sat there in a state of turmoil. He was unable to make sense of his own feelings; in fact, he did not even know how to start sorting them out. The sky above his head was full of stars, but he could not make out the horizon. Everyone was going about their usual daily routine underneath the pagoda. Lights would go on and off at irregular intervals, like the stertorous breathing of a dying man.

Suddenly, Luo Yinan thought: What's the point of all this studying? Why should I try and make something of myself? What's the point of even being alive? How ridiculous it is that people make such an effort to survive in such a disgusting and evil society, in such a dark and difficult world.

At that moment, he made a decision for himself: leave! Leave the college, leave Wuchang, leave this dreadful situation, and never have anything more to do with any of these horrors. Having made this decision, Luo Yinan's mind began to wander. His thoughts went back to a temple to the god of Earth, a small temple in the mountains near his hometown. It had stood in the same place for hundreds of years, as if everything that was going on around it had nothing to do with it. He had been there countless times with his grandmother, and there was always an old monk sitting there impassively, reciting the scriptures, meditating, or hunting for lice in the sun. After each visit, his grandmother's face would always look more tranquil and kind. Luo Yinan thought: Oh, I could go there. That would be the right place for me to go – I can spend the rest of my life there. He knew full well that the old monk would take him in. The old monk had once looked deep into his eyes and said: "You have a destiny to fulfil." At this thought, he began to calm down, and the expression in his eyes turned cold.

This icy feeling quickly spread through his entire body, and Luo Yinan immediately realised how exhausted and unwilling to exert himself he was. He couldn't even bear the thought of returning to his dormitory, so he put his hand into his trouser pocket and felt for his money, decided that he had enough to get home and then stood up and walked down the pagoda stairs.

Luo Yinan walked down Hong Mountain in a daze, crossed South Lake and made his way to the train station. Wuchang City lay before him, bathed in the early morning light. Luo Yinan did not so much as give it a second glance; for him, it was another of the things he was leaving behind. The hustle and bustle of carriages coming and going grew louder with the rising of the sun. These sounds enveloped Luo Yinan like a fire burning; he felt that he was the firewood, blackened and burned by the flames. When it burns out, only the ashes are left.

2

THE MILUO RIVER had come into sight. Liang Kesi suddenly felt excited. He ran forward until he reached the water's edge. Then he bent down, cupped his hands and splashed his face over and over again. He had been feeling hot and sweaty, but now he felt refreshed. After washing his face, he also drank his fill from the river. Then he stood up and took a deep breath.

The evening sunshine fell on the river, and all of a sudden the waters turned into a sheet of gold. Liang Kesi thought to himself: The great poet Qu Yuan must have stood right here just before he died. Maybe just like me, he came from far away and was terribly thirsty, so he crouched down by the water's edge and cupped his hands to drink. But these waters did not save him – they drowned him instead.

> *My heart has long been racked with pain,*
> *Sorrow and worry have succeeded each other.*
> *The journey from Ying has proved long and hard,*
> *The Yangtze and the Xia I will not cross again.*

The clear and clean waters of this river should have washed away all of Qu Yuan's sorrow and grief. What a pity!

Liang Kesi looked up at the darkening sky and thought: He can't have been here at dusk. How could he bear to throw himself into the river to die when the landscape here looks so beautiful? No matter how terrible the things that have happened to you, how dark it seems once you are dead – it will only make things worse. If you stay alive, even if you have nothing but your bare hands, you may still be able to make things a little better.

Liang Kesi stayed by the banks of the river until the sun had completely set, and his sentimental mood disappeared with the last ray of light. What came next was a gnawing sensation of hunger; the moment he realised quite how starved he was, the more insistent the feeling became. So he left the Miluo River and headed back down the road.

The streets here were paved with stone and so narrow that the eaves on the houses on either side of the road almost met. If it rained, the water would fall like a curtain in the middle of the street. Liang Kesi looked at it and thought it was interesting. In the battle that had just been fought, the Northern Expeditionary Army had swept away the enemy here like a tornado, and now they were moving on. A festive atmosphere still pervaded the whole town; you could feel it, just standing there.

Right at the far end of the street, there was a lantern shining. The sun had already set, so the narrow road was wrapped in darkness and shadows. A small rice-noodle stall was still open for business. Liang Kesi stepped forward and shouted: "Boss, bring me a bowl of noodles – not too many chillies."

The boss immediately smiled and said: "If you don't put a lot of chillies in, it won't taste of anything!"

Liang Kesi sat down on the wooden bench, looking at the sign on the wall, but when he turned his head he suddenly realised the man sitting opposite looked very familiar to him. His clothes were filthy, and he was picking at his food. He would raise his chopsticks and pick up each noodle really slowly and listlessly, as if the bones in his arm had been removed. Liang Kesi stared at him and gave a start of surprise. He tried to speak to him: "Luo Yinan?"

The man slowly raised his head, and his eyes were full of painful confusion. Liang Kesi could now see him quite clearly; it was his classmate Luo Yinan. Liang Kesi was delighted: "It is you! Why are you here?"

Luo Yinan was still in a daze and muttered: "Where else would I be?"

"Why aren't you back at the college?" Liang Kesi said. "Aren't you reading Su Manshu day in and day out?"

Luo Yinan said: "Is the college still even there? Didn't Su Manshu die?"

By this point, Liang Kesi realised that something must be seriously wrong. He quickly broke in and asked: "What's wrong with you? What happened? Is it Shuya again?"

Luo Yinan said: "Have you seen Chen Dingyi's head?"

"What do you mean?" Liang Kesi asked. "What has happened to Chen Dingyi?"

"His head is hanging over Government Gate," Luo Yinan said.

Liang Kesi was shocked: "What do you mean?"

"I saw his head," Luo Yinan said.

"Chen Dingyi was beheaded?" Liang Kesi said.

Luo Yinan muttered: "They cut the heads off three men. The head at Government Gate is Chen Dingyi's."

"How is that possible?" Liang Kesi said. "Did you see it with your own eyes?"

"He looked just the same," Luo Yinan said. "He was smiling, and his eyes were open."

As Luo Yinan said that, he threw up the noodles he'd just been eating. A little piece of red chilli pepper was stuck to his lip. Liang Kesi was sitting there in a daze, unsure of whether his disgust was because Chen Dingyi had been beheaded, or because Luo Yinan had vomited. The owner of the noodle stall was scared, and he rushed over to say: "What on earth is the matter? My noodles are really good quality, though you may have found them a bit hot…"

Luo Yinan had now thrown up to the point where there was nothing left, and he began to cry. The sound moved through the shadows and went gently out into the gathering night. Everything suddenly seemed very sad.

Liang Kesi was still sitting there in a daze. It was hard for him to imagine that someone as alive as Chen Dingyi could have had his head hacked from his body and strung up over the city gate. Life can be very cruel. When he left Wuchang to follow the Northern Army in their revolution, Chen Dingyi had seen him off at the train station. On the way, he said: "Brother, we will meet again at Wuchang before the autumn leaves have turned yellow." He was so excited, his eyes glittered with the light of victory. And where was he now? Liang Kesi could almost imagine the sight of his head, with its eyes wide open, before him.

It was now quite dark, and the bowl of rice noodles in front of Liang Kesi was already cold. The owner of the noodle stall seemed in a hurry to close up and said: "Gentlemen?"

Liang Kesi took out the money to pay him, and, when he handed it over to him, he said: "I'm sorry to have caused you all of this trouble. We'll be on our way." Then he turned to Luo Yinan and said: "Is that why you've left college?"

"I couldn't stay in that kind of place a minute longer," Luo Yinan said. "I had to leave."

"Where are you going now?" Liang Kesi asked.

"I am going to leave this world behind," Luo Yinan said.

That gave Liang Kesi a shock: "You are going to kill yourself?"

Luo Yinan smiled bitterly: "How could someone like me find the courage to commit suicide? I am completely useless. My only idea was to run as far away as possible – so far away that no one could ever find me and I don't have to see anyone else."

Liang Kesi knew perfectly well that Luo Yinan was not only obsessed with Su Manshu's writings but also liked to hang around temples. There were plenty of occasions when he'd mentioned wanting to take Buddhist vows. And so he said: "OK... Do you really want to... become a monk?"

"I don't know that I have any other choice," Luo Yinan said.

"You don't want to avenge Chen Dingyi's death?" Liang Kesi asked.

"I wouldn't dare," Luo Yinan said in a low voice.

Liang Kesi got angry at that: "This isn't about whether you have the courage or not, but whether you care enough about it. Look at the state of our country: it has been completely devastated, and people are suffering terribly every day. One more monk just means one more waste of space."

"So in this life I am a waste of space," Luo Yinan muttered. "Just treat me as though I have never existed."

Liang Kesi got even angrier, and his voice was now much

louder: "Did you really see Chen Dingyi's head with your own eyes? If you did, how can you possibly say something like that? Have you forgotten that Chen Dingyi saved your life?"

"He saved my life, yes, he saved my life," Luo Yinan said, "but there is nothing I can do to pay him back."

"You have to pay him back come what may," Liang Kesi said.

Luo Yinan was looking off to one side, clearly unable to concentrate, and he said: "How do I pay him back? To whom should I pay back?"

"OK," Liang Kesi said, "I'll tell you how you should pay him back – with your life! You should devote your life to getting rid of the people who killed him!"

Luo Yinan stared at him without speaking.

Liang Kesi said: "Didn't you just say that we should all treat you as though you had never existed?"

Luo Yinan stretched out his hands and said: "You think I should kill them? How? How could someone like me do a thing like that?"

"Let me tell you again," Liang Kesi said. "Come with me and join the Northern Expeditionary Army. They are fighting just up ahead – in fact, they have already entered Hubei Province. Wuchang is going to be next. If you feel we should all carry on as if you never existed, if you die in the fighting, that's the end of it. But if you're alive when the war ends, you've paid Chen Dingyi back."

Luo Yinan seemed to pull himself together at that, and he stared straight into Liang Kesi's eyes. Remembering the circumstances under which Liang Kesi left the college, he suddenly asked: "Liang Wenqi, did you leave to join the Northern Expedition?"

"Of course," Liang Kesi said. "Now, I am no longer a student called Liang Wenqi – I have changed my name and become Liang Kesi, a soldier of the Northern Expeditionary Army."

"Liang Kesi?" Luo Yinan murmured. "That name sounds somehow familiar."

Liang Kesi smiled naively: "Can't you guess? The 'Ke' bit comes from Karl Marx's Chinese name, Ma-ke-si, and the 'si' from Engels, En-ge-si."

"Oh," Luo Yinan stammered. "That's very brave!"

"Exactly," Liang Kesi said. "We need people who are prepared to show courage right now."

"What are you doing here?" Luo Yinan asked.

"I promised my cousin I would follow his regiment when they headed off with the Northern Expeditionary Army," Liang Kesi said. "When I arrived in Guangzhou, I discovered that they had already arrived in Hunan. I have been chasing after them all the way, from Guangdong to Hunan, from Changsha to Yuezhou, but I still haven't caught up with them. An officer in Yuezhou told me that he was just ahead and that I should follow the railway tracks."

"Yuezhou has already fallen?" Luo Yinan asked.

Liang Kesi said: "The Northern Expeditionary Army is really great! Nobody was expecting that Yuezhou would surrender pretty much without a fight. You wouldn't know but I was right there on the spot, and they were setting off firecrackers all over the city, and it went on all night."

"Oh," Luo Yinan said, "I wanted to go to Yuezhou, but the trains weren't running, so I had to walk."

"And a good thing that you did," Liang Kesi replied. "Now I have got you here, come what may I am going to drag you along with me until we catch up with the Northern Expeditionary Army. I am not going to let you become a monk. I am going to make you one more soldier in the revolutionary ranks – if that means you end up as cannon fodder, it is still better than being just a mere parasite on society. Besides which, you aren't predestined to become a monk, and you have no right to take vows. Your benefactor Chen Dingyi has been killed, so you have to fight for him. You owe him that – it is the least you could do. Anyway, if you are going to live as if you were dead, you might as well be dead. But more likely" – and here Liang Kesi threw his arms wide and spoke categorically – "if you've been through a fight like this and you're still alive, you really understand the meaning of living."

Luo Yinan looked at him. He did not know why his classmate seemed so passionate; he was so excited that his spittle was already spraying him in the face. He did not want to say anything; he just felt tired.

That night, they could not find an inn to stay in, so Luo Yinan and Liang Kesi ended up in a peasant's house. They were put in a side room, full of firewood and tools. Liang Kesi was so exhausted that he fell asleep as soon as he lay down. Although Luo Yinan was tired too, it took him a long time to get to sleep. Mosquitoes were whining in his ear, and Liang Kesi also kept shouting in his sleep: "Attack them! Go!" It seemed that he was dreaming of the field of battle.

Yeah, Luo Yinan thought. It is only by being as tough as Liang Kesi that he could pay Chen Dingyi back. He also felt that since staying alive was pointless and there was no way to survive with dignity, he might as well go with them, and if he got killed, so what? He had already given everything else up, so why not his life? If he managed to survive, he could always become a monk later on – it wouldn't make any difference. It would all be the same in the end. If nothing matters to you, it doesn't matter if you do what Liang Kesi tells you.

3

THE BATTLE for Tingsi Bridge was pretty nasty. That whole summer, the Tingsi River was flooded, and the waters spread out from the southwest towards the north, pouring into the town by Tingsi Bridge, inundating the whole community on three sides and engulfing them many feet deep. All the local people's houses were underwater, and the whole place seemed dead. Even when shots rang out from time to time and the sharp sound rasped at the nerves, it didn't bring forth the slightest sign of life. The small town was surrounded by mountains, and the railway tracks wended their way in and out. They were guarded by Wu Peifu's Beiyang Army, which occupied the heights of Da'nao Mountain, a location that gave them a commanding position and good view, so that they could see anyone coming to attack them from a very long way away.

If the Northern Expeditionary Army wanted to attack Wuchang, they would have to pass Tingsi Bridge. Because the terrain was so difficult and the Beiyang Army was defending it so vigorously, the Thirty-fifth Regiment fought fiercely the whole day only to find themselves pinned down, unable to advance or retreat. Night fell on this stalemate, and a fog arose; mists mixed with countryside smells. Sporadic gunfire broke out like the blade of a knife cutting through the thick fog, adding a strange note of tragedy to the village's summer evening.

From his position on top of the wall, Mo Zhengqi was feeling frustrated. Tiny mosquitoes bit his neck, but he could not be bothered to swat them. Mo Zhengqi served as a company commander in Ye Ting's Independent Regiment. On 9 July, when the Northern Expeditionary Army set out from Guangzhou, their regiment had already gone on ahead. Counting it up, it had only taken them a little more than one month to get this far, but the heroic enthusiasm that had sustained him this far now had no outlet. They had done so well up until now, so if they ended up going no further – how could he bear it? It would be better to attack them under cover of darkness, Mo Zhengqi thought. That might just do it…

But no orders came.

Wu Baosheng slipped out of the house and came up to him and said: "Why don't they send us out to fight?"

Mo Zhengqi shouted at him: "Go to bed!"

Wu Baosheng countered: "Why aren't you asleep yourself then?"

"Do you get to order me about? Do I have to obey you?" Mo Zhengqi asked.

"Of course I have to obey you! You are our company commander!" Wu Baosheng replied.

"I am glad to hear it," Mo Zhengqi said.

"I guess you are worried about your cousin?" Wu Baosheng enquired.

Mo Zhengqi could almost see his cousin's face before him, and he could not help saying: "Yes. He said in his last letter that he was on his way to Guangzhou and he would join us for the Northern Expedition. I don't have a clue where he is now though. We've been advancing so fast. How could he possibly find us?"

"He is a pretty bright guy," Wu Baosheng said. "Don't worry about it – he can definitely find us."

"It doesn't matter how clever he is," Mo Zhengqi told him. "We've been fighting the whole way, so how can he possibly find us?"

"It would be hard for him to locate us if we weren't fighting," Wu Baosheng said, "but once the shooting begins, he just needs to head to where the guns are pointing, don't you think?"

"That's why I'm worried," Mo Zhengqi said. "He is just a kid –

student who has read a lot. I don't even think he knows how to run. Will he be able to dodge the bullets?"

"Don't worry," Wu Baosheng said, "he isn't stupid, and he's sure to get the hang of things round here right off. Last time your uncle brought him home, he came out mountain-climbing with me, and he was very quick on the uptake."

Mo Zhengqi thought about it and smiled: "I remember that too. In his letter, he said that he had changed his name to Liang Kesi because of his admiration for Marx and Engels."

Wu Baosheng almost laughed himself sick at that, saying: "Isn't his father going to have a fit at him changing his name to something weird and foreign like that?"

Mo Zhengqi also started laughing and said: "When you think of my uncle's stuck-in-the-mud face, I really can't imagine what he must have looked like when he heard about the name change."

Given what Mo Zhengqi had just said, Wu Baosheng now laughed even more happily: "Your uncle lives in the big city, and he's seen plenty of things in his time, so how can he have stayed so strict and stuffy in his ideas?"

"What are you laughing at?" Mo Zhengqi asked. "When your father finds out you've joined the army, you are in for the thumping of your life!"

"It's all your fault," Wu Baosheng said. "You told my father that you had found a job for me as a carpenter, so if he thumps anyone it's going to be you."

They both laughed at that. Mo Zhengqi and Wu Baosheng came from the same village, where they had grown up together. Wu Baosheng had followed Mo Zhengqi into the army, but he told his family that he would be working as a carpenter. After he enlisted, Wu Baosheng always had enough to eat, so he thought being a soldier was great. Mo Zhengqi pointed out that while getting enough to eat was good, fighting in battle was life-threatening. Wu Baosheng hadn't yet fully grasped just what 'life-threatening' meant.

Just as they were talking, someone suddenly shouted: "Mo Zhengqi! Where are you?"

It was Battalion Commander Cao Yuan's voice.[1] Mo Zhengqi immediately got himself down off the wall, almost falling on top of

Cao Yuan as he shouted: "Here I am! Battalion Commander, are we going to be on our way?"

Cao Yuan looked to see where he had climbed down from and said curiously: "You weren't asleep?"

"No," Mo Zhengqi said, "I was waiting for your orders!"

"Well, here they are," Cao Yuan said. "Starting right now, you are to move into position to flank the enemy."

Mo Zhengqi said happily: "I knew it! We fought for a whole day with no progress – we have to move! We are in no position to fight this war slowly. If the enemy can bring up their reinforcements, we are going to find ourselves on the back foot."

"Well," Cao Yuan said, "you've obviously thought a lot about it."

"This isn't my idea," Mo Zhengqi answered. "Regimental Commander Ye Ting has said it loud and clear plenty of times. Our weapons aren't a patch on theirs. We can attack, but nobody here knows the first thing about defence, so we have to fight fast, win and move on. We didn't take them during the day, so we have to carry on overnight."

"Do you know what Wu Peifu said?" Cao Yuan asked. "He said that ever since ancient times, it has been northerners conquering the south – no southerners have ever conquered the north. So when people from the south head north, they are marching to their deaths."

"That's just because our Revolutionary Army hasn't headed north before," Mo Zhengqi pointed out. "After a month of fighting, we've made a pretty good name for ourselves. The northerners are all scared of us, especially us in the Independent Regiment."

"You can boast as much as you like," Cao Yuan said, "but you need to remember that it is all just hot air – when you start fighting, for heaven's sake be careful!"

"Of course," Mo Zhengqi said. "During the course of the day, sir, I made a plan of the terrain here, and one of the villagers said that there is a path that goes past Gutangjiao and then a little bit further on you get to Tingsi Bridge. He also said that the waters there look deep, but there is a shallow channel where you can simply walk across."

"Great!" Cao Yuan said. "Find someone who knows about the channel to lead the way. Get ready!"

It was already long past midnight, and they set off at the crack of dawn. Mo Zhengqi was keyed up for a fight, but he soon realised that the enemy had already retreated. He looked over at Cao Yuan and could not stop himself from going up and asking: "What on earth is going on? Why have they run away without a fight?"

"There'll be a fight when we catch up with them," Cao Yuan said. "If they withdraw, we chase after them and have our battle then."

The enemy troops were indeed pulling back. One unit after another from the Northern Expeditionary Army had attacked under cover of darkness, and as soon as they got close they had charged them with their bayonets. Although they only cut a handful of holes in the enemy's lines, this was enough. Everyone in the Northern Expeditionary Army wore a bamboo hat and a red, white and blue cockade to symbolise liberté, egalité, fraternité, so that even in the darkness, engaged in close combat, the two sides had no difficulty in distinguishing each other. By dawn, victory was assured, and as the Northern Expeditionary Army marched forward they could see the corpses piled up under Tingsi Bridge, and the waters under the bridge running red with human blood.

In fact, the news that the Revolutionary Army had won a great victory in Hunan in their Northern Expedition was already common knowledge, and when the Beiyang Army heard that they had arrived, they were so terrified they could barely stand up. They had absolutely no intention of trying to fight, and after just a couple of engagements they had already lost. They began negotiating their surrender immediately, with a couple of conditions: first, the soldiers and their belongings were not to be searched for cash; secondly, any soldiers who wished to join the Revolutionary Army should be allowed to do so, and anyone who did not should be repatriated to the north, not just turned out to starve. The Revolutionary Army was somewhat surprised to be told this, and they commented privately to themselves: How could such a thing be, that conditions like this would be set? But in order to bring the fighting to a quick conclusion, they agreed. The Battle of Tingsi Bridge was over.

Mo Zhengqi felt that this was something of an anti-climax. The enemy troops on the front line had simply surrendered, and the reinforcements ran away as soon as they heard this. He was very upset and complained: "What's the point of chasing after these deserters? Why can't we go and bayonet the enemy?"

"Whoever you fight with, you are still fighting," said Cao Yuan. "It is all part and parcel of our victory! Get on with you! Catching up with the retreating army is an important part of the fighting."

Before the command had arrived to pursue the retreating enemy and attack their rear, Mo Zhengqi was already on the march with his men, following on behind Cao Yuan. They were so quick off the mark that they could almost see the enemy in front of them.

The Xianning Railway Station was full of wounded soldiers. There was a canal between the town and the station, and running alongside it was a dirt road crowded with people and horses. Some of them were travellers; others were there to transport the wounded. There were also the walking wounded, who had made their own way here to seek treatment for minor injuries. The cacophony was terrible as it rose and ebbed like the tide.

Given that a couple of soldiers in his company with minor injuries were refusing to leave their units and go for treatment, Mo Zhengqi went in person to the battlefield dressing station to collect the necessary medication for them.

As he stepped over the casualties, heaped one against the next, Mo Zhengqi was looking around for someone. The busy nurses all looked identical, dressed head to foot in white, thin and elegant, walking as if they were floating along. He grabbed hold of a nurse and asked: "Do you know Guo Xiangmei?"

The nurse did not even raise her head. She simply said: "No."

"She's a nurse like you," Mo Zhengqi said.

The nurse looked irritated: "With so many nurses here, how can you possibly expect me to remember all their names!"

Mo Zhengqi was feeling lost, when suddenly he heard a crisp voice saying: "How did that happen? He's a wounded man. What on earth have you been doing to him?"

Mo Zhengqi smiled; that voice warmed his heart. He made his way through the crowd, following the voice, and shouted: "Xiangmei!"

Guo Xiangmei turned her head and caught sight of Mo Zhengqi. A smile spread across her face, but all she said was: "You are a member of the Revolutionary Army! Help me carry this wounded man over there."

Mo Zhengqi immediately said: "Yes, ma'am!" He bent down and was about to pick up the wounded man, when suddenly he stopped: "He's a Beiyang soldier!"

"I don't care which army he belongs to," Guo Xiangmei said, "if he's wounded then he's one of my patients."

"You should care!" Mo Zhengqi retorted. "Yesterday, our unit lost Pockmarked Zhang and Li Fuguo, killed by the Beiyang Army, and today I have to carry this one about? None of the lads would ever forgive me."

Guo Xiangmei raised her eyebrows and said: "On the battlefield, he's an enemy combatant. Wounded and off the battlefield, he's a patient. Are you going to help or not? If you don't help, don't bother coming around again."

Mo Zhengqi was shocked and said: "I'll help, of course I'll help you."

Mo Zhengqi stretched out his arms and picked the wounded man up. As he did so, he muttered: "I wanted to hug you, and I've ended up hugging him – to be honest, it's not quite the same thing…"

The wounded man in his arms had some broken ribs and a broken leg, and his head was encased in blood-soaked bandages, with only one eye showing. This eye now looked at him sideways, with a very unfriendly gaze. Mo Zhengqi straightened his face and said: "If you glare at me like that, you'd better watch out. I could easily just let go."

Guo Xiangmei heard what he said, and though she laughed to herself, she ignored it.

Mo Zhengqi lifted the wounded man into the room and propped him up on a wooden bench. When he came out again, he could not see Guo Xiangmei anywhere. Looking around, he still couldn't find her. He had no idea what to do, so he went and found a military doctor and got the medicine he needed. Just as he was leaving, Wu Baosheng came flying down the dirt road, shouting: "Hurry up! We are all due to move out immediately!"

Mo Zhengqi craned his neck as he looked back. All he said was: "Where can that tiresome girl have gone?"

"You don't need to worry about any tiresome girl," Wu Baosheng said, "but Wu Peifu. He's arrived at Hesheng Bridge, and it looks like he wants to make a stand there. The battalion commander says that we've got to capture the bastard alive."

Mo Zhengqi immediately gave Wu Baosheng his full attention: "What? Wu Peifu is here in person to command the battle? He must have a death wish!"

"Exactly!" Wu Baosheng said. "Hurry up, because Regimental Commander Ye Ting has the horses ready to move."

As they spoke, the two of them hurried out of the station. As they hit the dirt road, Mo Zhengqi was still looking back.

At no point did he catch sight of that familiar figure.

The Independent Regiment chased the enemy all the way, fighting them whenever they caught up with them. The road was full of things dropped by the fleeing troops; besides clothes, guns and ammunition, there was also money. Mo Zhengqi also picked up an opium pipe, which he showed to Cao Yuan. Cao Yuan laughed: "Chen Jiamo smokes opium, maybe this is his."

"If you have to bring this kind of thing along," Mo Zhengqi said, "how can you expect to win?"

There were dead bodies everywhere, and their stench was everywhere too; even if you plugged your nose, it was unbearable. Some of the bodies had been chopped into pieces and were scattered through the undergrowth, and there were also plenty without heads, making an appalling sight as they lay there in the sunshine, with white maggots wriggling through reddened or blackened flesh. There was a copse of willows off to one side, and several heads were hanging from the trees. Mo Zhengqi couldn't understand who had killed these men. Was it the local people? Wu Baosheng arrested a villager who he caught in the patch of forest up ahead, and when he questioned him he was told that the Beiyang Army had been terrified by the news that the Northern Expeditionary Army had won victory after victory in Hunan. When the officers fled, the troops fell into anarchy, so Wu Peifu set up a military police unit that he armed with huge swords, and they killed any deserters they caught. Their leader was personally responsible for chopping a good few men to death. Wu Baosheng pointed to a headless corpse and said: "This one, the villager told me, was still running even after his head had been cut off."

When Mo Zhengqi heard this, all his muscles tightened. He just wanted to scream abuse at someone.

Then Wu Baosheng said: "Do you know why they wanted to forbid searching prisoners as one of the conditions of surrender?"

"Wasn't it because they had come by a few silver dollars?" Mo Zhengqi asked.

"And where did they find the cash?" Wu Baosheng enquired.

"How should I know?" Mo Zhengqi replied. "Maybe they robbed some rich man?"

"They haven't been robbing the rich," Wu Baosheng said, "it's robbing the poor, more like."

"Rubbish!" Mo Zhengqi said. "The poor round here don't have any silver dollars to be robbed of."

"OK," said Wu Baosheng, "let me explain. Of course, ordinary people don't normally have any silver dollars for them to steal. But I heard that a couple of days ago there was a crash at Tingsi Bridge where one of Wu Peifu's military trains ran into a train transporting silver for the Allied Command payroll. Four freight cars of money! The railway tracks were completely buried in silver coins."

"Gee, I'd have loved to see that! So what happened?" Mo Zhengqi enquired.

"What do you mean, what happened?" Wu Baosheng asked. "They stole it! The Northern Army[2] and the local people grabbed as much as they could, and nobody could stop them, so round here everyone has a heap of silver tucked away. With cash in hand, who wants to fight? They all want to go home and buy land and build houses for themselves. It's a pity that I wasn't there."

Mo Zhengqi was shocked to hear that, and it took him a while to recover. Eventually, he said: "Is that really the only reason why you've joined the revolution?!"

Wu Baosheng took out a couple of silver dollars, looked around, and then handed them over. He whispered: "I found these on one of the dead bodies. The terms of surrender didn't say anything about not searching corpses."

Mo Zhengqi also looked around and whispered back: "Give

them to your father when you get home, and say that you earned them as a carpenter."

Wu Baosheng said: "I will. But these are yours, since I knew you wouldn't look for any for yourself."

Mo Zhengqi glared at him: "Do you know what you've done?"

Wu Baosheng was cross: "Even if you don't want them for yourself, you should take them for your fiancée. When we get to Wuchang, you can buy something nice for her in one of the shops. What girl wouldn't want a pair of gold earrings or a silver bracelet, and some decent makeup, or maybe a silk skirt?"

Mo Zhengqi was silent for a moment, and he seemed to see Guo Xiangmei's smiling face before his eyes, with her eyebrows shaped like crescent moons. He took the coins out of Wu Baosheng's hand and put them in his pocket. Then he said: "I'll keep them for her."

Hesheng Bridge was just in front of them. When they were still ten kilometres away, a halt was called. Regimental Commander Ye Ting had sent scouts on ahead, and they reported back that Wu Peifu had ordered Liu Yuchun's[3] Eighth Division to guard the bridge and that the embankments on either side of the railway tracks and the surrounding hills and roads had been very thoroughly mined. Many deep trenches and shallow ditches had been dug, and the breastworks were ten kilometres wide. This was not a situation in which to underestimate the enemy.

Mo Zhengqi's company lay in ambush to the right of the main battlefields, on a small plateau. There was a patch of mixed woodland there, so although they were not too far from the enemy lines, neither side could see the other because of the thick grass. "What with so many trees," Mo Zhengqi explained, "and the dense undergrowth, nobody can see anyone else. Once the fighting starts, each platoon and each squad will decide what to do for themselves. I just want to say one thing – you have to advance! Under no circumstances whatsoever are you allowed to retreat!"

The order to attack came at dawn. In the blink of an eye, the shelling began, and you could see explosions everywhere. Mo Zhengqi cried: "When you see a break in the lines, charge! If you see the enemy, kill them!" Then he ran forward, hunched over all the while. The enemy's machine guns and artillery were also firing, making it impossible to see a thing: they were firing at random. As

Mo Zhengqi dodged and scrambled forward, he kept his eyes moving from side to side. He saw men blown to bits; he saw people scream and die. His heart was torn, but at this moment he couldn't stop. There was no point in trying to save them; he had to keep moving forward.

He would advance, then there would be a bout of hand-to-hand combat, then he would advance again, with more hand-to-hand combat, and it went on like that until he could hardly see what he was doing anymore. When Mo Zhengqi was covered in blood and so tired he could hardly stand, the enemy lines suddenly collapsed, and the sound of gunfire and killing slackened. Mo Zhengqi was so tired that he sat straight on the ground and could not get up again. Then he looked up at the sky and realised that the sun had already set and night was closing fast.

Battalion Commander Cao Yuan's voice rang out again: "After them! The enemy should not be allowed to recover. We need to attack them again tonight."

Mo Zhengqi looked over in the direction the voice was coming from, but what with the darkness and the smoke neither could see the other clearly. Mo Zhengqi could not see Cao Yuan's face, but he took a few deep breaths and cried: "Anyone who is still alive, follow me!"

Mo Zhengqi had no idea what happened the rest of that night. He had this experience many times; whenever he went to the battlefield and faced the enemy, time and space disappeared, and his mind went blank. All that remained was the need to kill the enemy.

They crushed the enemy's first line of defence, then they chased the retreating troops and broke through the second line. By that time, a new day had already dawned. They found that the enemy had already disappeared, leaving only some scattered corpses and a few laggards on the field of battle. Soldiers who had not closed their eyes for a day and a night sat scattered at random, and some of them fell asleep even before they could sit down.

Mo Zhengqi collected the laggards and counted up his surviving soldiers. After two battles, one third of his men had died. A few days ago, they had been talking and laughing as they marched together after the retreating enemy; they did not understand that they were walking the line between life and death. Now the line was clear: he was still on the 'life' side, but so many of his lively comrades had disappeared onto the side of death. Mo Zhengqi was sad, but there was nothing he could do. This was their fate as soldiers; besides which, dying is something that happens sooner or later to everyone.

Mo Zhengqi made a quick headcount, and then he got ready to lie down next to Wu Baosheng and take a nap. However, his foot was caught by something. Mo Zhengqi looked down and saw a hand was holding fast to his trousers. The hand, though weak, was enough to stop him from moving on.

It was a Beiyang soldier, and he was alive. Mo Zhengqi bent down and then realised that it was an officer.

"Stand up!" Mo Zhengqi roared.

The Beiyang officer was dying, there was blood all over his face, and he was obviously seriously injured. He could not stand up but pointed weakly at his pocket. Mo Zhengqi reached in and pulled out a letter, though the envelope was streaked with blood. The Beiyang officer grunted: "Sir... help me... let my parents, wife and children know... I'm dead..."

Mo Zhengqi's heart thumped. He imagined the faces of his own father and mother. He squatted down and said: "What's your name?"

The Beiyang officer muttered: "Yuan... Zongchun."

Mo Zhengqi said: "Which brigade?"

The Beiyang officer managed to say: "Liu Yuchun's."

Mo Zhengqi thought about it, and then he stood up again and said: "You aren't going to die!" Then he shouted: "Baosheng! Come on, get this man to the dressing station!"

Wu Baosheng gestured to two soldiers, and they lifted up the man named Yuan Zongchun and headed for the dressing station. Yuan Zongchun? Mo Zhengqi thought about it. He grabbed a pencil from his pocket and wrote his name on the back of the envelope. Having written it, he considered the matter again: Do I really want to send a letter on behalf of a Beiyang Army officer? He looked at the address on the envelope: Yutian County, Hebei Province. Sighing, he said to himself: This is addressed to his parents, so I am doing it for them.

The order to attack came again. The order also contained exciting news. Wuchang was not too far away now, and they would be there in less than a day.

That night it rained heavily. Mo Zhengqi led his soldiers in a crazy pursuit of the fleeing enemy; they were actually moving much faster than the routed troops. Having chased after them for who knows how long, suddenly through the lashing rain they saw several fires in the distance, which seemed to be hanging in midair. Someone shouted: "That's Wuchang right up ahead!"

Mo Zhengqi waved his arms and bellowed: "Pick up your feet everyone! We'll have the best dinner of our lives tomorrow… after we've taken Wuchang!"

4

AFTER THEY CROSSED the Miluo River, the terrain became more mountainous. The hills crested and troughed like deep green waves, stretching out to the horizon. The peaks surrounded them so that Liang Kesi and Luo Yinan felt like two lonely little ants doomed to climb slowly over one mountain after another in an endless encirclement. All the way along the road, they passed through a series of run-down villages; although there were clusters of old houses here with high blank walls and long tiled roofs, the whole place still seemed isolated. It was as if a giant were lying there, still breathing but unable to get up. Occasionally, they would spot old people or children squatting down at the foot of the walls, and they would be terrified: apparently, they seldom got to see strangers. At night, they mostly stayed in these villages. The big ones would have about twenty families living in them; the small ones had two or three. They wanted to find a guide, but while they were searching for such a person they realised that the recent passage of the army had left many obvious signs, and they could easily find which way they had gone by following them.

Although Luo Yinan remained depressed, Liang Kesi's optimistic cheerfulness caused his despair to gradually begin to fade; in just a couple of days, the pain seemed to have eased. He didn't think about it anymore; he just followed Liang Kesi. What Liang Kesi told him to do was what he did. Liang Kesi knew perfectly well that Luo Yinan never thought for himself: he just followed the crowd. Right now, he was in charge, so Luo Yinan did whatever he said.

It was quiet in the mountains, and the trees provided shade against the sun. Although they were travelling through the dog days of summer, it was not too hot. During a day's walk, it was rare for them to see even an occasional passer-by, since both woodcutters and villagers seemed to be hiding themselves away.

Liang Kesi recited: *"The wind and smoke have stilled, / Leaving mountains and sky the same colour. / Time is running out, and I still have far to go, / How much longer will I stay in the world of men?"*

"That's very nice," Luo Yinan said. "You've put one couplet from Wu Jun's poem on top of one from Yu Xin."

"And I didn't fool you in the slightest," Liang Kesi said. "You spotted it right away. It just came into my mind – right here and now I can't stop thinking about Yu Xin's *Lament for the South*"

"I have been thinking about that too," Luo Yinan said, "but it was the bit after the lines you quoted: *Once the general has departed, / Even the greatest tree will bow. / Once our knights have gone, / The cold wind will sough."*

"Ah, I know why it was these lines that came to mind," Liang Kesi said. "Now that Chen Dingyi is dead, you feel that even the great trees are bowing – since he has gone, the cold wind is soughing. That's right, isn't it?"

"You got it," Luo Yinan said sadly.

"What can you do?" Liang Kesi heaved a deep sigh. "Chen Dingyi was so much looking forward to the arrival of the Northern Expeditionary Army. When he heard that they were setting out, I took a boat with him to a meeting at Qingshan to discuss how we could support the Northern Expeditionary Army. On the way, I told him that I was going to go and join them. He said he would meet me in Wuchang in a few days. But they cut his head off before the Northern Expeditionary Army could even get there…"

Luo Yinan was silent, as if the wound in his heart was beginning to bleed again. He could almost see the severed head hanging before his eyes.

When Liang Kesi saw how upset he was, he said: "But I tell you that the tree is still there, and it will flourish once more. You mustn't spend all your time being sad and miserable. You have to harden your heart. Living in this kind of world, you have to get used to people dying. Yes, it is upsetting, but you have to dry your tears and carry on living. All too soon, you'll see more people dying. Maybe next time it will be me, or maybe it'll be yourself."

"I really don't care anymore," said Luo Yinan. "But do you really think you'll get killed?"

"Of course I don't want to die," Liang Kesi carried on. "But if that is what the revolution requires of me, I would not fear death."

"What about Lan?" Luo Yinan said. "What would happen to her if you died?"

It was now Liang Kesi's turn to fall silent.

He could almost feel Lan's tears falling on the back of his hand. Liang Kesi looked up at the sky; it was just starting to rain. The raindrops pattered down lightly, falling one at a time on his clothes and sitting there: a clear bead of water.

Yeah, what would Lan think if he died? Before leaving Wuchang, he told her that he had decided to give up his studies and join the army and that he was going to Guangzhou to join the Northern Expedition. Even though she was very unhappy about this, she knew that she could not stop him. When she came to see him off, before they could even say goodbye, her tears were falling in torrents, and the whole front of her shirt was soaked. He promised her that when the Northern Expedition ended they would never be apart again, that they would live happily ever after. Lan was very sad and said: "I don't know when the Northern Expedition will ever be over or whether we will ever meet again. Maybe when I see you next, it won't be in this world..." Face to face with the woman he loved, Liang Kesi was left speechless for a moment. It was quite true that he had deliberately chosen a career that would put him in harm's way. He had realised his ambition; this was the life he had always wanted. But for all that, he knew that when he went off to save the nation, he would make the woman he loved suffer. The sound of Lan's sobs followed him as he went – although it was like a knife twisting in his guts, he felt he had to go. When the country is in danger, everyone has to help. His journey would bring him face to face with heavy artillery fire and relentless bullets. But even if it killed him, he knew he had no other choice.

CHAPTER 4 | 33

As the rain hit the leaves, there was a rustling sound, almost as if they were talking. The two of them had nothing to say, so in the silence you could hear the sound of their footsteps and the occasional roadside insect or bird, startled by their passing.

Liang Kesi suddenly started shouting at the mountains:

"Holding a bamboo stick, with straw sandals on my feet – I will go far!"

"I am not afraid!"

"My rain cape will withstand the storm for the rest of my life."

Luo Yinan was alarmed at first, but when he listened to what he was shouting he smiled gently: "Although you and I have bamboo sticks in our hands, straw sandals on our feet, not to mention being dressed in rain capes and bamboo hats, it seems more appropriate to say: *Having looked back towards that bleak place, I set off homewards; regardless of whether there is stormy weather or sunshine.*"

"No!" Liang Kesi said. "I'm going to change a couple of words in Su Dongpo's lines: *Having looked back towards that bleak place, I move forward; regardless of whether there is stormy weather or sunshine.*"

Just as Liang Kesi finished speaking, the rain really did stop. He clapped his hands and laughed: "It's the will of heaven!"

Luo Yinan sighed deeply: "It may be the will of heaven, but you've just turned Su Dongpo's line upside down."

In the hope of finding a shortcut, they decided to take the woodcutter's path through the peaks. The path wriggled its way up and down the mountainside, with thickets of brambles and thorn bushes everywhere. There were a few scattered villages in these deep valleys, and the houses, with their black tiled roofs and grey walls, were hidden away under the green trees. It seemed that the war had not touched these isolated communities, so here thin lines of smoke arose from their kitchens, hidden away by the forest trees, giving a timeless impression.

While they were resting, for all that he was desperate to reach the battlefield as soon as possible, standing looking out at the mountains, Liang Kesi could not stop himself from sighing. "It would be wonderful to live in one of these villages where nobody bothers you, and you can spend your whole life in peace."

"Yes," Luo Yinan said, "but other people won't ever let you achieve such a humble ambition."

"From a distance, all these villages look terribly picturesque," Liang Kesi said, "but I don't know what they will look like if we get closer."

"When the nest falls from the tree," Luo Yinan remarked, "all the eggs get smashed. I reckon they won't have an easy life there either."

Liang Kesi agreed. He sighed again: "So Tao Yuanming's utopia at *Peach Blossom Spring* is always just a dream. It might seem to be within reach, but in fact it is as far from you as ever."

It's a dream people have had for more than a thousand years, but it is still just a dream, Luo Yinan thought to himself.

It was late when they arrived in Chongyang, and it was raining, so the slate-paved road was slippery and slick. Someone was galloping down the street – someone who looked like a soldier. Having been standing under the eaves to shelter from the rain, Liang Kesi chased him for a few steps, shouting: "Where is the Revolutionary Army fighting?"

A voice came out of the rain-soaked darkness: "After they crossed through Yanglou, I heard that they captured Hesheng Bridge and are now heading towards Wuchang!"

"Great!" Liang Kesi said excitedly.

"Isn't it odd," Luo Yinan asked, "that the Northern Expedition is going so smoothly? We haven't seen anyone fighting at all."

"Yeah," said Liang Kesi, "we're chasing after them without any baggage or anything, and we still can't catch up with them. Do you suppose Wu Peifu's people have simply run away?"

"Can the Beiyang Army be that useless?" Luo Yinan asked.

"I guess they can," Liang Kesi said. "Why is that?"

"How should I know?" Luo Yinan asked.

"Have you never heard the saying that water can float a boat or sink it?" Liang Kesi said. "The Northern Army is all out of water."

Luo Yinan thought about that for a moment: "Well, maybe it is."

That night, they stayed in an inn. After travelling for several days, they finally found themselves a comfortable bed. They also took a bath, washing off the accumulated filth, and they felt much more light-hearted. Liang Kesi fell straight onto the bed, but even though he was already half asleep he suddenly asked: "Do you think the Northern Expeditionary Army has already made it to Wuchang?"

Luo Yinan had no idea and said: "I don't know."

"I've been chasing after them all the way," Liang Kesi said, "but I can't catch up. If I had known they would move so fast, I would have waited for them at the city gates."

Luo Yinan did not say a word. He thought: If that was the case, we would not have met at the Miluo River, and perhaps by this time I would have received the tonsure and become a monk. I would have had a sutra to hand, getting up at dawn and going to bed at dusk, each day passing by as slowly as an entire lifetime, and yet my entire life would also have flashed past like a single day.

After Chongyang, the terrain was flatter, and their journey became much easier. It was also much hotter than in the mountains. When they passed through Puqi, they could see more and more serious destruction from military units, and the atmosphere was noticeably tense. Every so often they would pass a soldier; some had fallen behind because they got sick and were now trying to catch up again, but others were wounded and forcing themselves to keep moving.

"The battle must be underway just ahead of us," Liang Kesi said. Then he approached a wounded soldier to enquire.

The wounded soldier said: "You're too late! Two days ago when the fighting at Tingsi Bridge was wrapped up, the Northern Army ran away like the rats they are."

Liang Kesi was very excited: "Another big victory?"

"Sure!" the wounded soldier said. "We only fought for one day and one night, and it turned out that the Northern Army was even more useless than anyone had imagined. They all seemed to agree that their arms weren't long enough."

"What on earth are you talking about?" Liang Kesi said.

"They would have run away on all four legs if they could," the wounded soldier said.

The wounded soldier had an interesting way of putting things, and Liang Kesi burst out laughing. Even Luo Yinan, who was still depressed, found himself laughing out loud.

Originally, Puqi had a railway connection with Wuchang, but, because of the fighting going on up ahead, the trains could not go further than Xianning. Liang Kesi dragged Luo Yinan along with the idea that they would make it as far as Xianning and then decide what to do. However, the station was full of smoke, and there were wounded soldiers everywhere, with screams and moans filling the air, interspersed with the occasional laugh or giggle. After all, the battle was won: their injuries afflicted their flesh but not their spirit.

The train had been commandeered by the army. Liang Kesi tried to make his way on board unobtrusively, but he was immediately kicked off. A man who looked like an officer reprimanded him: "If civilians just crowd into the car, how on earth are we supposed to carry on fighting?"

"We aren't ordinary civilians," Liang Kesi said. "We are going to join the Northern Expeditionary Army."

"I can see at first glance that you're just students," the officer said. "Go back to school and study hard. Leave the fighting to us. You don't have a clue what you're doing."

Liang Kesi wanted to argue with him, but Luo Yinan tugged at him and said: "Even if you win the argument, do you think he'll let you get on the train?"

Liang Kesi was cross: "How dare he look down on us students! I wanted to tell him that we are at the forefront of the revolution."

"Forget it," Luo Yinan said. "He won't believe you, whatever you say. Let's hurry and find our own way there."

"It would be much faster if we could get on the train," Liang Kesi pointed out.

"Do you think we have more right to take the train than the wounded soldiers?" Luo Yinan asked.

Liang Kesi was speechless for a moment.

The town by Tingsi Bridge, which overlooked the Guangdong-Hubei railway line, had grown rich thanks to its convenient transportation links. Even the smallest alleys had been paved in stone, and it seemed that every door opened into a shop. But at this moment in time, the doors were all locked and bolted. Although the battle was over, the inhabitants were still far too frightened to show their faces.

As the sun rose ever higher in the sky, the reek of blood and the stench of rotting corpses filled the air; the closer they got to the main battlefield, the stronger it became. The Tingsi River had flooded, and the waters filled the plain. The banks were covered in corpses, and there were plenty more floating in the water. Some were face up, some face down, and in every kind of position. Luo Yinan suddenly turned pale and sat down on the ground with his legs buckling underneath him.

"What is the matter with you?" Liang Kesi exclaimed.

Luo Yinan could not speak. His heart was hammering, his throat could not make a sound, and his bones could no longer support his body.

"Is it heatstroke?" Liang Kesi asked. Then he picked him up and ran as quickly as he could towards the trees by the river.

There was a copse here, with lush undergrowth, and the wild flowers were also in full bloom. Their fragrance was swallowed up in the miasma of blood, and the beauty of the scene quarrelled with the disgusting stench all around.

Liang Kesi was panting from his exertions. He was about to put Luo Yinan down under one of the trees when he suddenly realised that each of the three trees opposite him had a person tied up in front of it. The three men had their heads bowed, and they were kneeling down. There was a bullet hole in each of their chests, from which the blood flowed down to the ground. It had already gone from red to black in the sun. They each had a placard hanging around their necks, with the words *Prisoner XXX* written on them. It seemed that they were deserters.

Liang Kesi shouted at Luo Yinan: "Close your eyes!" Then he turned him round so that he would face the other way. Luo Yinan seemed to be barely conscious. Liang Kesi was frightened and shouted: "Is anybody here? Can anyone help me?"

The woods were completely silent, and there was so little wind that you could not even hear the rustling of the leaves. "Hold on," Liang Kesi said, "I'm going to go and find someone." After that, he ran a few steps only to see a couple of horses come galloping towards him. Liang Kesi rushed over to them, shouting: "Help me, please! Help!"

It was a group of soldiers on horseback, and they stopped when they caught sight of Liang Kesi running towards them. Liang Kesi could see at first glance that they were all soldiers from the Northern Expeditionary Army, and among them was a woman soldier. One of the older soldiers asked: "What has happened?"

"My friend is sick," Liang Kesi gasped out. "Can you help him get to the hospital in town?"

A couple of the soldiers looked at each other. One of them, a man wearing glasses, said: "We are on our way to join the main army, so I'm afraid we don't have time."

"We are going the same way," Liang Kesi said. "We have been chasing the Northern Expeditionary Army all this way because we want to join you." As Liang Kesi said this, he gestured proudly.

"Oh?" the older soldier said. "You are a student?"

"Yes," Liang Kesi said, "and I am studying at Wuchang. When I heard about the Northern Expedition, I rushed to Guangzhou, but the army had already set off, so I ended up chasing it all the way. If I'd known that you would just waltz straight in, I would have waited for you at the gates of Wuchang."

Several soldiers laughed at what he said. The woman soldier said: "Where is your friend? Take me to see him."

"He's over in the forest ahead," Liang Kesi said.

The older soldier said to the woman: "Go and see him, but don't be too long about it. After you've checked up on him, follow along the railway line until you catch up with us."

"Yes," she said.

Liang Kesi took her over to the tree. Luo Yinan was still very pale and not properly conscious yet. The woman soldier checked his pulse and tried to bring him round with acupressure. Then she took a small bottle out of her pocket and asked Liang Kesi to help her to get Luo Yinan to drink the contents. "Is he going to be OK?" Liang Kesi asked.

The woman soldier said: "He may be suffering from stress, or it might be heatstroke. You can give him a drink of water and let him rest for a while. He'll be fine. The kinds of things that you can see round here aren't good for anyone."

"Aren't you afraid yourself?" Liang Kesi asked.

"I'm used to it," the woman said.

Liang Kesi was surprised: "You've fought in battle?"

"Sure," she said. "I took part in the Eastern Expedition. And in the Battle of Huizhou, I was right there at Feige Ridge. That was much worse than this."

Liang Kesi was even more amazed: "You? You don't look much older than me!"

She laughed and said: "Ambition is more important than age."

They sat under the tree and chatted about the Northern Expedition. She said that there were an awful lot of people who had set off with the Northern Expedition, and plenty more people had joined along the way. There were peasants and businessmen, as well as loads of students, and it was not only the students who'd come but also their teachers.

Liang Kesi was very happy. Suddenly, he lowered his voice and asked: "I heard that there are a lot of CYs in the Northern Expeditionary Army, and also plenty of CPs.[1] Which are you?"

The woman soldier smiled and said: "I'm nothing; I'm just a nurse."

Liang Kesi stared at her, as if he didn't quite believe her.

She laughed and said: "What about you?"

Liang Kesi was embarrassed but managed to say: "I am nothing, just like you. My classmates said that I was nothing but a playboy, and they did not believe that I cared about the revolution. So I'm going to take part in the Northern Expedition to show them."

She laughed and said: "Then you are not like me at all. I joined the National Revolution in the hope that the Chinese people will have a better future."

Liang Kesi was impressed and gave her the thumbs-up, saying: "You're right. Actually, I think the same."

Luo Yinan, who had been unconscious, was woken by the sound of their laughter. He was somewhat confused, and for a moment he did not know where he was or why there was a woman soldier sitting next to him. Her eyebrows were beautifully curved like willow leaves, and she had a bright smile on her lovely face. That smile made the whole world seem brighter: how much he loved their possessor. He suddenly remembered – Shuya! Luo Yinan shouted her name as he sat up.

The woman soldier was surprised: "He woke up!"

Her surprise brought delight to Luo Yinan's heart. Since he had seen Chen Dingyi's head hanging in the air, he had not been able to take pleasure in anything; it was as if he were shut in an airtight iron box. Now, the box had opened a crack, releasing the joy that was enclosed in it. "Shuya?" Luo Yinan said. "Is that you?"

"You've been unconscious," Liang Kesi said. "This is a nurse serving with the Revolutionary Army."

Luo Yinan shook his head in an attempt to wake himself up. When he calmed down, he realised he had been hallucinating.

The woman soldier explained: "I am a nurse with the Fourth Army's ambulance team. I happened to be passing here when I met your classmate trying to find someone to rescue you."

"You should thank her!" Liang Kesi said. "Oh, I forgot to ask you, what's your name?"

The woman soldier said: "My name is Zhang Wenxiu." After that, she turned towards Luo Yinan and held out her hand, saying: "I believe you are also our revolutionary comrade, so shake hands."

Luo Yinan sat upright and stretched out his hand. "My name is Luo Yinan," he said.

"I was originally intending to go to university," Zhang Wenxiu said, "but later I thought that with the country in a state like this, it was pointless, so I decided to take part in the revolution first. How do you feel now?"

"I am fine," Luo Yinan said. "Seeing you, I am feeling much better already."

Zhang Wenxiu giggled. The sound seemed to dispel the depression and stench around Tingsi. Luo Yinan felt as if fresh air was now blowing against his face. Liang Kesi also started laughing and said: "That's the first time in many days he has said anything so sensible. It seems you're a real lifesaver, Miss Zhang."

Zhang Wenxiu stopped laughing and stood up. She knocked the soil off her trousers and said to Liang Kesi: "As a revolutionary, you can't call me Miss Zhang. Just call me by my name, or even comrade." After that, she turned to Luo Yinan and said with a smile: "Although I'm not Shuya, I'm still very happy that you are feeling a bit better."

"Of course you are right," Liang Kesi burst in. "I am completely stupid – a revolutionary cannot possibly be called Miss. So can I call you Comrade Wenxiu? Oh, that sounds awkward."

Zhang Wenxiu grinned and said: "I don't like the sound of that at all. Just call me Zhang Wenxiu."

"Then how about Comrade Zhang?" Luo Yinan asked.

Zhang Wenxiu laughed again: "You can call me anything as long as you don't call me Shuya."

Luo Yinan felt embarrassed.

"I can't hang about here any longer," Zhang Wenxiu said. "I have to catch up with the rest of the team. You don't have to travel alone either. The Northern Expeditionary Army is recruiting over at Tingsi Bridge. You can go there and enlist straight away. If you are following the army, you won't get lost."

"Really?" Liang Kesi asked. "But I want to join the Independent Regiment because my cousin is there."

"You tell the man in charge that," Zhang Wenxiu said, "and he might be able to help you. I wouldn't know about that kind of thing."

"Can we go with you?" Luo Yinan asked.

"I'll be riding my horse," Zhang Wenxiu said, "so you can't keep up. I need to get to the front line at Hesheng Bridge immediately. The battle there is only just over. Although it's another big victory, there must be a lot of wounded people in need of help."

"Will we meet again?" Luo Yinan asked.

Zhang Wenxiu jumped on her horse and smiled back: "Maybe we will meet in Wuchang, but only if you make good time." As she said that, she whipped up her horse.

Luo Yinan gazed at her retreating figure.

Liang Kesi suddenly thought of something and said: "You're quite right – she does bear a very strong resemblance to Shuya."

"Yes, she really does," Luo Yinan said gloomily. "Their eyes are almost the same. I thought it was Shuya sitting next to me."

"Just before I left," Liang Kesi said, "I heard Lan saying something about how Shuya was going to get married. Is that right?"

"I think so," Luo Yinan replied. "They said she was going to marry her cousin."

"Last year, when you two got together," Liang Kesi said, "everyone said that you were a perfect couple – there were loads of people who envied you. Why did you break up?"

"It wasn't my idea," Luo Yinan said, "it was hers."

"Lan told me that Shuya's cousin was going to take her to live in England," Liang Kesi said.

"Yes," Luo Yinan replied. "She likes a quiet life."

"And is that why you split up?" Liang Kesi asked.

"Isn't that enough?" Luo Yinan said. "I can't give her the peace that she wants."

"It isn't yours to give," Liang Kesi pointed out. "It doesn't really exist. You are better off without her if she's that unreasonable."

"You can't say that," Luo Yinan mumbled. "She is right. With all of this violence going on around us, I simply cannot make her happy or make her feel safe. Since I can't do it, I should let her look for someone who can."

"Since when has anyone felt happy or safe?" Liang Kesi asked. "It is only when everyone is happy that any one individual can be happy."

"Not everyone can consider the bigger picture the way that you do," Luo Yinan said.

Liang Kesi stared at him and said: "What about you?"

Luo Yinan stood up and looked around. It was an idyllic scene of green fields and trees basking in the summer sunshine, but when you looked more carefully there were signs of damage and destruction everywhere. There was the smell of blood and smoke blowing in the wind, and it wrung Luo Yinan's heart. That's the way the world is, he thought to himself. Then he considered the matter more deeply and said: "It is the same for Shuya and me, but she can get the peace she needs through marriage, and I can't."

Liang Kesi sneered at him: "So you went off to become a monk."

"That was the first thing that came into my head," Luo Yinan said. "I don't even know if I can follow you going forward. I have been so shocked by the cruelty of all of this, and I really don't want to see any more."

Liang Kesi shouted at him: "Well, I want to tell you that you don't have a choice – you have to keep on going forward. We are going to Tingsi Bridge to enlist. It is because we want to put an end to such horrors that we are going to join the Northern Expedition."

Liang Kesi was always in high spirits. Occasionally, Luo Yinan found him very like Chen Dingyi. He felt overwhelmed and just whispered: "I don't want to argue with you. I'll do as you like, but I really don't know what it is that I am doing."

Liang Kesi pointed ahead proudly and said: "Wherever I go, you go. If I become a general in the future, you will be my deputy. Whatever happens, I refuse to allow you to become a monk." At that, he burst out laughing, which made Luo Yinan feel even more put upon.

5

BY THE TIME Mo Zhengqi and his soldiers reached Baoding Gate, it was getting dark.

The streets around Baoding Gate were in a dreadful state, as if there had just been some terrible fighting. The signs above the stores were hanging crooked, and the streets were covered with debris which crunched underfoot, though you had no idea what it was you were walking over. If you were unlucky enough to accidentally kick something, there would be a clang: it might be that you kicked over a tin can or a chamber pot. Many of the houses here were no longer habitable. The doors along the street were all closed with no lights showing, but there might be some suppressed commotion inside. Mo Zhengqi could feel that he was being watched from behind each door, and the peering eyes were tense and frightened.

His frontrunners were almost caught up among the last of the enemy as they retreated. It was so dark you couldn't see your hands in front of your face, and neither side could see the other clearly. The pursuers were pursuing, those running away were fleeing, both sides were right there together, but neither side realised who the others were or what they were doing. They were all so frightened they had gone numb.

From the watchtower on the city wall, someone suddenly shouted: "Close the gate! Close the gate!" For those running through the pitch-black night, this was a terrifying moment: with a thunderous crash, the gate immediately closed. At that moment, Mo Zhengqi realised that they had reached the front line and could not go any further. He stopped and turned back to shout: "Don't go into the city!" His voice was hoarse and strange, and those following on behind him suddenly stopped and asked each other: "What's wrong? What's going on?" The fastest runners had already made it into the city, their guns at the ready. Mo Zhengqi watched the huge gate swing closed. He knew that the soldiers in front of him would not be able to escape.

Guns were firing from the watchtower on the walls, and someone right beside Mo Zhengqi collapsed. Only then did people come to their senses and scatter in all directions. Fortunately, the houses near the city wall had not all been completely demolished, and they could now serve as shelters. Mo Zhengqi ordered his men to return fire. A few minutes later, they realised this was futile. The walls were so high that the guns had to be fired almost straight up into the night sky, which made a racket but otherwise had no effect at all. They might as well just retreat.

The troops who were following on behind also stopped. There was a firm, low voice somewhere in the procession saying: "Line up! Line up! Besiege the city! Besiege the city!" The command spread out like ripples in the water, until it reached the very outermost edges of the crowd.

Mo Zhengqi pulled back beyond the moat. When he counted his men, he discovered that he had lost more to rushing into the city and being shot on the retreat than he had imagined. He took a deep breath and decided that he had been far too precipitate.

By dawn, a really large number of soldiers and horses had gathered under the city walls. The whole of Wuchang lay before them. The ancient walls snaked across the low hills, and the streets of the city were empty; the houses were standing higgledy-piggledy, and there was fresh fire-damage and the scars of recent artillery bombardment everywhere. Clearly, a terrible battle had just taken place here. They could see the lamps hanging on the city wall, the gun barrels poking out of the battlements, the gate encased in iron sheeting and even the nails that held it fast. At some distance from the walls, the bolder inhabitants of the city had opened their doors and started to trade with the Northern Expeditionary Army. Mo Zhengqi suddenly felt hungry and took Wu Baosheng around to find somewhere that did noodles. Having made the rounds of several restaurants, finally he found a small place that sold them. He went up and asked for a bowl, which he guzzled straight down, so fast he almost choked. Compared with the rice noodles they made in his hometown, these were really nothing special. But he was hungry and didn't care about how they tasted. After he finished eating, Mo Zhengqi thought to ask the shopkeeper: "Aren't you scared by all the fighting?"

The shop owner said: "Of course! But I have got two kids in school here – if I don't go to work, how are we supposed to survive?"

During the conversation, stray bullets flew past from time to time. One of them hit the door opposite, and in the blink of an eye, a hole appeared there. Mo Zhengqi said: "If that got you in the head, what would you say?"

The owner of the noodle restaurant turned pale with fear. Mo Zhengqi told Wu Baosheng to pay the bill, and as he handed over the money he said: "Your noodles were delicious. However, while it is important to go to school and you need to make money, it's even more important to stay alive."

The shop owner was busy tidying up and kept repeating: "Yes, yes, you are quite right, sir. Staying alive is the most important thing."

The walls of Wuchang were very ancient. In fact, there was a city wall here already in the Three Kingdoms era, eighteen centuries ago. This wall had seen the rise and fall of dynasties, people had come and gone, it had been built and rebuilt, repaired and re-repaired over the course of more than a thousand years. The city wall was seven metres high and five metres thick and stretched for thirty kilometres, with ten gates allowing communication in and out of the city. Hanyang Gate, Pinghu Gate and Wenchang Gate all faced the Yangtze River; Tongxiang Gate, Binyang Gate and Zhongxiao Gate fronted onto the railway; Wangshan Gate, Bao'an Gate and Zhonghe Gate were on the southern side of the city opposite the Xunsi River; and Wusheng Gate to the north backed onto Sha Lake. The moat, with a depth of three metres,

CHAPTER 5 | 47

formed a further boundary between the city and the suburbs. There had been no major war for a long time, so people had built houses right up against the city walls. In addition, there were now stone bridges spanning the moat by every gate to the city, connecting up with the roads leading out of the city. The ridge of Snake Mountain cut across the city in a sinuous line like a serpent: its head was by the river, and its tail petered out by Binyang Gate, dividing the city into north and south. Both its head and tail had been equipped with sentry posts and batteries of guns. All along the ridge from the Yangtze River to the Han River, from Sha Lake to South Lake, from Gui Mountain to Hong Mountain, the highway and the railway, everything had been fortified and entrenched. Defending this city would be easy; attacking it virtually impossible.

The bulk of the Northern Expeditionary Army now came up and surrounded Wuchang completely. The Seventh Army was stationed outside Zhonghe Gate, Bao'an Gate and Wangshan Gate; the Fourth Army was at Zhongxiao Gate, Binyang Gate and Tongxiang Gate. Liu Yuchun and Chen Jiamo of the Beiyang Army, whose units were tasked with defending the city, kept the ten gates tightly closed. Liu Yuchun, as commander-in-chief, had assured Wu Peifu that he would hold the city at all costs. The huge and heavy gates now served to constrain a small, isolated world within them, and even the bustling sounds of Long Street could not be heard outside.[1]

The headquarters of the Northern Expeditionary Army was established at the Nanhu University of Arts. The task of leading the assault on the city was assigned to Chen Keyu and his Fourth Army, and the Seventh Army led by Li Zongren. As the commander-in-chief of the Fourth Army, Li Jishen, had stayed behind to guard Guangzhou, it was Chen Keyu, deputy commander of the Fourth Army, who was acting commander; while the commander-in-chief of the Seventh Army, Li Zongren, was in charge of the campaign as a whole. The attack on Hanyang and Hankou would be dealt with by the Eighth Army, under the leadership of Tang Shengzhi.

Mo Zhengqi was ordered to take his troops to Changchun Monastery. The Independent Regiment of the Fourth Army was stationed here, opposite Binyang Gate. This was to be their target. Mo Zhengqi had never been to Wuchang before, even though his uncle lived there. Everything he had ever heard about Wuchang came from his cousin Liang Wenqi. In spite of everything his cousin had said, he still couldn't see any difference between Wuchang and Guangzhou. Looking out into the distance at the huge city wall and Snake Mountain rising beyond it, he suddenly felt a strange sense of disquiet. If there was no gunfire, no fighting, and one lived somewhere among the hills of this city, planting one's crops there, life would probably be very comfortable. He thought: If I have to die, it might as well be here, and then maybe I can be reborn here in the next life. At that time, when the war is over, I will be able to live the kind of ordinary life I have always wanted. He told Wu Baosheng his idea.

Wu Baosheng never normally dared to answer back, but this time he did speak up. "I still prefer my hometown," he said. "I've heard that it gets so cold in winter here your fingers freeze off. If I've got to die, it is not going to be here. I want to go home to die. If I'm reincarnated and still living near your house, when other people bully me, you have got to help me."

Mo Zhengqi didn't know whether to laugh or cry and gave him a slap on the head: "If I get reborn here but you go back home, how do you think you can still live near me?"

The front-line command of the Independent Regiment was based at the Three Sage-Kings Hall at Changchun Monastery. Changchun Monastery was a Taoist institution named in memory of Qiu Chuji, also known as Changchun, the seventh disciple of the founder of the Quanzhen sect. Legend has it that Qiu Chuji once urged Genghis Khan, the founder of the Yuan dynasty, to govern with benevolence, and the khan admired him greatly for his insistence on preventing violence. Because of that, Changchun Monastery was built here above the Taiji Hall, and that was more than six hundred years ago. By the middle of the Ming dynasty, there were tens of thousands of Taoists here, and thousands of buildings. The Three Sage-Kings Hall was the most important building in the whole Changchun Monastery complex, and it enshrined statues of Fuxi, Shennong and Xuanyuan. Now, with the addition of a few tables, it had become the headquarters of the Independent Regiment attached to the Northern Expeditionary

Army. The idea that anyone might try to prevent violence seemed laughable now.

Most of the Taoist priests attached to the monastery were cowering in their rooms, afraid to come out. There were a few fresh-faced young Taoists, however, who came to talk to the soldiers of the Revolutionary Army and said that they had been looking forward to the revolution for a long time. As soon as Mo Zhengqi and Battalion Commander Cao Yuan entered the outer gate of Changchun Monastery, they saw a Taoist giving a military salute to every soldier who came past. Mo Zhengqi was somewhat surprised and asked what he was doing. Cao Yuan said: "He wants to show his support for the revolution."

When the Taoist priest heard what they said, he quickly answered: "Yeah, our founder, Master Changchun, was always in favour of revolution!" He also said that when the Manchu Qing dynasty was overthrown in the Xinhai Revolution of 1911, there were plenty of Taoists from their monastery who participated.

Mo Zhengqi couldn't help laughing.

Cao Yuan said: "That's great. Now you go to rest, and when our revolution is over you can tell us all about your founder."

Headquarters decided that the attack on the city should begin on 3 September. From the brief exchange of fire with the enemy on 1 September, it was clear they were determined to hold the walls, which would make it significantly more difficult to attack. The decision from on high was that they must advance and conquer, without giving the enemy the chance to breathe. They were to attack with ladders, forcing a breakthrough. The Fourth Army and the Seventh Army were both ordered to create suicide squads. Anyone who wished to volunteer could do so; otherwise, commanding officers could pick suitable candidates.

Mo Zhengqi stood up and shouted: "No need to call for volunteers! We joined the revolution of our own free will, and we are fighting for our principles. Every single person here is a member of our suicide squad! Pick anyone you like! None of us will back out!"

When Mo Zhengqi said this, everyone echoed his sentiments. On all sides, people were shouting that they were not afraid of death.

Anyone picked would go without a word! Ye Ting, the commander of the Independent Regiment, looked at his men sternly. After a moment's hesitation, he began to call out the names. There were three units in the suicide squad: the first battalion led by Cao Yuan formed the attack team; the second battalion led by Xu Jishen were the advance guard; while the third battalion and the special brigade led by Zhang Bohuang were auxiliaries. Ye Ting told them: "Taking Wuchang will almost assure victory for the Northern Expeditionary Army. If we throw enough at it, we are sure to win. No matter how difficult it is to take this city, it must be conquered at all costs."

Everyone answered: "Understood!"

The houses clustered around the city walls had all been dynamited, and the streets outside the moat were in ruins, which appeared to form an open break. However, there were still low broken walls here and there that could be used as shelter, allowing them to get close to Binyang Gate. There was a little hill over at the northeastern corner of Binyang Gate, and because of this the city wall appeared low. The Northern Expeditionary Army's artillery was mounted on the heights of Hong Mountain, and it was relatively convenient for them to concentrate their fire there. The attack was set for midnight. Four hundred suicide squad members were divided into groups of ten men, with two ladders to each group.

Mo Zhengqi led his group over to receive orders; once night fell, they set off in silence. He was very excited, thinking that tomorrow he might be standing on the walls of Wuchang, looking out at the rivers and lakes, the monarch of all he surveyed. Wouldn't that be great? He also thought about going round to his uncle's house in uniform to frighten the old idiot.

Wu Baosheng came over and asked in a low voice: "Will we really have breakfast in Wuchang tomorrow?"

"Do you ever think about anything that isn't food?" Mo Zhengqi asked. "Tomorrow will be my treat!"

The eastern corner of Binyang Gate did not look very far away. You had to cross a depression, climb over the hill, get over the moat, and then you would be at the foot of the city wall. With the hill where it was, the wall was only a couple of metres high. It was obviously much lower than the wall elsewhere. When the ladders went up, you could grab the top of the wall with your hand. Standing over at Changchun Monastery, you could see any movement on the walls quite clearly, and the same was true for them. It would be madness to attack in the daytime; only once the darkness of night made it impossible for them to see each other could they strike.

Cao Yuan was right out in front, but he seemed hesitant. There simply had not been enough time to prepare for battle; they didn't even know which route would be the most convenient for crossing the moat and which points on the city wall would be the easiest to climb with ladders. There were no pre-arranged signals for contact between different teams... in fact, they didn't even have time to choose long enough pieces of bamboo to make the ladders. When the ladders were finished, they were obviously not going to reach, and one ladder broke halfway. Cao Yuan's heart sank a little. If things go badly and you hit a landmine, that will kill you; if the ladder isn't long enough and you can't climb the wall, that will also kill you; if you can't keep your lines of communication open, and by the time everyone is in place it is broad daylight, that means you die right then and there. Headquarters was eager for another victory. They had been winning one battle after another, but in point of fact they had been fighting without ever achieving a proper understanding of the enemy's position. They had got this far on courage and speed alone. It seemed as though heaven were looking out for the Northern Expeditionary Army, and everyone thought that, with the courage shown by their soldiers, it ought to be possible to conquer Wuchang with one concerted attack. However, no battle is won by wishful thinking from one side. Cao Yuan had gone to Regimental Commander Ye Ting and told him it was too dangerous. Ye Ting had thought about it for a moment and then said: "I agree. But headquarters has already given orders. We have to carry them out, even though they are damn dangerous."

It was a night without a star to be seen. It was absolutely black. Moving forward, nobody could see anybody else, and they relied entirely on sound to keep up with their comrades. The ladders were heavy, and the road was difficult to negotiate at night. By the time the attack team had fumbled their way through the darkness to their positions, the horizon was already showing a streak of light.

Cao Yuan said to Mo Zhengqi: "If you see an opportunity, then get up the walls. If you can't, I am ordering you right now to withdraw immediately, and don't waste any time."

Mo Zhengqi said: "Rest assured, sir, that every time we crossed swords with them in the past, they did not stop to fight. We'll get up there no problem."

Cao Yuan looked stern: "That was then, and this is now. Have you not seen their entrenchments? If you hesitate, that could mean the deaths of dozens of your comrades! If you get them killed, I swear I will have your head as a sacrifice to them!"

Mo Zhengqi had never seen Cao Yuan so angry, so he made haste to agree. But all the time he was thinking: We're the greatest, aren't we? How could the Northern Expeditionary Army be defeated by the likes of them?

As soon as all the suicide squads were in place, the order to attack was given. Four men from each team carried a ladder across the depression, almost running, then they made their way over the moat and arrived at the foot of the walls. Negotiating the moat was easier than expected, but before they had even got the ladders up they were spotted by the soldiers in the watchtower. Overhead, someone shouted: "The enemy is coming!" Suddenly, all the lanterns on the tower were lit, and the oil lamps hanging on the walls were burning bright. The Northern Expeditionary Army was completely exposed. Bullets beat down on them like hail, and it was at this moment that they discovered that instead of providing covering fire, the suicide squads behind them couldn't shoot as far as the enemy on the walls but were hitting their own side instead. They could also hear the artillery firing. Although they failed to hit any of the attack teams, the sound was terrifying. At that moment, battle was joined; ladders fell and people dropped with them. Cao Yuan broke out in a cold sweat all over. If he continued the attack on the city, every single one of them would be killed. "Withdraw!"

When Mo Zhengqi heard his cry, he was in the process of falling off a ladder. A splinter of bamboo stabbed him in the leg, and he felt a spasm of pain. He wished he could fly straight up to the watchtower and slaughter everyone there. But he also knew that if they carried on fighting like this, all his comrades would be killed. So he did not hesitate; immediately, he echoed Cao Yuan's cry and had his men retreat. He himself was already incapable of walking, and his trousers were soaked in blood. Wu Baosheng had to help him along. The machine gun in the watchtower swept back and forth relentlessly; they had almost made their way across the moat when Mo Zhengqi suddenly stumbled and fell to the ground. Before he could get up, a man rushed over and pressed him as flat as he could. The gunfire rang in his ears as the sand on either side of him exploded.

A few seconds later, shooting began from the perimeter wall of Changchun Monastery; Ye Ting had ordered them to provide covering fire for the retreating troops. The machine gun in the watchtower stopped for a moment. Mo Zhengqi turned over and realised that it was Wu Baosheng who had fallen on top of him. He had been shot, and blood was pouring down his back. Mo Zhengqi was so shocked and horrified he forgot all about the pain in his leg. He took his friend up on his back and set off at full speed.

Wu Baosheng was still conscious, but only just. "It didn't hit my heart," he said, "it just got me in the shoulder. There's no hurry. You can't run, you have a leg injury."

"Bastard!" Mo Zhengqi said. "Why did you lie down on top of me?"

Wu Baosheng giggled and said: "If I hadn't, you'd be dead. I saved your life. When we go back home, if ever my arm hurts, you'll have to help me get the crops planted."

Mo Zhengqi had no intention of arguing with him. He knew that Wu Baosheng had just saved his life, and his eyes were damp. "I promise to get Xiangmei to look after you," he said, "and I promise you that it won't hurt."

By the time they got back to Changchun Monastery, the sun had risen. The smoke was gone, and the air was fresh. Hong Mountain lay quietly behind Snake Mountain, and the forest trees were lush. The late summer sunshine fell on the leaves, swaying in the breeze, as if scattering the light around. A breath of freshness came with this light and followed the gentle wind. Up on the walls of Wuchang, there were triumphant cheers and laughter. This sound flew like a dagger, piercing Mo Zhengqi's heart and lungs. Since the

Northern Expedition first set out, the Independent Regiment had fought one bloody battle after another, but never had they been so badly defeated.

Everyone who had stayed behind came to offer their condolences. The suicide squads looked devastated, as if this failure was their fault. Cao Yuan counted the survivors, but casualty numbers were not serious because they had pulled back so quickly.

Mo Zhengqi saw Ye Ting coming over and felt a little guilty; at that moment, he felt that it would have been better to die on the battlefield. Ye Ting came up to him, stopped, and saw the blood on his trousers. Mo Zhengqi said hurriedly: "It's just a bamboo splinter. It's already stopped bleeding."

Ye Ting did not say anything and patted him on the shoulder.

Cao Yuan, who was standing behind Ye Ting, said hurriedly: "Go to Baotong Temple and have it dressed."

"Yes, sir!" Mo Zhengqi said in a low voice.

Looking at his bedraggled forces, Ye Ting's face wore a dignified expression. After a long pause, he said: "Everybody needs to rest and recuperate. Anyone who has been injured needs to get treated straight away because we are going to attack the city walls again immediately."

6

LIANG KESI and Luo Yinan arrived at Wuchang just after the battle was over. The sun glinted on the watchtowers, so looking at them from afar they seemed touched with gold. Luo Yinan had never seen Wuchang from such an angle before. He felt a little surprised and could not help sighing: "Oh, how magnificent Wuchang looks from here!" Liang Kesi had much the same feeling, and he too sighed and exclaimed at the majestic sight.

It was here that they heard the news: the attack on the walls had failed.

Liang Kesi was shocked: "How could they possibly fail? No way!"

Luo Yinan was surprised by his certainty: "Why is it impossible? Isn't it true that battles are lost all the time?"

Liang Kesi asked the people around him: "Did the Independent Regiment take part?"

The answer came: "They were the main attack force."

"Then it's absolutely impossible that they could lose," Liang Kesi said firmly. "It must be a strategic withdrawal."

Luo Yinan thought his confidence was misplaced and said: "Why?"

Liang Kesi smiled, utterly convinced of the truth of what he was saying: "Well, even if I told you, you would not understand."

Liang Kesi and Luo Yinan were directed to go to the

Department of Political Affairs of the Northern Expeditionary Army to work on one of the propaganda teams. When they enlisted at Tingsi Bridge, the officer in charge of allocating recruits realised that they were students and was delighted to see them. Then he looked depressed and said: "Great – finally we get some educated recruits. We simply don't have enough propaganda people." After that, he sighed again and said: "Students should not be allowed to fight – we have peasants for that. We ought to be protecting you so that you can study properly."

"With things the way they are," Liang Kesi pointed out, "how can we study? We are better off joining the army and saving our country."

The officer was much impressed: "Well said! That's what we like to hear! Once we have saved the Chinese people from suffering, you can always go back to your studies."

Liang Kesi and Luo Yinan made their way to the headquarters of the Northern Expeditionary Command at Nanhu University of Arts as they had been directed. Luo Yinan felt he might be quite good at propaganda work, but Liang Kesi was furious. He repeatedly proclaimed that he was there to fight, not to write slogans or draw pretty pictures. All the way to the Department of Political Affairs, where they were supposed to report, Liang Kesi kept complaining, and even after he walked through the door he made it clear he was there under duress. He managed to annoy one of the officers there, a man in glasses, who retorted: "Do you really think that writing slogans and painting pictures isn't part of the fight?" Liang Kesi was struck dumb.

The soldier who took them to where they were to report was called Huang Jiezi. He had been a middle-school student in Hankou when he heard that the Northern Expeditionary Army had arrived at Wuchang, and he crossed the Yangtze River to enlist, whereupon he was enrolled in the propaganda team.

Liang Kesi said: "If only I had known, I would have done the same thing. I didn't need to do all this rushing about."

Huang Jiezi laughed: "I wanted to go to Guangzhou, but my mother locked me in my room. I didn't manage to escape, but as it turned out it was just as well that she did have me under lock and key."

Liang Kesi also laughed at that: "It sounds like your mother is a pretty clever lady."

They were sent to a classroom to write leaflets and slogans. Everyone was quite convinced that the Northern Expeditionary Army would take Wuchang in a day or two. Not only did they want leaflets printed, but they also wanted slogans written out in advance, and even the glue to paste them up was ready. As soon as the army entered the city, leaflets were there to be distributed, and slogans were to be pasted up on the walls. Luo Yinan had always enjoyed practising his calligraphy, and he had learned to write beautiful Yan-style regular script. He was perfectly happy writing away. This kind of work suited him down to the ground. He was quite sure he would be useless in any kind of battle – even if he wasn't scared of getting killed, the sight of blood made him go weak at the knees. Some people are just not cut out to be soldiers, Luo Yinan thought, and I'm afraid I am one of them. He was quite sure he did not have a heroic bone in his body.

But Liang Kesi was desperate to fight. He was determined to join the Independent Regiment, and he had promised his cousin Mo Zhengqi that he would follow him on the Northern Expedition. The whole way, they had been hearing tales of how the Independent Regiment won every battle they fought. Ye Ting, the commander of the Independent Regiment, was called "Zhao Zilong come back to life" in the newspapers, and he was being described as some kind of invincible warrior. Liang Kesi's imagination was on fire. He thought to himself: What greater glory could there be than to follow a hero like that onto the battlefield! Since the Independent Regiment is so great, of course they are going to be right on the front line.

After dinner, Huang Jiezi finally told Liang Kesi what he really wanted to know: the Independent Regiment was bivouacked at Changchun Monastery. Liang Kesi knew exactly where that was because he had been to the house of his classmate Chen Mingwu, and from his front door you could see the yellow roof of the Three Sage-Kings Hall at Changchun Monastery. Knowing that it was not far away, Liang Kesi immediately got restless, as if he wanted to set out straight away.

Luo Yinan said: "You are a soldier now, so you can't just go! What did the officer with the glasses say earlier?"

That seemed to remind Huang Jiezi of something. Lowering his voice, he said: "Do you know who the man wearing glasses is?"

"No idea," Liang Kesi said.

"It's Guo Moruo, the great poet!" Huang Jiezi whispered.

That came as a big surprise to Liang Kesi, so he squawked: "No way!"

Luo Yinan was even more amazed.

Huang Jiezi said: "The director of the Department of Political Affairs is Deng Yanda. He told me that from now on, Guo Moruo is going to be the deputy director. He only got here a day or two ago."

Luo Yinan turned to Liang Kesi: "Didn't you tell me you admire his poems very much? I remember you read his 'Goddess' some time back."

Liang Kesi's heart was hammering. He had read many of Guo Moruo's poems and particularly loved his 'Goddess'. That description of true love, fearless of the consequences, made his heart beat faster each time he read it. Now, Guo Moruo had been standing right opposite him, and he didn't recognise him! Or perhaps it was because he had never imagined that a famous poet like him would join the Northern Expedition! They had made the same decision. Liang Kesi was thrilled at the thought.

The three of them were walking along the edge of the quad at the Nanhu University of Arts. They had all fallen silent at the mere mention of Guo Moruo's name. Suddenly, there was a loud bang, as if there had been an explosion nearby. Huang Jiezi and Luo Yinan fell to the ground, but Liang Kesi stood still. He looked around and saw smoke rising somewhere beyond the wall.

"They aren't shooting at us!" Liang Kesi exclaimed.

Meanwhile, someone was shouting: "It's the artillery on Snake Mountain that's firing – they are aiming somewhere outside the wall, but they haven't hit anyone!"

Huang Jiezi got to his feet and looked at Liang Kesi admiringly. "You seem very calm," he said. "On the field of battle, you'd be a hero."

"Of course," Liang Kesi said.

Huang Jiezi kept his voice down, pretending to make a big mystery: "Let me tell you, when Generalissimo Chiang Kai-shek arrives, you should get him to send you to the front line. That would work!"

"You're having a laugh!" said Liang Kesi.

Huang Jiezi grinned wickedly: "Nobody else would dare to send a student out to fight. Director Deng Yanda would never agree. He says that all the students are needed to stay behind to write slogans."

The next morning, there was exciting news. The story was that the various senior officers had held an overnight meeting at headquarters, with the Russian military advisers participating. As a result of their overnight discussions, it was decided that they would use the same technique as in the conquest of Huizhou: an all-out assault on the city walls. With more people, more scaling ladders, more firepower, they would conduct a frontal attack. They had a deadline from Generalissimo Chiang Kai-shek: forty-eight hours to take Wuchang. Each and every person who made it to the top of the city wall would be generously rewarded. They would attack at midnight on 5 September, and their forces would be concentrated at Binyang Gate and Bao'an Gate. The other gates would also be attacked, but that would be a feint to distract and draw off the enemy forces.

Liang Kesi did not know how many people he had pleaded with in his efforts to be sent to the front. Although he did not dare to go directly to Generalissimo Chiang Kai-shek, he did make the rounds of other senior officers until he found one who agreed to transfer him to the Independent Regiment.

When he set off that morning, Luo Yinan went to see him on his way. Liang Kesi's face was flushed, and Luo Yinan had to ask him: "Are you really so sure you want to fight?"

"Of course!" Liang Kesi said. "You don't really count as a revolutionary until you have been to the front line and exchanged fire with the enemy."

"Are you really not afraid to die?" Luo Yinan asked.

"No," Liang Kesi said. "With things the way they are, it is better to die gloriously than live like a slave."

Suddenly, Chen Dingyi's head appeared in Luo Yinan's

imagination, and his heart ached for a moment: "I don't want you to die. I want to see you come back alive."

"Sure," Liang Kesi said, "but as long as I'm alive, you can't become a monk."

"OK," Luo Yinan laughed.

"We have a deal?" Liang Kesi asked.

"Yeah," Luo Yinan said.

They walked together as far as the crossroads. One way took you to Tongxiang Gate, the other to Bao'an Gate and the third to Hong Mountain. Liang Kesi went in the direction of Hong Mountain. He said: "I'm going to go first to Baotong Temple Field Hospital to see a relative of mine. She is my cousin's fiancée."

"There's a field hospital at Baotong Temple?" Luo Yinan asked.

Liang Kesi laughed: "Yeah, I thought you knew. I'll have a look and see if Comrade Zhang Shuya is there. How about it?"

Luo Yinan laughed nervously, then they said goodbye.

Looking at his back as he walked away, Luo Yinan suddenly felt uneasy without being able to explain why. He shouted: "You've got to come back alive!"

Liang Kesi waved and yelled back: "Of course I will! Remember that as long as I am alive, I will not let you become a monk!" His smiling face was lit up by the dazzling sunshine, so bright it gave the whole scene a transcendental air.

Suddenly, Luo Yinan felt that something about his expression looked like Chen Dingyi's head when it was hanging high above Government Gate. His heart skipped a beat, and he thought: No! I don't want you to die! If you do, I really will become a monk!

As he made his way back to South Lake, Luo Yinan bumped into Huang Jiezi. He was sitting in a carriage. When he spotted Luo Yinan, he called him loudly, and he jumped up into the carriage with him. "I knew I would find you here," Huang Jiezi said, "so I didn't wait around at home."

"Quite right," Luo Yinan said. "Where are we going now?"

"Yesterday," Huang Jiezi explained, "they used up all the bamboo around here trying to clamber over the city walls. So we have to go a bit further or we won't be able to find any at all."

"If you head out towards Xianning," Luo Yinan said, "when I arrived, I saw a lot of bamboo round there."

"Great!" Huang Jiezi said. "Let's go there."

Luo Yinan didn't write a single slogan all day. Their task now was to collect bamboo from one village after another; in fact, almost everyone had been sent out to collect material. They were now planning a much bigger attack with many more people, so they would need a lot more ladders. Collecting bamboo and making ladders was going to be vital for attacking the city walls. Having had ladders fall apart last time, not to mention splitting as soon as anyone tried to scale them, now there were strict requirements in place concerning the quality of bamboo and how the ladders were going to be constructed.

Far away from Wuchang, the fields in these late-summer-to early-autumn days were still green. The smoke rising from the little villages and the occasional barking of dogs reminded Luo Yinan of his hometown; his mother squatting down in front of the hearth to light the fire; his grandmother tapping on her wooden fish in front of the statue of Bodhisattva Guanyin; and his father reading a book by the light of an oil lamp. His father was a primary school teacher and taught little children from his clan to read and write in a classroom attached to the ancestral temple. He even called to mind their neighbour, old Mr Zhou, who was blind and claimed to be a fortune teller. When telling Luo Yinan his fortune, he would always grab his hand and say: "You're a lucky man. Even if everyone you know gets killed, you'll still be alive." At that moment, Luo Yinan wondered whether he might not have been telling the truth. But if it did happen, it would be a dreadful thing... What's the point of being alive if everyone you know is dead?

They were now on the outskirts of Xianning. The villagers were all very enthusiastic. Whether rich or poor, when they heard that the Northern Expeditionary Army wanted bamboo, they rushed out to cut it and promised to transport it safe and sound to South Lake. Just in case there was not enough, some young people simply grabbed their machetes and headed up the mountain. Luo Yinan was moved. Why should they care if Wuchang City is captured? After all, it is nothing to do with them.

Luo Yinan asked an old woman who gave them water to drink what she thought. The old woman said: "Last time when they came through, one of the officers said that all the poor people in the world are from the same family. That's true. I had a couple of officers billeted on me, and they helped me tidy up and swept the floor clean before they left. There was one soldier who was about the same age as my grandson. He helped me haul water from the well and fed the pig for me. He also chatted to me, and he could explain things so much better than my grandson. Oh yes, and he said his grandmother also worshipped Guanyin."

Luo Yinan listened to the old woman's words and was silent for a moment. Then he said: "My grandmother also prays to Guanyin."

The old woman was delighted: "Exactly! When they say that all the poor people in the world are one family, they've got it right!"

It was not just Luo Yinan who was busy; the entire staff from headquarters were rushed off their feet. Bamboo was coming in from all directions, and it was slapped down in heaps around the southern quad. All the people who usually worked in supplies were now enrolled in the teams constructing scaling ladders. Eventually, even the villagers who helped transport the bamboo were staying behind to make ladders. Tying them tight enough required a lot of strength; if they weren't tight, they would break when someone tried to climb them, and that could kill or injure the soldiers. The officer in charge kept repeating this while he made his checks. Luo Yinan understood the problem, but when he looked at his hands he saw how pale and slender they were... and how feeble. He felt deeply ashamed. The best he could do was to keep carrying bamboo over to the ladder makers and then take the finished ladder over to the pile by the wall.

The work lasted all day and all night, and he soon lost count of how many ladders had been produced. Even as the suicide squads assembled at the south quad on the evening of 5 September, the production of scaling ladders was not complete.

It was already getting dark, and the officer in charge shouted: "Hurry up! Hurry up! All the ladders need to be completed before the squads assemble!"

Luo Yinan's hands were cut to ribbons by moving bamboo, and, when he accidentally caught hold of a knot, the pain was unbearable. However, he did not complain because he thought that this hardship was part and parcel of his duties as a soldier. Even if he had become a monk, it would be hard work to go down the mountain and haul water up again. When he explained this to Huang Jiezi, the latter said: "Hey! You are a revolutionary now. How can you still be going on about becoming a monk?"

By the time the order was given for the suicide squads to assemble, the ladders needed for scaling the walls were pretty much complete. Luo Yinan sighed; he just wanted to rest and relax, but suddenly he caught sight of an official pointing to the quad and saying something to Huang Jiezi. Luo Yinan recognised him: Director Deng Yanda. Huang Jiezi saluted him and was about to leave, when he looked up and spotted Luo Yinan. He gestured to him urgently. Luo Yinan did not know what could have happened, and he ran over. Huang Jiezi said: "Quick, follow me! We need to get more lamp oil. Look, a lot of the lights have already gone out."

The night was already very dark. There were a few scattered lights showing at various points around the quad at the Nanhu University of Arts. A couple of paraffin lamps were burning the very last of their oil, glowing dimly, making the atmosphere of the whole place seem depressing and sad. Luo Yinan and Huang Jiezi set off at the double, bringing oil to each expiring lamp. As they lit up again, the light bounced off the ground, making a soft glow, sweeping away the sad air that had afflicted the scene. The assembled multitude no longer seemed so distressed, and there were now even some people laughing amidst the crowd. Luo Yinan was amazed at the power of light. No wonder, he thought, that everyone eulogises it when it is so important. It does not just expel darkness but also takes away the sadness in people's hearts.

When Luo Yinan heard the laughter ring out a second time, he suddenly felt that there was something familiar about it. Following the sound, he tracked down Liang Kesi, who was chatting and laughing with another man, a gun in his hand. Luo Yinan cried out: "Hey, Kesi!"

When Liang Kesi turned round to look, he pointed at Luo Yinan and said to the man he had been laughing with: "That's him. He is the one who wanted to be a monk, but in the end I just dragged him north with me. I told him there wasn't much difference between being a monk and being dead." There was a smile on his face as he said this.

Luo Yinan felt a little embarrassed. He went over to Liang Kesi and looked at his costume. Then he said in wonderment: "Are you in one of these suicide squads? Are you going to attack the city wall tonight?"

"I told you right from the start," Liang Kesi said, "that I was here to fight."

"Do you really know what you are doing?" Luo Yinan asked.

"Hey," Liang Kesi said, "you'd better not underestimate me, you know?"

"It's going to be a terrible fight," Luo Yinan said. "You've never been on the field of battle before, you..."

Before he could finish speaking, Liang Kesi grabbed hold of his shirt and dragged him to one side. Then he whispered: "I've been practising shooting all day. You can't say I can't do it." Then he said happily: "Come on, let me introduce you. This is my cousin Mo Zhengqi – he's a company commander. He is a hero in the Independent Regiment – a real hero, who has won countless battles."

Luo Yinan looked closely at Mo Zhengqi and saw that his hair was cropped short, his face had been burned dark by the sun, and his eyes were sharp. He did indeed look positively heroic. He nodded a greeting to Mo Zhengqi.

Liang Kesi laughed and said: "Don't you think he looks like a textbook hero?"

"Yeah," Luo Yinan said. "He could double for Guan Yu, God of War." The idea had just popped into his head.

Liang Kesi was not very pleased: "That is really not a good comparison! Our regimental commander, Ye Ting, is often said to be Zhao Zilong come back to life. If Zhengqi here is like Guan Yu, then wasn't Zhao Zilong his blood brother?" He burst out laughing as he said this.

Luo Yinan considered the point: it really was not a good comparison. He wanted to laugh like Liang Kesi, but he couldn't.

The night was warm. Before they assembled, the officers told everyone to write a final message for their families. The soldiers all knew the risks they were running. Whether they would come back alive or not would depend entirely on luck. This was a suicide mission. Only Liang Kesi found it in himself to laugh. But the sound did not dissipate the oppressive atmosphere. His laughter seemed to bounce from one wall to the next, rebounding here and there, until it came and landed in front of him again. Even he now realised that his mirth was not only out of place, it was bizarre.

The commander began to speak. His voice was extremely low, and as he spat out the first few words they seemed to harden in mid-air. Luo Yinan moved away in a hurry and stood off to one side of the quad. Guo Moruo, Deputy Director of the Department of Political Affairs, also made a speech. Luo Yinan could tell that the poet was conflicted about what he was saying, and that made his voice even deeper. That depth made a fire appear in front of Luo Yinan's eyes, and a phoenix flew in and out of the flames. Under the wings of the phoenix, he could see Liang Kesi's sunny face. Luo Yinan's legs began to shake. The city walls were going to be attacked in a full-frontal assault. Forty-eight hours. Generous rewards. Nobody would be allowed to retreat. Deserters would be killed. These words leapt across the quad. Blood was about to be shed; the battle was about to begin. Luo Yinan thought: Did you really laugh just now? Are you really happy? How can you smile in the face of death?

Luo Yinan did not hear the rest of the speech. Looking at the suicide squads lined up in there, he thought to himself: Maybe tomorrow, these people will all be dead and buried at the foot of the walls of Wuchang. He was terrified at the thought, and the trembling of his legs progressed until he was shaking all over. Even as the troops began to move off, he could not control himself.

The paraffin lamps were almost burned out, and the light grew faint again.

It was zero hour, and the suicide squads were leaving. In the dim glow, Luo Yinan watched Liang Kesi leave. He was not laughing now, and he walked close behind Mo Zhengqi. His appearance once again made Luo Yinan's heart beat faster: he looked just like Chen Dingyi when his head was hanging over Government Gate.

7

THE NIGHT WAS VERY DARK. It was also quiet, except for the sound of hurrying footsteps and the occasional smack of a leg against a ladder. These noises, filled with tension and unease, merged into the blackness. All the houses around were dark, their lights out. Even if there were lamps burning somewhere, the windows and doors were all covered with thick blackout curtains so as not to attract the attention of the gunners.

Liang Kesi still felt not the slightest fear. He did not know why he was not afraid. He thought he ought to feel scared; after all, he had never been in battle before, but he simply didn't. He was just excited. He seemed calmer than Mo Zhengqi, who had been through many fights before – almost as if he were not heading off for battle but rather going to take part in a performance; and for him, it was not going to be a tragedy.

Liang Kesi thought to himself: That's the sort of person I am. I am that brave. My courage comes from my resolution. I am willing to die – to be destroyed – for my principles, and that is why I am not afraid. I've always been different from other people in that way.

But Mo Zhengqi, who was walking just ahead of him, was in a serious mood. The presence of his silly little cousin by his side made him significantly more nervous than he had ever felt going into any previous battle. He had fought before. He was not indifferent to the prospect of his own demise; from experience, he had worked out some basic skills of survival on the field of battle. But his cousin had no idea of the dangers, so he was completely unconcerned. He was naively determined to fight on the battlefield, as if idealism could stop bullets. He was asking to get himself killed. What should I do? Thinking this, Mo Zhengqi felt a knife twist in his heart.

Liang Kesi was happily bouncing along. Suddenly, he quickened his pace and caught up with Mo Zhengqi. He whispered: "Have you often had to march in the middle of the night like this?"

"Keep your mouth shut," Mo Zhengqi snapped back.

It was a starless night. Mo Zhengqi deeply regretted boasting to his cousin about the revolution underway in Guangzhou; he should never have told him what a great thing the Northern Expedition was. It was his letter that brought his cousin to this. His enthusiasm about the revolution started burning even brighter because of this letter, and this sustained him on the long and difficult journey to Guangzhou without a murmur, and then from Guangzhou all the way to Wuchang. When Mo Zhengqi was sitting on one of the wooden stools at Baotong Temple Field Hospital to have his dressings changed, he was wondering where his cousin had got to, and then Guo Xiangmei brought him in. They had been delighted to see each other. He was so happy his cousin had made it all the way safe and sound: it was an enormous relief. However, only a few minutes later, he realised that a new burden awaited him.

Liang Kesi was insisting on joining the Independent Regiment.

Mo Zhengqi categorically refused. He tried to persuade him to stay in the Department of Political Affairs, saying that it was the best possible option for him, but Liang Kesi just kept repeating that he was determined to fight. Mo Zhengqi was adamant. This was no ordinary battle, but a suicide mission. If something happened to his silly young cousin, how could he ever face his uncle again? Liang Kesi didn't agree and kept pestering him. He demanded to see Regimental Commander Ye Ting and was not going to go away until he did. He said that he had already obtained approval from one of his superior officers for his transfer.

Mo Zhengqi had no choice but to take him to headquarters at the Three Sage-Kings Hall.

"Have you ever fought in a battle before?" Ye Ting asked.

"Not yet," Liang Kesi said, "but I will have soon."

"Can you use a gun?" Ye Ting asked.

"I can learn today," Liang Kesi assured him.

"You have never fought in battle, and you don't know how to use a gun, but you still want to go. Aren't you afraid of getting killed?" Ye Ting demanded.

"No," Liang Kesi said.

"Why not?" Ye Ting asked.

"For the sake of revolution," Liang Kesi said, "Tan Sitong was prepared to use his death to awaken an entire generation. And I am happy to die if that is a call to arms for a new generation of revolutionaries. Tan Sitong wrote a poem that says, *I will laugh though the sword falls, my head to sever, / My courage and daring will be beacons forever.*"

Ye Ting stared at the chatty and always insouciant Liang Kesi and meditated for a moment. Then he remarked: "Well said."

That seemed to serve as further encouragement for Liang Kesi, and he became much more confident. He now mentioned that Tang Caichang, Tan Sitong's classmate and good friend, had been executed right here in Wuchang. Before he died, he said that he was happy to be executed since so many heroes had died the same way. "These two great men are my role models," he said. "I would be happy to follow their example if my death meant that people in the future would be able to lead a better life."

"That sounds wonderful," Ye Ting said, "and I am very touched. But I can tell you right now that my men are not allowed to go to battle expecting to die. I want my men to think about killing the enemy and how to survive themselves. So I am willing for you to join the Independent Regiment, but I am not going to send you to the front line. You will be part of our propaganda team."

Mo Zhengqi heaved a sigh of relief, but Liang Kesi was very upset. He wanted to argue, but Ye Ting did not give him any opportunity to speak: "I would like to give you a piece of advice. People who talk too much don't make good soldiers. On the battlefield, it can sometimes almost seem that the bullets have eyes, and they are looking for people like you to slam into. Mo Zhengqi, I want you to keep an eye on him." Having said this, Ye Ting walked away.

Just as the regimental commander had indicated, Liang Kesi was not allowed to join one of the suicide squads. Cao Yuan, the battalion commander, was repeatedly pestered by him as he organised his attack team, but he just said: "If the commander won't let you go and get killed, do you really expect me to disagree?" However, Erqiangzi, one of the soldiers chosen for Cao Yuan's attack team, developed diarrhoea, and when the time came for them to set off he was too weak even to stand up. Liang Kesi, who had been looking for any opportunity to join in, lowered his hat and answered to his name at roll call. By the time Mo Zhengqi discovered what he had done and reported it to Cao Yuan, the attack team had already arrived at South Lake. Cao Yuan said: "If you are so worried about him getting himself killed, why on earth did you write to him like that in the first place? What did you expect?"

Mo Zhengqi gulped and could not answer; he had no idea what to say.

At three o'clock in the morning, Li Zongren, as the commander-in-chief of the entire campaign, gave the order to attack. The batteries of guns placed around Hong Mountain shook the heavens as they fired. Shells rained down on Binyang Gate, Zhongxiao Gate, Wusheng Gate and Snake Mountain. In an instant, the earth and the sky were rent with thunder and lightning, as the city of Wuchang seemed to explode. The sound of shouting and screaming rose high into the sky and seemed to hang in the air for a long time.

With the artillery barrage providing covering fire, Cao Yuan ordered his attack team forward, moving as quickly as possible. There were ten men carrying each scaling ladder as they forded the moat and marched straight to the foot of the walls. Behind them, the advance guard and the auxiliaries also fired at the watchtowers so that the attack team could make it up the walls without coming under attack.

However, the ladders still weren't long enough, and the enemy was defending the walls with all its might. Quite apart from bullets, fireballs were also now coming down on them. The sound of bamboo breaking and the screams of soldiers falling from the ladders was appalling. Cao Yuan shouted: "Go on! Go on! Don't stop!" The first batch fell, and then another rushed to take their place, then they fell too, and the next batch attacked. There was soon heap after heap of bodies under the city wall, and the people coming up behind them almost had to clamber over their comrades-in-arms to charge forward. The ladders were now placed pretty much directly on top of the stack of corpses.

In the heat of battle, Mo Zhengqi could no longer look out for his cousin. He didn't even know where he was. Jacked up on a pile of corpses, four of the bigger scaling ladders did now reach to the top of the city wall. If they didn't get up there now, by the time it got light, it would be too late and all their sacrifices would be in vain. "Follow me!" Mo Zhengqi roared at the top of his voice. "Anyone who is still alive, climb!" As he shouted this, he advanced a few steps and began to make his way up the ladder. He climbed quickly and soon reached the top of the city wall. He could clearly see the faces of the enemy soldiers there; he noticed particularly the pimples on the nose of one of them. Mo Zhengqi roared again at his men, struggling to climb over the edge, leaping onto the top of the walls.

There was a cry of alarm from the watchtower, and all of a sudden Mo Zhengqi found himself in the midst of a melee. Following close behind him, several more soldiers bellowed as they leapt on top of the walls.

The enemy panicked. They had fought with the Northern Expeditionary Army before and were well aware of their skill in fighting hand-to-hand. They were starting to retreat. Suddenly, a man shouted: "Anyone who retreats will be beheaded! Bayonets, advance! Kill them all! Burn their ladders!"

Immediately they started destroying the ladders behind Mo Zhengqi and his men. Soldiers armed with bayonets emerged from the watchtower on the northeastern corner of the walls and, without the slightest hesitation, charged at Mo Zhengqi and the others. The troops in the advance guard, who were supposed to move on and attack the city itself, were now not able to climb the walls, so Mo Zhengqi and his men were isolated. Now they were the target of both bullets and bayonets. In the space of just a few minutes, they were either cut to pieces under the watchtower or fell from the top of the walls. They could not move forward, and the only way back was down.

Mo Zhengqi took a bayonet wound to his shoulder, and when a group of enemy soldiers lunged at him he decided to jump off the walls.

As he fell, he had only one thought in his mind: This is the end.

However, as it turned out, the fall did not kill him. There was now layer upon layer of corpses at the foot of the city walls, and he landed on them – his deceased comrades saved his life. He was covered in blood, but he didn't know where he was injured other than his shoulder. He felt no pain.

People were still trying to climb the walls, and the scaling ladders were being positioned willy-nilly, anywhere they could get them set up. As the sky began to get light, Mo Zhengqi straightened up and looked around for his soldiers. He was shocked to find that there were only a few left. Just at that moment, he heard a voice in mid-air, coming ever closer as someone fell: "Help! Zhengqi!"

Mo Zhengqi's heart gave a horrible thump: it was his cousin. He struggled to get up and shouted: "Where are you, Kesi? Where are you?"

A little voice spoke near him, faint and quavering: "I am over here, but I think I have broken my legs... both my legs are broken." Mo Zhengqi scrambled over in the direction of the sound, but bullets and artillery shells were still flying around in all directions. He saw Liang Kesi lying on the ground, his face contorted in pain, unable to move.

Mo Zhengqi clawed his way over to him and tried to comfort him: "Thank goodness you're alive. If you've been injured, you will heal; if you've broken your leg, that'll heal. In fact, you can break as many as you like and you'll still get better." As he spoke, he moved round behind Liang Kesi and dragged him into the lee of the wall. "We're out of range here," Mo Zhengqi said, "so it's completely safe. Don't move. When the battle is over, I'll get you out of here. If you think you can manage it, try to make your way over to the barbican under the watchtower: that's the very safest place. Try to conserve your energy; I will come back to save you. You must not be afraid."

"I am not afraid," Liang Kesi said. "Be careful! I'll wait for you here."

"I'll be back as soon as I can," Mo Zhengqi said.

The attack on the walls was now clearly slackening, and fewer and fewer soldiers were coming forward. However, from time to time, people were still falling off the scaling ladders, and the pile of corpses at the foot of the city walls was getting higher and larger. Mo Zhengqi moved closer to the heap and shouted: "Zhou Sen! Li Donglin! Li Jishan! Tang Laiqiao!" No one answered. He shouted again: "Li Shengbiao! Fu Ba! Zeng Xiangfeng! Tan Yunsheng!" There was still no response.

A faint whisper came to him: "They are all dead…"

He went cold all over. "Who are you?" he asked.

The voice answered: "I am Liu Zhengbao, from the second platoon."

"How are you doing?" Mo Zhengqi asked him.

The voice replied: "My back is broken, and I can't move."

"Lie still and keep breathing," Mo Zhengqi said, "I will rescue you."

From across the corpses, another voice now spoke: "Company Commander, I can't move… It's me, Zhang Desheng."

"You both lie right where you are," Mo Zhengqi said, "and stay still. I'll find an ambulance team to rescue you. Hold on for me! Liu Zhengbao, can you see if there are any other casualties? Tell them to stay safe and wait for rescue."

"OK," Liu Zhengbao said. "Actually, Zhao Huzi and Li Sanfu both seem to still be alive."

The sky was now getting light, and Mo Zhengqi felt that something was now very wrong. If they carried on fighting like this, even if each and every one of them was prepared to risk their lives, they would not make it to the top of the walls. At that very moment, he heard Cao Yuan cry: "Withdraw! Pull back to the plateau!"

Mo Zhengqi ran as fast as he could towards the little plateau. Cao Yuan's face was a mask of blood. Mo Zhengqi was shocked and asked: "Battalion Commander, are you hurt?"

"No," Cao Yuan said, "that's He Changhua and Huang Zhenxiang's blood. They died right in front of me."

"It is already daybreak," said Mo Zhengqi, "and we only have a dozen people left. We're far too exposed. What should we do?"

"I swore before we set out that I would not return until we had control of the watchtowers," Cao Yuan replied. "We haven't had any further orders, so I guess we are all going to die here."

"If we die here," Mo Zhengqi said, "we will have achieved nothing. And we've already lost plenty of comrades."

"How about this?" Cao Yuan answered. "I will write an urgent dispatch and you can take it to Ye Ting and see what he says. I'll stay here and try and hold on."

"Yes, sir!" Mo Zhengqi cried.

Cao Yuan took pen and paper from his jacket pocket and wrote quickly: *It is now light and we can't get into the city today. We are now down to our last dozen men, but the Revolutionary Army never retreats. What should we do?* Then he signed it: *Cao Yuan.*

Just as the last stroke of the last word hit the piece of paper, there was a sudden volley of bullets from the top of the walls, all aimed at the small plateau. Several bullets hit Cao Yuan in the head, and he collapsed. The paper fell to the ground, while the pen bounced down the slope.

At the same time, Mo Zhengqi also collapsed to the ground, a bullet carrying away one of his ears. He was standing below Cao Yuan anyway, who now lay on top of him. Mo Zhengqi struggled to push him off. When he saw Cao Yuan's head, he cried out in horror: "Battalion commander! Battalion commander!"

Cao Yuan was dying, and he gasped: "I swore… if I survived this, I would come and live… right here in Wuchang. Hurry up… regimental commander… Call for reinforcements… Save our men… Order the men… to move back, and take… the wounded soldiers… take… take… back…" Then he died.

Mo Zhengqi was devastated by his loss, but he had no time to waste. He picked up the piece of paper and ran to headquarters as fast as he could, ignoring the pain in his body.

It was not far to go, but Mo Zhengqi felt as if it took a lifetime to get there. There seemed to be someone in front of him, running with him, and that was Cao Yuan, a man he admired more than he could say. Ever since he joined the army, he'd been under Cao Yuan's command. Now he was running along, but he couldn't keep up with him. He didn't know how long he had been running for, when suddenly the figure in front turned around, and it was

Regimental Commander Ye Ting come to meet him. He wanted to shout but could not; instead, he fell to the ground.

When Mo Zhengqi regained consciousness, it was already early afternoon. He was in pain all over his body. When he opened his eyes, he realised he was in hospital. An anxious face floated in front of him, a face that had appeared countless times in his dreams, and which he associated with all the warmth and sweetness he had ever known. He moaned and spoke a name: "Xiangmei."

Guo Xiangmei was startled: "You're awake? Thank goodness you've finally come round!"

Mo Zhengqi thought of the message he had been carrying. He struggled to sit up and said: "Where is the regimental commander? I need to talk to Regimental Commander Ye!"

Guo Xiangmei forced him to lie back down and said: "Stay right where you are. It is the regimental commander who sent you here."

"Where are my men?" Mo Zhengqi asked.

"Everyone has retreated," Guo Xiangmei said. "The attack failed."

Mo Zhengqi suddenly remembered everything. He remembered Cao Yuan, covered in mud and blood and shot in the head; Liang Kesi, propped up under the city wall with both his legs broken; and the soldiers who lay in heaps at the foot of the walls, dead or injured. A faint voice also floated past his ear: *My back is broken and I can't move.* Mo Zhengqi sat up again and said: "What about Battalion Commander Cao?"

Guo Xiangmei said nothing.

"Did they get the wounded men out?" Mo Zhengqi asked. "They were my men. And my cousin. Has Kesi come back yet?"

Guo Xiangmei paused for a long time and then said cautiously: "There are still a lot of bullets flying about and the ambulance team hasn't yet been able to reach the casualties. The wounded have not been evacuated, and I have no idea what has happened to your cousin."

Mo Zhengqi felt as if his head had just exploded, and he fainted dead away.

8

LUO YINAN DID NOT CLOSE his eyes all night.

The attack was underway. Artillery fire made the ground shake, and he could feel the whole room rocking. Everyone was quite sure that the Northern Expeditionary Army was such a fine fighting force, its men so fearless and brave, that it seemed certain Wuchang would be taken by morning. Victory was in sight, and everyone was all keyed up. Even Luo Yinan, who was normally so solemn, was infected by their cheerful anticipation and spent the whole night writing slogans. It wasn't just him either; even Guo Moruo, deputy director of the Department of Political Affairs, was also up all night writing. In his eyes, Guo Moruo's calligraphy was almost perfect. But because he admired him so much, Luo Yinan did not dare to get too close to him.

Just before dawn, Luo Yinan and Huang Jiezi were sent to headquarters at Changchun Monastery to find out what was going on. "You have two missions," Guo Moruo told them. "Your first task is to report back here immediately if we have been victorious. The second task is to write an account of the battle and get it sent to the newspapers."

Luo Yinan was excited because he had never written anything for the papers before. If his account of the battle was published, it would be a great event in his life.

They groped their way through the darkness and made their

way as quickly as they could to Changchun Monastery. During their journey, the fierce gunfire did not let up for a moment, and several shells exploded near them. They had no idea where the shells came from and, hearing the roar, they were so terrified they fell down on their faces. When they exploded, earth was sprayed all over them. At this moment, they felt that death was hovering close to them.

Luo Yinan and Huang Jiezi were absolutely petrified. But they couldn't go back with nothing – everyone would despise them. They had to conquer their fear and keep on moving forward. To make themselves feel better, they talked about Liang Kesi. He was so brave that he wasn't afraid even when shells exploded all around him. There was no way either of them could match up to him. Now Liang Kesi was right there on the front line, charging the enemy's guns. They were not sure what would happen to him in such a fierce firefight: whether he would become a great hero, praised to the skies, or a corpse that they would have to sadly lower into the ground. At that moment, anything seemed possible.

Cheered by the thought of Liang Kesi, they finally arrived safely at Changchun Monastery. The horizon already showed a streak of pale light.

The attack was still underway. The enemy's artillery fire was unusually fierce. Director Deng Yanda, who was right there on the front line watching the assault on the walls, had his sleeve pierced by a bullet and his horse shot and killed under him. When Luo Yinan heard that, he could feel his skin crawl.

Changchun Monastery stood almost as high as the watchtower by Binyang Gate. In front of them was an embankment with soldiers lying in wait behind it. From this position they could exchange shots with the garrison in the tower, providing covering fire for the suicide squads climbing the walls. Luo Yinan wanted to move up to the embankment to see what was going on over at the front line, but he was stopped by a soldier. He said: "Director Deng told me not to let you go any further." Luo Yinan obeyed orders and found a stone pillar to squat behind instead, and from there he watched the battle unfold.

There were several people over on his left who took turns looking out to see what was going on. He recognised several of them: Director Deng Yanda; one of the Russian military advisers; and another man, who was usually quiet and stern-looking, and who Luo Yinan recognised as an interpreter for the Russian military adviser. Except for Director Deng, Luo Yinan did not know the names of any of them, but their position in the army was quite clear to everyone. The reason the Northern Expeditionary Army has always fought so well, Luo Yinan thought, is because all the senior officers are always right there at the front themselves.

Suddenly, there was a violent commotion among them. He could hear Deng Yanda, who was normally so calm, screaming: "Quick! Come quick! Help!" Luo Yinan was startled and jumped up. He had just gone a few paces when a bullet whistled past him. He felt a searing red-hot pain in his arm. When he looked down, there was a hole in his nice new uniform, and the pain went straight to his heart. He wondered to himself: Have I been shot? At the mere thought, he fell to his knees in terror.

Several soldiers rushed past him, all hunched over but moving at the double, and, having hesitated for a few seconds, Luo Yinan followed on behind them, crouching down low. When he got to the embankment, he saw that it was the interpreter who had been shot. Deng Yanda was trying to lift him up, and there was blood everywhere. Even as the world turned dark, he was still trying to speak: "Don't worry about me. You need to be careful of the enemy." Having said this, his eyes completely lost their focus.

Deng Yanda gave his orders: "Carry him out back and call a doctor immediately."

Luo Yinan, who always fainted at the sight of blood, was useless for carrying purposes. He sat in a miserable weak-kneed lump behind the embankment, closed his eyes and felt unable to move. His arm also began to bleed. He couldn't accept what he had just seen at all. Just a few minutes ago, he had watched the interpreter gesturing and talking, and now he was dying.

A soldier came up and saw his plight. He was shocked and said: "Are you injured?"

Luo Yinan was silent. He was feeling dizzy. The soldier helped him up and had him stretchered over to the main hall. He was sat down on a cot in front of the hall. By this time, the doctor had finished examining the interpreter. He spoke in a low voice to the horrified Director Deng Yanda: "The bullet hit him in the back of the head; there is nothing I can do." This voice drilled through Luo Yinan's semi-conscious brain, and all of a sudden he called to mind the name of the interpreter: Ji Defu.[1]

When Luo Yinan remembered the name, the mists in his head seemed to clear. He took a deep breath. This attracted the attention of one of the nurses. She went over to Luo Yinan and said: "Oh, it's you!" He stared at her and thought of Shuya. The nurse suddenly asked: "Did you faint at the sight of blood again?"

Luo Yinan now completely came to himself again. He remembered this was the nurse, Zhang Wenxiu, who had looked after him on the journey here. "It's you?" he asked. "Is it really you again?"

Zhang Wenxiu saw the blood on his arm and exclaimed: "Did you hurt yourself? Come on, let me look at that for you."

"The bullet just clipped me," Luo Yinan said. "It doesn't hurt anymore."

"Even if it's not paining you I still need to have a look," Zhang Wenxiu informed him. "I told you when we said goodbye, I don't want you getting injured!" As she said this, she reached out and helped him take off his uniform. Luo Yinan did not dare to look. He was afraid he might pass out if he did. Zhang Wenxiu said: "Well, you're lucky. The wound is not deep, and it didn't touch the bone, and it's already stopped bleeding." As she spoke, she took some gauze and ointment out of a small bag by her side and bandaged him up. Then she said: "Be careful not to get that infected. It should be fine in two or three days."

"Are you based here?" Luo Yinan asked.

"The field hospital is actually over at Baotong Temple," Zhang Wenxiu told him, "but because the fighting has started, we have to be on the front line, since we need to be able to provide first aid to the wounded as soon as they come in. By the way, what happened to your companion? Your Marx-and-Engels friend?"

Luo Yinan jerked his head in the direction of Binyang Gate: "He wangled his way onto the attack team, so I don't know whether he is alive or dead." As he spoke, he grew sad. He said to himself: Kesi, where are you now?

Zhang Wenxiu couldn't help expressing her admiration: "Ah, he's a pretty amazing guy!"

Just as she said that, Zhang Wenxiu had to rush off to treat another wounded person. Luo Yinan looked at her back and repeated in a low voice: "He *is* a pretty amazing guy!"

The gunfire at Binyang Gate gradually began to lessen. Although he could not even begin to imagine what the attack team members of the suicide squad had been through, Luo Yinan kept seeing Liang Kesi's face. He couldn't understand why he felt so sure that something bad was going to happen.

When Luo Yinan walked over to the Three Sage-Kings Hall, he could see that everyone was looking tense: he knew that the situation on the front line could not be good, so he headed in the same direction they were going. There was a small garden in front of Changchun Monastery, and from there you could see the watchtowers in the distance, but because of the houses in between it was not easy to shoot across them. Luo Yinan could see Ye Ting's solemn face; he was striding towards the small plateau over by Binyang Gate. As he walked along, Luo Yinan saw a soldier come running towards him, soaked from head to foot in blood. He couldn't help quickening his pace, and he ran towards the man.

The man's arm was up, and he saw that he seemed to have a note clutched in his hand. He was running towards Ye Ting, and when they were only a few paces apart he fell to the ground without saying a word. He was still trying to reach out to Ye Ting when he fainted. Ye Ting squatted down and shouted: "Quick! Bring a stretcher over here!" Then he said: "Mo Zhengqi, I want you to hold on for me!" Then he took the note out of his hand.

Ye Ting looked at the note. His face went grey, and his lips were shaking. Each word seemed to come out between gritted teeth as he said: "Withdraw! Get everyone out of there!" His voice was low and depressed.

Someone said: "Generalissimo Chiang ordered us to capture Wuchang in forty-eight hours."

"Do you know how many people are left in that battalion?" Ye Ting said with barely suppressed rage. "Do all of them have to die below the walls of Wuchang? And Cao Yuan..." He seemed unable to carry on.

Luo Yinan was no longer thinking about Ye Ting. He remembered that the company commander named Mo Zhengqi was Liang Kesi's cousin. What had happened to Kesi? Luo Yinan's heart sank until he could barely breathe.

The attack on the walls was a complete failure. Countless soldiers from the Northern Expeditionary Army had died – so many that Luo Yinan was shocked and panic-stricken. The soldiers who managed to retreat from Binyang Gate were all in a terrible state; the high morale shown by their confident smiles as they set off had now been entirely swept away. Luo Yinan thought that their feelings about all this must be very complicated. Thinking of this, his own feelings became complicated too. He kept going up to the soldiers to ask if any of them had seen Liang Kesi. They did not speak, but just shook their heads. Hardly any of them seemed to know who he was. Of course, Luo Yinan thought, he was only there for two days. He could hardly believe it: in just two days, he and Liang Kesi had been separated, the living forever apart from the dead.

Huang Jiezi rushed over to him and said that Director Deng had given orders for Ji Defu's body to be carried back to headquarters.

Luo Yinan had no choice but to accompany Huang Jiezi. "But I haven't found Kesi yet," he said to Huang Jiezi.

"If he's still alive," Huang Jiezi pointed out, you will find him. "If you don't, that means he is dead." His words were very calm, almost cold.

Luo Yinan looked at him, and Huang Jiezi seemed to understand what he meant.

"I was a friend of the interpreter who got killed," Huang Jiezi said. "Did you know that? I used to ask him about Russian words, and every time he explained it to me really well – he said that after the war he would teach me Russian properly. And now? He's just lying there dead." Huang Jiezi's voice was tragic.

Ji Defu's body was placed on a stretcher, and a raincoat completely covered his upper body. Deng Yanda sent soldiers to provide a guard of honour.

Not far from Hong Mountain, they met some soldiers coming the other way. These men were waving flags and laughing with delight. As they got closer, Luo Yinan realised that it was Guo

Moruo from the Department of Political Affairs who had brought his people out to hear about the victory. Just as he was about to say something, he heard Deng Yanda's guards shout: "Deputy Director Guo!"

When Guo Moruo heard him call out and saw the man lying on the stretcher, he was deeply shocked. He ran over quickly and said: "Who is this? Is it Director Deng? Has he been shot?"

The guard said: "No, it is..." And then he couldn't continue.

Guo Moruo went over and lifted the raincoat. He recognised Ji Defu straight away. His face had gone a pale grey – he was obviously dead. Guo Moruo felt stunned, and tears welled up in his eyes. The guard came forward and said: "Director Deng gave me a letter for you."

Huang Jiezi noticed that the propaganda workers from the Department of Political Affairs were all holding bunches of red paper and slogans and asked: "What is all this in aid of?"

One of them replied: "Haven't we already captured Wuchang? They said the battle for control of the city was underway. We thought that by the time we got there, the battle would be over."

"Who said that?" Huang Jiezi said angrily.

Guo Moruo had now read the note. Turning his head, he asked: "We haven't taken the walls?"

"No," the guard said. "The attack failed, and we've suffered serious casualties."

Guo Moruo looked horrified: "We heard from the commander-in-chief that the Fourth Army had already entered the city and was fighting from street to street. Is that a lie?"

"I don't know where you've got that story from," the guard said. "The whole of the Fourth Army has suffered heavy losses, particularly Ye Ting, who's lost more than half his men. He's so upset his eyes are completely bloodshot, and his whole face is swollen with grief."

"Is Director Deng OK?" Guo Moruo asked.

"Director Deng has been lucky," the guard said, "but his horse was killed under him, and he took a bullet in the arm."

Guo Moruo whispered: "Oh my God, that sounds terrible!"

The procession preparing to go to the city to celebrate their victory had now turned around, and their joy turned to sadness in the twinkling of an eye. They joined the guard escorting Ji Defu's body and walked along in silence. Who lied? Luo Yinan wondered. Why would anyone say that the Fourth Army was already inside the city? How could anyone be cavalier about something so important? But he did not ask, nor did any of the others. The team was so depressed that no one said a word all the way to South Lake.

9

THIS WAS the worst day since the Northern Expedition first set out. Everyone had been so sure that today they would be inside Wuchang by lunchtime. Or in Huang Jiezi's words, if they were too late for lunch, they would definitely be in control by dinner time. As a result of this hubris, they simply could not get their heads around the fact that the Beiyang Army, which they had defeated over and over again, was managing to defend the gates so strongly this time. The Northern Expeditionary Army, having won one victory after another, had now fought for half the night, and all they had to show for it were piles of corpses everywhere, while the survivors had retreated to the far side of the moat. The enemy troops in the watchtowers and on the walls had suffered a lot in previous defeats, but this time they had won: the happy sounds of their victory could be heard all around. They drank to their hearts' content and threw empty bottles out over the tops of the walls. Against such a background, the soldiers of the Northern Expedition finally came to understand: the walls of Wuchang were more than a thousand years old; it might seem that the city was on the brink of collapse, but the walls were still standing strong, in spite of their age. They would be easy to defend but difficult to attack – just as had always been the case.

Depression, resentment, anger and sadness could be read on everyone's faces.

After dinner, Luo Yinan went to the field hospital at Baotong Temple. When he set out, it was still light, but by the time he had Hong Mountain in view it was dark. It was very quiet all around, and the windows of all the houses he passed by were covered with blackout curtains. In some places, even though the houses were relatively close together, he could not hear the slightest noise. Everyone was trying to attract as little attention as they could.

Occasionally, gunfire sounded behind him. He could hear that it was the batteries on Hong Mountain; they were firing in the direction of Binyang and Bao'an Gates. The guns roared, but it seemed as if nobody had bothered to aim; they were just bombarding in the general direction of Wuchang. It was intermittent and absolutely terrifying. But since he knew what direction they were firing in, he wasn't scared.

When he arrived at Baotong Temple, he wasn't sure whether he wanted to look for Mo Zhengqi or go and see Zhang Wenxiu first. He had been through a lot during the course of the day; the racket and tension had not bothered him at the time, but now, in the evening, when everything started to calm down, wave after wave of anxiety seemed to pour over him and oppress his spirit. He felt as empty as he had when he first left Wuchang a few days earlier. But now, Liang Kesi was gone. Since the two of them had met by the banks of the Miluo River, he had done whatever Liang Kesi told him to, one way or another. Liang Kesi's demands had felt like a lump of iron pressing down upon him, forcing his anxious and uneasy heart to gradually settle down. Now, he was missing, and he did not know if he was alive or dead. Without that lump of iron in his heart to keep him stable, his hard-won veneer of composure had begun to crack again. Kesi, he said to himself, I now know how important you are to me. But do you know?

As he got closer to Baotong Temple, he realised that there was a commotion going on all around it. As he advanced, he could hear all kinds of moans and screams from every direction. Those sounds were more painful than bullets. Luo Yinan's heart began to hammer; he clenched his fists as tightly as he could to stop his hands from shaking.

Luo Yinan found Zhang Wenxiu first. She had just finished assisting a doctor during an operation. Her eyes were bloodshot, and her exhaustion could clearly be seen on her face. "Another young man lost a leg," she said.

Luo Yinan heard the news with a tremor in his heart. After a long pause, he said: "Are you very tired?"

"Yes," Zhang Wenxiu said, "I haven't slept for two days and two nights."

Luo Yinan didn't like the sound of that and said: "How on earth can you carry on like that?"

"I will try and nap this evening," Zhang Wenxiu said. "Are you here to change your dressing?"

Luo Yinan explained that he was looking for a man named Mo Zhengqi, a company commander with the Independent Regiment, who had been injured and sent there. "He is Liang Kesi's cousin, so I want to ask him if he knows what happened to him."

Zhang Wenxiu said: "I know him. His fiancée, Guo Xiangmei, is a friend of mine."

Luo Yinan did not expect it to be this easy. "Great!" he said. "Can you take me to see him?"

"Sure," she replied. "But he doesn't seem to be in a good state."

"I won't keep him long," Luo Yinan hastened to assure her, "I just want to ask about what has happened to Kesi."

"He's upset because of his cousin," Zhang Wenxiu said.

Luo Yinan's heart almost turned to ice: "What about him?"

She did not reply but shouted to one of the other nurses: "Xiangmei, this comrade is here to talk to Company Commander Mo."

The nurse came over, and she looked sad. Luo Yinan's heart was pounding. She came forward, stretched out her hand and said: "My name is Guo Xiangmei."

Luo Yinan made haste to take it and said: "Luo Yinan – I am a classmate of Liang Kesi's."

"I know," she said, "you came with him all the way from Hunan. What did you want to see Mo Zhengqi about?"

"I want to know about Liang Kesi," he said.

Guo Xiangmei hesitated for a moment, but in the end she said: "Come with me."

Luo Yinan followed Guo Xiangmei to the ward where Mo Zhengqi was recuperating. As they came through the door, a soldier stopped them and said: "Nurse Guo, I've been looking for you. Company Commander Mo has run away."

Guo Xiangmei was shocked: "But he's injured! Where can he have gone?"

"I am afraid he's gone over there," the soldier said, and he pointed in the direction of Changchun Monastery.

Guo Xiangmei swore and rushed out as fast as she could go. Luo Yinan was right behind her and asked: "What's wrong?"

"Mo Zhengqi's been badly upset about two things," Guo Xiangmei explained. "Battalion Commander Cao's body is still over there – they've been together for years, and he just can't bear to think of his corpse being left exposed. The other thing is that his cousin is still waiting under the walls for him to come back and rescue him."

"Kesi is somewhere under the walls?" Luo Yinan was horrified.

"That's what Zhengqi told me," Guo Xiangmei said. "He said Kesi fell off the ladder and broke both his legs, so he couldn't move. Zhengqi dragged him under the watchtower, to somewhere the enemy couldn't see to shoot him. He promised that he would come back to save him. But without help, there is nothing he can do."

Luo Yinan immediately started to panic: "He broke both his legs? Oh, my god! How can we get him out of there?"

"I am sure Zhengqi can do it," Guo Xiangmei said. "I won't go with you any further. I have to go to Changchun Monastery because he is sure to be there."

"I'll go with you," Luo Yinan said.

Guo Xiangmei thought about that for a moment and looked carefully at him. Without saying anything, she took him to a tent, where she grabbed two first-aid kits and a couple of water bottles which she handed to Luo Yinan. "We'll need to find a cook and get him to give us some buns," Guo Xiangmei said. "There are more casualties out there than just Kesi. They've been injured, but they will also be hungry and thirsty. If we are going to save them, we need to build up their strength."

Luo Yinan was much impressed by her thoughtfulness. He hung his first-aid kit and the water bottles across his body and then followed her to the camp kitchen, where she begged for a bag of buns and got all their bottles filled with water. They managed to find their way to Changchun Monastery in the dark. Fortunately, there was some moonlight, which allowed them to see the road under their feet. Although Guo Xiangmei was a woman, she walked very fast. Luo Yinan had to work hard to keep up with her.

"I grew up in the mountains," Guo Xiangmei said, "and it was a long way from anywhere. You learn to walk fast like that."

Soon they found themselves at Changchun Monastery, which loomed high above their heads. They could see more than a dozen people with stretchers heading off in the direction of Binyang Gate. Guo Xiangmei whispered: "I'm afraid it's them." As she said this, she quickened her pace and shouted at the top of her voice: "Mo Zhengqi!" The soldiers slowed down, and one of them turned round and came to meet Guo Xiangmei. Another man trotted along behind him.

By the light of the moon, Luo Yinan could see that the man was Mo Zhengqi. His head was swathed in bandages and his shoulder was the same. As for the person behind him, he could not see who it was; but even if he could have seen him clearly, he wouldn't have recognised him. But Guo Xiangmei knew exactly who he was: Wu Baosheng. Before Mo Zhengqi had even opened his mouth, Wu Baosheng said: "Xiangmei, what are you doing here?"

"If you are here, why shouldn't I come along too?" she snapped.

"You see how well she knows me," Mo Zhengqi remarked to Wu Baosheng. "I simply could not forgive myself if I did not try to save them."

"If we are going to go and rescue these people, how about we get going?" Guo Xiangmei said. "What are we standing around here for? Stop yapping!"

Mo Zhengqi started to smile: "Xiangmei, you're a girl after my own heart."

"What are you talking about?" Guo Xiangmei said. "If I don't understand you, who could?"

Mo Zhengqi looked at her, and suddenly his face darkened. "There's one other person, but he's dead now. He knew me better than anyone. I can't let him lie there out in the open. I want him to be at rest in a coffin."

Guo Xiangmei's tone softened, and she said: "I know. I'm here to help you." She pointed to the water bottles and the bag of steamed buns that Luo Yinan was carrying.

When Luo Yinan noticed Mo Zhengqi's eyes turning towards him, he quickly said: "Company Commander Mo, I am a friend of Kesi's, and I want to go with you to save him."

"I want the two of you to wait back at the monastery for me," Mo Zhengqi said. "We don't need you. Baosheng, ask the others to take the first-aid kits and water, and make sure everyone has something to hand out. Since you're hurt, I don't want you carrying anything – just make sure everyone knows what they are supposed to do."

"I can carry this stuff," Luo Yinan said.

"Hand it over," Mo Zhengqi said. "As long as someone makes it out to the injured men, they will get something to eat and drink." Then he turned back to Luo Yinan: "If you have all the supplies and something happens to you, even if everyone else makes it over there, there won't be a thing for them to eat or drink. Understand?" During this conversation, Wu Baosheng unhooked all the bottles and bags slung around Luo Yinan's body. Suddenly, Luo Yinan realised that he didn't understand a thing about being on a battlefield.

"Comrade Luo," Mo Zhengqi said, "you go back to the monastery with Nurse Guo and wait for us there."

"There'll be a lot of casualties around the city wall," Guo Xiangmei said firmly, "and you might kill them if you move them without proper care!"

"I can't let you risk it," Mo Zhengqi said stubbornly. "Even if it kills me, I can't send you out there to die."

"And if you get killed, what am I supposed to do?" Guo Xiangmei asked.

Mo Zhengqi stared at her and did not speak, but his eyes showed just how much he loved her.

"Stop this right now!" Wu Baosheng said. "What is all of this about the two of you dying? We are here to recover the corpses and rescue our casualties – everyone is going to be coming back alive."

Mo Zhengqi thought about that. He bowed his head and said: "Let's go! We don't want to delay any longer."

The soldiers moved forward, but since no one had said whether

Luo Yinan could go or not, he decided that it would be OK if he just followed along behind them. He was feeling excited all of a sudden, and his fears had vanished. He remembered how fearless Liang Kesi had been; now he himself understood what it was not to be afraid.

As they approached the position where the worst of the fighting had taken place, they were almost crawling. Since Mo Zhengqi had already been through here twice, he knew the way, and they were still moving pretty quickly. Soon they reached the entrenchments. The city walls soared up majestically in front of them. The watchtowers were silent; since they had just been through a terrible battle, they had come to a pause. Both sides were resting and licking their wounds; no one imagined that, on such a night, anyone would come back to the walls.

At that moment, Luo Yinan still felt no fear, but he was overcome with disgust. There should be a special freshness to the air on such a late summer's night; a coolness after the heat of the day, a period of rest for the intensely green leaves that covered every tree, and which would all too soon turn sere and yellow. But now there was blood everywhere, rank and metallic-smelling, so that even the wind, passing through, would be infected and carry that gruesome stench to other places.

Mo Zhengqi divided the soldiers into two groups. One group was to cross the moat and crawl over the open space beyond, and then make their way to the foot of the walls to look for any survivors. The other group was to search the small plateau for Cao Yuan's body. Both missions were extremely dangerous. If they were spotted by the enemy in the watchtowers, they would be completely exposed to their guns. Particularly right under the city wall, where the terrain was flat and the distances longer, it would be easy to attract attention.

Mo Zhengqi decided that he himself would lead the team going to rescue the wounded under the walls, and he ordered Wu Baosheng to take charge of the soldiers going to rescue Cao Yuan's body. Guo Xiangmei had hoped that Mo Zhengqi would be directing operations from somewhere in the rear. He was injured, after all, and did not have to go himself.

"Nonsense!" Mo Zhengqi said. "If I just stay here, why bother coming in the first place?"

Guo Xiangmei made it clear that she thought he ought to realise what he could and could not do, and that come what may he was in no fit state to direct the wall mission. He would have too far to go, it would be too difficult for him: they needed to get this done fast. In his present state, he would just put everyone else to unnecessary trouble. They were supposed to be going to rescue people, but he might prove to be one more person they had to save.

This was the truth. He was not afraid to risk his life, but his presence might influence the outcome of the whole mission. Mo Zhengqi thought about it for a while and decided that he was so badly injured he simply did not have the strength anymore to run over to the wall.

Just as he was hesitating, the soldier named Erqiangzi said: "I'll go. Your cousin ended up in the attack team because he was replacing me. I'd feel bad if I didn't do my best to save him."

Wu Baosheng also pointed out that he wasn't seriously injured and that he hadn't participated in the suicide mission the night before, so having had a few days' rest he was feeling much better. He ought to be the one to go over to the walls to save people, not to mention the fact that Liang Kesi was like his own brother.

Mo Zhengqi thought about it and agreed, saying: "OK, in that case I will put Baosheng in charge, and you, Erqiangzi, will cooperate with him. I will lead the search for Battalion Commander Cao."

"You are so badly injured you can't even lift a stretcher," Guo Xiangmei said, "so you will be directing operations from back here."

"I have to be there when Battalion Commander Cao's body is recovered," Mo Zhengqi said. "Apart from anything else, who other than me knows where to find it?" When he said this, everyone was silenced – even Guo Xiangmei was left with nothing to say.

Guo Xiangmei decided that she would go with Wu Baosheng to rescue people under the walls. Mo Zhengqi glared at her and refused to permit it. "What am I here for, then?" Guo Xiangmei enquired.

"You just stick with me," Mo Zhengqi said.

"It is my job to rescue injured men," she pointed out, "not to search for corpses. And besides, today's mission is to save the wounded. You promised your soldiers, and you promised Battalion Commander Cao, that you would get them out of there. It should have been your job to see them back safely. Now that you are out of action, it's right for me to go instead of you. It's going to be very dangerous, but I'm your future wife, and if I go it's the same as if you go yourself. No one can complain. Why are we even arguing about this?"

Mo Zhengqi was feeling confused, and he didn't know what to say. He looked at the woman he loved more than anyone else in the world, and he knew that she was doing this because she loved him. He had no choice but to agree. Mo Zhengqi told everyone that all along the way the road would be covered with corpses of their comrades-in-arms. When they saw the bodies, they must not get upset. Their mission was to save survivors. If there was the slightest movement in the watchtower, they must fall flat on their faces and not move, pretending to be dead. When they were about to set out, he took Guo Xiangmei's hand and said: "If you don't come back, I will never forgive you."

Guo Xiangmei smiled: "I am an old soldier, and I have come back alive from far more battles than you."

Luo Yinan was amazed by everything Guo Xiangmei said and did. He had never seen a woman like her before. She was so open, so strong in her love. Every word she said reminded him of a saying about how some things cut to the heart. His admiration for her drove out the feelings of loathing for the world around him that had been lingering in his mind. He decided to follow Guo Xiangmei; after all, he had come with her in the first place in order to save Liang Kesi.

Mo Zhengqi gazed at him as if trying to take his measure. "You'd better come with me," he said. "You're just a student, and you'd better not slow everyone else down. I know you faint at the sight of blood, and there'll be blood everywhere over there. And there'll be nobody to look after you."

Mo Zhengqi spoke so seriously that Luo Yinan was filled with shame. He thought about the way he got dizzy when he saw blood. If that happened, he really would be putting everyone else at risk, and he did not dare to insist on going. "Be careful!" he said to Guo Xiangmei.

"Rest assured," she said, "I will tell Kesi how worried you have been about him."

Having watched them make their way through the moat and crawl over to the wall, Mo Zhengqi took his soldiers over to the plateau. Soon they were in the midst of a heap of corpses. When Luo Yinan looked around, he could see the aftermath of all the fighting. It was the first time he had ever seen a battlefield, and there were bodies everywhere, lying on their backs and on their sides, twisted this way and that. No matter how often you read about such scenes in books, no matter how well they are described, you cannot even begin to understand the shock of actually seeing it for yourself. It is truly unimaginable.

The moon shone like water, and the stars glittered in the sky. These are the people he saw marching away a day ago, with the lamplight shining on their faces; he had himself added paraffin oil to the lamps and seen the light shine more brightly. Now, those faces and bodies lay rigid in the moonlight, motionless, never to move again. The grass around them was moving; the grass growing freely in the gaps between the stiff bodies was swaying in the breeze just like before. The grass lived on, but what about them? An infinite sorrow struck at Luo Yinan's heart. "What kind of world is this?" he murmured. "Why are we fighting like this?"

"This is not the time or the place for sentimentality," Mo Zhengqi said. "This is war. War means that people get killed. You may kill the enemy, or you may die yourself. So the first thing you have to learn is to be cruel. You have to get used to that."

Having made a mental note of its location, Mo Zhengqi was quick to find Cao Yuan's body. In the moonlight, the blood that covered his face was clearly visible, but his expression was very calm, as if he were in a long, deep sleep and nobody should think about waking him up. Mo Zhengqi burst into tears. He wiped Cao Yuan's face clean with his sleeve and said in a low voice: "Put him on the stretcher!" Two soldiers lifted Cao Yuan's body up. They crawled along, dragging the stretcher, till they had him in a place of safety.

Whether it was the movement of the stretcher bearers or the people crossing the entrenchments, a voice in the watchtower started shouting: "Here they come again!" Next came a scream of confusion: "Light the lamps! Get them lit!"

Shots rang out immediately. Mo Zhengqi whispered: "Quick! Otherwise we'll all be killed." They no longer took into account the noise made by the stretcher and dragged it as fast as they could, with Luo Yinan pushing it towards them with all his might. Once they got in among some dense undergrowth, a couple of people lifted the stretcher and ran. One of the soldiers was shot, and one corner of the stretcher fell to the ground. Luo Yinan went over and picked the man up. The soldier said: "Go and get Battalion Commander Cao away from here. I can crawl back." So Luo Yinan ran over and lifted up the fallen end. They kept on running until they were behind the wall of a dilapidated house: there they were safe. As he was gasping to get his breath back, Luo Yinan suddenly realised that Mo Zhengqi was not with them. His heart tightened, and he immediately turned back. After running a few steps, he saw that he was lying on a bank of earth.

Luo Yinan ran over to him and crouched down. "What did you come back for?" Mo Zhengqi asked.

"I was worried that you'd had an accident," he said.

"Look after yourself," Mo Zhengqi said, "I have to go."

"You're going to the walls?" Luo Yinan said in alarm.

"Yes," Mo Zhengqi said. "They are in terrible danger over there. I can't just ignore them."

Luo Yinan recalled Guo Xiangmei's face when she said she would go in Mo Zhengqi's stead, and he immediately said: "You mustn't."

"It's not up to you," Mo Zhengqi sneered. "It's my decision."

"No," Luo Yinan said. "You are quite right that I don't have a say in it, but then neither do you – it's the enemy up in the watchtower who has the power to decide."

"Are you scared of them?" Mo Zhengqi sneered again, "because I'm not."

"I am not afraid of them," Luo Yinan said, "but I am afraid that if we carry on like this, Liang Kesi and the others will not be able to survive. Before the shooting started, our people might already have got out of range and been tucked away safe and sound under the wall. The enemy could not see them there, and they might think it was only a false alarm. There was a bit of shooting, but it stopped pretty soon. If you go parading over there with all the lights along the wall blazing, doesn't that tell the enemy that our men are right there underneath them? You can still run, but what about Liang Kesi? What is he supposed to do? Are you trying to save him or get him killed?"

Luo Yinan had no idea how he could have said such a thing, but his words rendered Mo Zhengqi speechless. He was absolutely right, and he had to agree. He shouldn't make things worse by doing something so reckless. "We've already got one soldier shot in the leg," Luo Yinan reminded him, "and two others injured."

Mo Zhengqi held his breath for a moment, and then sighed and said: "Let's get out of here."

When they arrived back at Changchun Monastery, Regimental Commander Ye Ting was waiting for them with a face like iron. The three casualties were immediately picked up by field doctors. Ye Ting went over to Mo Zhengqi and said sternly: "Are all my men back yet?"

"Not yet," Mo Zhengqi muttered. "There are a few more..."

"How dare you go without express orders!" Ye Ting demanded. "You've already been wounded – do you want more people to be injured like you? How many more casualties have we got now?"

Mo Zhengqi's voice was even smaller: "At present... three."

"What sort of heroic idiot are you?" Ye Ting asked. "Did you really imagine you could take the watchtowers with so few men? Aren't you afraid that I will punish you severely for such insubordination?"

At this point, one of the soldiers who'd gone with him on the mission couldn't stop himself from saying that Company Commander Mo had gone to recover the body of Battalion Commander Cao. He didn't want the battalion commander's body lying exposed out in the wilds.

Ye Ting was shocked, and he softened his tone: "Did you bring it back?"

"Oh, sure," Mo Zhengqi said. "I got it back."

Ye Ting's voice was even softer: "Where is it?"

"By the door," said Mo Zhengqi.

Ye Ting walked over to the stretcher. Cao Yuan's body was lying there uncovered. His face looked up into the starry night sky, as if enjoying the quiet evening. Ye Ting squatted down beside him. He looked at his face carefully. Tears fell on the bloody face drop by drop.

When Mo Zhengqi saw this, he couldn't help but cry. He knew how fond Ye Ting had been of Cao Yuan, and he himself had followed him for many years, never thinking for a moment that he would be killed like that. He fell to his knees.

Many sleeping soldiers heard the noises outside and got up to see what had happened. When they saw Cao Yuan lying there, with Ye Ting and Mo Zhengqi crying, they knelt on the ground too, and the sound of sobbing could be heard all over.

Ye Ting wiped his eyes and said in a choking voice: "Can someone bring me a sheet to cover the body? I want him cleaned up and dressed in his uniform. We are going to bury him properly."

Then he turned to Mo Zhengqi and said sadly: "Don't take any more risks. I don't want anybody else to die here. You have to leave some people alive so that the Independent Regiment can carry on!"

Luo Yinan was the only person who did not kneel or shed tears. He did not know Cao Yuan, or even what he did. But he was trembling inwardly. His mind was still filled with the horrible scenes he'd just seen on the battlefield, and the voice of Mo Zhengqi was still ringing in his ears: *This is war. War means that people get killed. You may kill the enemy, or you may die yourself. So the first thing you have to learn is to be cruel.*

10

IN ALL HIS LIFE, Liang Kesi had never spent a night like this one. He never thought that he would have to live through such a day, leaning completely helplessly against the massive walls of one of the barbicans guarding a gateway to Wuchang City, just twiddling his thumbs. He had gone through Binyang Gate loads of times; on one occasion, he and his classmate Chen Mingwu had carved a line of poetry into the wall of the barbican with their penknives. Chen Mingwu had carved a line from one of Li Bai's poems: *I look up at the sky and laugh as I head out of the gate*; while he had written, *Even if the son of heaven calls, I will not get on board*. Both of them were very young, and they liked Li Bai's untrammelled freedom. Now these two lines were hidden away behind the locked gates. Looking in through the crack at the bottom of the gate, there were sandbags piled up behind it, and Li Bai's words must now be hidden behind those sandbags.

When he fell off the scaling ladder, he had no idea what would happen next. His cousin Mo Zhengqi dragged him to safety under the wall, said a few words and rushed off. The battle was at its height, and he was a soldier, so of course he could not take personal considerations into account. He quite understood that. Liang Kesi knew that his legs were both broken, but he was convinced that no matter how limited the conditions at the field hospital, he would be up and walking around normally after a few months' rest. With this firmly fixed in his mind, he was not afraid at all and could face the situation in which he found himself with complete equanimity. Even though gunfire resounded in his ears, he fell asleep leaning against the wall. He had not had a good sleep for many days and nights because he'd been so desperate to fight in this battle.

The sky began to turn pale, but, even though the gate was still as tightly closed as ever, the gunfire gradually slackened. By the time the sun rose in the morning, it had completely stopped. When Liang Kesi opened his eyes, still waiting for rescue pretty much where he had fallen, he suddenly realised that none of the others who had jumped with him had survived. Right in front of him, there was a sea of corpses and bits of broken ladders as far as the eye could see.

There was a watchtower directly overhead, and the enemy's movements were clearly audible. They whistled in surprise, then they cheered and celebrated their victory. Then someone was drinking, and the empty bottle he let fall almost hit him on the head. Suddenly, Liang Kesi understood what this must mean. The battle he had imagined would prove an easy victory was over, and they had not won. His side had lost. He, and all the other wounded soldiers who could not move, had been left behind on the battlefield.

It was time to face the facts. As the sun rose, Liang Kesi knew he could not just lie there like that. If he stayed where he was, by noon, the sun would burn him to a crisp, and he'd get heatstroke. He'd already smashed both his legs, so if anything else went wrong he'd be dead. He had no idea where Mo Zhengqi could have gone, but Liang Kesi was sure he would not have been killed, and that he would definitely come back to save him.

I need to conserve my strength and wait patiently, Liang Kesi thought, that's all I can do. Mo Zhengqi said that I should try and crawl into the lee of the gateway if I could. That would be safe, and it would get me out of the sun. With that in mind, he tried to move. However, his legs were broken. He had struggled up the city wall during the battle, but just as his hands were almost touching the parapet, the ladder underneath him was shattered by a missile thrown from above. He fell from a great height and now could not move. He felt a little guilty at the thought that he had been chasing the Northern Expedition all this way so that he could join in the fight, and then before even firing a shot he fell off the ladder and instantly found himself a burden on everyone else.

Liang Kesi crawled forward, inch by painful inch. Although the injury was in his legs, it was agony to make any movement at all. From the barbican wall to the gateway was only a couple of steps, a distance he could normally cover in a hop and a skip, but now it took him all morning to crawl that far. When he got near the gateway, he came across a soldier who was moaning with pain. "What is wrong?" Liang Kesi asked.

"I broke my back," the soldier said.

"With me, it's my legs," Liang Kesi told him. During their brief chat, he noticed that there were a couple of other soldiers clawing their way slowly towards the gateway, but not one of them could stand up.

By afternoon, everyone had made it into the gateway. The soldier with the broken back, Liu Zhengbao, was completely incapacitated. With him were two more slightly wounded soldiers, one named Zhao Huzi and the other named Li Sanfu, who had managed to manhandle him into the gateway, one on each side.

"If they open the gate," Liu Zhengbao said, "we are all going to die."

"That's not going to happen," Liang Kesi told him. "My classmate said that when he left, lots of the city gates had already been completely blocked with sandbags. I reckon Binyang Gate is one of them."

There were seven of them in total. One soldier was wounded in the head, and by the time he managed to get to the gateway he was already beyond speech. He quickly slipped into a coma. They could see how much he was suffering, but there was nothing they could do.

Zhao Huzi started to cry and said: "I don't know whether we are going to take this city or not, but if we don't all of us are going to die here."

"No we aren't," Liang Kesi said, "none of us are going to die. My cousin is Mo Zhengqi, from the First Battalion. Do you know him?"

"Of course I know him," Liu Zhengbao said. "He is my company commander. Are you the cousin who just arrived? I heard the company commander say that he wanted us to keep an eye on his cousin."

"That's right," Liang Kesi replied, "that's the kind of person my cousin is. You all know him, so you should know he will come to save us. So we just have to hold on."

"That's right," Liu Zhengbao said, "Company Commander Mo told me to hold on too – he said he would come back to save me."

Zhang Desheng, one of the other wounded men, now chipped in: "I heard Company Commander Mo say that too, and he is sure to come."

"I trust him," Zhao Huzi said, "but if he doesn't come for a day or two, we'll die without food or drink, let alone the fact that everyone here is injured."

Liang Kesi comforted him: "Let's not move around – let's keep our strength up because we've got to be alive when they come to rescue us."

"Why are you being so miserable?" Liu Zhengbao asked Zhao Huzi. "He's just a newly enlisted student, and he's trying to keep cheerful. We've won one battle after another all the way here, and we're sure to capture Wuchang too any day now. Are you saying we can't even hold on for such a short time?"

"Are we really going to win in a day or two?" Li Sanfu asked. "We've already tried to attack the walls twice and failed."

Liang Kesi said: "Although we have failed twice, there will be a third attack soon, and the commander-in-chief will not let us be defeated again. Do you really think the Northern Expedition will just turn around and go home because they can't deal with Wuchang? They are going to keep attacking it until it falls."

Everybody thought carefully about that and decided that he was right, so they calmed down. Even though they were hungry and thirsty, even though their wounds were painful, even though they felt blank and empty, they had to force themselves to wait patiently.

Liang Kesi fell asleep while he was waiting, and he slept the long afternoon away. When he woke up again, it was dark. His legs had gone numb ages ago, but so long as he did not move they were not too painful. It was hunger that woke him up. He had a full meal the night before when he was about to set out, and not a drop of water or a mouthful of food had passed his lips since then. Such hunger and thirst made him hesitate to think about what tomorrow would bring.

The soldier wounded in the head was no longer breathing. Nobody noticed when he died. Liang Kesi was sad: the man died right next to him, and he didn't even know his name. He hadn't said a word from beginning to end; he just gave a few low moans and then passed into eternal silence.

The moon rose, and there were a million stars sparkling overhead. The weeds and scrubby trees around the moat faded into the night. In the darkness, it was impossible to make anything out. Only the yellow roofs of Changchun Monastery not far away could still be dimly made out in the moonlight. It was a beautiful night, but the smell of blood in the air all around was strangely disgusting. The bodies beneath the walls had been exposed to the sun all day and in the damp night air; they were beginning to decompose. What will they be like tomorrow? Liang Kesi didn't dare to imagine. These were the comrades-in-arms who rushed so enthusiastically to the battlefield with him last night; even though he hadn't been able to see them clearly, they had fought together side by side, they had lived and died together, and now they would never know each other.

The survivors in the gateway were suffering. In addition to the pain, there was hunger and thirst to deal with. Everyone woke up one after another, and the first thing they all said was they were hungry.

Zhao Huzi, who was always a worrier, said: "Do you think they will attack the city again tomorrow?"

"Stop going on about it," Liu Zhengbao said, "because it just makes you more nervous. Hey, kid, are you studying in Wuchang?"

"Oh, yes," Liang Kesi replied. "Our college is right by the foot of Snake Mountain."

"Is that were the artillery is?" Liu Zhengbao asked.

"Yeah," Liang Kesi said, "I've seen it with my own eyes. If I'd known how damaging it would be, I'd have gone undercover in the city and waited for the right moment to blow the guns up."

Liu Zhengbao laughed: "You may be just a student, but you are still pretty brave. Just like Company Commander Mo, you'd make a great general in the future."

Liang Kesi laughed and said: "If that ever happens, we'll definitely make you all colonels or majors or something like that."

Several of the soldiers who had been asleep were now awake, and they all laughed when they heard him say this.

The nervous Zhao Huzi also seemed to relax. "I'd like to be a staff officer," he said, "so that I don't have to be there on the front line with my gun. When I see that the enemy soldiers look more or less the same as me, I really can't find it in myself to kill them."

"Hey!" Liu Zhengbao said, "this is war! We are on different sides. Even if the guy opposite is your own brother, if you meet on the field of battle, the knife goes in, and it comes out red."

Liang Kesi was shocked and said: "I couldn't do a thing like that."

"Have you been reading too many books or what?" Liu Zhengbao asked. "If you don't kill him, you're going to die. Even if he doesn't kill you, your commanding officer will. And he won't survive either because his commanding officers will kill him too. That's how it works on the battlefield."

"That's horrible," Zhao Huzi said. "That's exactly why I want to be a staff officer."

"You are so timid," Liang Kesi said. "Why on earth did you join the Northern Expedition?"

Zhao Huzi pulled a long face: "My family got caught by a famine, so we didn't have enough to eat. At least they don't let you go hungry when you're serving as a soldier."

Everyone was silent. After a long pause, Liu Zhengbao said: "I was bullied in my home village, so I decided to enlist. At least that way I might be able to help my family."

Zhang Desheng, who had generally kept quiet up until then, now opened his mouth: "I come from a really poor family too, so I had to enlist."

All the others whispered: "Me too."

Liang Kesi now realised that he was the only one who was fighting out of principle. He felt depressed, but on second thoughts he decided that they must be telling the truth. Then he asked: "And why don't we have enough food? It is because warlords are in power, and they don't care about the people, so whatever food you grow isn't enough to keep you properly fed. The Northern

Expedition is going to overthrow them and build a society where everyone can eat as much as they like."

"We know all that," Liu Zhengbao said. "Regimental Commander Ye has told us about that over and over again. Otherwise, why would we fight like that when attacking the walls? If we die, we die, but at least it will have been worth it. We all want our families to have a better life in the future!"

"You're right, there is no reason to be scared of dying," Liang Kesi said. "Besides which, we are not necessarily going to get ourselves killed."

When he said this, another silence fell, and everyone felt depressed. Suddenly, Liang Kesi remembered something he had been taught at school and said: "Do you know about Spartacus?"

Everyone shook their heads.

"Then let me tell you a story," Liang Kesi said.

It was now late at night. All around there was silence, and the quiet was only broken by the occasional chirping of an insect, throwing the peace that otherwise reigned into relief. In a low voice, Liang Kesi began to tell the others about how Spartacus had fought so bitterly for survival against the Roman Empire. He also explained gladiatorial games to them in great detail.

He had barely begun his story when suddenly there was a burst of gunfire from the watchtower. The crisp sound of gunshots was as loud as thunder in the night sky, and there was shouting as well. The people in the gateway were shaken by it all. Then Liang Kesi said happily: "They are attacking the walls again!"

Liu Zhengbao cocked an ear and then said: "It isn't loud enough for that. Do you suppose it is our fifth columnists at work?"

The lamps on the walls were now lit and shone brightly all around. After a while, the gunfire stopped. There was silence. "What was that all about?" Liu Zhengbao asked. "Surely that's not how we do things?"

While he said this, he caught sight of a couple of people crawling quickly towards them. "Don't make a sound," Liang Kesi said. "Somebody's coming."

A number of people quickly scrambled into a corner, away from the light. One of them stood up and then ran towards the gateway, all hunched over. They were all alarmed. The newcomer whispered: "Kesi!"

Liang Kesi burst into tears and immediately responded: "Over here! Is that you, Baosheng?"

It was indeed Wu Baosheng. What surprised Liang Kesi was that he was followed by his cousin's fiancée, Guo Xiangmei. In total, four people had come, and the last of them, Erqiangzi, was dragging a stretcher.

Wu Baosheng said: "Company Commander Mo sent us to get you out of here." Guo Xiangmei immediately started handing out water and steamed buns, and all the injured men in the gateway became agitated. Liang Kesi made haste to say: "Keep your voices down! We don't want the enemy upstairs to hear us."

Guo Xiangmei opened her first-aid kit and set to dealing with their injuries. "There were six of us originally," Wu Baosheng said, "but we were spotted by the watchtower, so only four of us have made it. How many are there of you?" He counted up as he said this and announced: "Seven. Are you all injured? Is there anyone who can walk by himself?"

No one answered. "I'm afraid not," Liang Kesi said. "Liu Zhengbao's back is broken. I've got both legs broken, and so has Zhang Desheng. The other two have been shot in multiple places. They are pretty badly injured. It's not been easy for them to make it this far. Li Sanfu is less badly wounded, and Zhao Huzi is the best of us, but he certainly can't run."

"We can crawl," Li Sanfu said.

"Yes," Zhao Huzi said. "We can crawl back if we have to."

Wu Baosheng hesitated for a moment and then said: "It's impossible to crawl all the way back. OK, you have managed to crawl here, but you can't get across the moat that way. Besides which, now the lamps on the walls are lit, and you are injured so you can't move quickly, so it will be really easy to spot you. Let's all eat something, drink some water, and keep your spirits up. Then we'll discuss how to get you out of here. But we'll have to wait for the lights to go out before we can leave."

"Where's my cousin?" Liang Kesi suddenly asked.

"He got injured," Wu Baosheng said.

"Badly?" Liang Kesi asked. "Otherwise he would never have let Xiangmei come."

"Yes," Wu Baosheng said, "he was insisting on coming, but Xiangmei was afraid that he wouldn't be able to make it and would just be a burden on everyone else, so she said she would go in his stead, that she would represent him. However, Zhengqi is out here as well. He took people off to go and collect Battalion Commander Cao's body. He didn't want his corpse lying exposed in the wilds. You know how fond he was of Battalion Commander Cao."

Liang Kesi was shocked: "Battalion Commander Cao has been killed?" A couple of the soldiers beside him were also shocked into speech.

Wu Baosheng paused and said: "Yes. It has really upset the whole regiment from top to bottom, and Ye Ting has been miserable all day."

"Sure," Liu Zhengbao said, "the whole regiment knows how much he loved and trusted our battalion commander, and our battalion commander really loved and trusted Company Commander Mo."

"Exactly," Wu Baosheng said. "So Company Commander Mo was refusing to stay in hospital even though he was so badly injured. He said that there were two things he had to do. One was to save you lot. The other was to recover the body of Battalion Commander Cao and bury him properly."

Liang Kesi stopped talking. Mo Zhengqi had come through for him. The reason why he had never been afraid through all of this was his complete faith in his cousin. He knew that he would never abandon him.

Guo Xiangmei inspected the wounds of each of them in turn, cleaning them and wrapping them in bandages. She was in a sad mood. The reason these men had not been evacuated was because none of them could move. If they did not get to hospital immediately for surgery, once their wounds became infected, they would die of blood poisoning and other complications. It was unclear whether the more severely injured ones would survive another day. But she could not say this to them; she could not allow them to panic. "Don't worry," Guo Xiangmei said, "I am a doctor. With me here, your injuries are under control. As long as we have food and water, and everyone conserves their strength, we'll be fine here for a few days. Once we can get you away, we'll take you straight to the field hospital. We've got good doctors there, and you'll soon be well again."

"We believe you," Liu Zhengbao said. "Having you here is like having Company Commander Mo. On the battlefield, as long as I see Company Commander Mo, I am not afraid because he will always find a way to bring us home safe and sound."

"I'll tell him that," Guo Xiangmei said. "He'll be pleased to hear it."

Guo Xiangmei checked on Liang Kesi last of all. She complained in a low voice: "What do you think you are doing, Kesi? You're a student, and you come from a rich family – you've been pampered all your life. What on earth are you doing out on the field of battle?"

"If Regimental Commander Ye heard you say that," Liang Kesi smiled, "he'd have you shot."

"I don't care about anyone else," Guo Xiangmei said, "but you are my fiancé's cousin! Zhengqi almost went mad when he heard you hadn't made it out."

"When I get back," Liang Kesi said, "I will really owe my cousin for this. In the future, just hand over your children to me, and I promise I will teach them how to read and write free of charge."

"Do you never stop joking?" Guo Xiangmei asked.

Liang Kesi had one injured calf and one injured knee, which was already very red and swollen. Guo Xiangmei judged that he had badly smashed the bones in both his legs. If not treated quickly, he would probably lose both of them. Already, Liang Kesi was in no state to walk and would have to be stretchered out. They had only two soldiers and one stretcher with them; as to what had happened to the other pair and their stretcher, who knows? With only one stretcher, who should they take out? How could they get out? Guo Xiangmei was more than a little anxious. Looking at Wu Baosheng, she saw him frowning and knew that he must be worrying about the same thing.

Guo Xiangmei, while dressing Liang Kesi's wounds, said: "Your classmate, Luo something, is a really good person."

"Luo Yinan," Liang Kesi said. "How is he?"

"He was very worried about you," Guo Xiangmei said. "Last

night, he came to the hospital to ask about you. I heard that Zhengqi was coming out to rescue you, so I tagged along too. He was supposed to come with us, but Zhengqi wouldn't let him. He knew that he faints at the sight of blood, so he was afraid that if he fainted out here, he would just cause more trouble for everyone."

"Wow!" Liang Kesi was shocked. "Did he actually make it out to the front line? Because he wanted to save me? He's a real scaredy-cat. In fact, the only reason he wants to be a monk is so that he doesn't have to deal with any of the grim realities."

"Yes, he told me about that," Guo Xiangmei said. "He said I should tell you that you must live. As long as you're alive and refusing to allow him to become a monk, he can't go and take religious vows."

Liang Kesi laughed. He remembered the scene when he met Luo Yinan by the Miluo River and felt a little touched. He thought: He wanted to come out here to save me?

It got later and later, until it was almost morning, but none of them felt like sleeping. Sometimes they looked up at the sky, and sometimes they whispered to each other. Everyone was waiting anxiously for the lamps on the walls to go out.

However, that night, the lights stayed on until the sun began to rise.

11

THE OFFICERS and men of the Northern Expeditionary Army felt that this was the most awful day they had endured since setting out; they were not prepared for the fact that the next few days were going to be worse.

There were corpses of soldiers of the Northern Expeditionary Army everywhere under the walls of Wuchang. If you stood on one of the higher slopes, you could clearly see them sprawled across the ground. Those brothers-in-arms had now passed away, but they were left lying out there in the wilds, exposed to the heat of the sun, crawled over by every manner of insect. When the wind blew, it brought the stench of the corpses with it. Everyone for miles around could smell it. Even if you were sleeping in your bed inside a house, the smell of corruption was right under your nose. The living had no way to collect the dead; they had to look on helplessly from a distance.

A handful of impulsive soldiers ran to headquarters at South Lake, and when they saw their commanding officers they demanded to be allowed to fight. "Let's go!" they shouted. "Let's go and fight again!"

Their officers were too sensible to allow this: "If you fight like this, you'll just get yourselves killed. You have to have a plan."

The soldiers ignored this advice and cried: "If we die, at least we'll die with our comrades! This is unbearable!"

Their senior officers were hard men, but at this moment they also shed tears and said: "Do you think we like this? They were our brothers-in-arms too!"

Ye Ting looked as black as thunder all day and was reluctant to speak to anyone. Nearly two thirds of the Independent Regiment had fallen below the walls of this millennium-old city; they would never be coming back. He had sent them out but would not be welcoming them home again. One of the dead was Cao Yuan, his favourite of all the officers under his command. He had buried Cao Yuan at the foot of Hong Mountain. When his body was consigned to the grave, all the soldiers of his battalion came, but there were only a few of them. Ye Ting was furious and said: "Get everyone here!" Mo Zhengqi, his eyes red, told him that everyone was there: all the survivors had come. When Ye Ting heard this, he started to shake and almost fell. Fortunately, Mo Zhengqi was there to prop him on his feet.

Investigations revealed exactly what had happened with the rumours that they had already entered the city. It turned out that some people were convinced that the Independent Regiment was so competent they would take Wuchang with no problem, so they might as well jump the gun a bit. They then lied and said that the city had been captured and their troops were inside, which, as it turned out, simply caused more casualties. Everyone in the Department of Political Affairs was very angry because they had been in such a festive mood as they held their flags and slogans, ready to march into the city. When they met civilians fleeing for their lives, they shouted: "Don't run away! We have taken Wuchang! You should join us and celebrate our victory!" Most of the civilians turned round and went with them. As a result, they ended up being part of this fraud. This was deeply humiliating for them, and everyone was clamouring for justice. However, the situation was complicated, and there were numerous factions at headquarters all fighting tooth and nail. Apart from Chiang Kai-shek throwing a fit, nothing happened and nobody was punished.

At dawn on the sixth day, a shell fired from Gui Mountain landed right next to Wu Peifu's headquarters at Zhajiadun in Hankou. The commander of the defence of the city of Hanyang was

Liu Zuolong. Wu Peifu immediately phoned him to complain about this incident. Liu Zuolong said: "Oh, they must be firing in the wrong direction." A few minutes after he put the phone down, another shell landed. At that moment, Wu Peifu realised that he had lost Hanyang.

Soon enough, news of their triumph arrived in Wuchang. The Hanyang garrison had risen up, and Liu Zuolong then surrendered to the Northern Expeditionary Army. Chiang Kai-shek immediately put him in charge of the Fifteenth Army. Hanyang having changed sides, the Northern Expeditionary Army took advantage of the situation to build a pontoon across the Han River. They expected to take Hankou any moment now.

This news wiped away all their sorrow at the previous day's appalling defeat. All eyes were on Hankou; the Department of Political Affairs was rife with stories about how they were going to attack Hankou and capture Wu Peifu alive. Once they caught him, people claimed that they would dismember him and eat him in revenge for what had taken place at Wuchang.

The attack on Wuchang seemed to have been put on hold.

All the troops were pulled back, out of the line of fire. Headquarters decided to reorganise its forces, prepare the equipment necessary for an assault on the walls and, having first encircled Wuchang, they would wait for the opportunity to attack.

Mo Zhengqi, lying in the hospital, was out of his mind with worry at this. Not only was his cousin Liang Kesi lying somewhere at the foot of the walls, but so were Liu Zhengbao, Zhang Desheng and a number of his other soldiers, and he still didn't know if they were alive or dead; but Guo Xiangmei and Wu Baosheng, who went to rescue them, were also out there, and this tore at his heart. His wound had not even begun to heal: the injury to his ear was infected, and he could not so much as raise his arm, which had several stitches in it. The doctor told him that if he didn't calm down and rest, if the infection got any worse, he would probably lose the hearing in that ear.

Ye Ting went with him in person to Baotong Temple and told the doctor that he must save him. "Don't do anything stupid," Ye Ting said. "I want you to stay as part of my Independent Regiment."

"It's not as bad as they say," Mo Zhengqi said through his tears. "Give me another chance, will you?"

Ye Ting ignored him and ordered his bodyguards to stay behind and keep a close eye on him. He went over to the headquarters by South Lake alone.

Another terribly anxious person with not the slightest interest in what was going on over in Hankou was Luo Yinan. He returned to the Department of Political Affairs, where he spent the whole time on pins and needles, worrying about Liang Kesi and Guo Xiangmei. He did not know what had happened to them. He wanted to go to Baotong Temple to ask Mo Zhengqi; he knew that he was seriously injured and would definitely be there. However, the work of the Department of Political Affairs was endless. He and Huang Jiezi spent an age buying a coffin and shroud for Ji Defu. Then there was all the fuss about the fighting over in Hankou and Hanyang. It felt as though a new task was landing on their plate every five minutes, and they had to work through the night without any time to rest. He could not get away at all.

Early that morning, all the members of the Department of Political Affairs gathered at the small warehouse where Ji Defu's body was lying to hold a memorial service for him. Director Deng Yanda delivered the eulogy, telling the story of Ji Defu's life and death. His voice was filled with emotion. In the hot weather, the body in the coffin had begun to decompose, and from time to time body fluids seeped out from between the boards and fell, drop by drop, to the ground. There was a horrible smell hanging in the morning air. Luo Yinan remembered how Ji Defu had collapsed, and his heart twitched as he thought about it. It was the first time that he had witnessed someone's death, and now he was witnessing his corpse rotting away. All of a sudden, Luo Yinan was overcome by the horror of what he had seen and began to cry. His crying triggered other people's tears, and those who had known Ji Defu well now all began to sob.

The walls of Wuchang were very close to where they were standing, and there were bursts of artillery fire every now and again. These shells were being fired from Hong Mountain and Gui Mountain on the north bank of the Yangtze River towards Wuchang, almost as if it were a gesture of respect for the dead Ji

Defu. It was to the sound of the guns and sobbing that Ji Defu's coffin was lifted onto a carriage and sent to a nearby small temple for storage. Once an appropriate cemetery had been located, they would arrange for a burial to be held.

Luo Yinan was silent all day. "Are you thinking about being a monk again?" Huang Jiezi asked. He shook his head. At this moment, he really wasn't thinking about it anymore. There were too many things that he still had to do. For a start, he didn't know what had happened to Liang Kesi, Guo Xiangmei and the others. Were they even still alive? Shouldn't he be making an effort to contact Mo Zhengqi? Surely he couldn't just hang around here, as if none of this had ever happened?

Lots of people had now come from the Party headquarters in Hankou to help them. Several factories in Hanyang came out on strike, saying that they were doing this in support of the Northern Expeditionary Army's attack on Wuchang. People crossed the river to the south bank in droves to offer their condolences or to help. The situation, which had seemed hopeless, now unexpectedly started to look a lot more cheerful.

The warlord-controlled newspapers were praising Liu Yuchun, commanding the defence of the city, as "Zhao Zilong come back to life". This epithet had originally been applied to Ye Ting, but now the enemy borrowed it for Liu Yuchun. Huang Jiezi was much irritated by this: "If it weren't for the terrain here, not to mention the guys back in history who built Wuchang's city wall so strong, he would have fuck-all chance to defend anything!"

When Luo Yinan heard the news, he was stunned. He had only one thought in his mind: What about Liang Kesi?

It was already very dark. That evening, Luo Yinan slipped quietly away from South Lake and walked alone through the night. He was going to find Mo Zhengqi. He was sure that Mo Zhengqi had not given up trying to rescue his men.

There were now loads of doctors and nurses at the field hospital at Baotong Temple, and volunteers had come over to help from various charitable institutions in Hankou, as well as students from the medical school. It took a lot of time for Luo Yinan to find Zhang Wenxiu.

Zhang Wenxiu was surprised: "What are you doing back here again?"

Luo Yinan was a little embarrassed, but he was happy to see her again. "I want to ask you to help me find Mo Zhengqi again," he said.

"What's wrong?" she asked. "Didn't you just find him the other day?"

Luo Yinan now realised that she had no idea what had happened. He explained that after Guo Xiangmei took him to see Mo Zhengqi, they discovered that he'd run away. Then they went to Changchun Monastery to find him and ended up going to rescue Liang Kesi.

Zhang Wenxiu listened with her eyes popping and could not help asking a barrage of questions. So you all went off late at night to save people over by the walls? So Guo Xiangmei crossed the moat and never came back? Liang Kesi hasn't been rescued either? And Mo Zhengqi went even though he was injured? You don't know whether Xiangmei is alive or dead? No wonder I haven't seen her for the past two days! Is she really over there, pinned down under the walls?

Luo Yinan was so confused by her enquiries that he could only say yes, yes, yes.

Zhang Wenxiu did not speak for a long time. Luo Yinan was feeling uneasy and asked: "What's wrong?"

"You are amazing!" Zhang Wenxiu said. "I should have gone with you. What are you going to do now?"

"I don't know," said Luo Yinan. "But I think Mo Zhengqi will have come up with a plan."

"I'll take you to him," she said.

Many of the wounded were lodged in nearby houses, but some were kept inside Baotong Temple. Luo Yinan followed Zhang Wenxiu as she made her enquiries from one room to the next, and finally they located Mo Zhengqi in the side room of a house under the hill.

Mo Zhengqi was feeling restless and impatient. Seeing Zhang Wenxiu and Luo Yinan coming through the door was a godsend. When Luo Yinan saw that Mo Zhengqi was now wrapped in even more bandages than before, he was shocked and said: "Have you been injured again?"

"The doctor insisted," Mo Zhengqi said. "They like to scare people, but it is actually much better than before. What's so special about being got with a bayonet? Just sew it up and I'll be fine! I got stabbed in the back one time before and didn't even go to hospital for it, and it healed up fine."

"How about Xiangmei?" Zhang Wenxiu asked. "Has she come back yet?"

Mo Zhengqi immediately looked upset and said: "No. It's good you're here. If I don't go and save them, they're going to die. If anything bad happens to them, how can I carry on living?"

"What is your plan?" Luo Yinan asked.

"I'm going to rescue them!" Mo Zhengqi said. "Before Battalion Commander Cao died, he asked me to make sure our injured brothers-in-arms got back safely. If I don't go to save them, he'll come back to haunt me."

"If the enemy spot you," Luo Yinan said, "won't they just kill you?"

"So you think I shouldn't go because they might kill me," Mo Zhengqi said. "When we attacked the city, weren't we risking our lives? I have to go, even if I know I am risking my life."

"Your life is important too," Luo Yinan pointed out.

"But my conscience also matters," Mo Zhengqi said. "That's my family out there, and my comrades. If I have to abandon them, I would rather be dead."

Luo Yinan looked at Mo Zhengqi and thought to himself: Yes, he is that kind of man – chivalrous and courageous. No wonder Guo Xiangmei loves him so much; she does not just care about him but also his reputation. She would rather put herself in danger than risk her wounded lover getting injured again. Luo Yinan admired him very much and decided that, come what may, he would do his best to help him.

"What about your wounds?" Luo Yinan asked.

"I went out the other day," Mo Zhengqi said, "and the last couple of days I've been feeling much better than I did that day. You don't have to worry about me. You just find a way to get me out of hospital."

"OK," Luo Yinan said. "But I think if we go and try to rescue them a second time, how about we don't go straight there? It's a little bit shorter, but it's too exposed. Can we go around a bit and get over the moat somewhere less obvious, and then work our way round the wall to Binyang Gate? Although it is further, it will be dark, and there won't be many guards out, so it will not be so easy to spot us."

Mo Zhengqi was amazed and said: "Do you know the way?"

"I remember it from trips to the walls when I was at school," Luo Yinan said. "For example, we can cross the moat at the wastelands between Zhongxiao and Binyang Gates. The grass there is very high, and there are a handful of houses we can use for shelter."

Mo Zhengqi suddenly asked: "Didn't you want to go off and become a monk?"

"Yes," Luo Yinan said, "but I want to save Liang Kesi more."

Mo Zhengqi looked at him with approval and said: "Good stuff. I've underestimated you. But you won't be able to fight. I'll have to take my men."

"I will go too," Zhang Wenxiu said.

"You can't," Mo Zhengqi said. "If anything happens to you, Regimental Commander Ye will have me shot out of hand."

Zhang Wenxiu looked very stern: "My responsibility is to save lives and help the wounded. It's not up to you to decide whether I go or not. If there are wounded men out there, it is my duty to go."

Mo Zhengqi and Luo Yinan looked at her, not quite sure what to do. "It's too dangerous," Luo Yinan said. "You'd better stay here. If you can help Company Commander Mo to get out of the hospital undetected, you will have done your bit."

"I don't care if I have 'done my bit' as you call it," Zhang Wenxiu said. "You see, they're in danger, they're wounded, and maybe they need some treatment before they can be moved. That's the most important thing."

"Listen, honey," Mo Zhengqi said, "that's exactly what Guo Xiangmei said. But the thing is we are acting in secret and against orders."

Zhang Wenxiu smiled: "I am in the same profession as Guo

Xiangmei, and this is our duty. I guess I'll just have to break the rules with you, and I promise not to tell anyone."

Mo Zhengqi pointed to Luo Yinan and said irritably: "He is already enough of a problem for me, and now I have you too. If anything happens, how can I explain it to my superiors?"

Luo Yinan and Zhang Wenxiu spoke almost with one voice: "We are volunteering for this mission."

Mo Zhengqi sat down by the window and considered the matter. The clouds were thick that night, and the moon was obscured. On moonless nights, the sky is gloomy and dark.

Luo Yinan looked out of the window and suddenly remarked: "The moon is not bright tonight. If we're careful, maybe we can succeed."

Mo Zhengqi, as if he had made up his mind at that very moment, stood up and said: "OK, we go tonight. If it succeeds, the credit is yours."

"I don't want any credit," Luo Yinan said. "I just want to save Liang Kesi. I am doing this because he wanted to save the world, but I only wanted to find a temple where I could spend the rest of my life in peace. So the world needs him to survive and not me."

Zhang Wenxiu looked at Luo Yinan and said: "The world needs you too – we all need you. I am not only going to save Liang Kesi, but I will also rescue you from this dream of becoming a monk."

Luo Yinan looked at Zhang Wenxiu in some surprise. Suddenly, he really wanted to ask: "What do you mean – you need me too?"

Zhang Wenxiu told Mo Zhengqi's guards that the doctor would be operating all night and had no time to come over. She would therefore be taking him to the doctor to have his wounds examined. She asked the guards to stay there until they came back. Knowing that Zhang Wenxiu was a nurse, the guards nodded and agreed.

They went first to the kitchen to get food and water and then quietly left the hospital.

Mo Zhengqi did not go to Changchun Monastery since his company was now billeted in nearby houses. They had now attacked the city twice, on the third and the fifth of September, and there were not many survivors left. There was an endless stream of recruits coming in, many of them students, and those cheerful and childish faces made Mo Zhengqi think of Liang Kesi. He went straight back to his own company, where the remaining veterans were all living in the same house. Mo Zhengqi felt sad. When they first arrived, his company had needed several houses to live in, but now there was room for them in one house, with plenty of space to spare.

Too many of their comrades died, and their bodies were still lying out there in the wilderness, exposed to the sun and the rain. They could smell the stench of corpses day and night but could not bury them. They suffered a lot from this. When they saw Mo Zhengqi, they burst into tears and asked if they could go and collect the bodies of their brothers-in-arms.

Mo Zhengqi also shed tears, but after only a few drops he wiped his eyes with the back of his hand and said: "The most important thing right now is not the dead, but our comrades left alive outside the walls. They are injured, and if we do not save them they will die." When they heard that he was going to save their casualties that night, everyone stood to attention and asked to join the mission. Mo Zhengqi indicated to four strong soldiers and told them to bring a stretcher. Then he said: "This time, there is no need for so many people. You should take advantage of this opportunity to rest up, get fit and well, and help train the new recruits. You are the backbone of our company, and I need you to stay safe."

A soldier said: "Company Commander, you're the backbone. You need to be careful."

"Don't worry about me," Mo Zhengqi said. "The king of hell knows that I haven't fought anything like enough battles yet. Oh, and by the way, don't say a word about this to Regimental Commander Ye. Otherwise, he'll shoot me, and you'll have my blood on your hands."

The soldiers all said: "Company Commander, don't frighten us like that."

"I am not saying this to scare you," Mo Zhengqi said. "It's the truth."

Seven of them set off on their mission. Outside the walls of a couple of the houses, there were scaling ladders that hadn't been taken across the moat. Luo Yinan suddenly had an idea and said: "Company Commander Mo, shouldn't we take this ladder with us?"

"We aren't going to be climbing the walls," Mo Zhengqi said. "What do you want ladders for?"

"Maybe we can use this ladder as a bridge and cross the moat faster," Luo Yinan said.

When Mo Zhengqi heard that, he immediately ordered the two soldiers to pick it up and muttered: "It seems that you are pretty bright. If I become a general in the future, you can be my staff officer."

"I'm afraid he'll already be an old monk by then," Zhang Wenxiu said.

"Do you think it'll be easy, being a monk?" Mo Zhengqi asked.

Luo Yinan did not say anything. He thought to himself: A sparrow cannot understand the ambition of a swan, but can a swan know the feelings of a sparrow?

It was not far from Binyang Gate to Zhongxiao Gate: a mile plus a hop, a skip and a jump, as the locals said. There was a stone bridge across the moat outside Zhongxiao Gate, but this was now under strict guard. Mo Zhengqi knew full well that they could not just walk over the bridge. They had to find a way through somewhere between the two gates.

On the eve of the siege, the people living outside the city walls had fled. In order to prevent the Northern Expeditionary Army from using their houses in the attack, Liu Yuchun had ordered that all houses near the city wall be burned or blown up. The scene by the moat, a hundred metres in each direction, was terrible to see. All the way, Mo Zhengqi kept repeating: "Look, you see, this is why we have to fight them! This is how they treat people!"

Having gone about a mile, they suddenly heard gunshots. The shots were scattered, first coming in a burst and then tailing off. At first, it seemed there might be a target, but then it seemed that there wasn't – they were just testing. Slowly, stopping and starting, they crawled forward in single file. Although they were covered by the undergrowth, they were clearly visible from the watchtowers. These days, the enemy guarding the walls were on high alert and frightened. They were afraid that the Northern Expeditionary Army would assault the walls at night again, so they lit all the lamps on the four corners of towers. From the moat to the foot of the walls – a distance of some ten metres – it was as bright as day. The open land beyond the moat, almost one hundred metres, was also somewhat lit up. Mo Zhengqi cursed bitterly: "How much oil are they wasting on this?"

Mo Zhengqi had been injured, so he crawled forward only slowly. After crawling for about half an hour, he arrived at the moat. Two soldiers passed the scaling ladder carefully across, and it was just long enough. But if a man clambered across it, it would need to be supported. Otherwise, once he started moving, the ladder would fall into the water. Mo Zhengqi gave his orders: "Students and women will stay here, holding the ladder. We'll go over." Without waiting for their reply, he added: "There are only orders on the battlefield, no explanations."

That served to silence Luo Yinan and Zhang Wenxiu, who wanted to complain. "Once they've gone over," Zhang Wenxiu said, "you take hold of the ladder, and I'll climb over. The wounded over there can't be moved without me. Company Commander Mo is an ignorant fool – he doesn't understand."

Luo Yinan felt that she had a point, so he gave a grunt of agreement.

Four soldiers quickly climbed over the scaling ladder. Mo Zhengqi had just hoisted himself up on it when suddenly a soldier on the opposite bank whispered across: "Someone is coming." Mo Zhengqi speeded up, and the ladder shifted with his movements. Luo Yinan and Zhang Wenxiu gripped the ladder desperately, one on each side, so as not to let it slide into the moat.

Mo Zhengqi managed to get across safely, and he ordered everyone to lie down in the grass. From the other side of the moat, Luo Yinan and Zhang Wenxiu could also see a shadow moving. Looking at this person's figure, Mo Zhengqi decided that it was a stranger. He would wait for whoever it was to come closer.

Bullets were being fired at random from the watchtower, and the crouching figure fell to the ground. Mo Zhengqi said: "It's one of ours! Otherwise, they wouldn't be out here dodging bullets." Then he and his four soldiers crawled swiftly over towards the visitor.

As they got closer, they saw it was a foreigner. When the foreigner saw Mo Zhengqi and the others suddenly materialise in front of him, he jumped and said quickly: "I am not an enemy."

"Who are you?" Mo Zhengqi asked.

"The woman who got shot," the foreigner said, "I guess she's one of yours."

When Mo Zhengqi heard that, he didn't have time to ask any more questions; he was too busy clambering towards him. He saw at a glance that it was Guo Xiangmei on the foreigner's back! It was a heart-stopping moment. He called softly: "Xiangmei!"

Guo Xiangmei was unconscious. "She needs help right now," the foreigner said. Two soldiers helped put Guo Xiangmei on the stretcher.

"Is she out here alone?" Mo Zhengqi asked.

"There are more back there," the foreigner said, "but I think one of them has already died. Another one is injured, but he's still able to crawl. I could only carry one of them, so I took the woman."

As the foreigner's voice tailed off, one of the soldiers said: "Company Commander, you go with your fiancée, and we'll save the others." Then two of the soldiers turned and started crawling towards the wall.

Guo Xiangmei was completely covered in blood. Mo Zhengqi looked at her and felt as if a knife were twisting in his heart. It was a terrible struggle, even with the foreigner there to help, to get her across the moat. Zhang Wenxiu rushed to her rescue, but as she worked she said: "She has lost too much blood – we need to get her to the hospital as soon as possible."

"Since the enemy isn't shooting this way," Luo Yinan said, "you get going, and I'll stay here and wait for the rest of them."

"There is another casualty coming on behind," Mo Zhengqi said, "maybe Liang Kesi, maybe one of my men – I have to wait for him. Nurse Zhang, you will take Xiangmei to the hospital at once. Comrade Luo, you can't let this foreigner run away. I want you to escort him over to headquarters at Changchun Monastery."

The foreigner quickly said: "I don't need to be escorted anywhere – I am not going to run away. I came to see you on purpose. I have something important to say to your officers."

"In that case," Mo Zhengqi said, "you must see him handed over to Regimental Commander Ye in person."

"OK," Luo Yinan said.

While they were talking, the two soldiers and Zhang Wenxiu

were already heading off towards Hong Mountain with the stretcher, running as fast as they could. Luo Yinan and the foreigner also set off at a sharp pace for Changchun Monastery. Mo Zhengqi could not cross the moat again because he was needed to hold the scaling ladder. He didn't know who the injured person coming up behind could be. If it was Liang Kesi, that would be great.

It was a very long wait.

12

IT WAS SO LATE at night that few people were abroad in the streets. Luo Yinan escorted the foreigner to Changchun Monastery, and when the foreigner saw the dilapidated streets and tumble-down houses he could not help sighing: "Lord, is it by Your will that this flourishing community should be destroyed? Come and save them!" When Luo Yinan heard him say that, he couldn't help turning around to look at him.

When the foreigner saw Luo Yinan turn, he also took this opportunity to consider him. Suddenly, the foreigner said: "You look familiar to me. Are you by any chance a student in Wuchang?"

"Yes," Luo Yinan said.

Then the foreigner asked: "Do you know Shuya? She lives over on Garden Hill."

Luo Yinan suddenly called him to mind and said: "Are you Mr Meng? Mr Meng, the foreigner who works for Wenhua University?"

"That's me," the foreigner said happily. "One Christmas, was it you who went to the church to collect Shuya when she was singing in the choir?"

"That was me," Luo Yinan replied. "But how do you remember me?"

"I was the choirmaster," Mr Meng told him. "I remembered you the moment I saw your eyes – at that time they were full of distress, like a lamb that had gone astray. I wanted Shuya to enrol you in the choir because I thought that praising the Lord in song might help you find a way out of your confusion. But Shuya explained that you are a Buddhist."

"Oh, that," Luo Yinan said. "Shuya mentioned it to me."

"It seems to me," Mr Meng went on, "that your eyes show much more distress now."

Luo Yinan was reluctant to talk to him about it. He was even more reluctant to mention Shuya: her name always seemed to open a gaping wound in his heart. He didn't even want to know how Shuya was faring; after all, her family was rich. No matter how much chaos is inflicted on others, the rich people will always be spared, or at least that is what Luo Yinan thought.

"What are you doing here?" Mr Meng asked.

"That is exactly what I wanted to ask you," Luo Yinan replied. "What on earth were you doing outside the walls? How did you end up saving one of our people?"

"Your artillery has been bombarding the city day in and day out," Mr Meng explained. "It has been terrible. You've been knocking people's houses to pieces, and it's the poor who have been dying. I want to ask your officers to stop."

Luo Yinan was amazed: "Was that why you came out of the city? You took such a big risk for that? How on earth did you get out? Did you go through Binyang Gate? I think you came from that direction."

"I didn't come through the gate," the foreigner explained. "All the city gates are blocked. I used a rope to let myself down from the top of the city wall."

Luo Yinan was now even more surprised: "They let you leave?"

"I was planning to just sneak out," Mr Meng said, "but I was caught."

"And then?" Luo Yinan asked.

"The reason why I went to Binyang Gate," Mr Meng explained, "was that the officer guarding the city wall there is a relative of some friends of mine. I know him, and I know he's a reasonable man. I told him why I wanted to leave, and he let me go – in fact, he helped me let myself down over the city wall with a rope."

"Do you think you can change our commanding officers' minds?" Luo Yinan asked.

"I don't know," the foreigner said, "but I have to at least try to persuade them. I do not want to see tens of thousands of ordinary civilians die from your shells, nor do I want to see their homes destroyed by gunfire. The Northern Expeditionary Army said when they set out that they were coming to help the people and save them from suffering – but if this rescue should be at the cost of so many civilian lives, who would want you to come? Who in the future would want you to save them? There is an old Chinese saying that he who wins the hearts of the people wins the world. Once you start butchering them like this, will you still have the hearts of the people? Not only will you lose their support but you will also be condemned in the court of public opinion around the world. I believe they will not ignore the consequences. What do you think, young Buddhist?"

Luo Yinan was shocked by what he had said. He recalled Liang Kesi saying that the reason the government of the Beiyang warlords would collapse was that they had lost the support of the people. In answer to the foreigner's questions, he said: "I think you're right. I agree with you." After that, feeling that he hadn't fully expressed his meaning, he added: "I think that I have learned a lot from what you said."

"Let us hope that your senior officers will agree," Mr Meng said in a satisfied tone.

Luo Yinan took the foreigner as far as Changchun Monastery. Ye Ting wasn't there. Apparently, he had gone round to headquarters at South Lake. The foreigner asked Luo Yinan to take him there. He did not dare to refuse, and he quickly headed out towards South Lake. After locating Ye Ting, he explained why Mr Meng had come and brought him over. By this time, the sky in the east was already brightening with the dawn of a new day.

The foreigner chatted with several of the officers inside, while Luo Yinan waited outside on the pavement. When he got tired of standing, he sat down on the ground. His thoughts were far away as he considered what had just happened. He wondered what had happened to Mo Zhengqi and whether the wounded soldier coming along behind was Liang Kesi, and he worried about whether Guo Xiangmei had reached the hospital in time. He wanted to rush over and ask them, but Ye Ting had not said anything about him being allowed to leave. He did not dare go anywhere without authority, so he ended up waiting.

The sun had already risen above the horizon when Ye Ting and a couple of other officers came out, escorting Mr Meng. Luo Yinan hastily stood up. "Take Mr Meng to somewhere where he can get accommodation," Ye Ting said. "He said he knew you before?"

"Oh, yes," Luo Yinan answered. "I used to study here in Wuchang."

"Then he can stay with you in the first instance," Ye Ting said. "Let him get some sleep."

"No need," the foreigner made haste to say, "I have to go back to the city."

"How are you going to get past the walls?" Ye Ting asked. "All the gates are closed."

"I can discuss that with them," Mr Meng said.

"How are you going to get close enough to them to do that?" Ye Ting asked. "You are going to have to leave it to us. You go and get some sleep."

There was nothing that the foreigner could do, so he simply said: "OK."

Luo Yinan took Mr Meng to his own accommodation. Then he said: "Are you really going to go back into Wuchang?"

"Of course," the foreigner said. "I didn't come here to persuade the Northern Expeditionary Army to stop the bombardment just to run away afterwards! I have to go back. The city people are in terrible trouble, and I have to be with them."

"I had no idea you were so brave," Luo Yinan said admiringly.

"Just like you Buddhists," Mr Meng carried on, "if it helps other people, we can sacrifice ourselves."

Luo Yinan wanted to ask about Shuya. He hesitated for a moment but did not say anything.

After arranging for a place for the foreigner to lay his head, Luo Yinan decided to go and find Mo Zhengqi. He wanted to know whether Liang Kesi and the others were alive or dead. As he had spent the whole night running back and forward, he was absolutely exhausted and staggered as he came out of the door. It so happened that Huang Jiezi needed to go to Baotong Temple Field Hospital to get some stomach medicine for one of the officers and didn't feel like walking, so he got up early that morning and found a place for himself on the cart that the canteen used for hauling vegetables back from the market. Just as the cart pulled out onto the main road, he spotted Luo Yinan weaving along. Huang Jiezi was surprised and called out to him.

When Luo Yinan looked back, he saw Huang Jiezi on top of the cart and stopped in his tracks.

"Where are you going?" Huang Jiezi asked.

"To Changchun Monastery," Luo Yinan said. "What about you?"

"I'm off to Baotong Temple to collect some medicine," Huang Jiezi explained.

Luo Yinan now wondered how badly Guo Xiangmei had been injured. Moreover, if Mo Zhengqi had rescued anyone, he would probably have sent them over to Baotong Temple. So perhaps it would be best to go to there. Having come to this conclusion, he said: "I'll come with you."

Huang Jiezi asked the driver to stop, and Luo Yinan clambered in awkwardly. When Huang Jiezi realised just how tired he was, he was very surprised and insisted on knowing the reason. Luo Yinan interspersed the story of how they had gone to rescue people with his yawns.

Huang Jiezi's eyes were practically popping out of his head. He shouted: "If you are going to do this kind of thing, you ought to tell me. I want to be a hero too!"

"I don't want to be a hero," Luo Yinan said. "I just wanted to save Liang Kesi."

"And isn't Liang Kesi my brother-in-arms too?" Huang Jiezi demanded. "Of course, I have only known him for a very short time, but we are both revolutionary comrades! Will you tell me next time?"

"I don't know if there is going to be a next time," Luo Yinan pointed out.

As he said that, he fell asleep. By the time Huang Jiezi woke him up, they had already arrived at the foot of Hong Mountain. Looking up, over the treetops, they could see the spire of Baotong Pagoda.

Luo Yinan went looking for Zhang Wenxiu. Someone told him

that she was at work in the Dharma Hall behind the main courtyard. A shell fired from Snake Mountain in the early hours of the morning had exploded near the Dharma Hall, bringing part of the roof down. The hospital had decided to transfer the wounded to the houses below the mountain.

That was a dreadful shock to Luo Yinan; he was so frightened that he ran through one building after another and rushed straight out to the back of the main courtyard at Baotong Temple.

The Dharma Hall was a place of worship for Tantric Buddhism, and it had only been built two years earlier. Luo Yinan had been present when it was consecrated, and he knew that it was built in the form of the Five Mandalas prescribed by the Tang dynasty Tantric Vajrayana Sect. Because the abbot, Master Chisong, had just come back from Japan, Luo Yinan had been reading Su Manshu very enthusiastically at that time. In order to understand Su Manshu's theories about Buddhism, he had come specially to visit, but Master Chisong was in Shanghai at the time, so he had not been able to meet him.

The Dharma Hall was indeed in confusion when he arrived: the north-facing corner of the roof had collapsed. Medical staff were busy moving the wounded out. Luo Yinan spotted Zhang Wenxiu in there, bending over, as she readied herself to carry a soldier with two broken legs out on her back. Luo Yinan pulled her away and took the wounded man on his own back.

"Why were they shelling you?" he asked.

"For the last two days," Zhang Wenxiu said, "it has almost been like competitive bombardment. This side hits the other side, and that side hits us back. Shells have been landing all over the place around here. This one has landed the closest, and it almost brought down the whole roof. Fortunately, it did not fall anywhere near the middle, or we'd all be dead."

The wounded were all sitting quietly in the sun outside the Dharma Hall, waiting for the transports going up and down the hill. Everyone looked calm, not at all like when they had just come from the front line. Zhang Wenxiu had no time to waste on Luo Yinan, and he did not mind that. Seeing that she was so busy, he kept quiet about all the questions he wanted to ask and just followed around behind her to help.

CHAPTER 12 | 127

When there was a lull, Zhang Wenxiu said: "I know why you are here – come with me."

With that, she took him to a room within the Dharma Hall that was still entirely undamaged. There was a bed on which a body was lying, covered by a white sheet. Luo Yinan went cold all over: "Who is it? Is it Liang Kesi?"

Zhang Wenxiu wiped her eyes with her hand and said: "It's Guo Xiangmei."

"You couldn't save her?" Luo Yinan was shocked.

"No," Zhang Wenxiu said. "She never regained consciousness and died this morning."

"What about Company Commander Mo?" Luo Yinan asked. "Does he know?"

"Yes," said Zhang Wenxiu. "He tried to kill himself but was restrained by two soldiers. I don't know where he is now."

Luo Yinan stood in front of Guo Xiangmei, trembling all over. He did not dare to lift the sheet to see her face, which had always seemed so happy and confident. He had gone with her to save people; he had known her for only two or three hours; but she had allowed him to see another kind of person, a sort of person he had never met before. It never occurred to him for a moment that the hand of death would claw her away so soon. Now, he was standing there, and she was gone forever. It's too easy to die. But in that case, what's the point of being alive? Luo Yinan felt drained. That night, she'd said: "I'll tell Kesi that you're worried about him." That was the last thing she said.

He stood there, not knowing what to do. Zhang Wenxiu tugged at his sleeve, and he followed her out of the door. The sun was now high in the sky, and the shadows thrown by the trees were short.

Luo Yinan had now calmed down. "Where is Liang Kesi?" he asked.

"He never came," Zhang Wenxiu said.

"Wasn't there another wounded person yesterday who was coming along behind?" Luo Yinan asked. "Was that not him?"

"No," Zhang Wenxiu replied. "That was a soldier from the Independent Regiment, Zhao something-or-other. Mo Zhengqi brought him here in the middle of the night. He had a leg wound, but his life was not in any danger."

"But…" Luo Yinan said, "is Liang Kesi still alive?"

"Oh, yes," Zhang Wenxiu said. "The soldier called Zhao said that there were seven of them to begin with, but one of them died the first night, and then six were left. Four of them were badly injured and could not move. One of them would not have survived yesterday if Xiangmei hadn't gone out there. They have no food, and water is a problem. Xiangmei decided to bring the two least injured men back and then afterwards try to come up with a plan to rescue the others. They were moving across towards the moat when they were spotted by the enemy up in the watchtower. That foreigner rescued Xiangmei, but unfortunately… she didn't make it. All the people who went with her were killed too. If it hadn't been for Company Commander Mo's men turning up in the nick of time, the other soldier would never have made it back alive. However, one of Company Commander Mo's people also got killed."

Luo Yinan was appalled. He worked it out: two attempts at rescue had cost the lives of so many people, but only one casualty had been saved – it wasn't worth it.

"Would you like to meet the other soldier?" Zhang Wenxiu asked. "He's called Zhao Huzi, I think. I'll get someone to take you to him."

Luo Yinan nodded.

Originally, there had not been many people living in the village at the foot of Hong Mountain. Almost all the houses were now occupied by the Northern Expeditionary Army's casualties. Those with minor injuries were being transported south in an endless stream. Those so badly wounded that they could not be moved were left here, and then taken to Hankou. Luo Yinan found Zhao Huzi easily enough. He was lying in bed with no colour at all in his face. Luo Yinan asked the nurse about his injuries. The nurse said that his leg had already turned gangrenous and that they might have to amputate. But his mental state was more concerning; he seemed to have been deeply traumatised by his experiences, and he was suffering a great deal of pain and restlessness. Luo Yinan was silent for a moment and left without going over to speak to him. There was a deep sorrow in his heart and an agony that seemed to etch down to the marrow of his bones.

Luo Yinan needed to find Mo Zhengqi. Now that he knew Liang Kesi was still alive, he couldn't just ignore him; he had to go and rescue him. He did not ride with Huang Jiezi on the cart going back to headquarters at South Lake. When they came to a fork in the road, he jumped out. Huang Jiezi wanted to join in the rescue of Liang Kesi too, but he had to take the medicine back to the senior officer who was waiting for it, and he did not dare to disobey orders.

"Liang Kesi is a friend of mine too," Huang Jiezi said, "so if you need me for anything, just tell me."

"I will," Luo Yinan said.

Luo Yinan went first to Mo Zhengqi's billet. The soldiers there said that the company commander had been summoned to the Three Sage-Kings Hall by Regimental Commander Ye. Luo Yinan rushed off to Changchun Monastery, but the moment he entered the main gate he realised that something was very wrong. There were some soldiers running towards the Three Sage-Kings Hall. Luo Yinan grabbed one of them and asked: "What's the matter?"

The soldier said: "I heard that Company Commander Mo has been making a formal apology to the regimental commander, but he still wants to go back out to save his men."

Luo Yinan now set off running towards the Three Sage-Kings Hall himself.

By this time, there was a crowd jammed into the door, and the atmosphere was stern. Luo Yinan wriggled through and looked into the hall. Mo Zhengqi was standing off to one side, his head bowed, with a bundle of thorns tied to his bare back. The white bandages wrapped around his shoulder really caught the eye. Regimental Commander Ye Ting was pacing back and forth, shouting at him. His voice rang out like a bell and resounded through the hall.

"You say that Cao Yuan ordered you to do this," Ye Ting bellowed, "but Cao Yuan took orders from me! Look at you! Standing here making an exhibition of yourself by apologising with a bundle of thorns like something out of feudal history! How many comrades have we lost because of you? Tell me that! The lives of the wounded matter, but so do those of my soldiers! They are lying there outside the walls injured and can't come back – that hurts me too! If I could help them, I would. But don't you see how bad the situation is? I can't risk the lives of any more soldiers trying to bring them back. That's my duty! I am ordering you, under no circumstances whatsoever are you allowed to cross the moat! Our Independent Regiment cannot afford to lose any more men!"

Mo Zhengqi looked at him sadly and muttered: "But... But..."

Ye Ting interrupted him: "No more buts! If you do something that stupid again, I'll have you shot!" As he spoke, he took out his revolver and put the muzzle right up against Mo Zhengqi's temple.

Luo Yinan was horrified. A soldier cried out: "Regimental Commander! Please don't..."

Another soldier shouted: "We are willing to risk our lives if that means we could save our brothers! We volunteer to go with Company Commander Mo!"

Ye Ting ignored them and went on: "You answer me! Are you going to obey orders or do I have to kill you?"

Mo Zhengqi raised his head and said slowly: "I will obey orders!"

Luo Yinan breathed a sigh of relief. But in that instant, he saw that Mo Zhengqi's eyes had filled with tears. Ye Ting put away his gun and stood there for a moment without saying a word, and then he walked out of the door. The soldiers thronging around the door moved aside to let him pass, and Ye Ting told them, enunciating each word carefully: "Even if you are willing to die for your brothers, I can't let you do that. Some facts have to be faced up to, and this is one of them. Go back to work!" Then he turned around and left.

The soldiers gradually dispersed. Mo Zhengqi stayed where he was, unmoving. Luo Yinan went over and took the bundle of thorns away from him. He squatted down beside him and said: "What happened, Company Commander Mo?"

Mo Zhengqi looked over and saw that it was Luo Yinan. He took a note from his pocket and said: "I found this in Xiangmei's pocket."

When Luo Yinan saw that it was Liang Kesi's handwriting, his heart beat faster. Liang Kesi wrote that all four of them were badly wounded and could not move. It was impossible to get them out from where they were with the enemy watching, so there was no need to send anybody to save them. But if someone sent out food, water and medicine, they would be able to hold on. He hoped that they would attack the city as soon as possible, and they firmly believed that they could stick it out until the day of the attack. The note also specifically included a line or two destined for Luo Yinan: I am really glad that you have become a proper warrior so soon. Maybe I will see you among the soldiers who take the city. I believe that victory is not too far away.

Luo Yinan held tight to the note, his hands trembling. He thought: Am I a warrior? How could that possibly be? As he thought that, he asked Mo Zhengqi: "When will we attack the city again?"

Mo Zhengqi said: "Headquarters says there will be no attack on the city in the foreseeable future." His voice was low, full of sadness and helplessness.

Luo Yinan was horrified: "How can that be? What about Liang Kesi and the others?"

'Don't think about it anymore,' Mo Zhengqi said. "Go back. Where is the foreigner? I want to thank him for everything he did."

A flash of an idea sparked in Luo Yinan's mind. "I think I have a plan! I am sure we can save them!"

Mo Zhengqi immediately grabbed hold of him with both hands and asked eagerly: "Tell me! How?"

"Mr Meng, the foreigner, said that he wanted to go back to Wuchang," Luo Yinan said. "He knows the officer guarding Binyang Gate. He'll enter the city there, so they'll have to open the gate. We can ask him to save Liang Kesi."

"How?" Mo Zhengqi asked.

"Mr Meng can take Liang Kesi and the others into the city with him," Luo Yinan said. "He can arrange for them to go to a hospital there. Would that be OK? They are all seriously wounded. Would the enemy mind that they participated in an attack on the walls?"

Mo Zhengqi stood up indignantly: "What on earth are you thinking? Do you remember that they are the enemy over there? What does the enemy do? They try to kill us! Would you like them to be captured alive by the enemy and dragged into the city and then have their heads cut off like your classmate Chen Dingyi, so that they can hang them from the watchtowers to show us all how brave they are?"

Luo Yinan's head was spinning, and he felt as if someone had hit him with a club. He remembered Chen Dingyi and how his head had hung up all by itself over the city wall. Fear swept over him like a wave, and he stared at Mo Zhengqi as if in a trance.

"If they want to keep their heads," Mo Zhengqi continued, "they have to betray the revolution. It would be better to let them die where they are, under the walls. What were you thinking! Besides which, that foreigner cannot be allowed into the city through Binyang Gate! If he goes that way, all of our people over there will be killed!"

Mo Zhengqi's last words came out in a roar, so loud that Luo Yinan's mind went completely blank at the sound.

13

WITH LIU ZUOLONG'S SURRENDER, Hanyang fell without a fight. With his cooperation, the Northern Expeditionary Army built a pontoon bridge at Hanjiang, forced their way across the Han River and attacked Hankou. Fighting raged at various locations along the banks of the Han at Zongguan, Jijiazui and Dakou Alley; with every minute that passed, so many people were killed that the river ran red with blood. But in the end, the enemy was defeated and withdrew from the city, and Wu Peifu fled north to Xiaogan by car. Hankou soon raised the flag of the Northern Expeditionary Army all along the river, and those standing on guard at the Bell Tower atop Snake Mountain could almost hear the enthusiastic cheering coming from the opposite bank. The steamers patrolling the Yangtze River were immediately placed on high alert. They kept a close eye on both the northern and the southern sides of the river, though they did not dare to fire shots unless absolutely necessary, fearing that any escalation in the conflict would only place their families in even greater danger.

Wuchang was now completely isolated.

At the same time, fighting in Jiangxi Province was ongoing, and the situation of the Eastern Expedition was critical. The headquarters of the Northern Expeditionary Army had decided to postpone its attack on Wuchang and redeploy its troops to Jiangxi, leaving the Fourth Army behind to keep up the siege of Wuchang.

They were completely cut off now: there was a land blockade, a water blockade, and a communications blockade; no food was being allowed in, no information either, and no residents were allowed in or out of the city gates; and if anyone attempted to open the gates and break through the siege, they were beaten back without mercy. With no food, no way to leave, and no news from outside, when the morale of the garrison defending the city collapsed because of starvation, it would all be over.

The soldiers of the Northern Expeditionary Army seemed relieved. It's easier to lay siege to a city than to attack it. Ever since they had started out from Guangzhou, they had fought all the way, one battle after another with almost no pause. There had been bloodshed and terror day after day. Now, everyone could finally relax and rest.

But Luo Yinan was in a terrible state.

What about Liang Kesi? He was still alive, though he had been wounded and was lying hidden within the entrance to Binyang Gate. Although he could not see him all the way across the battle lines and entrenchments, he could well imagine how he looked, propping himself up against the wall. He was waiting, full of confidence, for the army to attack the city, for it was only by an attack on the city that he could survive.

Now, all attacks had temporarily ceased, and they were prohibited from attempting a rescue. This meant that the four wounded men hiding in the fortified gateway would die. Luo Yinan couldn't bear to think of it: he knew that Liang Kesi was not far away, living in anticipation of rescue, while he was over here watching and letting him slowly die. How could this lively and ambitious young man, this romantic and impressionable young man, be allowed to die before he had achieved anything?

Luo Yinan was so upset that he could not sleep at night.

The Department of Political Affairs was kept very busy during this time. They had been ordered to print a leaflet as part of their political propaganda work. This particular leaflet was entitled "A Letter to the Enemy" and addressed to "Our brothers opposite". In the letter, the strength of the two armies and their treatment of their soldiers was compared, and the enemy were advised to put down their weapons as quickly as they could. It was signed "The

Department of Political Affairs at the Headquarters of the National Revolutionary Army".

Huang Jiezi cursed while he ran off more prints: "How can we call them brothers after they have killed so many of our comrades?"

Luo Yinan bowed his head in silence as he cut the greaseproof paper, but in his heart he agreed: Yes. How can we call them brothers?

There were other leaflets calling on the people of Wuchang to take action to support and foster the National Revolutionary Army.

Luo Yinan questioned Huang Jiezi: "How are these leaflets going to be delivered?"

"No idea," Huang Jiezi replied.

But they soon found out because the aeroplane arrived.

The aeroplane arrived just as the bulk of the army was about to march on Jiangxi Province. At first, everyone was very excited and felt that Wuchang would fall quickly with aerial bombardment. Needless to say, if they blew a hole in the walls, the Northern Expeditionary Army would be able to pretty much walk into the city. Luo Yinan was worried whether the bombs dropped by the aeroplane would hit Binyang Gate. Liang Kesi and the others trapped in the entrance could not move. He was worried that falling walls might bury them. He even thought about talking to the pilot to explain the situation: he could blow up anything, providing he did not blow up Binyang Gate. But soon everyone came to realise that it wasn't a bomber that had flown in.

The Department of Political Affairs had the leaflets everyone had been writing bundled up and taken out to the aeroplane. The plane circled in the skies over Wuchang a couple of times, dropping the leaflets, and several hand grenades were also thrown, and then it flew back. Although this frightened the people inside the city badly, it was not as though they had managed to blow a hole in the walls. Luo Yinan, who had been worried about this prospect, was now very disappointed.

After dinner, Luo Yinan took a break and rushed over to Baotong Temple to find Mo Zhengqi again. He felt helpless; he did not know what to do. He had to go and find him. It was almost as if Mo Zhengqi had become his prop and mainstay.

The most badly injured casualties from Baotong Temple had

now been moved over to the hospital in Hankou. There were a lot fewer people, and the houses had begun to empty one after the other. Only some of the less seriously injured, who had not yet been transferred, sat in the doorways, chatting with each other as they waited. Suddenly, the bitter atmosphere of wartime had gone. Although gunfire occasionally sounded, a leisurely and relaxed atmosphere prevailed at the foot of Hong Mountain.

Mo Zhengqi's bed was empty. Luo Yinan asked several people about him, but none of them knew where he had gone. They also said that he was ignoring everybody and had spent the whole day looking as stiff as a poker, interspersed with throwing things and losing his temper. Luo Yinan understood exactly why he was behaving so. He had lost one loved one after another on this campaign, so it was no wonder he was so very unhappy.

Having failed to find Mo Zhengqi, Luo went to look for Zhang Wenxiu again. Zhang Wenxiu was not on duty that day. She had been washing her hair, and it was lying loose all over her shoulders as she sat under Baotong Pagoda and chatted with another nurse. They both looked particularly beautiful in the moonlight. If it had not been for the occasional gunshots shooting through the sky, how charming and attractive the whole scene would have been! Luo Yinan looked at them and was moved. He did not want to disturb the two of them because he wished to keep this sight before his eyes for as long as possible.

Zhang Wenxiu raised her head and saw him. "What are you doing here?" she asked.

Luo Yinan now had to go over and explain: "I've come to see Company Commander Mo."

"He isn't here," Zhang Wenxiu said. "I was about to go over to Changchun Monastery to see if I could find him. He has to have his dressing changed, or that wound is never going to heal."

Luo Yinan was shocked: "Didn't he come back here? Is he going out to try and save them again?"

"No," she said and shook her head. "We all heard that if he dares to act off his own bat, against direct orders, Regimental Commander Ye is going to have him shot."

The nurse sitting next to her now moved round to comb Zhang Wenxiu's hair and put it into braids. "I heard that Regimental

Commander Ye put his gun up against Company Commander Mo's head," she said.

"He did," Luo Yinan replied. "I saw it with my own eyes. But what about the four casualties over by the walls? Are we just going to let them die?"

"Exactly!" Zhang Wenxiu said. "We were both talking about it just now. We know they are waiting for help over there, so if we don't go to the rescue we're going to feel really bad about it. Besides, did Guo Xiangmei die for nothing?"

At the mention of Guo Xiangmei, Luo Yinan's heart ached a little. Every time her face came to his mind, he felt an infinite sadness. "Yes," Luo Yinan muttered, "how can she have died in vain? She was an amazing person, and I can't even begin to match up to her."

Stars filled the sky. Luo Yinan left Baotong Temple in a daze, with no idea what he should do. When he got to the fork in the road, he looked up at the sky. He wondered if Liang Kesi might not be looking up at the starry sky just like him at that very moment. Perhaps he too was sighing. What was he sighing about? His helplessness or the cruelty of life? Thinking of this, Luo Yinan felt more and more uncomfortable. Suddenly, someone called out to him. In the darkness, he couldn't see clearly, but hearing the voice he knew it was Zhang Wenxiu.

She came running over. She was carrying a first-aid kit on her back and panting as she said: "You walk so fast."

"What's happened?" he asked.

"I am going to Changchun Monastery," she said. "I told you I need to change Company Commander Mo's dressing."

"I'm thinking about going there too," Luo Yinan told her.

"Great!" Zhang Wenxiu said. "Let's go together."

Together they turned down the road leading to Changchun Monastery. The moonlight was very bright. Luo Yinan walked in silence.

"You are much braver than I thought," Zhang Wenxiu told him. "I remember when I first saw you, I thought you were completely useless for all that you wanted to join the army."

"That's just because Liang Kesi forced me to do so," Luo Yinan said. "I wanted to go home, but the train stopped halfway, and then we ended up meeting by the Miluo River. He forbade me to go home and said he would make me go and join the Northern Expeditionary Army. I just thought life was boring, so I obeyed his commands."

"I heard you wanted to go back home to become a monk?" Zhang Wenxiu asked.

"Well," he said, "I am tired of life."

Zhang Wenxiu laughed and said: "You didn't become a monk. You joined the propaganda department instead – that's a really big difference."

"Once you have seen through all worldly lures," Luo Yinan said, "you can follow where fate leads. Liang Kesi was so positive and optimistic – I didn't want to brush the bloom off the peach. I am here, but my heart is there – that is all."

Zhang Wenxiu was surprised and said: "You mean, you are still physically present here now, but in your heart you have already taken the tonsure to become a Buddhist monk?"

"You could say that," Luo Yinan said.

"Ah!" Zhang Wenxiu exclaimed again. "I've never met a revolutionary soldier like you before! Why would you join the revolution if you don't believe in it?"

Luo Yinan laughed and said: "Why not?"

"That's odd," she said. "The Revolutionary Party welcomes real revolutionaries, eliminates counter-revolutionaries, and shows no mercy to the false revolutionaries. I guess you count as a false revolutionary, don't you? Do you understand that? Many people want false revolutionaries to have their heads cut off, not just counter-revolutionaries!"

Luo Yinan was shocked and blurted out: "So a revolution requires you to cut the heads off other people?"

"I have to correct you there," Zhang Wenxiu said. "We aren't cutting other people's heads off – we are cutting *enemy* heads off. Because if we don't kill them, they will kill us."

"If you end up dead either way," Luo Yinan said, "what's the difference between the two of you?"

Zhang Wenxiu glared at him and said in a disdainful tone: "It seems to me you really are a false revolutionary!"

"I don't care about the revolution one way or the other," Luo

Yinan said. "I just follow my destiny."

Zhang Wenxiu stood still and said: "If this wasn't right on the front line, I would report you to the authorities."

Luo Yinan couldn't understand her sudden volte-face and muttered: "But am I not part of the revolution right now? Why should my motives be so important?"

"Of course they are important," Zhang Wenxiu said. "Because what you think forms your belief. If you don't truly believe in the revolution, you can change your mind at any time. So if the enemy catches you, you will immediately betray us."

Luo Yinan didn't know how to exculpate himself. He thought: That's not the kind of person I am. But he didn't say it. Suddenly, a strange sadness overwhelmed him.

Mo Zhengqi's company was billeted in a house about fifty metres away from Changchun Monastery. When Luo Yinan and Zhang Wenxiu arrived, they saw a soldier, coated in mud, washing himself down at the basin. Luo Yinan went over to ask where Company Commander Mo was. The soldier said: "Keeping an eye on things over at the tea shop."

Luo Yinan didn't understand what he meant. "Huh?"

Zhang Wenxiu thought that fighting might have broken out again and said: "I don't hear any shooting."

The soldier smiled, pointed a finger and said: "Go to the corner, turn left, walk seven or eight metres, and then you'll see Zeng's tea shop. Go in, and you are guaranteed to find Company Commander Mo."

Luo Yinan nodded, turn around and went out.

Following the soldier's instructions, they did indeed arrive at the tea shop. The owners had already gone to bed, but there were lights on in the front room. The windows were covered with thick blackout curtains, and several soldiers were carrying baskets of earth out. Luo Yinan stepped in and was immediately stopped in his tracks. Zhang Wenxiu was surprised into saying: "What on..."

A soldier quickly explained: "We're digging a tunnel."

Zhang Wenxiu was even more amazed: "You're tunnelling into the city from here?"

The soldier said: "Of course!"

Mo Zhengqi was squatting off to one side and did not stand up when he saw them coming. He just remarked coldly: "We don't have to make it all the way into the city, only as far as the wall. We put down explosives there, and then we blow a hole in that motherfucking wall."

This time, it was Luo Yinan who was shocked into speech: "You're going to blow up the city wall? How long will that take? If the wall collapses, won't it land on Liang Kesi and the others? Besides which, will they still be alive by then?"

Mo Zhengqi got angry and shouted: "Don't mention his name to me! What are you doing here anyway? If you haven't got anything useful to contribute, then go away. Don't just stand there, getting in the way!"

Luo Yinan was stunned by his irritability. He opened his mouth and tried to say something, but nothing came out, so he stood there awkwardly.

"Stop being so aggressive, Company Commander Mo," Zhang Wenxiu said. "Be careful of that wound. We are here to change your dressing." Mo Zhengqi wanted to say something, but Zhang Wenxiu carried on regardless: "You can't refuse treatment. If that wound gets infected, you won't be able to do anything. In fact, you won't even be able to squat here. In that case, you'd be better off if Regimental Commander Ye did just shoot you."

Mo Zhengqi was still angry, but he changed his mind about making any more fuss when he heard that. "If you want to change my dressing, go right ahead," he said. "There is no need to make a song and dance about it."

On one side of the counter, there were a couple of chairs, apparently set aside for customers who came to the shop to drink tea in situ. Zhang Wenxiu pulled Mo Zhengqi over to one of the chairs and made him sit down. There was a huge hole in the ground on the other side of the store, and soil was being hoisted up there. The soldiers carrying the earth away shouted: "Get out of my way! Move!"

Luo Yinan, standing by the door, dodged first this way and then that. He thought to himself: How many days will it take to dig as far as the wall? Can Liang Kesi hold out until then? Thinking of this, he could not help looking over at Mo Zhengqi.

Mo Zhengqi allowed Zhang Wenxiu to change the dressing, but

his face was still set, and he did not once look over towards Luo Yinan. His eyes were fixed on the soldiers digging, as if he were supervising their every move. Luo Yinan knew that he was entirely surplus to requirements here and decided that Mo Zhengqi was probably still angry about his ideas earlier in the day. Then he said in dismay: "I'd better go, Liang Kesi is waiting for me." As soon as he said that, he left.

The road from Changchun Monastery to South Lake took him through farmland and wasteland, with a few scattered houses. Luo Yinan was walking down the road alone. He remembered Tao Yuanming's poem: *The road is narrow, and the grass is long; the evening dew wets my robes.* He decided to change it to, *The night-time dew wets my clothes.* This reminded him of travelling by night with Liang Kesi. When they had been studying together, they had not had very much to do with one another. The quiet and diffident Luo Yinan had always watched from the sidelines as the passionate and idealistic Liang Kesi and his companions had rushed about so busily. They were always so full of vigour; always so lively as to infect others with their passion. Luo Yinan decided that Chen Dingyi and Liang Kesi were actually quite similar, but their ambition had brought them nothing but bad luck. Chen Dingyi was dead; Liang Kesi was dying. Even if the wall was blown up and the army attacked the city, what would that matter if Liang Kesi had already starved or died of thirst over in the gateway? He trembled at the mere thought of it.

Having made his way back to where he was living, he was almost at the door when suddenly he saw a couple of scaling ladders left under the wall of the quad. It occurred now to Luo Yinan that he might not be able to rescue them, but he could at least take them some food and water to help the four of them survive until the tunnel had been dug. In fact, as long as they got a little food and a few mouthfuls of water every day, they would be able to survive. Once the tunnel had been dug, he was quite sure that Mo Zhengqi would rescue them first and then blow up the wall. All he needed to do was to transport food and water out to the barbican, and Liang Kesi would be saved! With this in mind, Luo Yinan felt a great deal better.

He went to find Huang Jiezi and explained his plan.

Huang Jiezi was shocked and said: "Just you? How is that going to work?"

"I thought one person would be enough," Luo Yinan said, "because the more people go, the easier they are to spot. One person doesn't make much noise and won't attract attention from the watchtowers, not least because no matter how great a warrior he is, he cannot possibly attack the walls by himself."

"What about me?" Huang Jiezi said. "What can I do to help?"

"You can help me get the scaling ladder to the edge of the moat," Luo Yinan said, "so I can use the ladder as a bridge. I need you to hold it for me as I cross."

"Then how do you get back?" Huang Jiezi asked.

Luo Yinan thought for a moment and said: "How about you wait there for me? After I deliver the food and water, I'll come back the same way."

"OK," Huang Jiezi said, "but you must come back safe and sound!"

"Of course, if it works out today, we can climb over there every two or three days so that they don't die of hunger," said Luo Yinan. "Sooner or later, Wuchang will fall, and then they can be rescued."

"That's a good idea," Huang Jiezi said. "Do you want to tell one of the officers what you are doing?"

"Not at all," Luo Yinan said. "Even if we are successful, we cannot say a word."

"Why not?" Huang Jiezi asked.

He explained: "The commanding officers all want us to preserve our strength as much as possible, and we want to save our comrades. We have different priorities and different ideas."

"I don't understand," Huang Jiezi said. "Don't the officers want to save them?"

"A rescue attempt may not succeed," Luo Yinan pointed out. "At the same time, there may be further deaths. From the point of view of our commanding officers, they need to stop any more people from getting killed, so they have to let the people over in the gateway die. But we think differently – they are our brothers. As long as they are alive, we have to go to rescue them. Even if we get killed, we can't turn a blind eye to their fate, or we will never forgive ourselves."

Huang Jiezi now felt he had some insight into the problem: "You are right. If it had been us out there, we would be thinking that our comrades will come to rescue us, so we would have the confidence to wait."

"I guess so," Luo Yinan said.

Luo Yinan felt he hadn't explained properly. He was sure that if he didn't save Liang Kesi, his whole life would be meaningless.

As they were speaking, they began to get ready. Huang Jiezi went to the kitchen to look for some food, while Luo Yinan gathered several water bottles to fill. Huang Jiezi packed a few steamed buns in a bag, along with a pile of pickles and several carrots. He seemed very excited and said that he had explained to the cook exactly what he was doing and the man had been really helpful, packing up everything that was not needed in the canteen. Luo Yinan looked at the heap and thought if they rationed their food there would be enough for up to five days. "We can't bring enough to keep them well-fed," he said, "but at least they'll get enough food to keep them alive."

Luo Yinan considered carefully exactly how to tie the cloth bags and bottles about his person so they would make no noise when he was crawling over the ground.

"I found a little cart," Huang Jiezi said. "We can put all of this stuff inside and tow it over to Changchun Monastery and then strap it onto you when we get there."

Luo Yinan thought that seemed sensible.

Huang Jiezi made Luo Yinan lie down on the cart too. He said that when he had to climb over the entrenchments to reach the city wall, it would really take it out of him, so right now he needed to rest and keep his strength up. Luo Yinan obeyed him, heaved the scaling ladder onto the cart, and then lay down beside it.

The cart rumbled and swayed gently on the dirt road. Luo Yinan was lying with his face looking up at the sky; there were so many stars shining there, and the moon floated in and out of a gap in the clouds. He felt as though he were the only person under the heavens. He felt that he too was spiralling into the abyss.

Trudging along, suddenly Huang Jiezi said that there was someone up ahead of them, and it looked like a woman. Luo Yinan sat up: "Would it be Nurse Zhang from the field hospital?"

"It looks a bit like her," Huang Jiezi said.

As they got closer, they recognised Zhang Wenxiu. She was surprised to see them, and then she spotted the scaling ladder. "You are going to..." she said.

"It's nothing," Huang Jiezi said, "we're just taking this up to the front lines."

Zhang Wenxiu noticed the bottles and bag. She pinched it and said: "You've got steamed buns in there! I know what you're up to. Tell me the truth!"

Luo Yinan had to be honest: "I want to take some food and water out to Liang Kesi."

"You were hinting something of the kind when you walked out," Zhang Wenxiu said. "I thought at the time that you were up to something, and sure enough so you are."

"I wasn't hinting anything," Luo Yinan said. "I decided afterwards that I could not bear for Liang Kesi to starve to death."

"You are right," Zhang Wenxiu said. "But they need medicine as well as food. They need experienced nurses."

Luo Yinan was shocked: "What do you mean?"

"I am going with you," Zhang Wenxiu said.

"You can't do that," he told her. "It's too dangerous!"

"Comrade future-monk," Zhang Wenxiu said, "I have been on the field of battle a lot more than you have. When we were fighting in Huizhou, I was right there at the front of the front line. Do you understand me?"

Huang Jiezi was impressed: "You were there at the Battle of Huizhou?"

"Of course I was!" Zhang Wenxiu said. "However, the city wall there was much lower than at Wuchang."

"Oh, sure," Huang Jiezi said, "the Wuchang city wall is over a thousand years old."

Luo Yinan made haste to cut in: "Go away, we need to hurry up. We aren't going to fight anyone – we just want to deliver some food as discreetly as we can. We can't save them, so I just want them not to starve to death before the army attacks. In a few days' time, the tunnels will be dug, and Company Commander Mo can go and rescue them."

"You have forgotten one thing," Zhang Wenxiu pointed out.

"They are all injured. If they aren't given medicine, even if they don't die of hunger, they will still die in agony because of their injuries. In this weather, without water to clean their wounds and without any antiseptics, do you think that their injuries will simply heal of their own accord?"

Luo Yinan and Huang Jiezi exchanged glances and could think of nothing to refute her point.

"If you can go," Zhang Wenxiu said, "so can I. And even if you can't go, I should still find a way to get over there."

"No," Luo Yinan said, "if anything happens, they will shoot me."

"If the enemy spots you," Zhang Wenxiu told him, "they will shoot you long before anyone else gets the chance. If nothing happens, then it's a secret between the three of us. How is anyone going to know?"

Luo Yinan and Huang Jiezi were silent.

After a moment, Zhang Wenxiu said: "Let's go." She turned around and walked in the direction of Changchun Monastery. Huang Jiezi and Luo Yinan followed her in silence, as if she were the leader of their expedition.

Not far from Changchun Monastery, Zhang Wenxiu turned in a different direction and headed for Zhongxiao Gate. Luo Yinan understood that she was going to the place where they had crossed the entrenchments last time. There were relatively few people there, so maybe they could get through.

Huang Jiezi asked in a low voice: "Is this right?"

"Just follow her," Luo Yinan said.

When they were nearly there, they abandoned the cart, and the three of them lifted the scaling ladder. Luo Yinan was in the front, Huang Jiezi was at the back, and Zhang Wenxiu was in the middle. The walls of Wuchang were right in front of them. It was not easy to slide the ladder across the moat. Last time, several soldiers were hard put to do it. But this time Luo Yinan had brought a rope. He tied the rope to one end of the ladder and had Huang Jiezi hold it tight while he and Zhang Wenxiu slowly lowered the ladder onto the opposite side of the gulf.

This time it went well. The scaling ladder lay straight across the trench in a trice, like a wooden bridge. Luo Yinan instructed Huang Jiezi to hold the ladder firm at all costs; in fact, he should tie the rope around his waist to prevent the ladder from slipping. "If it falls," Luo Yinan said, "that will not only kill us but you too. The enemy up in the watchtower will shoot as soon as they hear the sound. They are terrified of being attacked by the Northern Expeditionary Army – as far as they are concerned we are lurking behind every bush, and they won't know how many people we have out here. They'll just point their guns and shoot, so you'll have no chance at all to escape."

Huang Jiezi gave a nervous: "Oh."

Luo Yinan divided up the steamed buns and water bottles; half of them were tied to Zhang Wenxiu and the other half to himself. He had learned that from Mo Zhengqi: if either of them reached the gateway, Liang Kesi would be saved. The first-aid kit was a little bigger, so Luo Yinan decided that he would go over first, taking the kit, and then Zhang Wenxiu could follow him. He would help Zhang Wenxiu over and then go back to get the rest of their stuff.

Looking at Luo Yinan taking command like this, Zhang Wenxiu said: "I really can't understand why you want to become a monk instead of joining the revolution?"

"I agree," Huang Jiezi said, "I think he would make a good general."

Luo Yinan ignored them: "How could you possibly understand how I feel!"

There were corpses everywhere at the foot of the walls, and they had now been exposed to the elements for several days. The stench hanging in the air was getting stronger and stronger. In the middle of the night, mixed with the night-time breezes, it was especially noticeable. The smell made Luo Yinan feel sick to his stomach: he had seen all these men alive; he had watched them gather in the moonlight and then march away, never to return. Now, the moonlight was still shining, but he was looking at their decomposing bodies. Life is so cruel. These young men had met a terrible end!

That was what Luo Yinan was thinking as he clambered over the scaling ladder.

He climbed over the trench, followed by Zhang Wenxiu, who also made her way across successfully. Luo Yinan took off the first-aid kit and handed it to Zhang Wenxiu, then climbed back to fetch the food and water. "I'll set off slowly," she said. "If we go separately we'll make a smaller target."

"Be careful," Luo Yinan told her, "and keep out of the light. If it gets too bright, get down and play dead, lying on your stomach, and then move forward little by little, not too fast." Luo Yinan remembered what Mo Zhengqi had told him when he participated in their first rescue mission.

"I know," Zhang Wenxiu said, "I have done it before."

However, the second time Luo Yinan crossed the scaling ladder, just when he got to the middle, the enemy suddenly spotted something. The light came on, and gunshots rang out. First, it was just a few scattered rounds, but Huang Jiezi on the other side of the moat was already scared out of his wits and started to scream. The screams alerted the watchtowers, and now the firing became localised and intense. From his position in the middle of the moat, Luo Yinan made a clear target. He wanted to climb over quickly, but the ladder was swaying with him. Luo Yinan looked up to remind Huang Jiezi that he needed to hold the ladder, but he was lying on his stomach, motionless. Luo Yinan's heart sank. He cried in a low voice: "Huang Jiezi! Are you OK?"

As he said this, there was another loud burst of gunfire. He quickly fell flat on his face, oblivious to the searing pain in his back. He did not know whether he had been shot or not. He moved his body, only slightly, but now the whole ladder slid down into the moat. Before he could react, he was falling with the ladder. An appallingly loud splash rang in Luo Yinan's ears, but by that time he was beyond hearing anything.

14

THE SOUND of gunfire was sporadic. For several days now, there had hardly been any fighting during the day, and the silence at night was even worse. Suddenly, a gun would be fired from the watchtower above them, like a convulsion in the dark, which left everyone feeling frightened and on edge. However, stillness and silence reigned over the front-line positions. Liang Kesi fixed his gaze in that direction. He wanted so much to see the signal flares set off there, followed by a group of soldiers from the Northern Expeditionary Army launching themselves against the city walls, carrying scaling ladders. He wanted them to fight a bloody battle, just as he had that night, except that this time they would breakthrough into the city. Once that had happened, even if it only occurred one time, he and his fellow soldiers would be saved.

However, it seemed that it was never going to happen. The layers of corpses piled up under the city walls were giving off a worse and worse stench. As soon as the wind blew, a horrible smell of decay enveloped them. To begin with, they felt nauseated, and later it made them vomit, but finally they got used to it. By this time, Liang Kesi, leaning up against the entrance to the barbican, had come to realise that a large-scale direct attack on the city would not be taking place. Looking at the massive towering walls of Wuchang and the corpses of the Northern Expeditionary Army scattered everywhere, he understood that even if tens of thousands of people were prepared to risk their lives, they would never be able to take the city if they were armed with nothing but scaling ladders and courage. The enemy was right above their heads, and it was easy to hear the soldiers chatting up in the watchtower when it was quiet. They were clearly feeling quite confident. Liu Zhengbao said: "Don't think about it." Liang Kesi thought to himself: Yeah, I shouldn't think about anything.

Soon after Wu Baosheng and Guo Xiangmei left with the two most lightly wounded casualties, they had one more death. At present, Liu Zhengbao, who had broken his back, was speaking only two or three sentences a day, while another soldier was only hanging on by a thread and could no longer even eat. Liang Kesi's legs were both swollen, and pus had begun to seep from the festering wounds. He thought that even if he managed to get back alive, he would probably lose his legs. Worst of all, although they had rationed them as strictly as they could, they had now run out of food and water. During the day, he had eaten the last mouthful of bun and drunk the last two sips of water. Afterwards, he thought: Maybe this is the end.

The stars were shining as bright as ever, as dazzling points of light in the dark night sky. Ever since he had been injured here, Liang Kesi had been looking at the stars every night. He now realised that he had never noticed before how bright the night sky was. Perhaps these stars were his comrades who had died on the field of battle. It was they who had given their lives to illuminate a China mired in poverty and ignorance, just as the stars illuminated the night sky. Then he thought: Just think of yourself as one of those stars – all that matters is that you are shining. As to which one you are and whether anyone will pay attention to you – that does not matter in the slightest.

Liu Zhengbao, lying by his side, shifted uneasily. Liang Kesi quickly asked: "Are you OK?"

"I have been dreaming of my mother," Liu Zhengbao said. "I guess I am going to see her soon. She starved to death, you know, but I was not at home when she died. I heard her calling to me."

Liu Zhengbao said all this in one go, but when Liang Kesi questioned him further he did not make a sound.

It was now late in the night. Liang Kesi was tired and drowsy. As he dozed, he became aware of someone calling to him. He thought: Is this Death?

Suddenly, gunfire rang out again, and there was a terrible racket all the way from Zhongxiao Gate to Binyang Gate. This woke Liang Kesi up completely. He thought: Can they be attacking the walls again? Having thought about it, he decided that was impossible. He propped himself up and looked out towards the front-line position. There was no movement over there. He decided that it must be the enemy up in the watchtowers getting scared of their own shadows again. They had been jumpy and on edge for many days. Sure enough, the guns were fired for a while and then stopped.

At this time, Liu Zhengbao shifted again and whispered: "There is something going on out there! Maybe someone is coming."

Liang Kesi was delighted: "Really? Can that be true?"

He listened for movement outside the barbican. Time passed in silence, and then after a long, long time a tiny voice whispered: "Is anybody there?"

The voice came from just outside the barbican. It was a woman's voice, but it did not sound like Guo Xiangmei. When she came into the gateway, Liang Kesi could see clearly by the light of the moon that the visitor was the nurse at the field hospital, Zhang Wenxiu. He exclaimed: "What are you doing here!"

Zhang Wenxiu caught sight of Liang Kesi and Liu Zhengbao next to him, and tears welled up in her eyes. In a choking voice, she said: "Great! It's great that you're still alive! How many more people are there?"

Liu Zhengbao said: "There are three."

Suddenly, Liang Kesi felt sure that he was not going to die, and his eyes were wet with tears. He said: "If you hadn't come, we would have died here."

Zhang Wenxiu untied the food and water bottles strapped around her person and said: "You must be hungry. There is food and water here but not much. Luo Yinan is bringing more, but I don't know…" She paused there because she remembered that the gunfire seemed to have been directed towards the moat. She had even heard a huge splash, but she didn't know if it was made by Luo Yinan.

Liang Kesi was startled and said: "Luo Yinan? You mean, he is behind you? Who else is coming? What about my cousin Mo Zhengqi?"

Zhang Wenxiu was silent for a moment, and then she said: "Only the two of us came this time – Luo Yinan and me. Mo Zhengqi couldn't come."

Liang Kesi exclaimed again: "Just you and Luo Yinan?"

"Yes," Zhang Wenxiu said. "Luo Yinan insisted on coming to help you. He knows you've hurt your legs. He says he might not be able to rescue you, but at least he can keep you alive. Then when we attack the walls, we can bring you out. He wanted to come all by himself, but he bumped into me on the way. I thought you would need medicine as well as food, and I was right, wasn't I?"

Liang Kesi did not answer her but asked: "What about my cousin Mo Zhengqi? Is he dead?"

"No," Zhang Wenxiu said, "he's still alive. However, too many soldiers died trying to get you out of here, and he was injured again. His commanding officer has forbidden him to come over here, saying that he will be shot if he tries."

Liang Kesi remained silent for a long time.

"Did Zhao Huzi get back safe and sound last time?" Liu Zhengbao asked.

"He got back OK," Zhang Wenxiu said, "but all the others were killed."

"What do you mean?" Liang Kesi exclaimed. "Is Guo Xiangmei dead?"

"She was rescued by a foreigner," Zhang Wenxiu said, "but she was too badly injured to make it. Luo Yinan saw the note you left, so he insisted on coming out here to save you."

Liang Kesi had been propping himself up to talk to Zhang Wenxiu, but all of a sudden he could no longer support himself, so he fell back and knocked his head against the ground with a thud. Zhang Wenxiu was shocked and said in alarm: "Don't do that! We haven't given up. We're still trying to work out a way to rescue you!"

Liu Zhengbao said in a choking voice: "Please go back and tell our comrades not to make any more attempts to save us. It's not worth it – the price is too high. The regimental commander is absolutely right."

Liang Kesi whispered: "Wu Baosheng is... dead?"

"I guess so," Zhang Wenxiu said, "he didn't come back. From what that foreigner said, there was someone lying on top of Guo Xiangmei who took a lot of bullets for her – his body was riddled with holes. Company Commander Mo said it must have been Wu Baosheng. Company Commander Mo was almost howling when he said that. He told me that Wu Baosheng came from the same town as he did and was his best friend. Unfortunately, Xiangmei got really badly shot in spite of it all."

Neither Liu Zhengbao nor Liang Kesi said another word.

In silence, Zhang Wenxiu examined their wounds. The soldier who never spoke seemed moribund. Zhang Wenxiu knew that he would not survive the night. Liu Zhengbao and Liang Kesi's injuries were also very serious. If they stayed out here, even with food and drink, she was afraid they would not be able to hold on much longer. She was so worried that she didn't know what to do.

Liu Zhengbao suddenly said: "Nurse Zhang, would you give me a drink of water?"

Zhang Wenxiu quickly handed over a water bottle and gave him two mouthfuls.

"That feels good!" Liu Zhengbao said. "The water is very sweet. Thank you."

Zhang Wenxiu turned around and asked Liang Kesi: "Would you like a drink too?"

"I already had something to drink today," Liang Kesi said weakly. "Let's keep it until tomorrow – we could be here for a while."

When they were talking, they suddenly heard the sound of a dull thud. Liang Kesi immediately realised that something was very wrong with Liu Zhengbao. He had been lying on his back up until now, but somehow he had flipped to lie face down on the ground. "Could you see what the matter with him is?" he asked Zhang Wenxiu.

She crouched down and asked: "Liu Zhengbao, what's wrong?" As she whispered this, Liu Zhengbao convulsed all over. "What's the matter?" she exclaimed. "Are you OK?"

With great difficulty, Liu Zhengbao smiled and said: "Don't let our comrades come out here again." Then he died.

Zhang Wenxiu turned his body over and found a knife in his chest. There was blood on the ground; although not much, there was enough to soak Liu Zhengbao's body. Zhang Wenxiu burst into tears and sobbed: "Comrade, you shouldn't have done that! How can you do something like that?"

"What's wrong with him?" Liang Kesi hissed.

"He… he… he's killed himself!" Zhang Wenxiu said through her tears.

That was the most dreadful night of Liang Kesi's life. Even though he had suffered when he was first wounded there, even though he had been through many extremely difficult days since then, he had not experienced this kind of agony. It was not his own injuries or any concern that he might die that caused his pain; he could never have imagined that in the space of just a few days, so many people, including friends and relatives, would be killed trying to help him. He had always been so optimistic, waiting for the city to come under attack, waiting for rescue. He had been so sure that the Northern Expeditionary Army was invincible; so utterly convinced that someone would come to rescue him; he had never even considered how much such a rescue would cost. Guo Xiangmei had died trying to save him. Wu Baosheng had died too. He counted up those of his comrades who had been killed and found that ten fingers were not enough! He was shocked by his own selfishness. He had made the revolution pay an enormous price; the families of the victims would have suffered so much pain. He had joined the revolution intending to make a contribution to it, but before he had been able to do anything of the kind, he had already caused irreparable losses. He felt like a criminal! He deeply regretted his impulsiveness and recklessness. He had been so very enthusiastic about playing a role in the revolution, but this was its tragic conclusion. His whole life had turned out to be a failure.

After a very long pause, Liang Kesi said: "He's right. We should all have done that long ago. You get back as quickly as you can and don't try to rescue me again. Even if you could get me out of here, I don't want to be responsible for any more deaths. I want you to tell them that from me. And another thing, his name was Liu Zhengbao. Please write it down."

"Then what about you?" Zhang Wenxiu asked. "What are you going to do?"

"I know what I should do," Liang Kesi said.

"You aren't going to do the same as him, are you?" Zhang Wenxiu enquired, and she pointed nervously at Liu Zhengbao.

For a moment, Liang Kesi was sunk in depression. He thought: I should do what Liu Zhengbao did. The best thing I could do right now would be to die like him.

"You must not kill yourself!" Zhang Wenxiu said.

"Why not?" Liang Kesi asked. "I think he makes a fine role model for me."

Zhang Wenxiu lowered her face until it was right next to his and said: "If you die, then won't all the others have sacrificed their lives in vain?"

"I don't want my comrades to continue to sacrifice their lives for nothing," Liang Kesi said.

"But what about them?" Zhang Wenxiu pressed him. "What about those who are dead? They died to keep you alive. Do you think you have any right to cut your own life short?"

"What do you mean?" Liang Kesi said in a shocked voice: "Are you telling me I have no right to die?"

Zhang Wenxiu's eyes were fixed on him. Her gaze was strong and firm. Liang Kesi did not dare to look at her directly. "That's right," Zhang Wenxiu said, "you don't. The only way you can pay them back is to stick with it. No matter whether someone comes to rescue you or not, no matter how they try to rescue you, no matter whether or not you can bear the consequences in the future of so many people having been killed, you have to survive. You have to grit your teeth. You have to live no matter how hard it gets and stick with it until your final breath. This is your fate, and it is also your responsibility because this is how you will be paying back your dead comrades. Otherwise, how can you do right by the people who died to save you? How can you do right by me, knowing that I risked my life to come out here to help you? Down there in the underworld, if they know you've held on right to the bitter end, they'll think it was all worthwhile. But if they know that you ended up killing yourself, well, that would make their deaths truly worthless – how could they not feel the injustice?"

Zhang Wenxiu was in such a hurry to speak that she ended up surprising herself by what she had said. Liang Kesi was stunned too, for this was a question he had never thought about – your benevolent intentions don't necessarily bring about good things, and your death isn't necessarily something you can decide for yourself. He now realised that the world was much more complicated and difficult than he had ever imagined. He thought it was like the darkness of night: you can no longer distinguish shapes and colours; or make out slopes and depressions; you don't know whether something is beautiful or ugly; you don't know the secrets that are hidden there. You can't see anything clearly.

The two of them were silent. The sky was still very black.

"I have to leave while it is still dark," Zhang Wenxiu said, "so I can't stay here any longer. There won't be enough food and water for two anyway."

Liang Kesi did not say a word.

"You need to be patient," Zhang Wenxiu carried on. "Company Commander Mo has people digging a tunnel, and they are going to tunnel through to the walls and then pack it with explosives."

"Really?" Liang Kesi asked.

"Let me repeat," Zhang Wenxiu said, "you must wait patiently. I am sure that when Company Commander Mo puts the explosives down, he'll take the opportunity to get you out before they go off."

A smile seemed to drift across Liang Kesi's face.

"Once the tunnel is ready," Zhang Wenxiu said, "someone will come here to save you – but if it doesn't work out, I will come again and bring you more food and water. You just have to hang on."

"Do you really think so?" Liang Kesi asked. "Yes," Zhang Wenxiu said firmly, "you can't die – you aren't allowed to. You have to live for the sake of those who have already gone. No matter how hard it is, you can't let them die for nothing."

Liang Kesi fell silent again.

"Don't think there is anything noble about suicide," Zhang Wenxiu said. "It is a cowardly act. You need to be tough to live – surviving makes you a hero. Didn't you just join the revolution? You haven't achieved anything yet. If you live, that's an achievement right there."

"Is that so?" Liang Kesi muttered. "Can that be right? I guess I should listen to you. OK, no matter how painful it is, no matter how much I suffer, I will stick with it."

"It's a deal," Zhang Wenxiu said. "In two or three days, I'll come back again. I already know how to get here, and nothing will happen. But if you die, when I come again, it will be all in vain."

"There's no need for you to come back here," Liang Kesi said. "I promise to stick to it."

"I have to come back," Zhang Wenxiu remarked, "because I need to bring you more medicine. I'm going to be treating those legs for you."

It was at the very quietest moment of the night that Zhang Wenxiu climbed out of the barbican, and Liang Kesi watched her disappear into the darkness. About an hour later, the sound of heavy gunfire came from the direction of Zhongxiao Gate, but he did not know whether it had anything to do with Zhang Wenxiu or not. He was worried for her but would never know what had happened. The helplessness of human existence was something he now experienced over and over again.

And he would never know: Zhang Wenxiu quietly climbed to the edge of the moat only to discover that the ladder had gone. She knew something bad must have happened to Luo Yinan. She couldn't get across the moat that way, so in a moment of panic she decided to run the risk of trying to cross the stone bridge by Zhongxiao Gate. The stone bridge was not very wide, and she thought that if she caught the enemy off guard she ought to be able to run across, and then she could use the battered walls of demolished houses for shelter. But she could not outrun the bullets. No sooner had she set foot on the stone bridge than she was spotted by the garrison up in the watchtower. After a few shouts and a burst of gunfire, she fell to the ground just two metres away from the broken-down wall of one of the houses. After that, nobody ever saw or heard from her again.

15

When Luo Yinan woke up, he was completely confused. He did not know what had happened or where he was. A nurse came over to give him an injection, and the familiar white dress made him think it was Zhang Wenxiu. Suddenly, he wanted to ask: "Why am I lying here? What on earth is going on?"

The nurse in white turned around and said in a pleased voice: "Are you awake? Finally, you've come round!" It was not Zhang Wenxiu's voice, nor her face, nor her hands and feet. It was all very strange, very strange indeed.

Several doctors came rushing over to peer into his eyes and listen to his heartbeat. He heard a doctor heave a deep sigh and say: "Well, it looks like he's going to make it."

Luo Yinan was in terrible pain all over his body. He wanted to speak but found that he didn't even have the strength to open his mouth. He thought to himself: Am I dead?

This was one whole week after Luo Yinan was rescued from the moat by Mo Zhengqi.

September sunshine, warm and soft, had already taken over from the hot and bright summer weather. After a few more days, Luo Yinan was able to sit up. He realised that he was in one of the church hospitals in Hankou. Through the window, he could see the sign on the wall outside.

The leaves on the trees outside the window had begun to turn yellow, and the dazzling sunshine was becoming less bright. Luo Yinan leaned against the pillows and tried his best to recollect what had happened to him. He had suffered a head wound, and there were many things that he had forgotten. He could remember a nurse named Zhang Wenxiu, who had brought him round when he was lying under the tree and dressed his wound in the hall. And after that? He couldn't remember a thing. When he asked the nurses about what had happened to him, they were vague and could not explain satisfactorily.

One day, a nurse brought a man to see him. Luo Yinan felt he looked familiar. He decided they must know each other, so he thought as hard as he could. "Don't you remember me? I'm Mo Zhengqi," the visitor said.

Luo Yinan felt the name was familiar and said: "I know I should know, but I can't remember who you are. Did anything happen to us? Sorry, I can't even remember how I ended up in this state."

Mo Zhengqi smiled gently: "Yes, your head was injured."

"That's what the doctors say," Luo Yinan said. "What happened? Can you tell me?"

"Do you remember Liang Kesi?" Mo Zhengqi asked.

The name went straight into his head like a nail. Up until now, he felt as though he had been locked up in a dark room, but now, all of a sudden, a hole had appeared in the wall, letting in light from outside. Luo Yinan's mind lit up, and all his memories came floating up to meet it. He remembered Chen Dingyi's head; the streets at night along the banks of the Miluo River; travelling with Liang Kesi to catch up with the Northern Expeditionary Army; the soldiers setting out at night and marching away under the light of paraffin lamps; Ji Defu dying in front of him; bodies scattered across the ground and Cao Yuan's face stained with blood; the lights on the wall by Binyang Gate being on all night; he remembered Guo Xiangmei and the foreigner; he remembered the pistol pointed at Mo Zhengqi's head; the ladder across the moat; Huang Jiezi; Zhang Wenxiu clambering over the ladder; and finally, he remembered falling off the ladder and that last deafening splash.

"Where is he?" exclaimed Luo Yinan. "Is he still alive?"

Mo Zhengqi grinned bitterly and said: "Do you remember everything?"

"Oh, yes," Luo Yinan said, "it all comes to mind. What's happened to him?"

"I don't know," Mo Zhengqi said. "Maybe he's still alive, maybe he's dead."

"You didn't go to rescue him?" Luo Yinan asked.

"I saved you," Mo Zhengqi said. "My wound got infected because of that. I'm damn lucky to be alive – in fact, I'm in the ward next to yours."

Luo Yinan was shocked and said: "You saved me? From the moat?"

Mo Zhengqi nodded and told him that the more he thought about it, the more panicky he became after Luo Yinan and Zhang Wenxiu left that night. Guo Xiangmei and Wu Baosheng had already died trying to save Liang Kesi. If his cousin died out there, how could he live with himself? So he decided to go to the rescue alone. If his cousin was dead, he would let the enemy kill him too. He made his way quietly out to the front line, across the grassy fields and through the battered and tumbled-down houses, right to the edge of the moat. Suddenly, he noticed that Luo Yinan was climbing over the moat with the help of a scaling ladder. He was surprised but was just about to go and join him when the enemy started firing. He heard Huang Jiezi scream, and then the sound of the ladder falling into the water. He knew the moat was very deep and there were many bodies floating in it. If Luo Yinan had fallen because he had been hit by a bullet, it would be virtually impossible for him to climb out. So he jumped in himself. He dragged Luo Yinan a long way round the moat, until they were nearly at Tongxiang Gate, and then used the pile of corpses as a kind of ramp. A couple of people living in a house near Tongxiang Gate helped him. Together, they managed to get Luo Yinan carried over to the field hospital. He had been shot multiple times and remained unconscious throughout. The doctors really thought he was going to die. As for himself, all this violent effort didn't do his old wounds any good at all; in fact, the sewage in the moat infected them so badly that he almost died. It was more than a week before either of them had been considered out of danger.

Luo Yinan was appalled by what he now heard. A week. He had almost died. He had been unconscious for a whole week. But had anyone gone to rescue Liang Kesi during this time? How had that week gone for him, lying wounded in the gateway? If Zhang Wenxiu hadn't reached him, he would have had nothing to eat or drink. How could he survive? And what about Huang Jiezi? And where was Zhang Wenxiu who climbed the moat ahead of him? Luo Yinan had so many questions, but he did not dare to ask them. He was feeling very tense, too nervous to speak.

As if he could see what he was thinking, Mo Zhengqi said sadly: "Huang Jiezi is dead. He was holding up the scaling ladder with his head exposed and the bullet went smack into his temple. I didn't know to begin with that Zhang Wenxiu had gone with you. The day before yesterday, my deputy company commander came to see me and said that a nurse tried to run across the stone bridge over by Bao'an Gate and she was shot dead. Then I heard that Zhang Wenxiu, a nurse at the field hospital, had been missing for several days, and no one seemed to know where she had gone. I put two and two together – it must have been her."

At that moment, Luo Yinan felt as if his heart had been pierced by a thousand arrows. Of course it's her! So does that mean she's dead? Are Huang Jiezi and Zhang Wenxiu both dead? Why am I still alive? If only I could have died myself!

Mo Zhengqi laughed bitterly, stood up and walked over to the door. Then he turned back and said: "I know what you're thinking. You're thinking, why isn't it me who died? You're thinking exactly the same as me. However, there are some things that aren't up to you – it is fate, that's all. This is your fate."

After that, he left. As he disappeared from view, Luo Yinan watched him. From then on, there was one name that neither of them would ever dare to speak, and that name was Liang Kesi. Luo Yinan said to himself: Liang Kesi, are you still alive? If so... was this really meant to be your fate?

The attack on Wuchang had now completely stopped, and the focus of the Northern Expedition moved to Jiangxi. The Fourth Army that remained behind had orders to keep Wuchang under siege but not to fight. Occasionally, an aeroplane flew over to scatter leaflets.

One day, two colleagues from the Department of Political Affairs came to the hospital to see Luo Yinan and told him that the department had moved over to Hankou. The vice director, Guo Moruo, was presiding over the work there, while Director Deng had stayed behind in Wuchang. Fighting had already stopped in Wuchang, but both sides remained on high alert. The scheme to dig tunnels in order to lay bombs to blow up the city wall had utterly failed. First they dug too deep, and the tunnel filled up with water from the moat; then they dug too shallow, and the tunnel collapsed before they had even got halfway. Headquarters finally decided to give up on that idea for the time being and concentrate on the siege, so that the people in the city would have nothing to eat or drink, and they would have to surrender. Even if they didn't surrender, there would be an uprising inside the city. The Department of Political Affairs was very busy producing lots of leaflets which were dropped over Wuchang by aeroplanes; these were intended to destroy the enemy's fighting spirit and encourage progressive elements in the city to take action. General Li Zongren had gone to Jiangxi, so Chen Keyu was now in charge of the siege. General Chen had already asked for Krupp guns to be moved into position, in preparation for another attack on the city walls on 19 September. His plan was to begin by knocking down the wall and then order an assault all along the line, but later on he gave up this idea. First, he was afraid of killing too many people. He had been listening to what the foreigner, Mr Meng, had to say. Secondly, he was informed that the enemy had run out of food and was now prepared to negotiate.

As his colleagues explained what had been happening, Luo Yinan looked remote and calm. He let them talk. He was not interested in listening to them discuss the situation on the front line when he could only think of one thing: What about Liang Kesi? Is he still alive? How had he managed to survive? He could say nothing of this to his two colleagues. As their chattering voices swept over him, his mind was in a state of turmoil.

Luo Yinan's uncle and cousin also came to see him in the hospital. His cousin exclaimed: "How did you become a member of the Northern Expeditionary Army? And you've been injured! I simply can't believe it. I always thought you were going to become a monk."

Luo Yinan smiled: "I can't believe it either."

His cousin carried on: "Are you a hero now?"

Luo Yinan was surprised: "Am I a hero? No, no, no, I haven't achieved anything, on the contrary... on the contrary..." He could not carry on because Huang Jiezi and Zhang Wenxiu's faces had appeared before his mind's eye.

He felt that he had murdered two people.

His uncle said: "You've been very badly injured, so you have to take good care of yourself. Mr Bai, the one who let you use his telephone, has been a friend for years with an old monk at the Guiyuan Temple in Hanyang. I asked him to find a room for you there. It's nice and quiet. You've always been interested in Buddhism. It's just right for you to rest and recover. Your father wrote to say that the family had heard that there was fighting going on over here, so I should take good care of you. Your aunt says that it wouldn't be right for you to carry on being a soldier. When everything settles down, you'd better go back to college."

His uncle had a lot to say, and Luo Yinan listened but did not answer. He hadn't thought about whether he would ever go back to his studies. But his heart did beat faster at the idea of going to recuperate at the Guiyuan Temple. He really didn't want to be a soldier anymore. The bloody scenes of battle had shocked him profoundly. Moreover, he was now a murderer who had brought about the deaths of two Northern Expeditionary Army soldiers. He could hardly face his comrades. Chen Dingyi had been beheaded, and now he had no idea whether Liang Kesi was alive or dead – his mind had gone completely blank again. It would be good to go to the Guiyuan Temple to rest, to let himself recover and meditate on all that had happened. After all, that's a place he would like to go.

Although he was far from fully recovered, Mo Zhengqi was ready to return to his company and came to say goodbye to Luo Yinan. "Will the city be attacked again?" he asked.

"If we don't take Wuchang by other means," Mo Zhengqi said, "sooner or later it will have to be attacked."

"Can't we go around it?" Luo Yinan asked.

Mo Zhengqi looked at him with a strange expression on his face, as if to say, how could you say something so stupid?

This time, neither of them talked about Liang Kesi or how to rescue him. It was a painful subject that neither of them was prepared to raise.

There was no food at all in Wuchang now. Rumours were rife that there were more and more suicides because of starvation every day, and many people were dying of disease. The people of Hanyang and Hankou were getting increasingly upset about this. Although the two branches of the Yangtze River divide Wuhan into three parts, the people in each part of the city are connected by blood. Many families in Hanyang and Hankou had relatives over in Wuchang. Nobody knew anything about what was happening to the people trapped inside Wuchang, and the rich people who had escaped from Wuchang right at the beginning were especially nervous because most of them still had family left behind. They ran around begging for help from anyone they could think of. They were hoping that people might be allowed to leave Wuchang and that the Northern Expeditionary Army would not simply shoot them. The Chamber of Commerce and various charities in Hankou had also swung into action, and they were preparing to set aside money if that would bring the fighting to an end.

Negotiations were underway.

The Hankou Chamber of Commerce offered to pay 200,000 yuan towards the demobilisation of the Beiyang Army, but Liu Yuchun refused. He then put forward as a condition of opening the gates that his army should be allowed to retreat with its weapons. If he was to go north to Henan, he had to preserve his forces. This was rejected by the Northern Expeditionary Army. They said: "Lay down your weapons, open the city gates and surrender, and we guarantee preferential treatment for your prisoners – other than that, there is nothing to talk about." There were several rounds of negotiation, without the slightest progress.

Wuchang was still under tight siege, but, somehow or other, news about deaths inside the city managed to leap across the Han River and the Yangtze and make its way to Hankou and Hanyang. The people there, with relatives in Wuchang, were going crazy. Every day, people were crossing the river by boat and standing outside Hanyang Gate, Pinghu Gate and Wenchang Gate in the hope that somehow someone might open them.

The gates stayed closed.

Luo Yinan left hospital on the day of the Mid-Autumn Festival. His uncle escorted him to the Guiyuan Temple, where he was going to be staying. On the first day, he was very calm and felt that the quiet atmosphere was just right for his recuperation. But that night, he dreamed of Liang Kesi. He came walking towards him on a pair of crutches, without saying a word. He just looked at him, and there seemed to be a smile on his face. Luo Yinan woke up in a sudden panic. He had never had such a dream before, but now Liang Kesi had caught up with him in his sleep. Luo Yinan did not know what the dream meant, but it made his skin crawl.

Early the next morning, Luo Yinan made his way to Baishazhou and from there sailed across the river by boat.

He went straight to Binyang Gate, but there was no one there that he knew. Standing behind the wall surrounding Changchun Monastery, he looked over towards the watchtower. The soldiers there were idly basking in the sun. The gunfire had stopped. The two sides were no longer heavily barricaded, and it seemed they weren't even interested in shooting at each other anymore. But how had Liang Kesi spent so many days and nights all by himself over in the barbican? Could he still even be alive?

Luo Yinan made enquiries of people about Mo Zhengqi. A soldier told him that Company Commander Mo was over by Tongxiang Gate.

"Are you getting ready to fight again?" Luo Yinan asked.

"Maybe," the soldier said. "Regimental Commander Ye has ordered a lot of people to go over there."

Luo Yinan now headed in the direction of Tongxiang Gate. Because he was still so weak, he had to pause and rest every so often. By the time he reached the gate, the sun was setting.

Tongxiang Gate was the closest city gate in Wuchang to the railroad. The trains weren't running because of the fighting. However, several carriages were sitting on the rails, and a dozen soldiers were swarming around on top of them. Luo Yinan did not see why. Are they planning to use these carriages as battering rams against the gate? he wondered.

Luo Yinan asked everyone he met where Mo Zhengqi was. At this time, there was much disorder in the ranks and too many new recruits, so many people did not know each other. It took him a long time to find him in a house, where he was drawing sketch-maps under a paraffin lamp, with several other people in attendance. Luo Yinan recognised Ye Ting, the regimental commander. He did not dare force his way in, so he sat on a broken stone block outside the door and waited. It was another night full of stars. It was only one day after the Mid-Autumn Festival, and the moon was still bright. There was a gusty wind blowing that night, and floating clouds moved fitfully across the sky. Although the moon did not move, it seemed to be tossed among the billows.

After a very long time, Mo Zhengqi and his team came out. He spotted Luo Yinan sitting on the stone block, spoke a few words to Ye Ting and then walked over.

"What are you doing here?" Mo Zhengqi asked. "Have you recovered?"

"I'm OK," Luo Yinan said. "What about you? Didn't you nearly die too?"

"Oh, I'm tough enough," Mo Zhengqi said, "and I've been a soldier for a while. As long as I can walk and I'm not bleeding, I can return to the battlefield. Are you looking for me?"

"Yes," Luo Yinan said.

"What's the matter?" Mo Zhengqi asked.

Luo Yinan opened his mouth and could not say a word. He did not dare to speak Liang Kesi's name.

Mo Zhengqi was silent for a moment and then said suddenly: "Go back, go back to rest, there's nothing you can do."

"You are not going to save him?" Luo Yinan asked.

"I am afraid it is too late for that," Mo Zhengqi said.

"You can't be sure," Luo Yinan pointed out. "He said that he would hold on."

"How many days ago was that?" Mo Zhengqi asked. "How can he have held on this long? What about water? What about food? And remember that he was injured. Zhao Huzi told me that when Guo Xiangmei took him out, she said that if the remaining casualties were not treated immediately, they would die. How many days has Xiangmei been dead now? Two weeks! Give me a break, brother."

Luo Yinan was feeling disappointed. He thought: You have no

proof that Liang Kesi is dead, so how can you give up on him like this?

Mo Zhengqi seemed to understand what he was thinking: "You can blame me – fine, I blame myself. But think about it – how many of our comrades have died trying to rescue him? Let me tell you that pretty much every single soldier in the Independent Regiment has been killed trying to take Wuchang!"

Luo Yinan looked at him in shock.

"Do you know?" Mo Zhengqi said, "on the first day after I came back from hospital, I still thought that I would get him out no matter what. But that day, an old woman came looking for her son – she said that people from the same village wrote to her, saying that they had already got as far as Wuchang. She'd come just to see her son. Regimental Commander Ye had someone take her over to me. Her son, the one who went over to the barbican with Guo Xiangmei, was called Erqiangzi. He died out there. His corpse is still lying over there, and no one even knows where he fell. I had no idea how to face his mother. I didn't close my eyes that night. I'm the company commander, and it's natural to care about the people under my command. My cousin is in a very dangerous location, and every time we try to rescue him my men are risking their lives. I really can't let anyone else die. Kesi's life matters, but so do the lives of my soldiers. You have to understand that."

Luo Yinan was silent. He thought he was right, but his heart was still filled with disappointment. He did not know why; nor what he was disappointed with. He was just disappointed.

That night, Mo Zhengqi arranged for Luo Yinan to stay with him in a house near Tongxiang Gate. Now that the fighting had subsided slightly, people were returning to their homes. It was a family of three who lived here: their landlady and her two sons. The man of the house was not at home. He was a tailor. Their landlady explained that on the day the city gates were closed, her husband was helping some of his relatives make cotton-padded clothes, so he ended up being trapped inside the city. Now there was no food there and piles of corpses everywhere. She had no idea whether her husband was alive or dead. Luo Yinan listened to her story and did not interrupt; he just listened quietly. He thought:

How many people are in the same boat, not knowing whether their family and friends are alive or dead?

The next morning, when Luo Yinan woke up, he felt drowsy and confused. Mo Zhengqi had already gone out. The landlady told Luo Yinan that he seemed to be running a temperature and ought to go back to bed. He shook his head. He thought: I ought to go back.

Once he got outside, the sunshine was delightful. Wuchang was always lovely in the autumn. He remembered that when he was in school, they liked autumn outings best and went regularly to Changchun Monastery and Baotong Temple because they were nearby. Sometimes they would walk around the city walls and recite poems aloud as they went. It was on such a day that he listened to Liang Kesi reciting 'The Goddess'. Now, all of these places were battlefields.

Luo Yinan went out. The distant Tongxiang Gate was closed, and everything was quiet. It seemed inconceivable that any fighting was going on. There were neither pedestrians nor traffic passing by. The whole place seemed frozen. On the railroad tracks leading to the front line, the carriages had been encased in sheets of iron, like tanks, with sandbags piled up inside them. Some soldiers were slowly pushing the carriage forward, and it was Mo Zhengqi who was directing operations. Luo Yinan was amazed: Were they really going to use this carriage to smash through the city gate?

He stopped and stood to one side, watching them. Having been pushed to a particular place, the carriage came to a halt. A couple of soldiers jumped into the carriage and kept a close eye on Tongxiang Gate through the small holes left on the walls of the carriage. Others grabbed picks and shovels and began digging under cover of the iron-clad carriage. A deep hole had already appeared in the ground.

Luo Yinan went over to Mo Zhengqi to say goodbye. "What are you doing?" he asked.

Mo Zhengqi did not take his eyes off the soldiers and said: "Digging a tunnel."

"Again?" Luo Yinan exclaimed. "Are you going to try and blow up the wall here?"

"No," Mo Zhengqi said, "we're going to be digging into the city."

"It seems incredible," said Luo Yinan.

"The owner of the house over the other side," Mo Zhengqi explained, "is one of ours. We are going to tunnel into his house and then send elite troops in from there to attack the city."

Luo Yinan mumbled something incomprehensible and then said again: "It seems incredible."

"Don't you think incredible things are happening every day?" Mo Zhengqi asked.

Luo Yinan pondered this and could not help agreeing: "Yes, there are too many incredible things going on." Then he told Mo Zhengqi that he was leaving.

His toneless voice finally attracted Mo Zhengqi's attention. He turned to look at him and saw that his face was all red and his eyes were glassy. "Are you getting sick?" Mo Zhengqi wondered.

Luo Yinan grinned harshly: "I don't think I've ever been well."

"You can't just go like this," Mo Zhengqi said decisively. "I'll take you back home to lie down. It doesn't matter if you stay here for a few days. The landlady can take care of you."

"Never mind," Luo Yinan said, "I can still walk."

Mo Zhengqi ignored him, and he shouted in the direction of the iron-clad carriage: "Hey, Xiaozhuzi, come over here! Take Comrade Luo here back to my house, and tell the landlady to take care of him." A young soldier came running over.

Luo Yinan was unable to refuse and had to let Mo Zhengqi arrange everything. Back in the house, the landlady boiled him some porridge, made him soup and summoned a doctor to see him. Luo Yinan lay in bed, not wanting anything, at the mercy of others. He was in a trance-like state and felt as if his soul were already flying past countless floating faces. Liang Kesi, Guo Xiangmei, Zhang Wenxiu and Huang Jiezi were all there. They smiled at him and waved hello. Sometimes they came close, sometimes they were far away, but none of them spoke to him. He thought to himself: At last, I've come to join you.

16

THE TUNNEL PLAN didn't work.

That evening, the enemy troops up in the watchtower over Tongxiang Gate suddenly spotted a pile of soil next to an empty train carriage. They thought about where this heaped-up earth could possibly have come from and came to the conclusion that the Northern Expeditionary Army was digging tunnels into the city. This was very unwelcome news, and they were panic-stricken: they did not know how far the tunnels had been dug or how long they had been at work before they noticed; nor did they know where the exit was going to come out. In fact, given the fighting power of the Northern Expeditionary Army, even if only a handful of people made their way through the tunnel and opened Tongxiang Gate, Wuchang would fall. The soldiers inside the city had little stomach for a fight. Even if they filled the streets with barricades and fought from house to house, hungry soldiers could not possibly defeat well-fed ones. Actually, they could not have defeated them even if they had been properly provisioned and equipped. That night, the lights in Liu Yuchun's headquarters in Wuchang stayed on all night. He decided to create a suicide squad of three thousand men and make a surprise attack out of the city. The soldiers were divided into two groups. The first group had instructions to gain control of the armoured train carriages and then provide covering fire for the second group as they broke through the enemy lines. This second group was tasked with stealing as much food as they could from the storehouses beyond the walls. Even in the worst-case scenario where they failed to break through the lines and steal any food, at the very least they would put a stop to the Northern Expeditionary Army's plan to tunnel into the city.

After orders had been issued, though it was very late at night, the canteens inside the city started to put pots on the stove so that the troops could eat their fill. The cooks said sadly: "Today you are going out to fight, so even if you die in battle, at least you'll die with full stomachs."

The soldiers all said: "Yes! That's right!"

At four o'clock in the morning, Mo Zhengqi heard a cry of alarm from Luo Yinan. He got up as quickly as he could and went over to his bed. Luo Yinan was still running a high temperature. The doctors could not find any reason for this: they suggested it was because he had been so seriously injured and then been placed under great mental strain – if he stayed quiet for a few days, perhaps that might be able to alleviate it. Mo Zhengqi knew that he had been badly traumatised by the death of Liang Kesi. It would be true to say that Mo Zhengqi himself had also been traumatised by this. Every night he told his cousin: "I am so sorry, Kesi, I am sorry." But saying this didn't make him feel any better.

Mo Zhengqi went out for a pee after checking that Luo Yinan was all right. Afterwards, he walked over to the sentry post and asked about the situation. Suddenly, he noticed signs of movement over by Tongxiang Gate. He went right up to the front-line position and looked over at the city gate. At first sight, there was nothing much going on, then he realised that the gate was opening. Mo Zhengqi rubbed his eyes and asked the soldier on guard: "Look, what are that lot over there doing?"

"What!" the soldier cried. "They're opening the gate! Do you suppose they want to come out for a breather?"

"You keep an eye on things here," Mo Zhengqi said. "I'm going to wake everyone up."

He had just turned around when the guard suddenly screeched: "Company Commander Mo, look!"

Mo Zhengqi looked back and was almost struck dumb with amazement. A long line of troops was exiting the open Tongxiang

CHAPTER 16 | 171

Gate in an endless stream. Almost at the same time, another line of troops emerged from the small gate under the Chuwang Tower. Mo Zhengqi shouted: "No! The enemy is going to break through our lines!" Then he grabbed the sentry's gun and fired a shot into the sky.

A fierce battle began with that gunshot.

Thousands of soldiers from the Beiyang Army were pouring out from Wuchang, shouting despairingly. The Northern Expeditionary Army, stationed outside the city walls, was well aware that the troops inside the city did not have enough to eat and they just wanted to go home. For many days now, they had felt there was no reason to take them seriously. From their positions outside the city walls, they had been laughing at the defenders as they ate their meals, asking themselves how many more days they could hold on for. They had decided that they were all going to be for the chop; they were just waiting for them to lower their flags and surrender, and then they would simply march into the city unopposed. They had forgotten the old saying about cornered rats.

As soon as the enemy troops were out of the city, they divided themselves into two teams. Mo Zhengqi immediately worked out that one team would definitely be going to grab food, so he gave instructions to the soldiers in the iron-clad carriage that they should hold out for as long as they could, but if they could not defend their position they should withdraw. He rushed to the storehouses with as many men as he could commandeer. As he ran, he sent a soldier to report these developments to Regimental Commander Ye Ting, with a request for reinforcements. They had to protect their food stores; otherwise, the enemy would rob them, and, once they were resupplied, the siege they had imposed on the city for so many days would be rendered pointless.

There were only a few dozen troops from the Northern Expeditionary Army guarding the iron-clad carriage, and they now came under attack by more than a thousand enemy soldiers. Having held out for twenty minutes, they realised they would have no choice but to retreat. The enemy occupied the carriage and immediately became more cheerful: all their efforts could now be focused on the granaries. Mo Zhengqi was now completely reckless in the risks he ran. He kept screaming: "Think of all your brothers-in-arms who died on the walls! Kill them!"

The corpses lying unburied everywhere under the walls were a source of great pain for the soldiers of the Northern Expeditionary Army. For so many days, the smell of decay had been floating around Wuchang in a thick miasma, like countless souls in torment. With this in mind, the pain and anger that had been suppressed for so long could now be expressed in bullets. There were not many soldiers in the storehouses, but each of them now fought like a demon. Even when they were surrounded and outnumbered by the soldiers who had come out from the city, they carried on fighting. Their commanders had miscalculated, but they couldn't understand why.

This was the battle Mo Zhengqi had been looking forward to fighting. He wanted to bathe in blood as he fought to the death. He had lost too much already, too much to bear, outside the walls of Wuchang. He thought: If I die in battle, so be it – I will have requited my comrades and my family with my own blood.

It was getting light. Ye Ting had already heard the news and personally took command of his machine gun company as they rushed to reinforce him. Other regiments stationed around Wuchang also sent troops to help. When the enemy saw that they no longer had the upper hand and their positions were about to be overwhelmed, they had to give up their idea of stealing food and flee back to the city.

When he met with Ye Ting, Mo Zhengqi was coated in blood from head to foot. "Have you been injured?" Ye Ting asked.

"No," Mo Zhengqi replied, "it's blood from my comrades."

"You did great!" Ye Ting shouted. "Well done!"

"Regimental commander," Mo Zhengqi said, "they've opened one of the main gates. How about we take advantage of the situation to attack the city?"

Ye Ting did not speak; he just waved his hand.

Mo Zhengqi immediately grasped his intention: just like at the battle for Tingsi Bridge, he was to lead his men to chase after the retreating enemy.

The Beiyang soldiers guarding Tongxiang Gate saw that the Northern Expeditionary Army was launching a fierce counter-attack and realised that their vanguard was already engaged with the last of the retreating troops. Immediately, a loud cry went up to shut the gate. There were still more than six hundred Beiyang soldiers outside the walls who had not been able to make it back to the city. There was a huge force coming up behind them, their retreat had been cut, so they were now desperate: they had no idea what to do.

Mo Zhengqi rushed to the front and shouted: "Put down your guns! If you surrender, you will not be killed; anyone who fights back will be shot!" Behind him, a group of other soldiers roared the same message, and the six hundred men who had been caught outside the walls were terror-struck. Mo Zhengqi looked along the city wall towards Binyang Gate. He wondered: Can we attack Binyang Gate from here?

In this fight, the Beiyang Army had employed their very strongest forces in a sudden attack, and yet they were still defeated by the Northern Expeditionary Army. The defenders standing on top of the walls were really frightened when they watched what was happening to their own people: either they surrendered or they were shot. Although Wuchang, with its high and thick walls, was easy to defend, although they had caused five times more deaths and injuries to the Northern Expeditionary Army, they were unable to leave the city. Once outside these massive defensive walls, they were no match for their opponents. Once they actually crossed swords, it was immediately apparent who would win and who would lose.

The city was under siege, it was in terrible danger, and they had no wish to fight; indeed, they had entirely run out of food, and they knew the situation was hopeless. What was worse, the city was full of starving people – even if they still had the energy to walk, they could no longer speak. The streets were empty and cold, day and night. The shops were closed. If an open door was to be seen, it was not because they were open for business but because they had been robbed. At the foot of Snake Mountain, just inside the city wall, there were many new graves. Later on, so many had died that there was nowhere to bury them: those bodies were lying exposed. Even at street corners and by the sides of the roads, more and more corpses were to be seen. Someone would be walking along the road and then just fall down dead. This was an even more horrifying sight than the scenes outside the city walls. Even the most hard-hearted of soldiers could no longer bear such a dreadful situation. None of the defenders could relax. If they fought, they would die in a bloodbath; if they did not fight, they would die of starvation, or they would die because they were driven mad by the appalling sights they could not avoid seeing. Deaths happened all the time now. Everyone could see the end coming closer and closer. Despair, like a plague, spread through the barracks.

The Northern Expeditionary Army besieging the city was in a much better state. It was now obvious that the enemy could not hold out much longer. There was nothing for them to worry about; they didn't fire their guns or blast the place with artillery shells – they just waited. They were waiting for the enemy to collapse, waiting for the city gates to open of their own accord, and then they would go into action.

But the people in the city could no longer wait. All of the food in the shops had been expropriated by the military, and everything had been eaten up. Weeds by the lake, mice in people's houses, and feral dogs out in the hills had all been used by hungry people to fill their stomachs. Push open a door, and you might perhaps see a whole family that had starved to death, and stories of finding everyone in a particular building had hanged themselves were also passed from mouth to mouth. Every day, the death toll rose higher. If they waited much longer, more than half of the civilian population would have died.

The Chamber of Commerce that covered Wuchang, Hankou and Hanyang, not to mention various charitable organisations, finally decided that they had had enough, and they joined forces to negotiate with the armies on both sides: "Since you can't agree, at the very least you have to allow people to leave the city to get food. The garrison defending the city should regularly open the gates and allow people out; meanwhile, the troops outside the city should agree not to take advantage of this to attack."

The commanders-in-chief of both armies agreed. A notice was posted inside and outside the city: Beginning on 3 October, from 8.00am to 3.00pm, Wenchang Gate facing the Yangtze River would be opened to allow the old, the sick, women and children to leave the city to find food. After a month's desperate siege, Wuchang was finally opening a tiny crack to the outside world again.

Luo Yinan's temperature had also gone down. That day, his landlady cooked him a bowl of noodles. The last time he'd eaten noodles was on a street by the banks of the Miluo River, with a lively and energetic Liang Kesi sitting opposite. Where was Liang Kesi now? Nearly a month had gone by since the attack on the walls, and Luo Yinan knew that Liang Kesi must be dead, but he did not dare to think about it. The noodles were hard for him to swallow.

The landlady was surprised and asked: "You don't like it?"

"It's not that," Luo Yinan said. Then he began to sob. The landlady was puzzled, but she did not dare ask any more questions.

Luo Yinan decided to return to the Guiyuan Temple. Mo Zhengqi also felt that his physical and mental wounds were so serious that it would take a long time for him to recover from them. He too recommended that he go somewhere quiet to recuperate. Mo Zhengqi sent Xiaozhuzi to escort him back to Hanyang. "The situation out there is still very dangerous," he said, "and you are not at all well – you'd better not go out alone." He ordered Xiaozhuzi not to come back until he'd seen him safely ensconced in his room at the temple. Luo Yinan could not summon the energy to refuse, so he just did as he was told.

Mo Zhengqi found a carriage to take Luo Yinan to the banks of the Yangtze River. It was packed with people coming out of the city, like refugees. They were all pale, with bones jutting out from beneath their skin, and they moved slowly, so weak that it seemed as if they could be blown over by a gust of river wind. Nevertheless, they hurried as much as they could.

A huge barge from Hankou was anchored by the bank, all hung with white flags. Some people wearing white cloth armbands bearing a red cross were moving back and forth. They were setting up porridge stations along the shore. There were also some people from the Chamber of Commerce dressed in western suits and ties. From time to time they were cautioning everyone: "Slow down! Don't eat too much! In your state, you must be careful not to overeat!"

Luo Yinan got out of the carriage and looked at the crowd. He sighed deeply and said: "What kind of world is this?"

"This is our fate," Mo Zhengqi said. "These are the cards we have been dealt. So if we want to change our destiny, we have to change the world first."

Luo Yinan sighed again and said: "You sound just like Liang Kesi."

At the mention of his name, Mo Zhengqi's face changed dramatically. After a long pause, he said sadly: "You shouldn't hate me – I had no choice."

"I know," Luo Yinan said, "and I don't hate you – I guess this is the fate you were talking about."

"Yes," Mo Zhengqi replied, "such is fate."

"It's just that Liang Kesi had to pay a terrible price," Luo Yinan said.

"Oh, yes," Mo Zhengqi answered. "All of our comrades-in-arms who are lying out there under the city walls had to pay a terrible price. But none of us had a choice – we had to do this." When he said this, his face was filled with sadness.

For a long, long time afterwards, Luo Yinan remembered the sadness on Mo Zhengqi's face. This sadness pierced him to the heart, to the very marrow of his bones. Day after day, night after night, he found it coming back to haunt him, so he failed to recover. The old monk at the Guiyuan Temple came to talk to him several times, but he did not have the strength to say more than a few words. The old monk sighed and said: "You have to find a way to put it all behind you!"

But he thought: How can I?

That evening, it was getting dark, and Luo Yinan was about to light a lamp. Suddenly, Mo Zhengqi came in through the door. Luo Yinan wondered if he was seeing things. "It's me," Mo Zhengqi said. "I've come here specially to see you."

"What's up?" Luo Yinan asked.

"We're going to take Wuchang tonight," Mo Zhengqi told him.

Luo Yinan was shaken to the core.

"We've got someone on the inside," Mo Zhengqi explained. "He made contact when he came out of the city with all the other people to get something to eat. It's already arranged with headquarters – he's going to open the city gate for us at ten o'clock tonight."

"Which gate is he going to open?" Luo Yinan asked eagerly.

Mo Zhengqi spat out the name, one word at a time: "Bin... yang... Gate."

Luo Yinan, who had been limp and listless all this time, seemed to have received an instant injection of strength; it was as if he had just been waiting for this day, and he leapt to his feet with a cry.

"My mission will be to take my men straight to enemy headquarters," Mo Zhengqi explained. "There will be resistance in the city, we won't have much time, and I simply cannot go and deal with the people in the barbican. I'd like you to help me find Kesi after the gate has been opened and the fighting around there has subsided. It's been so long – I am sure that he is no longer alive. But you must find his body and bury him properly for me."

"Of course! Of course!" Luo Yinan made haste to say. "Naturally I'll do it. I will definitely find him. Who knows? Maybe he's still alive."

Mo Zhengqi smiled bitterly: "There is not much hope of that. If it really is so, then all I can say is that it will have been a miracle – but I don't hold out much hope. Anyway, I want you to help me take care of him."

"Of course!" Luo Yinan said. "We'll wait for you. We'll go and see him together."

Mo Zhengqi smiled gently: "There are going to be thousands of people fighting all across the city, so I have no idea what will happen. I don't know if I will survive this mission. So that's why I am begging you now – if he's dead, bury him at the foot of Snake Mountain. I'll ask the landlady's son to help you. And another thing, don't tell his parents that he died so miserably."

"I understand," Luo Yinan said. "But I think we still ought to wait for you. You have to remember that we'll be waiting for you."

Mo Zhengqi hesitated for a moment and then said: "OK. You've got to come back across the river with me now. Wuchang will fall tonight."

Luo Yinan was busy changing his clothes and putting on his shoes; all his health problems seemed to have vanished. They hurried to the river bank, and by then it was already dark. There was a ferry pulled up by the bank, and when the ferryman saw Mo Zhengqi in his uniform he seemed thrilled. "Comrade!" he shouted. "Hurry onboard! This is the last boat!" Mo Zhengqi hurled himself into the little boat, followed by Luo Yinan, who leapt aboard in spite of the many days he had just been lying in bed.

"It seems the temple has been looking after you well," Mo Zhengqi said.

"It's not that," Luo Yinan replied. "I have to get better for Liang Kesi."

It was the evening of 9 October 1926. Binyang Gate, just like every other night they had been there, was lit up with lamps that could illuminate a hundred metres. Soldiers with guns were still on guard in the watchtower, and even the stench of putrefaction on both sides of the moat was as strong as it had ever been.

Just before ten o'clock, the landlady's son arrived, bringing a stretcher. He was a young man of about sixteen or seventeen years old, and he looked a little like Huang Jiezi. Luo Yinan's heart immediately started hammering.

"Don't worry," said Mo Zhengqi. "When our men have control of the gate, I will use my torch to signal to you. I will draw three circles, and you'll know it's safe to come forward. Don't go into the city. It's going to be chaos in there, and there will be fighting. Your job is to find my cousin in the barbican and then carry him to Changchun Monastery and wait for daybreak. Once the whole city of Wuchang is secure, someone will come and help you bury him."

"I understand," Luo Yinan said. "But you must come back. We'll wait."

Mo Zhengqi smiled. He turned his head and looked at the dark shadow of Snake Mountain. "I know," he said. "The foot of Snake Mountain would be a good place."

Having said that, Mo Zhengqi set off with his men to assume his position on the front line. At ten o'clock sharp, someone up in the watchtower gave the signal. Mo Zhengqi whispered: "Advance!"

From his position flat on his stomach behind a small rise, Luo Yinan watched them cross the stone bridge over the moat without a hitch. Sure enough, the city gate opened, and the Northern Expeditionary Army slipped in. Immediately, the sound of gunfire could be heard within the city; shouts and screams also rose up into the quiet night sky over Wuchang. Half an hour or maybe an hour later, there was a torch drawing a circle up in the watchtower. Three circles. Luo Yinan knew that Binyang Gate was now under their control.

He and the landlady's son picked up the stretcher and headed for Binyang Gate. All along the way, there were corpses, and the landlady's son occasionally cried out in horror. Luo Yinan, compared to him, seemed to have already gone through many vicissitudes, and the sight left him unmoved. The gunfire in the city was louder and coming not in bursts but in full and constant flow. The sound of shrieking rose and fell like waves, rising from the bottom of the mountain to the top, and then pouring back down again.

They arrived at Binyang Gate without encountering any problems. Luo Yinan was feeling deeply nervous as he asked the landlady's son to put down the stretcher and lighten his torch so they could see a little better.

With the torch lit, the entire scene inside the barbican was instantly revealed. Six or seven people were in there; some lying on their backs, some on their sides, and some slumped across the ground. There was only one person sitting up against the wall. His hands were crossed in a very natural position, lying relaxed on top of his legs. But his head was hanging down onto his chest.

At a glance, Luo Yinan recognised him: the man sitting there was Liang Kesi! He looked just the same as he remembered him. He exclaimed in surprise: "Liang Wenqi!" This was his name back at college, and the name he was used to calling him by.

The landlady's son squatted down and asked: "Is that him? He's dead."

"How can that be?" Luo Yinan asked, and he squatted down too.

The landlady's son covered his nose and said: "He stinks."

He was quite right; now Luo Yinan could smell the stench of a decomposing corpse too. He did not cover his nose; in fact, he didn't even really mind the smell but sat down next to him. He thought: He's really dead! As he realised what that meant, he couldn't help bursting into tears. Although he had expected that this would be the case, when he saw his body, he was devastated.

Luo Yinan did not know how long he sat in the gateway for. He looked up and saw the stars out in limitless space. When he was here, did Liang Kesi look up at the stars at night? Looking at the night sky like this, what did he think? The landlady's son also looked up at the sky and kept silent. He just squatted quietly beside him, waiting.

The city gate was open, and now a few people began to flee. At first, the Northern Expeditionary Army troops left on guard there tried to stop them, but soon there were too many people to stop, so they let them go. The people coming out were all shocked at the sight of the bodies lying everywhere under the walls. Some people screamed, others started to cry, but the cacophony gradually lessened as they moved further away.

The landlady's son said: "It's almost dawn."

Then Luo Yinan said: "Let's go."

They carried Liang Kesi to Changchun Monastery but did not enter the hall. The Taoists had been up early, as if they knew what would happen today, and they were burning incense in all the halls. Smoke curled up and mingled with the slightly foggy air to turn it into a misty morning.

They put the stretcher down by the wall outside the main hall. Luo Yinan stood up and looked towards the city. Suddenly, he felt sure that he had been here before. Then he remembered that more than a month earlier, Ji Defu, the translator, had been shot right here and then died at Director Deng Yanda's feet.

17

THE DAY HAD FINALLY DAWNED. All the gates of Wuchang had been thrown open. It was the Double Tenth Festival.

An endless stream of people was leaving the city of Wuchang where they had been cooped up for so long; as if they needed to breathe freely the air from beyond the walls, or as if they wanted to bask in the sun outside the city. As they came through the gates, they had pained smiles on their faces. In these smiles, there was some measure of happiness, but sadness and tragedy were more strongly marked. However, all the people who came out through Bao'an and Binyang Gates looked thoroughly traumatised: they were appalled by the bodies lying heaped everywhere in the bright autumn sunshine. The stench hung heavily in the air. More and more people came to stand at the entrances to the watchtowers, beating their breasts and stamping their feet. Finally, the two gates had to be placed under armed guard, and the soldiers, armed with guns, announced that nobody was going to be allowed through for the time being.

Just before noon, a number of carriages arrived from Hankou with coffins. Soldiers from the Northern Expeditionary Army who had not entered the city began the work of collecting the dead with the assistance of the Red Cross. Rank weeds grew thickly in among the nooks and crannies of these corpses. As each body was lifted, the shape of a human figure appeared on the ground. They were outlined by the weeds, which had fed on their bodies and grown lush.

More and more weed outlines were revealed, making the ground appear something like a picture puzzle. Quickly, they discovered that they did not have nearly enough coffins. The message was handed on: "We need more coffins from Hankou. There are not enough here, and there are many more dead inside the city."

The shooting inside the city had still not stopped. Liu Yuchun was fighting every step of the way as he retreated to the foot of Snake Mountain with more than a thousand of his men. They kept up a valiant resistance and refused to surrender until the afternoon. But defeat was inevitable, and their valour was in vain. When enough of them had been killed off, they could no longer hold out. In order to avoid being captured alive, Liu Yuchun's staff officer took him to the home of Mr Meng, the foreigner who taught at the Wenhua University. They were old friends, and Mr Meng agreed to hide them in his house. However, his Chinese servants were fiercely resentful at the pointless deaths of tens of thousands of people in Wuchang, so they went to the Northern Expeditionary Army to turn him in. Within half an hour, soldiers had arrived and captured Liu Yuchun alive at the foreigner's house.

News of his arrest, like a whirlwind, swept across the whole city in an instant, and everyone seemed to know about it almost as soon as it had happened. They put Liu Yuchun onto a truck and paraded him through the streets. The people of Wuchang were given every opportunity to vent their anger against him, while the inhabitants of Hanyang and Hankou were ecstatic with joy.

Night fell. The battle was over, and the house-to-house fighting, which they had imagined would be necessary to capture the city, never even began. When they came to take control of the streets, pretty much everyone surrendered the moment they saw the Northern Expeditionary Army. For the first time in forty days, laughter could be heard in Wuchang.

Luo Yinan spent a day sitting in front of Liang Kesi's body, but Mo Zhengqi never came. The landlady's son and two soldiers carried in a coffin and said: "Let him rest in peace here. It will be more comfortable for him to wait for Company Commander Mo in his coffin." Luo Yinan thought that he had a point, so he allowed them to lift Liang Kesi in.

He lay on his back in that small wooden box, his features blurred by bloating, but his expression was the same as ever, and his mouth was curved in a smile that was very familiar to Luo Yinan. The landlady's son suddenly exclaimed: "What's that in his pocket?" Luo Yinan noticed that there was a piece of paper protruding from his jacket pocket. He pulled it out and discovered that it was a letter written on two pieces of paper. Luo Yinan spotted his own name at once and was shocked. He ran over to read his letter under the lamp.

It felt as though Liang Kesi were talking to him:

Luo Yinan, my dear friend,

This is the last letter I will ever write to you. I feel sure that you are still alive. Now I know that it is my destiny to die under the walls of Wuchang. It won't be long now before I am gone. However, I feel I should leave you a few words.

Zhang Wenxiu told me that I should not commit suicide; that it was my duty to hold on until my final breath, so that those who died to save me would feel that their sacrifice had been worthwhile. I think she's right. I am writing this letter to pass on my duty of perseverance. I'm going to write until the day I can write no more.

When I first picked up this pen and paper, I didn't know who to leave my message to. My parents? I couldn't bear to let them see my handwriting again because they must have been devastated when they heard about my death. I can't write to Lan either. I promised her that I would come back to her, and I have failed her terribly. My cousin Mo Zhengqi will have suffered greatly from Xiangmei's death, and he will want to avenge her even at the cost of his own life, so I'm afraid he won't live to read my letter. You are all I have left now, my friend.

I dragged you with me to chase the Northern Expeditionary Army all the way to Wuchang. Every time I think about you coming out to the front so many times to try to save me, I am so amazed and impressed. I know that in your weakness you wanted to avoid all the troubles of this world by becoming a monk. And yet now you are not afraid of the enemy's guns, and you have risked your life to try to rescue me in this dangerous situation – how much that has surprised and moved me. I used to feel guilty that I had not contributed anything to the revolution, and now you have helped me. I have made at least one man who wanted to be a monk become a fighter. From now on, you will have to fight for me; I am afraid that offering you in my place is the best I can do.

I have no fear of my impending death, nor have I ever regretted participating in this battle. We didn't win, and I never even got to shoot the enemy, but I was here, I took part, and I have become one of the countless victims of this war. I have paid for my ideals with my life, so I feel I have nothing to be ashamed of. Others may not understand this, but you will. You know what I wanted to do with my life.

In the future, please take care of Lan for me. Comfort her in times of frustration and pain, and help her when she needs it. After all, I owe her too much, too much that can never be repaid. I can only ask you, my friend, to help me make some recompense. Let her know that even though I am dead, I still love her and remember her.

I also want you to go and thank our teacher, Zhong Shuyu, for telling us the story of Spartacus. I spent several days reciting the story to my companions out here, and that gladiator helped us make the painful transition from this world to the next. When I started telling the story, there were six people in my audience, and when I finished there were only three left. By that time we no longer cared whether we lived or died.

At no time have I felt the slightest fear. I think I must be different from other people.

If you see Chen Mingwu, tell him to go and kowtow at my grave. He did not believe that I would go and join the Northern Expeditionary Army, or fight on the field of battle. He said that if I did, whether I was alive or dead, he would kowtow to me. You tell him that I did it and that I died on the battlefield. He's lost, so he needs to go and kowtow to me. Also, tell him to be good to Hong Peizhu.

How long have I been holding on for? I don't even know what date it is today.

There is no sadness in my heart. I am waiting calmly for death. I will die for what I believe in, so I am without fear.

Zhang Wenxiu suits you much better than Shuya ever did. Tell her I've been sticking to it.

They are firing the guns again.

This time there were fewer shots fired than before.

Even if I die, you must not become a monk.

There is no water.

I am still holding on.

The moon is so bright.

The way that his sentences became shorter and shorter seemed to mirror the way that his breath gradually became shallower, until in the end he died. Luo Yinan was sure that he really had held out until his final breath.

The landlady's son had followed him over and read the letter too. As he read it, he started to cry and said: "He must have written this over the course of many days! How on earth did he survive so long?"

Luo Yinan thought: Yes, he must have written over many days and held on for so long! But when did he in fact die? Can he really have managed to stick it out until the Mid-Autumn Festival? Where was I then? Luo Yinan remembered that he had been discharged from hospital that day and then moved over to the Guiyuan Temple. He had been sitting out in the temple courtyard, looking up at the moon over his head and feeling that the moonlight was shining unusually coldly. At the same time, Liang Kesi had been all by himself and seriously injured out in the gateway, trying to survive just because someone else had told him that he ought to. He felt very guilty at the thought of having imposed such a burden.

Luo Yinan said to the landlady's son: "You wait here for Company Commander Mo. I'll go into the city and look for him there. He's probably very busy right now dealing with his military duties, but I want him to come along tomorrow – we need to put the dead to rest. If he comes back after I leave, you tell him that. Whatever happens, I'll come back as soon as I can."

The landlady's son agreed.

Luo Yinan went out of Changchun Monastery and headed again in the direction of Binyang Gate. When he passed through the barbican, he paused for a moment by the wall where Liang Kesi had been discovered, as if mourning his dead friend in silence. There were soldiers standing on guard there. He asked them if they had seen Mo Zhengqi of the Independent Regiment. The soldiers did not belong to the Independent Regiment, so they said they had no idea who he was.

Wuchang had never seemed so bleak. There were few passers-by in the street except for the soldiers on patrol. The shops were all shut, and few of the streetlights still shone. The alleys stretched out into pitch darkness, and the people living there seemed to have all doused their lamps. Soldiers on patrol came past every so often, and each time Luo Yinan questioned them, but none of them could tell him what had happened to Mo Zhengqi.

Quite unconsciously, Luo Yinan walked in the direction of his college. The whole place was a mess, and in the darkness he could not find any of his classmates – not even in the dormitories. He made his way back to his old room, thinking that he might find a tea urn there and get himself a drink, but he found nothing. Then he went next door to see if his classmate Chen Mingwu was there. If he's not around, Luo Yinan thought, at least I can leave him a note. It turned out that an unexploded artillery shell was sitting right there on the bed. The shell was so huge that it frightened Luo Yinan into a cold sweat.

He decided he ought to go and find Lan at Juxian Hotel. He ought to tell her what had happened to Liang Kesi – after all, if they buried him tomorrow, she would want to be there to pay her last respects. When he came out of the gates, he met someone coming the other way. Both of them decided that the other looked very familiar.

Luo Yinan hesitated: "Are you Guo Wenjun?"

The other hesitated and then said: "Are you Luo Yinan? From Liang Wenqi's class?"

Luo Yinan breathed a sigh of relief and immediately replied: "Yes, that's me."

"What are you doing here?" Guo Wenjun asked. "When the siege was ongoing, I don't remember seeing you on campus." Guo Wenjun was so thin he was positively skeletal and barely had the strength to speak.

Luo Yinan stood there by the gates to the college and briefly described how he had met Liang Kesi and gone with him to catch up with the Northern Expeditionary Army. Of course, he also explained how Liang Kesi had died in battle under the walls of Wuchang.

Guo Wenjun was so shocked his mouth hung open, and for the longest time he could not say a word.

Luo Yinan followed Guo Wenjun back to his dormitory. Guo Wenjun poured a glass of water for Luo Yinan and then described what had happened during the forty-day siege. As he spoke, the tears rolled down his cheeks. "You know," Guo Wenjun said, "I thought it was the end of the world. I thought we were all going to die."

Luo Yinan was stunned by Guo Wenjun's statement. He had thought that what he had experienced were the most tragic and dreadful things that could possibly happen to anyone. He could never have imagined that while he was experiencing these things, events every bit as tragic and dreadful were being played out inside the city. Hong Peizhu committed suicide by jumping into a well. Zhou Jincheng was killed by an artillery shell. Chen Mingwu had simply disappeared. Shuya, who was newly married and pregnant, had been crushed by the crowds as she left the city, and she had lost the baby. And Lan, whom Liang Kesi had loved so much, had been thrown into prison as a member of the Revolutionary Party and gang-raped day after day. Now she had gone insane. Guo Wenjun cried: "Liang Wenqi is lucky to be dead! How could he live with what they did to Lan?"

Luo Yinan had no idea how he managed to get away. The pain he felt was like being hit by an axe, and it shook him to the core. What kind of world is this that such terrible things can happen?

It was nearly midnight when Luo Yinan finally returned to Changchun Monastery. The landlady's son was fast asleep at the foot of the wall, and there was another man beside him, wearing the uniform of the Northern Expeditionary Army, who was also sleeping. Luo Yinan, tired and distressed, blurted out: "Company Commander Mo!"

The uniformed soldier woke up and rubbed his eyes. Luo Yinan recognised him; this was Xiaozhuzi, who served under Mo

Zhengqi. "Is that you, Xiaozhuzi?" Luo Yinan cried. "Where is Company Commander Mo?"

Xiaozhuzi didn't say a word at first. Then he began to cry and said: "Company Commander Mo was killed in action yesterday! He died at the foot of Snake Mountain when they were fighting with Liu Yuchun."

Luo Yinan looked at him blankly. In fact, he had imagined that this might possibly be the case, but now that it was confirmed he was appalled.

"Did Company Commander Mo say anything?" Luo Yinan asked.

"No," said Xiaozhuzi. "When we caught up with them at the foot of Snake Mountain, the enemy counter-attacked fiercely. The company commander told me that if he died, I should come and find you."

As Xiaozhuzi said this, he took two letters out of his pocket and handed them to Luo Yinan. He said: "Company Commander Mo's own uniform was in tatters, so we were told to put him in a new uniform for burial. We found these in his pocket when we dressed him. That's all he left behind."

One of the letters was addressed to Liang Kesi's parents and consisted of a single line: "Uncle and Aunt, I'm sorry, I didn't look after him properly. Zhengqi." Another letter was addressed to someplace called Yutian County in Hebei Province, with a name on the back: Yuan Zongchun.

"Who is that?" Luo Yinan asked.

Xiaozhuzi shook his head: "I don't know."

It was another sleepless night for Luo Yinan. He thought over and over again about what Mo Zhengqi had said to him. He decided that he must have been ready to die; that he would have wanted very much to go and join his fiancée, his friends and his cousin. Perhaps this was a gift he had given himself. Thinking of it this way, Luo Yinan felt a little calmer.

The next afternoon, they buried Liang Kesi and Mo Zhengqi. The surviving soldiers who had served under Mo Zhengqi came to help bury him, as did a handful of students rounded up by Guo Wenjun. He said: "These are the only ones left – I have brought all of them."

They buried Liang Kesi and Mo Zhengqi on a small slope at the tail end of Snake Mountain. It faced Hong Mountain, with Zhongxiao Gate on the left and Binyang Gate on the right. The two cousins were buried in the same grave, as suggested by the landlady's son. He had admired Mo Zhengqi very much. When the coffins were carried to the foot of the mountain, he cried: "Let's bury Company Commander Mo and his cousin together so they can be companions for one another. Otherwise, Company Commander Mo will be lonely."

As it happened, it would have been difficult to dig two graves on that hillside, so everyone just said: "Let's put them together! We can call it the cousins' tomb."

Two cobbled-together coffins were placed side by side in the hole. When they began to fill in the soil, Ye Ting, the commander of the Independent Regiment, arrived. He was terribly depressed. He only said one thing: "I am sure I will never be able to replace Mo Zhengqi."

All the soldiers of the Northern Expeditionary Army who had died under the walls of Wuchang were buried on Hong Mountain, looking across at the cousins' tomb.

18

AFTER LIANG KESI and Mo Zhengqi were buried, Luo Yinan became seriously sick again. He was ill for a very long time, and his recovery was slow. There were bullets in his body that the doctors had been unable to extract, but the damage to his mind was even more serious. His doctors told him that if he could not deal with the mental scarring, he would never be able to recover physically.

That whole winter, Luo Yinan never left the house. A new term began, and he didn't go to college. His family decided that it was impossible to go on like this, so they wrote a letter to him summoning him home.

In the early spring, Luo Yinan went by boat from Hanyang to Hankou. He went to say goodbye to his aunt and uncle, in preparation for returning home. Walking along the street, he suddenly bumped into his landlady's son. He stood right there in front of Luo Yinan in full uniform.

"Have you joined the army?" Luo Yinan asked.

"Yes!" the landlady's son said. "I want to be a man like Company Commander Mo."

"He was indeed a great man," Luo Yinan remarked.

"And what about you?" the landlady's son enquired. "What are you going to do?"

"I am going back to my hometown," Luo Yinan explained.

The landlady's son was shocked and said: "Are you going to become a monk? Have you given up the revolution?"

Luo Yinan was stunned into silence.

"What about Liang Kesi's letter?" the landlady's son asked. "Have you forgotten what he said? I can remember every word."

Luo Yinan was speechless.

He did not return home after all but went back to the Guiyuan Temple. His uncle came to see him and said: "If you want to become a monk, I suppose we can all live with that."

"I haven't actually come to any decision yet," Luo Yinan told him.

His uncle sighed and said: "Think about it some more."

On the day of the Mid-Autumn Festival, Luo Yinan thought to himself: This is the day Liang Kesi died. So he crossed the river by boat. The walls around Wuchang had not been restored. Here there was a gap, there a corner was being torn down, and everywhere there were people with carts stealing bricks from the wall to rebuild their own houses.

Luo Yinan went to the cousins' tomb at the foot of Snake Mountain, burned incense for them and sat for a while. He was all by himself, thinking quietly. He could see everything that had happened, those scenes of corpses scattered everywhere, in front of his eyes. He knew then that last year's pain was still there in his heart, and he would be carrying it forward into this year.

The moon came out, as bright as it had been a year before. Its soft glow bathed the mountains, rivers, trees, flowers and plants. But it would never shine again on Liang Kesi, or on Mo Zhengqi, lying side by side in their quiet graves. Luo Yinan thought: Maybe the moon was the only witness to Liang Kesi's death?

Below him, at the foot of the mountain, was Binyang Gate.

Suddenly, a girl began to scream: a heart-rending wail. Her voice rang through the soft moonlight, as sharp as a knife. Everything seemed to collapse at this cry. The sound struck at Luo Yinan's heart, and he was overwhelmed with pain. Cry as loud as you can, he thought. That's the sound I want to make. Now you cry for me.

The next day, he left Wuhan and went north with the landlady's son...

Many years later, Luo Yinan, a teacher at a middle school in the north, was escorted back to his hometown to deal with his "historical problems". He sat numbly by the window until the train reached Wuchang, but then he began to feel more and more ill at ease. As the train passed Xiaodong Gate, he stood up. This had once been Zhongxiao Gate, where Zhang Wenxiu had been shot dead racing across the stone bridge. Next they came to the tail of Snake Mountain, where some houses had now been built on the slopes. The trees had grown so tall, he could not see whether the cousins' tomb was still there. Then there was so-called Dadong Gate. He burst into tears. Binyang Gate was a shadow of its former self. The corpses lying strewn across the landscape, the barbican, the gunfire, and the stench of putrefying human flesh had all vanished with the passing of time.

The train continued on its journey, and when he turned back he could only catch a glimpse of the roof of Changchun Monastery, which was still as yellow as ever.

Liang Kesi said: "From now on, you will have to fight for me. I am afraid that offering you in my place is the best I can do." He also said: "Even if I die, you must not become a monk."

He had done as he was told. He had fought for many years and then ended up staying on in the north. He had become a teacher, and he told all his pupils the story of Spartacus, which he said he had learned from his own teacher. But he never mentioned the Northern Expedition, nor did he tell them about the fierce battle fought beneath the walls of Wuchang. It was a source of endless agony to him; he could not bear to think about it. Now he had been labelled a "counter-revolutionary" and was being taken back to his hometown under guard. Many years before, he had been on his way home to escape the horrors abroad in the world and, having got halfway there, he had been dragged back by Liang Kesi to join the Northern Expedition. Since then, he had never gone back. The mountain temple, which he had otherwise long forgotten, once again came to his mind when the train skirted Dadong Gate.

A few years later, an old monk named Wuzhi arrived in Wuchang. People said that he was a very holy man. He searched all around the foot of Snake Mountain for something he called the cousins' tomb, asking many people where it was to be found, but they all said they didn't know. He stood there, looking at everything around him. Zhongxiao Gate and Binyang Gate had now completely disappeared. Only Changchun Monastery opposite him still had its yellow roof of yesteryear. He remembered Master Hongyi's saying about the intersection of sorrow and joy, and he wrote a line inspired by this on a stone at Snake Mountain: *As if present; as if absent.* No one understood what he meant. And after that, no one ever saw Wuzhi again.

Time never stops; the seasons roll by.

Life goes on, and the river is always the same.

PART II

DEFENDING THE WALLS

19

ONE AFTERNOON IN LATE SUMMER, Chen Mingwu was lying sprawled across his bed, fast asleep. He had managed to oversleep.

A loud bang woke him up. Suddenly, the roof tiles shook, and bits of gravel flew through the air. Chen Mingwu sat up and listened. He thought to himself: That was an explosion. The sound came from the top of Snake Mountain.

His cousin Daying ran into the room in a panic and said in a shrill voice: "Goodness that was terrifying! What was all that noise?"

Chen Mingwu explained: "That was a bomb going off." As he said this, he jumped out of bed and hurried out before even putting on his shoes.

"It's chaos outside!" his cousin warned him.

"I know," Chen Mingwu said.

"You must be careful!" his cousin instructed him.

Chen Mingwu just repeated the same words: "I know."

Dark clouds veiled the sky, as if it was going to rain. Chen Mingwu planned to go back to school. He was speculating about the cause of the explosion as he arrived at the crossroads with Yanzhi Road, when someone called out to him. Looking back, Chen Mingwu saw that it was Wang Zizheng.[1]

Wang Zizheng was hauling a bag with him as he ran forward.

He quickly came up to Chen Mingwu and asked: "Where are you going?"

"Back to college," Chen Mingwu said. "Was that an explosion just now?"

"Oh, yes," Wang Zizheng said.

"What is going on?" Chen Mingwu asked.

Wang Zizheng lowered his voice: "It was a student from the commercial college who did it. They say the bomber was arrested at the scene."

"Really?" Chen Mingwu exclaimed.

"These last few days," Wang Zizheng said, "everyone has been very tense and on edge, and many students have been arrested."

Chen Mingwu was indignant: "What's the point of arresting students just because you've been defeated in battle?"

Wang Zizheng stole a glance at Chen Mingwu: "I'm afraid the arrests are going to continue. You'd better shave your head. Long-haired students like you make an obvious target."

Chen Mingwu was surprised: "Really?" Wang Zizheng was in a hurry to leave, so Chen Mingwu asked him: "Are you up to something?"

"No," Wang Zizheng said, "but I have to get back in a hurry. I have some papers to deal with. If I read the current situation right, the defeat of the Northern Army is going to see Wuchang under siege pretty soon."

Chen Mingwu looked around, and the sky was getting even darker. He thought: It might well rain tonight. Every now and then people went past, carrying as much of their property as they could out of the city. Chen Mingwu had a faint sneer on his face: "These rich people are really pitiful." After thinking about it for a moment, he added: "I'm glad the Revolutionary Army is coming, I just wish they'd get a move on."

"Shhh…" Wang Zizheng said, "there's no need to make such a song and dance about it – you've got to be more careful."

"Well," Chen Mingwu said, "the same to you too."

They said goodbye. Wang Zizheng took a few steps, then he suddenly turned back and said: "You know, I heard that they are forcing everyone to leave the houses around Zhongxiao and Binyang Gates – I guess they are going to demolish them. If they are going to defend the city, they are going to have to stop the Northern Expeditionary Army using people's houses for cover. Doesn't your family live out there?"

Chen Mingwu was horrified: "Really? I haven't been home for days."

Wang Zizheng was also surprised: "What about your mother?"

Chen Mingwu did not answer; he was too busy running. Wang Zizheng shouted a few times, but he did not have time to respond. As he ran, he thought: "Oh, my God, please let nothing have happened to my mother!"

The area outside Binyang Gate had already been reduced to rubble. The houses close by the foot of the walls had been pulled down; there were broken tiles and mangled pipes, torn rags and shreds of clothing scattered everywhere across the ground. Women were screaming, and the sound rose and fell. Their resounding shrieks pierced the muggy air like knife blades.

The word 'Ji' on the wall of Old Ji's Barber's shop was still clearly to be seen. Chen Mingwu's home was a lean-to built underneath. Chen Mingwu and his widowed mother had lived in this shack for many years, the two of them alone against the world. He came running up, all out of breath, and when he pushed the door open he discovered the shack was empty: his mother was nowhere to be seen.

When a soldier saw there was someone inside, he came over and shouted: "Get out of there! The battle is going to begin any moment now – are you trying to get yourself killed?"

"Where is everyone?" Chen Mingwu asked.

The soldier said: "With the fighting about to start, everyone has run for their lives."

"Have you seen the old lady who lives here?" Chen Mingwu enquired. "Very thin, but not tall."

"I've seen loads of old ladies," the soldier said. "They are all thin. There are more than just one! Now get out of here!"

Chen Mingwu had to go. Outside the city walls, the shops were all shuttered, and their doors were bolted, while his neighbours had been forced to vacate the premises by the soldiers and were now fleeing. He felt confused and looked around blankly. He wanted to ask someone where his mother could be but couldn't see a single familiar face. Suddenly, on the ground by the side of the road, he spotted a familiar object. It was a laundry paddle; his mother's laundry paddle. On the handle, he could see the marks of her nails – she had gripped it so firmly, day after day, as to leave clear scratches. Chen Mingwu stooped to pick it up and looked at it. Suddenly, he felt heartbroken. He couldn't help shouting: "Mum! Mum! Where are you?"

He screamed like a woman. The sound was like thunder and struck the wall with a bang.

20

XIYUN FOLLOWED her mother and entered Wuchang City via Pinghu Gate.

The city people were all trying to leave; they rushed out of the walls under mountains of baggage, clutching a suitcase in each hand. They were bumping against one another, each more nervous than the last, each looking panic-stricken, but they tried not to make too much noise.

Xiyun felt this was odd and asked her mother: "Mum, what are these people doing?"

Her mother said: "Mind your own business!"

"Are they running away?" Xiyun asked. "What are they afraid of when Dad is here?"

Her mother repeated her instructions: "I told you to mind your own business."

"Will all the city people run away?" Xiyun asked. "It'll be no fun if they do. I don't like to play only with soldiers."

"What are you on about now?" her mother said. "When we find your father, I'm going to get him to give you a good talking to."

Xiyun's mother held her little brother, Xizi, by the hand. Xizi was only six years old, and he had never seen so many people before. He was enjoying all the hustle and bustle and said: "I like Wuchang very much!"

Someone shouted: "Out of the way! Get out of the way!"

Xizi decided to practice shouting the same thing. Xiyun gave him a quick slap and said: "You've been asking for that!" Xizi shrank back and said nothing.

A convoy of rickshaws came whistling past in a long line. Each of the rickshaws was piled high with boxes and trunks, and they were all sealed with wide bands. There was a foreign-looking young lady sitting in the last of the rickshaws. She spoke in a loud voice, using a very sharp tone: "Hurry up! If we miss the boat, the master will never forgive you."

"Young mistress," the puller said, "there are just too many people here – we can't get through."

"I don't care! Be quick about it," the young mistress said. "You can expect a beating if you don't get us there on time!"

Xiyun stared at the young lady. She thought: The ladies in the city are really beautiful. Xizi was also looking at her, and as the rickshaw passed by he twisted his little body into a knot.

"Sis, can we take a rickshaw too?" Xizi asked. "Sis, this gate is so big. Sis, will Dad be at this gate?"

Xiyun said: "Don't just call Sis, Sis all the time. Now hurry up! Dad's gate is bigger than this."

Their mother dragged Xizi along: "Walk properly!" After that, she turned back and scolded: "Xiyun, you keep close behind me! If you get lost, you're going to get killed – that's the way things are with the world in such chaos!"

Xiyun was frightened by her mother's words, so she hurried up and followed close behind her. She had little memory of her father; she only knew that he was fighting somewhere far away. Every year, her grandparents burned incense as they prayed that her father would not be shot dead. In the village, if anyone tried to bully Xizi, Xiyun would say: "You dare touch a hair on our Xizi's head and I will get my father to shoot you dead!"

Early one morning, bandits came to the village. They stole everything that the village headman, the third master, had and then they set fire to his house in front of all the inhabitants. The third master was an important figure there, and his son, Fusheng, had long been a good friend to Xiyun, close enough to make personal jokes. Fusheng liked to say: "Xiyun is the prettiest girl in the village, and we ought to get married as soon as possible." Xiyun found this intensely annoying and would always snap back with the same answer: "Dream on! That's never going to happen." It was the same Fusheng who tried to stop the bandits attacking his mother, and they cut his head off for it. The guy who did the cutting had a pockmarked face: he just raised his sword, and the next thing anyone knew Fusheng was in two pieces, and his head was bouncing along the ground until it came to rest up against a millstone. The whole village was petrified at the sight. Xiyun hid behind Grandpa, but she was so scared she wet herself. Later on, she found that many people in the village had a wet patch at their feet, including Grandpa.

Grandpa and Grandma didn't close their eyes all night. The next morning, they decided it was time for Mum to take Xiyun and Xizi away. "If you stay here, they'll kill you," Grandpa said.

Xiyun's mother wasn't so sure: "Outside there are soldiers everywhere, and just because we've run doesn't mean we won't be running into trouble. Besides which, when Zongchun comes back, what would he think of me if I've just abandoned his parents to their fate?"

"What do you think will happen if the bandits come back?" Grandpa said angrily. "Do you want to end up like Fusheng's mother?" Fusheng's mother had been raped by three bandits; once they'd gone, she jumped into the well.

Grandma also shouted at her: "If you want to die, that's fine, but what about the grandkids!"

"Go and find Zongchun!" Grandpa said. "He's a soldier, and he's got a gun. In this world, only men with guns can protect you and the kids."

Xiyun didn't want to leave. At dusk, she and Xizi sat on the big millstone out by the main square and sang songs. They kept singing as the sun set and the stars came out – just at that moment, they were both completely happy. Grandpa slapped Xiyun across the face and shouted: "Do you want to die here? Didn't you see how the bandits killed Fusheng? You were scared enough to wet yourself – have you forgotten?"

Xiyun's mother was helpless. She immediately packed a bag, grabbed Dad's latest letter home and headed out with Xiyun and Xizi. All that Mum knew was that Dad was in Wuchang.

The streets and alleys of Wuchang were packed with soldiers moving back and forward. A whistle sounded somewhere over to the east, and a whole troop would start jogging across in that direction. A whistle sounded over to the west, and a different troop trotted there. The chaos inside the city was terrifying; every rickshaw puller, porter, and sedan-chair carrier in the place was heading out of the gates as fast as they could go, as if the roof would fall in on them if they stayed. Only a couple of beggars, sitting in a corner of the walls, were still stretching out their hands to beg the same as ever, asking for coppers in their usual sad whine. Walking past them and hearing their voices was tranquillising. In that moment, it seemed that nothing very bad could possibly happen.

An old porter was heading straight towards them. Xiyun's mother stopped him and asked: "Excuse me, but could you tell us what's going on here?"

The old man stared at Xiyun's mother and said: "You're not from these parts, are you?"

"No," she said, "we've come looking for my kids' father."

The old man immediately started to scream: "Is this a time to be looking for anyone? You're going to get yourself killed! Get out of here as quickly as you can – the fighting is going to start any minute now!"

"We are not afraid," Xiyun said, "since it is Dad who's going to be leading his men into battle."

Xiyun's mother clouted her round the back of her head: "Children should be seen and not heard."

The old man's face changed: "Ah-ha, with the Northern Army? Why on earth didn't you stay safe and sound at home? Why risk your lives here?" When the old man finished speaking, he picked up the bags he was carrying and walked away.

"Grandpa said that Dad was always right on the front line," Xiyun said. "He must be here somewhere."

Xizi exclaimed in delight: "Sis, I want to fight with Dad too!"

Their mother looked deeply upset. She said fiercely: "Shut up, the pair of you!"

Xiyun's mother took out an envelope, since she wanted to ask passers-by for directions. But before she could begin her enquiries, a man suddenly appeared, as he came running out of one of the

CHAPTER 20 | 205

alleyways. He came to a standstill, sandwiched between Xiyun and her mother. Without saying a word, he picked Xizi up, and in a trice he put him on his back.

Xiyun's mother cried out in horror: "What are you doing?"

He whispered back: "Please, you've got to help me! I am begging you."

When Xiyun heard this, she also got a good look at his face. He was a young man, some years older than herself. His eyes were big, black and bright, like those of cats seen at night. His skin was beautifully pale, and his mouth turned up in a smile. He looked astonishingly like Fusheng. Xiyun's heart skipped a beat.

Xizi announced from his position up on the man's back: "I want to get down."

His sister patted him: "Just stay there for a moment."

Xiyun's mother wanted to say something, but when she heard her daughter's words she did not make a sound. She could see perfectly clearly that the young man with Xizi on his back was a student.

The young student walked along a few steps carrying Xizi on his back, and then they heard a group of people running out of the alley. Xiyun turned around and saw several soldiers with guns in their hands, shouting as they ran. Her heart was pounding. The young man carrying Xizi whispered to her: "Don't be afraid."

The soldiers ran forward, and when they reached the main road they stopped and looked around. Although there were many people out and about, they immediately focused on Xiyun and her family.

Two soldiers came walking over to them. One of them asked: "What are you doing?"

Xiyun's mother replied, her voice trembling: "We've come to find my kids' father."

The other soldier pointed at the young student and said: "Who is he?"

Xiyun rushed to answer: "He is my brother."

The soldier obviously did not believe a word of this: "He's your brother?"

Xiyun suddenly caught sight of the envelope in her mother's hand. She took it, handed it to the soldier and said: "Look, this is a letter from my father."

Xiyun's mother made haste to add: "My husband is a serving soldier like you. We've just come from Hebei Province."

An officer came across from the other side of the street. "Why don't you go and arrest someone," he roared. "What are you doing just standing here?"

The soldier saluted and said: "Captain Lu, this lady has just arrived from Hebei Province, and she says she's here to find her husband."

This Captain Lu looked at Xiyun's mother and asked: "Where in Hebei?"

"Yutian County," she said. "He wrote home saying that he was in Wuchang."

Captain Lu's tone was becoming more and more friendly: "Yutian, you say? What's his name?"

"His name is Yuan Zongchun," Xiyun's mother said. "He used to serve as Uncle Liu's aide – Uncle Liu Yuchun comes from our village too. When Uncle Liu became a major general, Zongchun – that's my husband – said that he got promoted too."

Captain Lu was shocked. He stared hard at Xiyun's mother and tried to say something but swallowed it back. All of a sudden, he was beaming, but it seemed forced and unnatural, as if someone was wringing his neck at the same time. "Oh, so you're Madam Yuan," he said. "I do apologise, please forgive my rudeness." After that, he spoke sharply to the soldiers: "Have you all gone blind and deaf? This is Staff Officer Yuan's family. Madam Yuan here speaks proper Hebei dialect, couldn't you tell? Hurry up and apologise to her." The soldiers were already busy bowing and scraping.

Xiyun had never heard anyone call her mother "Madam Yuan" before. She was amused and burst into laughter. Captain Lu glanced at her, but he went on speaking to her mother: "Staff Officer Yuan... Well, he ought to be over by Binyang Gate. I am afraid that I am busy right now, so I cannot escort you there in person. Hairy!" A young soldier came running up as Captain Lu shouted his name. "You take Madam Yuan round to Binyang Gate," Captain Lu commanded. "If something happens on the way, even if I don't kill you, the guys over by Binyang Gate won't spare you."

Xiyun's mother made haste to say: "No need, we can go there by ourselves."

"At present, there is chaos in Wuchang," Captain Lu said. "The Northern Expeditionary Army will attack at any moment now. You should be careful." As he spoke, he bowed to Xiyun's mother.

She returned the salute: "Thank you, sir."

Captain Lu waved to them as he walked away, but before he left his eye fell on the young student. He was amusing Xizi by trying to tickle him. Xiyun touched the student and said: "Brother, Captain Lu is leaving. You ought not to be so rude – say goodbye properly! And Xizi, you have to say goodbye too."

The young student quickly raised his arm and waved to Captain Lu, and Xizi followed suit. Captain Lu made sure that he beamed, and when he reached the other side of the road he turned back and waved a few more times.

Xiyun's mother watched him cross the road and relaxed. The little soldier called Hairy said: "Let's go. If we don't go soon, it'll be dark, and we won't be able to go anywhere."

They followed him in silence. Xiyun couldn't stop herself from stealing a glance at the student, and the student happened to be looking at her. He laughed, and so did Xiyun. He kept looking at Xiyun. She didn't understand why and wanted to ask, but he pointed at Hairy. She stayed silent; a moment's thought meant she understood the problem.

Xiyun went over to Hairy and asked: "Are you really called Hairy?"

"It's just a nickname," he said. "My real name is Li Guiyou."

"Should I call you Hairy," Xiyun asked, "or Mr Li?"

"Oh, you just call me Guiyou," Hairy said. "I wouldn't dream of asking a young lady like yourself to call me Mr Li!"

Xiyun clapped her hands and laughed: "If you are happy with that! If I ever meet you in the street and I call you Guiyou, you mustn't shoot me."

Hairy laughed and said: "I wouldn't dare!"

"What do you mean, you wouldn't dare?" Xiyun asked.

"Of course not!" Hairy said. "You are a senior officer's daughter, so it's my job to protect you."

"So do you have to do what I tell you?" Xiyun asked.

"Sure," Hairy said, "if I don't listen to you, I'm liable to get shot."

"OK," Xiyun said, "so I've got something to say, and you've got to obey me."

"Go right ahead," Hairy replied.

"You've escorted us this far," Xiyun said, "and that's enough. We will go on from here by ourselves."

Hairy was a little troubled and said: "Well…"

"We want to be able to tell Dad we found him all by ourselves," Xiyun explained. "We want to show Dad that we can look after ourselves. Otherwise, when Dad sees you, he will complain about me and my brother being useless, that we have to be escorted everywhere by soldiers."

Hairy hesitated: "Really?"

"Would I lie to you?" Xiyun asked. "Do you dare to disbelieve me?"

"That's not what I meant," Hairy said.

"I'm doing this for your sake too," Xiyun told him. "When we arrive at Binyang Gate, that's where we are going. But you have to walk all the way back. I don't think that's fair. You're going to be fighting in battle soon, so we shouldn't be tiring you out."

Hairy was very grateful: "That's very kind of you, miss."

Xiyun's mother also added her voice: "You can go back now. It's not too far, so I am sure we can find our way."

Hairy bowed to her: "Yes! If that is what you want, madam."

Seeing Hairy had walked away out of sight, Xiyun laughed loudly, and Xizi laughed with her. Their mother's face was stiff as she said: "I'm glad the pair of you can laugh! That nearly gave me a heart attack."

"Yes! If that is what you want, madam," Xiyun said, in imitation of Hairy's southern accent. Her mother could not help laughing. This was the first time Xiyun saw her mother smile since they had left home.

The young student put Xizi down and bowed deeply. "Thank you, madam," he said, "for saving my life. My name is Chen Mingwu. I will repay you if ever I have the chance."

"You should thank me too," Xiyun said.

"And me," said Xizi.

Chen Mingwu agreed: "Yes, yes, I want to thank both of you."

After patting Xizi and Xiyun on the head, he smiled and said: "I've never seen such a clever little girl before."

"That's what people in our village say about me too!" Xiyun cried.

Chen Mingwu turned to their mother and said: "Madam, the city is now so dangerous that I really ought to take you to Binyang Gate myself. But my house has been demolished, and my mother has disappeared. I have to find my mother..." As he spoke, he was overwhelmed with sadness.

"Of course you must go and find her," Xiyun's mother said.

Xiyun also chimed in: "There's nothing to worry about here, Mingwu. I can deal with things."

Chen Mingwu patted the heads of the two children again and then walked away quickly. Xiyun kept watching him until he had completely disappeared from sight. "If only he were really my brother," she said. "His name is Chen Mingwu, but unfortunately he didn't ask my name."

"I like him too," Xizi said. "It was really comfortable riding on his back. Unfortunately, he didn't ask my name."

"So you like him, do you?" Xiyun's mother said. "He must be one of these terrorists. If it hadn't been for your father's reputation, he'd have killed all of us."

In a flash, Xiyun was overcome by the memory of Fusheng's beheading, and her skin crawled with fear.

21

HONG PEIZHU WAS DRINKING tea when the bomb exploded on the top of Snake Mountain. The sound was horrendous and frightened her so much that her cup fell to the ground. Before she could overcome her terror, she suddenly thought: Could it be Chen Mingwu who did it? That thought made her feel quite limp; she almost passed out, and there was only room for one idea in her mind: to find Chen Mingwu.

Having passed through the barbican to Binyang Gate, she found herself outside the city walls and stood there in a daze. There were soldiers moving about, demolishing houses or driving people away, and the sounds of men shouting and people crying mingled together. Everything in that once-familiar vista had been destroyed, and the noisy streets seemed to be a place she had never seen before. This was a poor residential area; even the shops there were just small corner-stores. And Mingwu's house, which was just a shack after all, was somewhere there amidst the ruins, but Hong Peizhu couldn't even find where it once had been.

Hong Peizhu rushed back to Garden Hill again. At the gate to the Catholic church, she bumped into the foreigner called Meng.

"It's getting dark, Miss Hong," he said, "and it's not safe. You need to get home as soon as you can."

Mr Meng was a friend of Hong Peizhu's father. There were many foreigners living at Garden Hill, and they seemed to enjoy having dinner together more than anything else. Hong Peizhu's father was often invited, but her mother had bound feet, so it was Hong Peizhu who went with her father on these occasions. Hong Peizhu was a very beautiful girl, and the foreigners liked to chat to her. Chen Mingwu said that Mr Meng was completely hypocritical, and this meant that Hong Peizhu didn't like him much, but she was too lazy to think about the reasons for this. She now answered lightly: "I know." She walked away as fast as she could.

Mr Meng took a few steps and suddenly called out: "Are you looking for Young Master Liang?"

Hong Peizhu turned back and said: "Yes, I'm looking for Liang Wenqi."

"Wenqi went to Guangzhou a few days ago," Mr Meng told her. "The Liang family all crossed over to Hankou this afternoon, leaving a few servants behind to look after the house. Go home as quickly as you can and tell your father to go to Hankou and stay away for a few days. There'll be a terrible battle for possession of Wuchang starting pretty soon."

Hong Peizhu was stunned and did not know what to do. She stood stock-still for a few seconds, then as Mr Meng watched, she turned around and walked slowly away. When she got to the Gejiaying District, she remembered that the house Wang Zizheng was renting was over in the Taiping Planned Community. If she took this turning, she'd be right there – Chen Mingwu had taken her there. When Hong Peizhu remembered this, her footsteps turned in that direction.

Wang Zizheng's door was locked. Hong Peizhu knocked for a long time before the door opened a crack. When he saw it was her, he was surprised: "You...?"

"I am looking for Mingwu," Hong Peizhu said.

Wang Zizheng breathed a sigh of relief, but he still did not let her come in. "I saw him this afternoon before he rushed off," he said.

Hong Peizhu looked delighted: "Where did he go?"

"He went out to Binyang Gate," Wang Zizheng said, "but..." Suddenly, he fell silent.

"But what?" Hong Peizhu asked.

Wang Zizheng hesitated and said: "However, Guo Wenjun came

by just now and said that when he was on the way home, he saw the military police chasing after a student. He said that he thought the running student looked like Chen Mingwu. If that's true, I'm afraid he's going to be in serious trouble."

When Wang Zizheng said that, Hong Peizhu was so shocked that she burst into tears, but her throat was so tight that she could not speak.

"Go home," Wang Zizheng said. "I have to go out right away. These days, the Northern Army is trying to repair the city walls as best they can, and the battlements that have collapsed are all being put in good order again. I notice that the barbican around Government Gate has sandbags piled up everywhere, so I reckon that they are going to close the city any day now. The Northern Expeditionary Army is bound to attack us, and if the city falls they'll be fighting from street to street. I recommend that you get over to Hankou as soon as you can and stay with your family over there."

Hong Peizhu was terrified by the prospect Wang Zizheng had just described. She thought for a moment and said: "No, I have to find Mingwu."

"OK," Wang Zizheng said, "find Mingwu and tell him he needs to get across the river right now. If he wants to find me, he should go to the Spring-filled Teahouse over in Hankou and ask for Aqi."

Hong Peizhu nodded. She turned around and went away without another word. She was crying and praying: "Lord, you must not let anything happen to Mingwu. If you save him, I will help ten people in need in your name."

As Hong Peizhu walked on, the gloomy summer afternoon sky gradually turned a yellowish-grey. A wind arose, and a coolness came with the wind, like being sprayed with water. The number of people out on the streets was visibly decreasing. Anyone who could leave had already done so, and the few who remained were nervously making for home as quickly as they could.

There was a curfew imposed that night in Wuchang. All through the night, inspection patrols carrying their arrow-head tokens marched around, and the ancient bustling city of Wuchang seemed almost empty. The streets and lanes, apart from the flitting of the patrols, were denuded of passers-by. There was no laughter and singing, nor even shouting and cursing, to be heard. The patrols were nasty pieces of work; when they came across a pedestrian overnight, without saying a word they would begin beating him with their truncheons. If anyone tried to fight back, the guns and knives would come out. If you shouted, arrest was inevitable.

Hong Peizhu kept walking, her legs trembling, but Chen Mingwu was nowhere to be seen. Seeing that it was already dark, she had no choice but to go back home. Hong Peizhu's father was a government official, working in the provincial governor's office, so she had nothing to fear from the patrols. If she told them his name, they wouldn't do anything to her. However, Hong Peizhu had no intention of running up against soldiers on patrol if she could avoid it. It was best to avoid any attention.

Walking through an alley, a black cat leapt out of the corner and scampered across Hong Peizhu's feet, frightening her. She couldn't help screaming and backing against the wall. She banged her knee against the corner of the wall, and the pain was appalling. She leaned there and did not dare to move until she realised that it was just a black cat that had run past her.

The black cat disappeared. Even though it wasn't completely dark yet, the animal managed to suddenly disappear. Hong Peizhu felt that this was an ominous sign. She wondered what the appearance of a black cat could mean. She was sure that it was bad luck, but she was afraid to go any further down this particular avenue of thought.

Hong Peizhu used the very last strength she had to make her way back to the college. The patrol had already gone down the street; there were a couple of screams of pain from a corner somewhere far away in the distance.

No sooner had she arrived at the gate to the college than a man rushed up and pulled Hong Peizhu away. She was so frightened, she almost collapsed onto the ground. When she realised that it was the major-domo, Old Nuo, she was so angry she stamped her foot.

"Where have you been, miss?" Old Nuo was fretting. "The master and madam have people out looking for you everywhere. The whole family is waiting for you."

"Why?" Hong Peizhu asked. "I usually stay over at the college."

"It's not the same now," Old Nuo said. "The fighting is going to start soon – haven't you seen the chaos in Wuchang? The master has said that we are all going to cross to Hankou first thing tomorrow morning – we'll be staying with your older brother."

"I am not going anywhere!" Hong Peizhu cried. "I want to stay here!"

"The master has arranged everything already," Old Nuo said. "You will have to go home and talk to the master."

"I am not going anywhere," Hong Peizhu said, "I have things to do."

Old Nuo, with a mournful face, replied: "The master spoke to me this afternoon and said if I didn't find you today, he'd throw me out of the Hong house."

Hong Peizhu was shocked when she heard what the old man said. Her father had never said such cruel things before; it was a sign of how dangerous the situation had become. "What has happened?" Hong Peizhu asked. "Why are you so nervous all of a sudden?"

The old man lowered his voice and said: "Terrible things are going on. It's said that the Northern Army has been defeated, and that's why they've all fled to Wuchang. Even General Wu has been injured, and he's fled back to Hankou, with the Southern Army pursuing him all the way. General Wu ordered that the city be defended at all costs, and Snake Mountain's covered with artillery. You can see the guns from Tanhualin. Just think about it – when a battle is going to be fought right on your doorstep, how can you not be frightened? The two armies are going to confront each other right here, and there's going to be shells flying around, and they could hit anybody. If one of those shells falls on your house, nobody is going to escape alive."

"Stop trying to scare me," Hong Peizhu said.

"I am just telling you what the master said," Old Nuo told her. "That's not something I could have come up with on my own. But I've seen the rich people in Wuchang pouring out of the city – the officials aren't saying anything, but they are letting them go. The master said that hiding in the Hankou Foreign Concession would be the safest. The young master sent a servant over to tell us that the house is ready and waiting – all the master and madam have to do is get across the river tomorrow with you and your brothers and sisters. If you leave it any longer, it is going to be impossible to get out."

While Old Nuo was talking, there was an explosion somewhere nearby. After the sound ebbed away, there was the sound of screaming, and then there was silence. Never before had Hong Peizhu heard such a terrible explosion; she trembled with fear and could not say a word. Old Nuo dragged her to the side of the road, where they sheltered in the shadows of the eaves. They were making for home as quickly as they could.

22

MA WEIFU COULD NEVER HAVE IMAGINED a defeat like this.

At Tingsi Bridge, General Wu had vowed to fight with all his might; he had assembled vast quantities of ammunition and grain – they had so much food that they were able to build their breastworks with bags of white rice. Ma Weifu thought it was an incredible sight; half-jokingly, he pointed out to Staff Officer Yuan Zongchun that such a thing must be rare in the annals of war. It was quite unbelievable: the battle lasted only one day, and they were completely defeated. Ma Weifu followed the routed troops as they fled to the city of Wuchang.

The victorious Northern Expeditionary Army pursued them relentlessly, as if they imagined they could catch up with them before they got to Wuchang.

The moment Ma Weifu entered the city via Tongxiang Gate, he suddenly felt deeply tired of the war. Yuan Zongchun was dead. He had been hit by a stray bullet on the retreat: he just stumbled and fell to the ground. Ma Weifu wanted to turn back and help him, but someone beside him shouted: "Don't stop. Ye Ting's Independent Regiment is behind us. If you stop, they'll kill you!" Bullets fell around him like rain. Ye Ting's Independent Regiment fought as if each and every soldier was invulnerable: they seemed invincible. They also seemed to run like the wind, catching up with them without any apparent effort. Ma Weifu's hesitation lasted barely a second; then he carried on running. As he turned around, he could feel Yuan Zongchun's eyes boring into his back. But Ma Weifu could not stop. He knew that if he went to save him, he would end up dead beside him: the two of them would be ghosts in an alien land for the rest of time. However, he did not want to die yet. He was afraid of death. His only chance of survival was to join with the other soldiers as they fled, running as fast as they could towards Wuchang.

On his first evening back in the city, Ma Weifu had nightmares all night. Whichever way he turned, all he could see was Yuan Zongchun's face and particularly his eyes. The eyes were empty and stared at him without moving. The two of them had worked together for three years, advancing and retreating, never apart. But now they were separated by life and death. Although soldiers understand well enough that they may be killed in action at any point, to witness the sudden death of a close friend makes you feel as if you too have died. For days on end, Ma Weifu felt he was struggling against Death himself.

After they were defeated at Tingsi Bridge, General Wu swore: "We will win at Hesheng Bridge and defend Wuchang to the death."

The conference was held at the office of the military governor. At their meeting, General Wu ordered Liu Yuchun to take command of the defence of the city. Waving his fist, he proclaimed that he would stop the Northern Expeditionary Army at Hesheng Bridge but that Wuchang was the shield protecting his rear. As he spoke, his excitement grew, until he drew his sword and swung it against the table, vowing to unite his men, to protect the country to the very last drop of his blood, to hold Wuchang whatever the cost, to fight to the death, to never allow the Northern Expeditionary Army across the Yangtze River! The headquarters of the defence of Wuchang was established at the Jiangxi Guild Hall. After his orders had been issued, General Wu himself crossed the river by boat, heading for Hankou.

Ma Weifu did not initially take the Northern Expeditionary Army at all seriously, but after the Battle of Tingsi Bridge he seemed to come to his senses. Their opponents were no dilettante

Sunday soldiers, and they were facing an even more difficult battle. The fighting at Hesheng Bridge was going to be crucial for stopping the Northern Expedition; if they could win at Hesheng Bridge, it would be much easier to defend Wuchang. Perhaps it was because of this that Liu Yuchun appeared so upbeat; he said that defeats were nothing to worry about, so even though they'd lost at Tingsi Bridge they would definitely be victorious at Hesheng Bridge. The name Hesheng – congratulations on victory – was a good omen for them. Even if by some mischance they lost, well, way back when, he held out for forty-three days in Xinyang. Now Wuchang was a city over a thousand years old, and its walls are about ten metres high: how could they ever get in? They could hold it for much more than forty-three days!

Liu Yuchun was a hard man; he combined a chivalrous spirit with great courage, and Ma Weifu admired him very much. He had followed him for many years because of this. But right at that moment, he decided he didn't believe a word that he said.

Their plans for defending the city were almost identical to the defence of Xinyang the year before. For the defending troops, the most important issue is not the fighting, it is having something to eat. Without food, you have no hope at all of holding the city. All the grain stores and rice mills in Wuchang had been sealed. The two biggest millers, Cao Xiangtai and Zhang Wanshan, had all their rice requisitioned by the army. According to the quartermasters' survey, if they fed every person in the army two meals of porridge and one of rice per day, and the civilian population one meal of porridge and one of rice, they had enough food for about forty days.

Liu Yuchun slapped his thigh and said: "That's enough! Do we really have enough food for forty days? Our reinforcements will come up in ten days or so, and then the Southern Army will have to piss off with its tail between its legs."

He still spoke with great confidence, but Ma Weifu didn't really believe more than half of it. The half he believed was that they wouldn't have to defend the city for more than forty days, but he was not at all sure that it was the Southern Army that would be running away with their tails between their legs. Ma Weifu was filled with pessimism about this war. They had prepared for the fight at Tingsi Bridge, they had been very well equipped, but for all that they had been defeated. Why had they lost? After Ma Weifu had made it back to Wuchang and had nightmares all night, he came to understand: they had been defeated because the tide had turned. Once the tide starts running out, no man can hold it back. Afterwards, that one phrase stuck in his mind: the tide has turned.

Now, Ma Weifu was standing above Binyang Gate and watching a couple of soldiers hang paraffin lamps around the city wall.

The damaged battlements had all been repaired with fresh brickwork. In order to protect them, further brick walls had been built to the side and back of the defenders to prevent them from being injured by stray bullets. They collected all the cotton wool, wire and paraffin they could find in the city shops, as well as every chamber pot they could lay their hands on. Compared to paraffin lamps, the chamber pots were much bigger. They could fill a chamber pot with paraffin, stuff in a wad of cotton as a wick, tie it up with galvanised wire, and lower it halfway down the wall. Although it was not as bright as an electric light, when they were lit overnight, there would be quite enough light to keep an eye on the enemy and prevent any attack on the city.

Binyang Gate was located on the east side of Wuchang, and Changchun Monastery stood just outside the walls. Standing on top of the wall, Changchun Monastery lay revealed before you. It is said that Qiu Chuji, also known as Changchun, the seventh disciple of the founder of the Quanzhen sect, had died here, so this Daoist foundation was named Changchun Monastery.

A few months ago, Ma Weifu and Yuan Zongchun went to Changchun Monastery to pray. They had each lit one stick of incense and then offered up a silent prayer. Yuan Zongchun had asked Ma Weifu what he had prayed for. "Oh, nothing," Ma Weifu said. "My mind went blank."

But Yuan Zongchun had laughed at him and said: "You aren't married so of course your mind goes blank." He himself had far too many things to worry about: his parents, his wife, his children, and he'd prayed for them.

Ma Weifu looked out at Changchun Monastery beyond the walls, and Yuan Zongchun's voice seemed to resound in his ear.

Incense smoke arose in swirling curls above Changchun

Monastery, before dissipating into the grey sky. You know what? Ma Weifu thought. When this battle is over, will you still be sitting there unscarred? Will incense smoke still be curling up into the sky? Ma Weifu felt completely empty at that moment, as if he had been gutted.

A soldier carefully positioned an oil lamp and then climbed back on top of the walls on a rope. When he saw Ma Weifu, he stood to attention and saluted him. Ma Weifu saw that he looked familiar and nodded his head slightly. "Are you from Hebei?" he asked.

The soldier stood to attention again and replied: "Yes, I joined the army with Staff Officer Yuan..." Having said this, he paused, and after a short space of time he continued... "We come from the same village."

"I see," Ma Weifu said.

The soldier was about to go away, but he hesitated and then turned back to asked Ma Weifu: "Sir, can we hold this city?"

Ma Weifu raised his head: "What are you talking about? Don't you trust Major General Liu? Don't you trust General Wu?"

The soldier bowed and did not dare to say another word.

Ma Weifu calmed his voice: "I understand your concerns. Although we lost at Tingsi Bridge, we still have Hesheng Bridge. Even if we are defeated at Hesheng Bridge, I want you to understand that defending the city is playing to our strong suit, compared to offensive warfare. Last year, I was there when we fought for forty days in the defence of Xinyang, and we know what we are doing when it comes to holding a city. I guess that the walls of Wuchang are much stronger than those of Xinyang, aren't they? So you don't have to worry about us not holding this city."

The soldier answered carefully: "Yes, sir."

Normally, Ma Weifu couldn't be bothered to talk to the soldiers. But for some reason, today he had ended up saying a great deal to a raw recruit. It was all about raising morale, he thought, but did I want to persuade the soldier, or myself?

Hong Mountain was not far away. In the spring and summer, fresh air can sometimes seem like a fertiliser; the forest trees on the mountainsides were growing as fast as they could, and they were all lush and green. There was no doubt in his mind that there would be a vicious battle fought around Binyang Gate. Ma Weifu's gaze fell on the small hill outside the walls at the northeastern corner, which stood almost as high as the wall. If the Northern Expeditionary Army wanted to attack the city, that spot would be the springboard for their attack. Ma Weifu called the lieutenant over and pointed to the northeastern corner: "You need to keep an eye on this. You'll have to have people on it twenty-four hours a day. If you spot anything, please report it to me immediately, whatever the time." The lieutenant stood to attention and agreed. "You'd better drill a few more embrasures for machine guns in the walls here," Ma Weifu said. "They are really great when you have a city to defend." The lieutenant once again stood to attention and said yes.

Would drilling a few more embrasures for machine guns make any difference at all? Ma Weifu knew that he was just talking nonsense. Even though the walls of Wuchang were thick enough, how could they withstand artillery fire day after day raining down from the sky? And once the shelling started, surely it was not just the walls that would be damaged? What about Changchun Monastery? What about the soldiers defending the city? Once shells started exploding into shrapnel, how could the houses under the walls and inside the city, not to mention the tens of thousands of inhabitants, escape the carnage that would follow? Fortunately, his uncle and his entire family had followed his advice and decided to leave for Hankou tomorrow to take refuge there. It was fortunate too that his cousin Peizhu did not respond to his feelings for her. At that thought, Ma Weifu felt a little sad. Peizhu was quite right, he thought. If you fall in love with a soldier, you will suffer for the rest of your life. They are constantly under fire, and a soldier may have no choice but to risk his life. They could end up fighting in battle for some reasons beyond their comprehension, and then it turns out they will never be coming back.

Ma Weifu was quite sure that he would die at Binyang Gate within the next couple of weeks. He could feel Yuan Zongchun's shadow near him all the time, and those two black eyes, like two lights, stared in the direction that he was headed. He knew that sooner or later he would follow in Yuan Zongchun's footsteps.

This is my destiny, Ma Weifu said to himself.

Suddenly, the soldier who had just talked to Ma Weifu came

running up in a lather. Ma Weifu stared at him without saying a word, but his eyes questioned him.

The soldier stammered out: "Sir, the... the... they're here!"

Ma Weifu stiffened and said: "Speak properly!"

The soldier was still stuttering: "The... the... they're here!"

"Who are they?" Ma Weifu asked.

The soldier explained: "A woman and two... two children."

Ma Weifu was puzzled and asked: "Who are you talking about? What are a woman and two children doing here at a time like this? Get rid of them!" Ma Weifu's voice became sharp.

"But it's Staff Officer Yuan's family," the soldier explained, "and they're here to find him." He finally got the story out properly.

Ma Weifu was stunned.

"Sir, what should I do?" asked the soldier.

Ma Weifu was overwhelmed with sadness, and he said to himself: If only you'd lived just a few more days, Zongchun... What a time to pick to get killed!

"Sir, should I tell them to go away?" the soldier asked.

"Go away?" Ma Weifu said. "It's getting dark. Where can they go?"

"Yes!" the soldier said.

"You haven't told them about Staff Officer Yuan?" Ma Weifu asked.

"I wouldn't dare," the soldier said frankly.

Ma Weifu sighed and said: "Well, first arrange for them to rest and get something to eat. As for the rest, we'll have to break it to them slowly."

"Yes!" the soldier said and made as if to leave.

"Wait a minute!" Ma Weifu said. "Tell everyone that nobody is to tell them what happened to Staff Officer Yuan – just say that he is busy carrying out his official duties."

"Yes!" the soldier said.

By the time Ma Weifu got down from the wall, the sky was already turning grey. The breeze on his face was cool, and there was a roar in the distance. It was dry rumbling, like a thunderstorm stuck in the clouds. It seemed like fighting had already begun over by Hesheng Bridge.

By the side of the gate, Ma Weifu caught sight of a sad-looking woman. She stood leaning against the wall, and her posture showed just how exhausted she was. The two children were running around chasing each other and laughing. The sound of their laughter, like the chiming of silver bells, smashed the depressed atmosphere in Wuchang that evening into smithereens.

23

AT EIGHT O'CLOCK in the evening, Long Street, the busiest shopping street in Wuchang, was thrown into a sudden state of disturbance. Three young men were beheaded by the military police at Huo Alley, where it turned onto Long Street. Their heads were suspended up above.

The news spread through the night. It knocked on the doors of thousands of families, passed from one family to another through the whole of Wuchang, like ripples in water, spreading out one circle after another.

Three students had been killed.

Early the next morning, people went out to get more information. Anyone who went to Nianyutao got to see a human head. Anyone who went to Yuemachang got to see another head. And if you went out of Government Gate, there was a third head hung up over there. The people who had to walk underneath it came out the other side grey in the face and feeling weak at the knees.

Rich people were now leaving the city in even greater numbers than on the previous day. Luggage lay piled up on the docks like mountains, as the little steamers plying the river rushed back and forth from the south bank to the north bank as quickly as they could. There were so many carts carrying luggage sandwiching so many people dragging children along that they blocked Hanyang Gate, and nobody could get in or out.

Before daybreak, Hong Peizhu's eldest brother had sent people to collect all their luggage and row it across the river. The rest of the family were to follow by steamer once they had eaten their breakfast.

They had no idea how long the battle would last, nor when they would be able to return. Hong Peizhu's father sighed as he leaned against his walking stick, pacing up and down in his room. Her father was against all wars, but he was particularly horrified by the prospect of fighting in densely populated cities. When the two armies fought and there was shelling, it was the civilian population caught in the middle who suffered the most, and it was their houses and shops that were destroyed. None of the politicians or generals who decided to go to war in the first place would be killed. Hong Peizhu's father had spent some time studying in Japan; although he had subsequently learned to smoke opium, he was nevertheless an educated man who retained a sense of humanity. Looking through the window at the chaotic scenes outside, he chanted in a low voice: "Sooner or later every palace must come to dust. With the founding of each dynasty, the people suffer. When they fall, the people suffer too."

Hong Peizhu thought quite differently from her father. "China is in such difficulties," she said, "and so backward – warfare is inevitable. If you don't want to fight, then throw open the gates and let the Revolutionary Army march straight into Hankou. From here, they can take the train to Peiping; that would be best for everyone! If you aren't competent enough to govern the country well and you can't defeat them in battle, what are you trying to hold on for? You are just ruining everything and making ordinary people suffer unnecessary hardships."

"Have you been talking to that Chen Mingwu?" Hong Peizhu's father demanded angrily. "People like him need stringing up! They haven't learned anything worth a damn – instead, they are too busy bringing the country to rack and ruin."

Hong Peizhu now got angry too and said: "If you say that he needs stringing up, then I'm going to die too!"

Her father threw his stick at her and said: "If you want to die, go right ahead. My affection has clearly been wasted on you!"

Long after breakfast was over, the scheduled rickshaws started to arrive one after another, though none of them was on time. The major-domo, Old Nuo, was unhappy and asked: "Why are you so late?"

The pullers made a show of their efforts. One said: "There are sandbags piled up everywhere, and it's hard to get through."

Another said: "Yesterday, three people were killed. Their heads have been hung up at various crossroads, and there are loads of people standing around gawping, so it was impossible to make good time."

Hong Peizhu came out of the house just in time to hear about the killing. Her heart was thumping fiercely as she asked: "Who has been killed?"

"Students, of course!" the puller told her. "I saw two of the heads hanging there, and they both looked very young."

Hong Peizhu felt everything go black before her eyes, and she asked urgently: "Do you know who they are? What were their surnames?"

"I don't know," said one puller.

The other said: "I think one of them was called Chen."

The darkness in front of Hong Peizhu's eyes now engulfed her whole body. Everything went black. Chen Mingwu's face came floating towards her out of the darkness, his huge eyes were full of melancholy, and his mouth seemed first to be laughing, and then to be crying. All that was left of Chen Mingwu, as he appeared before Hong Peizhu's eyes, was his head. His neck was dripping with blood, drop by drop, falling directly at her feet. Hong Peizhu seemed to want to see the blood at her feet, and her body slumped towards the ground.

Hong Peizhu's father and mother had already boarded the rickshaw. The rest of the family were ready to go too. One of the pullers screeched in alarm: "Miss! Miss! Come quickly, master, she's fainted!"

Her parents clambered out of the rickshaw and rushed to her side.

Hong Peizhu's eyes were closed, and her face was grey. Her

mother burst into tears and screamed: "What's the matter, Peizhu? Peizhu, my darling, what's wrong?"

Her father demanded to know what had happened.

The puller explained: "When she heard about the students being killed, she just keeled over."

Hong Peizhu's father sighed: "If a student's been killed, what has that got to do with the rest of us? Old Nuo, call a doctor at once."

The major-domo arranged for one of the servants to call a doctor. When he saw that none of the family had gone, he started to panic. "You've got to get out of here, master," he said. "The boat won't wait. I'll look after Miss Peizhu. After she's seen the doctor, I'll escort her over there."

Hong Peizhu's father thought for a moment and said: "That's what we'll do. We can't all wait for her. There'll be more boats in the afternoon. You can be in Hankou by tomorrow morning at the latest. If they close the city, it will be very difficult for anyone left behind to make it out alive, so I want you to get out in time."

"Don't worry, master," said Old Nuo. "I would give my life to save Miss Peizhu. If I have to carry her across the river on my back, I will."

A long line of rickshaws went swishing out of the gate. The same sound could be heard everywhere in the noisy city of Wuchang.

The doctor was a German man, and he was called in whenever any member of the Hong family fell ill. By the time he arrived, Hong Peizhu was already running a high temperature. She was talking nonsense, but to her it made perfect sense. She knew why she had failed to find Chen Mingwu the day before: it was because he had already been cut in two. Although he had never responded to her affection, indeed he had avoided her pursuit, going so far as to tell her to her face that he did not love her, she still felt heartbroken for him because she knew the reason why he had so resolutely resisted and evaded her: it was not that he did not love her, but that he was unwilling to pursue a relationship with her. That unwillingness was because of her family; that fool said that he did not want to become part of a rich family, he did not want to have Miss Moneybags holding him back from joining in the revolution, and he did not want her to suffer for the rest of her life if one fine day they cut off his head. Hong Peizhu thought sadly: If you refuse me, won't I be sad about that for the rest of my life? Their love ran on parallel tracks, never crossing. It was like cops and robbers – one is always running away, and the other is always chasing. There had never been a relationship, and nothing had ever happened: they had both lost out.

The doctor said: "Miss Hong is over-anxious and over-stressed. That is why she fainted."

"In this city, they cut people's heads off all the time," the major-domo said, "and Miss Peizhu couldn't normally care less – what is different this time?"

The doctor smiled and said: "Who knows with psychological issues?"

The doctor gave her an injection, left some medicine for her, gave various instructions about how to look after her and left. The major-domo asked the doctor if he was going to go to Hankou. The doctor explained that he would not be leaving Wuchang; they were going to be fighting, and there would be a lot of civilian casualties. He was a doctor, it was his job to help save people's lives, so it was his duty to stay.

At noon, Hong Peizhu woke up.

"What is wrong with you, miss?" Old Nuo asked.

Chen Mingwu's face appeared again before her eyes, and her tears fell like rain. "Where are the heads hung up?" she asked.

Old Nuo told her: "I heard that one is up above Government Gate. Then there's one at Nianyutao and one at Yuemachang."

"Which is Chen's head?" Hong Peizhu asked.

Old Nuo was shocked and said: "They cut the head off one of your friends?"

Hong Peizhu cried impatiently: "Tell me, which one is Chen's head?"

"I don't know," Old Nuo said. "Don't think too much about it, miss. We've got to get across to Hankou by this afternoon's boat, or we won't be able to leave at all."

"I just want to know which head is Chen's!" Hong Peizhu insisted.

She now started screaming hysterically, but after only a couple of screams she fainted again. Old Nuo was frightened and summoned the doctor back again. "This is a psychological condition," the doctor said, "and medicine won't cure it. All we can do is calm her down for a while."

The major-domo escorted the doctor to the door and took this opportunity to ask: "Sir, do you know which head is Chen's?"

The doctor looked at Old Nuo in silence, and his eyes were filled with suspicion.

24

THERE WAS no news of victory from Hesheng Bridge. They could almost hear the crash of marching footsteps as the Northern Expeditionary Army advanced. The ten gates of the city of Wuchang were like ten big staring eyes, nervous and angry.

A siege of the city seemed almost inevitable. The message came down from on high that they would have to defend the walls for a maximum of ten days; after ten days, the main army would have come across the Yangtze River to relieve the siege. Headquarters decreed that all houses near the walls outside the city were to be demolished within a set time to prevent the Northern Expeditionary Army from getting inside and using them to attack the city.

As soon as the order had been given, several shells were fired on them, and hundreds of houses collapsed. The inhabitants, who had already been forcibly removed, suddenly reappeared en masse; when they saw their houses being reduced to ruins in the blink of an eye right in front of them, they began to scream and wail, and the angry shouting and cursing stretched for miles along the river.

In a cottage within Binyang Gate Barracks, Xiyun's mother had been unconscious for two days and two nights. She wore a white bandage around her head, and the blood that had oozed through it was now caked and dry. She no longer felt any pain; she felt that her whole body had been broken into pieces.

Ma Weifu did not know how to face this family. He had arranged for them to eat and rest, and he told them that Yuan Zongchun had not returned from his mission. They believed what he said, and they did eat and rest as he arranged.

That evening, Xizi and Xiyun ran out to Binyang Gate to play and saw that the gate was closed. "Don't close the gate," Xiyun said. "Dad hasn't come back yet."

"Dad is going to come back through this gate," Xizi echoed.

The soldiers on guard sighed: "Isn't it sad for these two kids!"

Xiyun told her mother what the soldiers had said, and she turned her face to the wall.

Xiyun's mother tied up her newly-opened baggage and then called to Xiyun and Xizi: "Let's go! We're going to find your father."

"Uncle Ma said that Dad would come and find us," Xiyun pointed out.

"I can't wait," her mother said. She then continued: "Wherever he is now, that's where we will go."

"But it's already got dark," Xiyun said, "so how can we possibly find him?"

Ma Weifu arrived as soon as he heard the news that they were leaving. He had no choice but to explain, hesitating and stammering, that Yuan Zongchun had died on the retreat.

Xiyun's mother stared straight at Ma Weifu with her eyes wide open, without shedding a single tear. Ma Weifu was in a panic and wanted to say something to comfort her, but before he could get the words out of his mouth Xiyun's mother tried to kill herself by dashing her brains out against the wall.

When Xiyun heard that her father was dead, she was about to burst into tears, but just at that moment she saw her mother was going to try to kill herself, so she rushed over to try and stop her. Xiyun wasn't nearly strong enough to do so, and she was knocked over by her mother. But because of this, Xiyun's mother didn't die; although she broke her head open and there was blood everywhere, her life was not in danger.

Ma Weifu was so frightened he felt limp. He had thought the worst had already passed, but now a new wave of horror engulfed him, and he broke out in a cold sweat, which soon soaked him from head to foot. He seemed to see Yuan Zongchun's eyes hanging over the city wall, as bright as torches, boring right into his heart.

Xiyun's mother fell to the ground, her legs twitching. Xiyun and Xizi were so frightened that all they could do was scream. Ma Weifu had absolutely no idea what to do. "Mrs Yuan!" he shouted, "Mrs Yuan!" Then he bellowed: "Help! Quick! Call a doctor!"

Before the doctor arrived, Xiyun's mother came to her senses and stared up at Ma Weifu. Just a few seconds later, a long scream rose into the sky. This was the sound of a widow wailing for her dead husband, and it tore a bleeding hole through the hearts of the soldiers guarding Binyang Gate.

After two nights, Xiyun's mother dried her tears and regained consciousness. She didn't want to come back to her senses, but at night Xizi's little hand held on tight to her nose: even when he was asleep he was anxious, fearing that she would just stop breathing.

Xiyun's mother woke up and got out of bed. Ma Weifu, who had been sitting next to her for two nights, said: "Don't move. If you want something to eat, I'll have someone bring it."

"I am sure you have better things to do," Xiyun's mother said. "You don't need to stay here with me. I won't try to join Zongchun again." She looked at Xiyun and Xizi, who were sleeping soundly, and said: "Zongchun wouldn't want me to abandon the kids. If I don't look after them properly, how could I ever face him when I die?"

Ma Weifu felt that was dreadfully sad, but all he said was: "It's good that you feel that way."

Throughout its history, Binyang Gate had always been a key strategic spot to be fought over. For both attackers and defenders, this would inevitably be where the fiercest fighting took place. As to just how bad it would get, Ma Weifu could not even begin to imagine. Intuition told him that although he had been lucky enough to survive Tingsi Bridge, once the battle here began, he was going to die. He had only needed to cross swords with the Northern Expeditionary Army once; then he knew that his side was fighting for their pay, while their strength was forged from blood and fire. If one side is holding a rattan cane and the other side has a sword, even if there is a mountain behind the rattan cane while the sword is only dangling from the ends of a couple of your fingers, it is the cane that will break first. And I am just a thread on the end of the rattan cane, Ma Weifu thought.

Civilians should not be hanging about anywhere in the vicinity of Binyang Gate. If a battle were to be fought here, the whole Yuan family would be in danger. Ma Weifu thought it best that they be sent out of the city to stay in a safe place. He said to himself: Zongchun, this is probably the only thing I can do for you.

He spoke about this to Xiyun's mother: "There's likely to be fighting here, so you need to leave as soon as possible."

Her eyes were blank.

"We are not afraid," Xiyun explained, "besides which, I want to fight like Dad."

"This isn't a game," Ma Weifu said with a bitter laugh.

Xiyun's mother whispered: "I don't really mind if we die here."

Ma Weifu jerked his head up and said: "You mustn't say that. What would Staff Officer Yuan say if he found out you thought that way? How old are your two children? Do you have the right to let them die? I am sure you understand, Mrs Yuan."

Xiyun's mother's eyes were even more unfocused and vague. She looked at Ma Weifu and said: "What will happen to us if we don't die? We've escaped from bandits back home, and it was a terrible journey to get here – if we go back, who's to say we won't be killed there?"

Ma Weifu heard her out in silence. Yeah, he thought, where can she go with her two children? How can I help them when I am soon going to be dead myself?

When the major-domo, Old Nuo, appeared at Binyang Gate, Ma Weifu was still worrying about how to make arrangements for the Yuan family. When he saw Old Nuo, Ma Weifu's eyes lit up.

"Young master," Old Nuo explained, "your cousin Miss Peizhu is very ill. Can you go over and see her?"

Ma Weifu was shocked: "Peizhu is still in Wuchang? Why hasn't she left?"

"We were just about to set off," Old Nuo said, "when one of the rickshaw pullers told her about three men being beheaded yesterday evening – Miss Peizhu was so frightened she just fainted dead away."

"How is she now?" Ma Weifu asked anxiously. "Aren't people

beheaded all the time in Wuchang anyway? Peizhu must know that."

"Oh yes," the old man said, "but this time is different. The doctor came and said that it was psychological. When Miss Peizhu woke up, she wanted to find out which head was Chen's."

"One of her classmates?" Ma Weifu asked.

"I don't know," Old Nuo said. "You come and talk to her, OK?"

"I'll come right away," Ma Weifu said, "but I'll bring three more people with me."

When Ma Weifu told the story of Yuan Zongchun's death and how his family had come all this way to find him, the major-domo listened and was appalled. "I'm telling you all this," Ma Weifu said, "because I want you to take Miss Peizhu out of town tomorrow, and while you are about it you can take them too. Once the war is over, if I survive, I will take care of them. If I don't make it, please ask my uncle and cousins to look after them. After all, my friend and I will both have given our lives for this country."

Old Nuo made haste to say: "You should not say anything so inauspicious. You were born to good luck, and I am sure you will live to be a hundred."

Ma Weifu smiled indifferently and said: "Even lucky people get shot sometimes. You've got to tell them that from me."

"I will tell them what you said," Old Nuo answered. "I will repeat it, word for word."

25

IT TOOK a long time for the major-domo to find a rickshaw. All the rickshaws in the city had been hired by rich people to haul their luggage over to the Hanyang Wharf. However, Old Nuo had lived his entire life in Wuchang, and when he spotted a rickshaw puller that he knew, he dragged him over and would not let go until he agreed to take him to Binyang Gate.

Xiyun's mother was sitting there, dead to the world. Ma Weifu spent ages explaining to her about Hankou, the Foreign Concession, his uncle and his cousin. She hardly responded. But Xiyun understood. "Uncle Ma," she said, "I know what to do. I promise we won't cause much trouble."

Ma Weifu looked at Xiyun and suddenly realised that this little girl was quite exceptionally clever. "I am glad," he said. "I was a good friend of your father's. Now I'm going to be taking care of you on behalf of your Dad, and you have to do what I tell you to. You are going to be looking after your mother and younger brother. You can't let anything happen to them, do you understand?"

"I understand, Uncle Ma," Xiyun said.

There was only one rickshaw, so Xiyun's mother sat on it with the two children. Ma Weifu had to walk. "You go on ahead," he said, "and I'll follow you in a minute."

"That'll be fine," the major-domo said. "Miss Peizhu is at home alone. I need to get back as soon as possible."

Xiyun jumped out of the rickshaw and said: "I'll go with Uncle Ma."

Ma Weifu thought for a moment and then agreed.

"One other thing, young master," Old Nuo said. "Could you please find out which of the three heads is Chen's?"

A light rain spun through the air, and the wind stopped, as if unable to make its way through the raindrops. Long Street, that great avenue, was soon sopping wet, and the dust turned into mud, which the pedestrians trampled absolutely everywhere with their hurried footsteps.

Ma Weifu had not been out of the barracks for several days, and the chaos in the city was worse than when he first arrived. The shops on Long Street were mostly closed for the duration, their doors bolted. The shopkeepers had cut small holes in the heavy wooden shutters covering their doors, and they could be seen peering out from behind, shaking their heads. There were no shoppers to be seen here; military police were tramping back and forth, though they were buying things – money and goods being passed through the small holes. At the wider junctions, soldiers were busy hauling in sandbags and building fortifications. It was obvious that they were preparing for street battles. With so many people inside the city, what should we do if there really is fighting from street to street? Ma Weifu asked himself.

When he passed his favourite barber's shop, the door was closed tightly, but there seemed to be voices coming from inside. Ma Weifu looked through the crack in the door and saw some people having their heads shaved. When the people inside saw Ma Weifu looking at them, they were scared witless. The barber just laughed, and he shouted through the shutters: "Sir, do you want your head shaved?"

"The fighting is just about to start," Ma Weifu said, "and you are still fussing about having your heads shaved?"

The barber whispered: "When the military police see you going about with hair, they arrest you and claim you are a terrorist. Didn't you know that?"

Ma Weifu fell silent and went away without saying another

word. He actually didn't know anything about that, but even though he knew now, he wasn't about to interfere. It was just another wound to his heart. He did not like the students who gathered to make public speeches and parade through the streets because he felt that things were already bad enough, but their childishness and ignorance were making things worse. Can we make our country peaceful, prosperous and strong by making speeches and marching through the city? What fools! But Ma Weifu was appalled that they were being arrested and beheaded. All of these young people, these precious lives, were being cut short – they were gone forever. What's more, he understood that it would be impossible to cut off enough heads to make any difference. For every one person they beheaded, dozens more would appear before the headman's sword. The end result would be even more civil unrest, and they would never know peace. Ma Weifu did not want to live in troubled times. He longed for a quiet world. That way, he could go to his cousin Peizhu bravely and openly: not worrying that she would turn against him just because he is a soldier; not afraid that he could never show his love for her in case he died young on the field of battle. In such chaotic and dangerous times, he had felt he had no other choice than to join the army; as one battle followed another, how dare he hold out any hope for the future? How could he imagine he would get what he so much longed for?

As they approached Government Gate, the head suspended above it was already in sight. Xiyun saw it first and cried out: "There's a head up there!"

Ma Weifu put his body in front of her, took her hand and said over and over again: "Don't be afraid, don't be afraid. Keep your head down and don't look at him – just follow my footsteps."

As they came closer, Ma Weifu could see the face, which was familiar to him. He remembered this man had the surname Chen. He was a member of the Revolutionary Party. Not long before, he had been arrested for instigating strikes by workers at the Anglo-American Tobacco Company and Tai'an and Shenxin Mills. Ma Weifu had met him occasionally, and his eyes sparkled with impatience and vehemence. At that time, he had thought that people with faces like that would not live long in this kind of world.

Well, he had been proved right. But what could Peizhu have to do with someone like him?

Ma Weifu was lost in thought until suddenly his jacket was tugged a few times. Xiyun had questions: "Uncle Ma, why did they cut off his head? Why did they hang his head here?"

Ma Weifu turned back and lowered his head. He saw Xiyun looking behind them. He was shocked and said: "Xiyun, look away – you will have nightmares."

"No, I won't," Xiyun said. "In our village, I saw the bandits cut off Fusheng's head. I also saw Fusheng's mother's body after she killed herself. I didn't have any nightmares at all." When Xiyun said this, she was completely calm – her face showed not the slightest trace of fear. Ma Weifu was amazed. "Uncle Ma," Xiyun asked, "are you afraid?"

"Yes, I am," he said. "I am afraid of getting killed."

Xiyun smiled: "How come? Aren't people killed every day? When we were on the boat, there were bandits chasing us on the shore, and the gunfire was really loud – lots of people on the boat died. One man died right by my brother Xizi's feet – they'd been looking out at the scenery together."

Xiyun's calm response left Ma Weifu speechless. He was unable to explain this entirely irrational situation to a child in any rational way because all these horrors were normal in Xiyun's eyes. Ma Weifu was sad, and he sighed: "Let's go. Your mother may well have arrived by now."

When Ma Weifu and Xiyun arrived at the Hong mansion, Xiyun's mother was already seated in the living room. Since this was a new place, Xizi did not dare make a sound. He just leaned against his mother and held her hand tightly. Seeing Xiyun, he started to feel much better and shouted: "Sis!"

The major-domo, Old Nuo, said: "Young master, Miss Peizhu has been asking after you, fretting about why you haven't arrived yet."

When Ma Weifu heard this, he was immediately agitated and said: "You look after Madam Yuan, and I'll go and see her."

Hong Peizhu lay in bed, her face entirely bloodless. Her big eyes looked even more huge than normal, and they were filled with sadness. Her former liveliness and beauty had disappeared completely. Ma Weifu felt his heart contract; he had been running, but now he slowed down.

Hong Peizhu looked at him and said nothing.

"What has happened to you?" Ma Weifu asked.

Huge tears rolled from her welling eyes. "Tell me, cousin," she said, "which head is Chen's?"

Ma Weifu hesitated for a moment: he could almost see the face hanging high in front of him.

"You know, don't you," Hong Peizhu said, "so please tell me which head is Chen's!"

Ma Weifu slowly said: "Just now, I passed Government Gate – that's where his head is."

Hong Peizhu burst into a storm of tears, which flooded down like torrential rain. Crying, she screamed: "Why? Why kill him? Why? He was so young, so kind. He just wanted to change China. He just wanted to make the country rich and strong. He wanted everyone to live a good life. How can a man like that be killed? Why kill him?"

Hong Peizhu's cry was bleak; in her sorrow, Ma Weifu saw right down to the bottom of her heart. He was a little sad as he thought to himself: Did she really love this guy called Chen? Peizhu had told him that she could not love a soldier in the Beiyang Army because they had the blood of the common people on their hands. Peizhu had become more and more estranged from Ma Weifu ever since she entered college. He didn't understand the reason before, but now he knew – in Peizhu's eyes, this revolutionary was more attractive than he was. However, Ma Weifu was very puzzled. How could this revolutionary, who now had his head hanging over Government Gate, want exactly the same thing as he did himself?

Ma Weifu sat down beside Hong Peizhu's bed, took her hand, and watched her cry in silence. Xiyun and Xizi heard the crying and came running over with thudding feet. However, they did not dare come through the door; they leaned against the doorframe and looked in. "Don't cry," Xiyun said. "Dad died too, and I didn't cry."

Hong Peizhu stopped crying and asked: "Who are you? Who is your father?"

"This is Xiyun," Ma Weifu said. "Her father was my friend, and during the fighting at Tingsi Bridge he was… killed in action."

"Why didn't you cry?" Hong Peizhu asked. "Didn't you love your father?"

"I didn't feel like crying," Xiyun explained. "Everyone dies sooner or later, and I've seen many people die. I've seen so many that I don't feel like crying anymore. Dad died. Maybe I will die tomorrow, and you will die the day after that. People die every single day, so are you going to spend every single day crying?"

Xizi, leaning against the door next to Xiyun, now piped up: "But Sis, I want to cry. When Mum cries, I want to cry. When this lady cries, I want to cry too."

Xiyun slapped him and said: "Kids cry when all they've done is to fall over on their bottoms. There's nothing special about that."

"I find this girl's conversation really depressing," Ma Weifu said. "It seems that she's got the whole thing wrong, but at the same time you feel that she's quite right. Peizhu, there are too many people dying right now, so death has become quite a normal thing to happen. Our tears have become meaningless."

"But I want to cry for Mingwu," Hong Peizhu said.

"Mingwu?" Ma Weifu said. "Is that this guy called Chen? Who was he? Your boyfriend?"

"Oh, no," Hong Peizhu said, "but I loved him."

"Since you loved him," Ma Weifu said, "doesn't he count as your boyfriend?"

"But he wouldn't love me," Hong Peizhu pointed out.

Ma Weifu raised his voice, and his tone showed his dissatisfaction: "Why not?"

Hong Peizhu bowed her head and said: "He didn't want to fall in love with a girl from a rich family. He knows who Daddy is."

"If he really didn't care for you," Ma Weifu said, "why are you so upset about him?"

"But I really loved him," Hong Peizhu said, "and all I wanted was for him to be happy."

Ma Weifu did not know what to say.

"Cousin," Hong Peizhu said, "I am begging you, please take me over to Government Gate. I want to see him for the last time."

"It is pretty hellish out there, Peizhu," Ma Weifu said.

"I am not afraid!" Hong Peizhu retorted. "I'm going to pay my last respects to him. I'm going to burn some spirit money and some incense for him. I'm going to pray that he can rest in peace..."

From her place by the door, Xiyun suddenly cried out: "Is the Mingwu you are talking about Chen Mingwu?"

Hong Peizhu looked at her with glazed eyes.

"He isn't dead!" Xiyun said.

Hong Peizhu was so shocked, she managed to throw herself straight from the bed to be standing straight in front of Xiyun in a single movement: "What did you say? Do you know Mingwu? How do you know he's not dead?"

"Mum and I saved Mingwu, and Xizi too of course," Xiyun said proudly. "He wasn't arrested. The head that they've got hanging up isn't Chen Mingwu's, it absolutely isn't. I took a good look."

Hong Peizhu hugged Xiyun and cried with sheer joy. "Really? Is that true?" she asked. "Xiyun, were you sent by God? You've saved Mingwu, and now you've come to save me, haven't you?"

There was a smile on Xiyun's face, but it was an odd one. "I haven't been sent here by God," Xiyun pointed out. "I was brought by Uncle Ma. You should thank him."

Ma Weifu was moved by Xiyun's words, which echoed his own thoughts. He hoped that as soon as he appeared, Hong Peizhu would start feeling better. Now she did, and the child he brought with him had played her part. He made Hong Peizhu sit down on a chair, but when he turned around he saw a smile on Xiyun's face, which seemed to be hiding something that he wasn't sure he could catch. Ma Weifu suddenly felt that this seemingly simple and straightforward little girl had a mind of her own.

He gave instructions to the major-domo: "Tomorrow, you've got to get them all away from the city."

"I will," Old Nuo said. "We'll take the first steamer in the morning."

26

IT WAS that night they suffered a terrible defeat at Hesheng Bridge.

The fleeing Beiyang Army had to run several miles to make it back to the safety of Wuchang. They crossed the moat and passed through Binyang Gate on their mad rush into the city. The gate was like a great big gaping mouth, fixed in a constant scream.

Ma Weifu climbed up to the top of the watchtower over Binyang Gate. Colonel He, who commanded the troops stationed at the gate, had ordered his men to light all the lamps. Ma Weifu went over to him and asked: "Have we been defeated again at Hesheng Bridge?"

Colonel He pointed to the fleeing troops pouring through the barbican and said: "With soldiers like that, how could we not be defeated?"

Ma Weifu looked gloomy. He thought Colonel He had hit the nail on the head.

Almost all the lamps around the city wall were lit. When he looked down, Ma Weifu suddenly realised that the Northern Expeditionary Army had almost caught up with the tail of the defeated army, and they were continuing their pursuit. The lead soldiers of the Northern Expeditionary Army and the stragglers of the defeated Beiyang Army were passing through the barbican together in a solid stream, with no break between them. If the Northern Expeditionary Army got into the city and started fighting, it would be easy for them to take control of Binyang Gate from the inside, and then the rest of their forces would be able to march straight in. In this way, Wuchang would fall without a fight – before dawn, their flags would be hanging over these walls. At this point, fighting between the two armies inside the city would become inevitable.

Ma Weifu thought of all that this would entail, and sweat broke out all over his body. He pulled Colonel He off to one side and said: "Look over there!"

Colonel He bent over to have a look, took a deep breath, and then started to bellow at the top of his voice: "Quick! Close the gate!"

With all the noise and chaos, it took two minutes for the gate to close.

After the gate had closed with a resounding thud, there was a fierce banging from outside. Colonel He stood on top of the walls and shouted: "Open fire!" That immediately drove all the people at the foot of the city walls over onto the far side of the moat.

One lieutenant hesitated and said: "But there are still many of our men who haven't made it in. Are you trying to get us all killed?"

Colonel He roared at him: "Have you not seen how many Northern Expeditionary soldiers have already made it into the city?"

The lieutenant was too frightened to say another word.

"I will inform headquarters about this immediately," Ma Weifu said.

All the oil lamps in the vicinity of Binyang Gate were lit. Gunfire sounded sporadically from the top of the wall. The people who had been running for the safety of the walls had all been beaten back, screaming and crying.

Ma Weifu walked down the stairs of the watchtower to the sound of the guns. The defeated troops who had run back to the city and the Northern Expeditionary Army soldiers mixed among them seemed to have completely vanished from sight; they were hidden somewhere in these deep and dark alleyways. Ma Weifu frowned and said to a junior officer: "From tomorrow onwards, every street and lane should be lit up all night long."

The sky was showing a faint glow when Major General Liu

came by on patrol. He thumped Colonel He on the shoulder and said over and over again that he had been right to close the gate. Then he asked how many soldiers from the Northern Expeditionary Army had managed to get in.

"Not too many, I think," Ma Weifu said. "Maybe a dozen or so."

"Well," Major General Liu said, "a few small fry can't do us much damage. Keep all of the city gates closed from now on, and don't let civilians come anywhere near them."

When the sun came out, Ma Weifu followed Major General Liu up the watchtower and looked around. They could see that the Northern Expeditionary Army troops were fanning out on both sides of the railway line and massing densely around Wuchang. Suddenly, a flag showing the white sun against a blue ground was raised above the pagoda at Baotong Temple over on Hong Mountain. There were no voices to be heard in the streets and lanes outside the city walls where they had not had time to demolish the buildings, but they could see one or two faces peering out, scanning the walls of Wuchang.

"I want you to take down those houses for me," Major General Liu commanded. "Nobody should be able to get anywhere near the walls."

When he gave the word, the machine guns and artillery swung into action. There was an earth-shattering racket, and the houses just collapsed in flames, as dust and rubble shot through the sky. The people who had been hiding in these houses to try and escape the fighting were now forced out, scattering in all directions.

After that, all ten gates to the city of Wuchang were closed. It was 1 September 1926; a rainy and windy day.

Old Nuo, the major-domo, had no idea what was going on. When he realised that the rickshaw he had ordered was not coming, he was so anxious he went out onto the streets to find another. There was nobody there apart from a handful of soldiers in filthy uniforms. Suddenly, there was an appallingly loud noise as the guns fired, and Old Nuo was thrown head-over-heels against the nearest wall. He righted himself and sat up, his eyes practically popping out of his head. Mixed in with the sound of the guns, he could hear people shouting: "The city is closed! There is no way out! Hide as quickly as you can! The fighting has already begun!"

It was only then that Old Nuo understood what a terrible mistake they had made by not leaving the day before; that was their last chance to get out of the city. Having failed to leave the city, they might well have failed to save their own lives.

Old Nuo picked up his feet and ran back; once he got through the main gate, he used a huge bar to barricade it shut.

Hong Peizhu heard the sound and came out. "Aren't we supposed to be leaving?" she asked.

"We can't leave," Old Nuo explained, "because they've closed the city."

"I don't care," Hong Peizhu said, "because Mingwu must still be at the college, so I want to go and find him."

"The streets are full of soldiers," Old Nuo said, "and they all have a very nasty glint in their eyes. It isn't suitable for women to go out."

"Then you've got to help me to look for him," Hong Peizhu said.

"They've got artillery pounding the place," Old Nuo pointed out. "Once they've finished this round of fighting and we've got a bit of peace and quiet, then I'll go, OK?"

"OK," Hong Peizhu said reluctantly.

When Hong Peizhu returned to her room, she did not see any of the Yuan family. This surprised her, so she called out for Xiyun.

The girl climbed out from under the bed, revealing an ashen little face, and said: "Were you looking for me?"

"What were you doing down there?" Hong Peizhu asked.

"Dad told me once that I should hide under the bed if the artillery starts firing," Xiyun explained. "That's because when the house collapses, there will be a bed to carry the weight and it won't crush you."

"Really?" Hong Peizhu said.

"Oh, yes," Xiyun said. "You should come and hide with us."

Hong Peizhu hesitated for a moment. She could not imagine herself crawling under the bed.

Xiyun seemed to read her mind and said: "If you don't want to climb under the bed, under the table is fine too. Dad said that hiding under the table works just as well."

There was an octagonal table right beside her. Hong Peizhu looked under the table as if she was thinking about something else.

Xiyun climbed out from beneath the bed and pulled Hong Peizhu under the table. At that moment, another huge explosion occurred, as if the shell had passed right over the roof. With a shriek, Hong Peizhu and Xiyun hugged each other as tightly as they could.

Old Nuo came running in, looked around and called out for Miss Peizhu. Hong Peizhu answered from under the table. "There's nothing to be afraid of," the major-domo said. "They are shelling targets outside the city."

"What happens if they misfire?" Hong Peizhu asked.

"The guns on Snake Mountain are all aimed at Hong Mountain," Old Nuo explained. "Even if they misfire, they won't hit us here."

Hong Peizhu jumped out from underneath the table and beat her clothes to free them from dust.

"I've been checking up," Old Nuo said. "We still have a lot of food left in the house – enough to eat for ten days to two weeks without any problem. Mrs Wu in the kitchen didn't buy many vegetables yesterday because she thought there weren't too many people left to eat them."

"Ten days to two weeks?" Hong Peizhu said. "Are we going to have to hide for that long?"

"I don't know," Old Nuo said, "but when the young master comes over, you can ask him. We've got a number of mouths to feed here, so I have to make sure everyone will have enough to eat. If you can eat your fill, there's nothing else to fear. After a while, when the guns stop firing, I'll go out and see if I can buy some rice, some noodles and maybe a bit of meat and vegetables."

"I'd like a bowl of Hai Tianchun's noodles," Hong Peizhu said. "You can bring some back for me."

Xizi now climbed out from under the bed and said: "Uncle Nuo, I'd like some noodles too."

"God knows whether they're open or not," the major-domo said.

27

CHEN MINGWU HAD BEEN all over Wuchang and still could not find his mother. He forced himself to think hard about where his mother could possibly be, but he could not come up with anything.

Passing Government Gate, Chen Mingwu saw that there was a human head hanging up over it, and then all of a sudden he recognised Chen Dingyi. Chen Dingyi had originally also been a student at the teacher training college, but he had been quietly engaged in counter-intelligence work with the Beiyang Army at the same time. Chen Mingwu's heart was beating so hard that when he moved away from Government Gate, he was in no fit state to carry on searching for his mother. Instead, he went to his cousin's house. After resting there for a few hours, he had calmed down.

When Daying asked what was wrong with him, he did not say anything about Chen Dingyi. He just said that he'd been chased by the military police while he was out looking for his mother. His cousin couldn't understand that and kept on asking questions. Chen Mingwu thought for a moment and couldn't come up with a good explanation, so he said: "I'm afraid it's all down to my hairstyle. They just can't get enough of arresting students."

His cousin was married to a barber called Shuigen. He had a stall that he took out onto the street every day. Seeing that Chen Mingwu had nearly come a cropper because of his hair, he insisted that he should sit down on the stool so he could shave his head. "No wonder everybody's been having their heads shaved just recently," Shuigen remarked. "Whatever kind of hairstyle they had – long or short, pudding-bowl, whatever – they've been coming to have it all shaved off. I ask them why? They are afraid of being suspected of being students. What a world!"

During this conversation, with a couple of strokes of the razor, Chen Mingwu turned bald. Looking in the mirror, he saw the skin on his scalp shining. "God almighty," Chen Mingwu said, "I look like some kind of gangster."

His cousin didn't like his new look either. She threw him a hat and said: "It's good that it isn't too hot. Let's cover you up."

The city had been sealed, so where could his mother be? Chen Mingwu was desperate. He went to Ziyang Lake again; for many years, his mother had washed clothes for several large households living by the lake. She had laundered for them until her hands were discoloured and hard. Would she have gone there to hide? Daying had searched there the whole afternoon the day before. Chen Mingwu thought: Maybe Daying and mother managed to miss each other. Maybe mother is back there now.

But all that he found there was further despair. The owners of the big mansions had gone out of town, leaving only one or two servants at home. The servants were only prepared to speak through the peephole; they didn't even open the door. He carried on until it got dark, but he got nothing at all out of it.

Chen Mingwu was so worried and hungry that he had to go back to the college. On the way, he saw numerous soldiers carrying sandbags in the direction of Binyang Gate. There were coolies in among them and even a few old ladies tottering on behind the rest with sandbags on their backs.

Chen Mingwu suddenly realised that one of the old ladies was known to him. He followed her and asked: "Ma'am, do you know Mrs Chen He?"

"I don't have time to talk to you," the old lady said weakly.

Chen Mingwu took her sandbag and put it on his shoulder. "I'll carry it for you," he said.

The old lady breathed out, straightened up and asked: "Who are you?"

"I'm Mrs Chen He's son," he explained.

"Didn't your mother come home?" the old woman asked.

"We live outside the walls," Chen Mingwu explained, "and none of us were allowed to stay in our houses. I can't go home myself."

"A couple of days ago we all got conscripted for labour," the old lady said. "I was sent to Government Gate, but I don't know where your mother went."

Chen Mingwu was shocked: "How can you possibly have been conscripted?"

"Your mother and I are both employed by people who've gone over to Hankou," the old lady said, "so we were sitting around idle that day, and someone came and asked if we could carry sandbags. We thought we might be able to carry a few, so we went."

"But my mother?" Chen Mingwu asked urgently. "Where did my mother go?"

The old lady said: "I don't know, but I think she was sent to the Nanlou area of the city."

Chen Mingwu repositioned the sandbag on the old woman's back and ran towards the Nanlou District.

It was already dark, and the streets were pitch-black, but there were a few lights shining here and there in the Nanlou area. The fortifications there were finished; the breastworks formed by sandbags made a terrifying sight. Chen Mingwu knew that his mother would not still be there at this point in time, but he could not stop himself from walking over to have a look. A soldier jumped out and shouted: "What are you doing?"

"I am looking for someone," Chen Mingwu said.

"Who are you looking for?" the soldier asked.

"Two days ago, my mother was here carrying sandbags," Chen Mingwu explained. "I want to see if she is still here."

"What, are you blind?" the soldier said. "Does it look like there are still any civilians around here?!"

"I know that," Chen Mingwu said, "but I still wanted to see."

"Go away!" the soldier said. "Get out of here! You look to me like a student, for all that you're wearing a hat. Go back to school as soon as you can, because if a patrol spots you, they'll cut your head off."

Chen Mingwu felt his legs begin to buckle. Not knowing where his mother could possibly be was causing him terrible anxiety.

Chen Mingwu was an only son; his father died young, and he and his mother had nobody else. Although his family was poor, his mother brought him up like any young gentleman from a good family, working herself to the bone so that he could study, so that he could have fun. Even if they had no money to buy rice, she would rather sell her own blood than let Chen Mingwu do any work. He enjoyed his mother's love and took it for granted; he was accustomed to it and sometimes even thought it was right that his mother should slave for him the way that she did. Now his mother had suddenly disappeared, and he felt empty, as if his heart had been scooped out. Only then did he realise how important his mother was to him. Chen Mingwu squatted down on the ground and burst into tears. When the soldier saw him crying, he seemed sympathetic and said: "Don't cry. You've got to get out of here. If the patrol comes past, there is nothing I can do to help you."

When Chen Mingwu returned to the college, he saw all his classmates were looking nervous. They were clustered together, discussing whatever news they had heard. Chen Mingwu had been rushing around all afternoon, and he was now so hungry his stomach was rumbling audibly – he couldn't stand it anymore. The school canteen had finished serving, and there was no food to be had. Chen Mingwu rummaged in his dormitory and found a bag of biscuits in the trunk belonging to his roommate, Guo Wenjun. He poured himself some cold water, ate the biscuits, and tried to quell his hunger.

Before he had finished, Guo Wenjun returned, carrying two bags of lily powder and a bag of mung beans. Seeing Chen Mingwu, he was obviously startled: "You didn't leave?"

"I wasn't ever planning to," Chen Mingwu said.

"Where have you been these days?" Guo Wenjun asked.

Chen Mingwu, with a sad face, said: "My mother is missing."

"Oh, dear," Guo Wenjun said.

"What about you?" Chen Mingwu said. "Why didn't you go home?"

"I was going to take a boat to Hankou first thing yesterday morning," Guo Wenjun explained, "and then go back to Zhenjiang. But as it turned out, the city was already closed."

"Are there many students left here?" Chen Mingwu asked.

"A couple of dozen," Guo Wenjun said. As they were talking, they could hear shouting outside. "What is it now?" Guo Wenjun asked. "Let's go and have a look."

They went out of the dormitory to find that several people were gathered out in the corridor. Chen Mingwu shouldered his way past them and saw that a member of the college staff was putting up the notice. The notice said that students were to be prohibited from going to the front gate or to the mountains behind the college, in case of trouble.

Guo Wenjun shouted: "Can't we even go for a walk?"

The staff member answered: "We've already had two students 'out for a walk' arrested, and we don't know if they are alive or dead. If you don't mind being arrested, go right ahead and take that walk."

Having said this, he walked away, leaving silence behind him.

There were bursts of gunfire every so often. Chen Mingwu was very tired, but he couldn't sleep. The sound of gunfire faded, and the night passed slowly. The more tired he became, the more impossible he found it to sleep. So he clambered out of bed, pulled on some clothes and went out.

Chen Mingwu simply could not understand where his mother had gone. The thought of this made his heart ache. Having climbed up to the third floor, he looked around. The lights around the gates seemed to sway gently in the distance. Around the hill the college was built on, there were occasional flashes from lamps. There seemed to be a lot of traffic on the neighbouring streets, and the rumbling noise made the atmosphere this morning very depressing.

> *Without a sound, I climbed up the western block alone,*
> *The moon hanging in the sky like a hook.*
> *The fallen leaves of one lonely parasol tree,*
> *Make deeper still the limpid autumn locked up in the court below.*

Chen Mingwu was feeling very anxious, and the words of the last emperor of the Southern Tang came to his mind. He was imprisoned in Wuchang, and he had no idea where his mother could be... the whole experience was deeply shocking to him.

A man in a long coat joined him on the third floor. In the dim light, Chen Mingwu recognised him as Zhou Jincheng, from the Physics Department. Zhou Jincheng was well known throughout the college as a radical. Once, during a protest march, he and Chen Mingwu had both been chased by the military police. They fled together and took refuge for a whole day in the same place. They knew each other well.

Chen Mingwu called his name. Zhou Jincheng was surprised to see Chen Mingwu with a smile on his face. "Mingwu," he said, "what are you doing up and about?"

"I can't sleep," Chen Mingwu said.

"Oh, sure," Zhou Jincheng said, "with the way things are right now, how can anyone sleep? There's going to be a terrible battle here, and who knows how many ordinary people will suffer and die here? Who knows whether you and I will even survive?"

When Chen Mingwu heard that and thought about his mother, he felt even more tense and nervous.

Zhou Jincheng saw that he had no intention of saying anything. He pointed to the street and said: "Do you know what all that foreign oil is for? It is for burning down all the houses near the city walls – they want to raze them to the ground in order to prevent them being used in an attack on the city. Today, they have knocked down some houses with machine guns and smaller artillery pieces. In order to save shells, it is going to be necessary to burn the rest with the foreign oil."

Chen Mingwu's heart was instantly aflame, just as if his wooden shack was burning in his chest. He stared at Zhou Jincheng, a little dazed, unable to say a word for a long, long time.

When Zhou Jincheng saw Chen Mingwu's strange expression, he was shocked and said: "What's the matter? ...Oh, your house is outside Binyang Gate, so..."

Chen Mingwu wanted to cry, but he had no tears. For a time, he was just choking, and then he said: "They've just made me homeless..."

Both men were silent. After a long pause, Zhou Jincheng said: "Our homes may be gone, but at least our families are still alive.

Our green hills will never grow old, the blue waters of the river will carry on flowing – as long as we still have our families, everything will be fine."

"Do you really think so?" Chen Mingwu asked.

After a long pause, Chen Mingwu said: "Chen Dingyi is dead."

"Yes," Zhou Jincheng said, "I saw his head. Do you know what happened to Wang Zizheng?"

"I saw him two days ago," Chen Mingwu said, "so I expect he's over in Hankou by now."

"Oh, you don't know," Zhou Jincheng said.

"Know what?" Chen Mingwu asked.

"He was carrying papers with him," Zhou Jincheng said, "and he was planning to cross the river at dusk. When he left the city by Pinghu Gate, there were some military police there, and I guess he must have panicked. He went off to one side and tried to tear up the documents he was carrying, but the military police spotted what he was doing and arrested him. They pieced together the torn documents and found a letter addressed to Chiang Kai-shek, the generalissimo of the Northern Expeditionary Army. He was shot dead then and there, and his body was thrown into Ziyang Lake."

Chen Mingwu was stunned by the news. Before he even began to recover from this shock, intense firing began around Binyang Gate, flashing like lightning before a thunderstorm. Subsequently, the artillery batteries on Snake Mountain started to fire one after the other, and the explosions almost tore him to pieces.

Chen Mingwu and Zhou Jincheng seemed to have been hit by the sound of artillery shells. Together, they fell to the ground and could not move for the longest time.

28

HOLDING Binyang Gate was going to be crucial for holding the city of Wuchang. Ma Weifu was keeping a close eye on the situation, as he had been instructed by Major General Liu Yuchun.

The Northern Expeditionary Army outside the walls was a hive of activity. Ma Weifu stood up high and looked down, and in the distance he could see the soldiers of the Northern Expeditionary Army moving back and forth in a constant stream. On the first day the city was closed, even though there was an exchange of fire, it was obvious that the other side was only testing the waters; the real dangers would be coming later on.

Ye Ting's Independent Regiment had occupied Changchun Monastery. At the Battle of Tingsi Bridge, Ma Weifu had only escaped from their grasp by the skin of his teeth. Now, once again, they were stretching out their hands towards him, across the city wall, across the moat, with a force that gave him a nearly physical jolt. Ma Weifu's mind had gone completely blank, and the fear that had settled in the marrow of his bones now spread throughout his body.

Once the fighting starts, he thought, I am going to die.

The Beiyang Army, up on top of the walls, was feeling very depressed. The two defeats at Tingsi Bridge and Hesheng Bridge had seriously damaged their morale. Ma Weifu wanted to say a few words to cheer them up, but he found he could not say a thing. The atmosphere in the watchtower over the walls, like the weather at the end of summer, was suffocating, and as dusk fell the gloom made them even more depressed.

The shades of night finally fell. It was the first night the city had been closed. The shining lamps strung from the walls flashed in the wind, now bright, now dim. The city was enveloped in darkness, and it was impossible to see the ground. Hong Mountain, like a black cloth, lay draped between heaven and earth, though sometimes you could see the light from a fire leaping out of the darkness. The pagoda on top of the mountain had been engulfed by the night, but the outline of Changchun Monastery was still dimly visible by the light coming from Binyang Gate.

For many, this night was the same as any other, but for the city of Wuchang this was the beginning of the nightmare.

Ma Weifu gazed out into space for a moment, and then explained to the officer on duty: "Tell your men to keep a close eye on things. If you so much as blink, it's going to be our people who will be killed."

Having said this, he was about to go downstairs when a soldier whispered: "Sir, there are loads of people from the Southern Army coming this way. If they set up ladders to attack the walls, can we hold out?"

Ma Weifu did not need to think about his answer; he just turned and said: "Why shouldn't you be able to hold out? Wuchang is over a thousand years old, the walls here are ten metres high and thick to match – this isn't some tiny little stockade that you can get a few ladders into position and just climb into. Besides, we are way up above them – we've got guns, ammunition, torches and stones all ready and waiting. They may attack in force, but that doesn't mean they can take the walls!"

The soldier thought about it and said: "I guess you are right."

As he walked down the stairs from the watchtower, Ma Weifu said to himself: The only thing is, surely they are not going to limit themselves to making a frontal assault on us.

Fierce gunfire started to sound at a few minutes past ten o'clock in the evening. At that time, Ma Weifu was forcing himself to rest.

He was lying in bed reading a book of Xin Qiji's poems. He had always appreciated Xin's heroism; in fact, his enlistment in the army was closely related to his admiration for Xin Qiji.

> *Drunk, I pick up the lamp to inspect my sword,*
> *I awake from my dreams to the sound of the horns*
> *blown to alert the barracks.*

He had hoped to experience such scenes for himself. But now, having retreated to Wuchang after a series of defeats in battle, having witnessed with his own eyes the deaths of his closest friends, his dreams were completely shattered. He had neither helped a rightful ruler to take power, nor had he won any kind of name for himself to be passed down to posterity. Although he was still young, he felt that his entire life had been wasted.

He could hear the bugle call interspersed with the sound of the guns. Ma Weifu had almost closed his eyes, but now he opened them at once. He jumped out of bed and went straight to the watchtower, without even thinking what it was he was doing. The watchtower was in chaos; several soldiers were running over to light the lamps. Ma Weifu shouted to them: "Light all the lamps around the city wall!"

When the lamps were lit, everything was as clear as day inside and outside the city walls. The soldiers of the Northern Expeditionary Army, who had rushed across the moat and were now erecting scaling ladders up against the walls, were completely exposed to view. So the machine guns on the watchtower went into action, and grenades were tossed down too.

Ma Weifu bent over to have a good look; even if the troops of the Northern Expeditionary Army managed to get up to the top of the scaling ladders, they were still more than two metres from the top of the walls. He breathed a sigh of relief.

It was a fierce battle on both sides. Colonel He, commanding the counter-attack from the watchtower, suddenly burst out laughing; Ma Weifu looked at him.

He seemed to have guessed Ma Weifu's question and giggled: "Isn't it great that the wall is this high! You see, they are firing to cover their attack, but the bullets just don't get this far, so they're shooting their own guys."

Ma Weifu looked closely, and sure enough he was right.

There were four big guns at the artillery battery at the Baobing Memorial Hall for the Revolution of 1911 on Snake Mountain. When they joined in the counter-attack and started shelling, the troops on the walls, who already had the upper hand, became even more confident of victory.

Colonel He shouted in the direction of Snake Mountain: "Aim carefully! Don't let anyone get over the moat!" But the gunners seemed to be entirely oblivious, and all the shells flew somewhere out into the distant dark wilderness. They were no deterrent to the enemy attacking the city. They seemed to be firing salutes: it sounded like a bombardment, but nobody was getting killed.

The people in the watchtower were cursing them heartily: "Bunch of clowns! Are you all completely blind!" But there was no point in yelling at them, and the shells continued to fly into the distance. The defeated Northern Expeditionary Army dragged away their wounded, and they retreated beyond the moat, leaving just a few corpses behind.

The battle was over. The soldiers in the watchtower suddenly realised that they had won, and it was an easy victory. Their excitement was uncontrollable; the emotions they had been bottling up for many days was now suddenly released. The cheers from the watchtower were thunderous, and for a time they resounded through the skies.

The victory boosted the confidence of the defenders enormously. They decided that their first two defeats had been accidental: it was because they had underestimated the enemy. Now, as long as they took the situation sufficiently seriously and fought all out, how difficult could it be to defeat the Northern Expeditionary Army? That afternoon, the defending garrison formed a mixed detachment of soldiers and attacked out from Bao'an Gate. The morale of the troops who joined this sortie was certainly strong; they hoped to open a gap in the Northern Expeditionary Army's siege of Wuchang. Ma Weifu ran up the steps of the watchtower when he heard the news. He knew that this sortie was very unlikely to succeed.

Intense gunfire could be heard throughout the day in the vicinity of Bao'an Gate. Soon the news came through: the units who had participated in the sortie had been attacked head-on by the Northern Expeditionary Army. After a few skirmishes, they had been defeated and turned back. Headquarters then gave orders that the army should stick to its guns and not attempt to leave the security of the walls to fight.

Ma Weifu stood by Binyang Gate, shouting at the soldiers to emphasise the seriousness of this order. "Don't think that defending the walls is going to be easy," Ma Weifu said, "because the worst is yet to come! The Northern Expeditionary Army has won every battle they've fought all the way to Wuchang – if they weren't pretty damn strong, how could they have done that? We're going to be doing well if we hang onto this city."

Over on Hong Mountain, this was a tragic moment. In the bitter silence, the determination to kill was growing. Ma Weifu shivered for no reason.

An even more dreadful attack now began, and again it took place overnight.

The Northern Expeditionary Army's artillery, located on Hong Mountain, was the first to fire, and in a flash the explosions rent the air. The noise and flash awakened everyone in the city. Zhonghe Gate and Binyang Gate were under attack simultaneously. In that instant, the artillery inside the city counter-attacked. With the artillery shelling from both sides, the explosions lit up Wuchang as if it were broad daylight.

Ma Weifu ran straight to the northeastern corner of the walls. The walls near Binyang Gate were clearly much lower than elsewhere because of the little hill just outside them. Sure enough, the Northern Expeditionary Army that attacked the city was using this small hill to make it easy for them. Both sides held their own heights, and the screaming shells crossed each other in a dense, horrifying barrage.

In the middle of the night, the defenders on the tops of the walls suddenly realised that the enemy's suicide squads had managed to cross the moat under heavy artillery fire and were now right under the wall. Four or five scaling ladders had already been put in position. Ma Weifu and Colonel He were screaming at their men: "Light all the lamps! Now!"

Instantly, Binyang Gate was lit up. In order to bring as much light to the scene as possible, the soldiers defending the walls had dipped lumps of cotton wool in tung oil to make flares, which they now threw out over the top of the walls. The Northern Expeditionary Army seemed unafraid as they attacked. One man fell, and another took his place. They held revolvers which they fired with a sound like thunder, as they desperately clambered towards the walls.

The main force of the defenders had gone up to the top of the watchtower. With the bright light coming from their home-made 'flares', they were lobbing down hand grenades to keep the walls impregnable. They significantly outnumbered the attackers, and they were also much better equipped. One reckless attacker came flying up one of the scaling ladders, ignoring the bullets and flames raining down on him, and managed to make his way up onto the watchtower, frightening the defenders who did not know what to do. As they hesitated, another man started to climb up the tower too.

From his position at the other corner, Ma Weifu saw that the situation had taken a turn for the worse. He shouted hoarsely: "Anyone who retreats will be beheaded! Bayonets to the front! Kill them all! Chop them to pieces! Burn the ladders!"

The bayonet squad came in from one side. Their weapons glittered with a silvery light under the lamps, as they flew through the darkness. The suicide squads, who had almost managed to get up to the top of the walls, were unable to withstand the ferocity of the defenders and retreated. Watching them getting killed or falling off the walls, Ma Weifu breathed a long sigh of relief.

As the morning sun grew ever brighter, the gunfire started to die away. The exhausted defenders carried the wounded down off the towers, one after another, and sent them to hospitals in the city. Ma Weifu stood at a gap in the city walls and looked towards the high ground where they had fought so fiercely. On that small slope, corpses were everywhere; the sun rose over the treetops on Hong Mountain, shining brightly on the grasslands and ponds and on those who had lost their lives. Ma Weifu had very mixed feelings about what had just happened.

> *Heaven and Earth are boundless and without end!*
> *I am all alone, and my tears keep rolling down my cheeks.*

That was the poem he called to mind just then.

29

FOR SEVERAL DAYS, gun and artillery fire resounded through the city with bangs like popcorn, and during the night half of the sky seemed to be lit up at any one time. The racket, the firing, the screaming, was truly daunting for the civilian inhabitants of the city. Spent bullets floated through the air like ghosts, passing here through a door and there through a window, silently embedding themselves into walls or hitting people. All of a sudden, the main topic of conversation in the streets and alleys had changed to concerns for who was dead and who had been injured. People came to believe that it was all a matter of luck: it was your fate to be killed by a stray bullet; if you were not killed, that too was a matter of luck. Who can control his own destiny when you are being shelled day after day?

The most terrible thing was the artillery fire from Snake Mountain. Because it was too close to the city, if a gun fired, the explosion flashed and the bang sounded right overhead. It shook the ground and tore through the sky: it was truly, truly terrifying. Every gun seemed to be aimed right at you. Every explosion forced people to crouch down on the ground.

Outside the city, the smoke was so dense that the streets and alleys were covered with dust – it got everywhere. Wuchang's busiest shopping street, Long Street, now had but few pedestrians to be seen. The radio had been issuing warnings to all inhabitants not to go out and not to try and watch the progress of the battle, so as not to be hit by stray bullets. They also warned you that before going to sleep at night, you should choose a place where you could be safe.

Hong Peizhu slept under the bed these days. Lying on the floor was damp and hard, which made her back ache. With the firing going on all night, she suffered from one nightmare after another. She shouted and screamed in her dreams, and often she had to be shaken awake by Xiyun who was sleeping beside her.

"You scream so loudly," Xiyun told her, "that it is even more terrifying than the cannons firing outside the city."

Hong Peizhu grimaced bitterly and said: "I don't hear myself."

In the middle of the night, she started screaming again, and the screaming made her feel dreadfully upset. Xiyun's voice seemed to come to her from far away: "Wake up! You are having a nightmare!" Hong Peizhu woke up. Xiyun looked at her and said: "Did you dream about Mingwu?"

"What was I shouting?" Hong Peizhu asked.

"You were shouting, 'Don't die! Don't die!'" Xiyun said.

Hong Peizhu tried to recall her dream; she was trying to return to the scenes she had witnessed in her sleep. Everything seemed to be covered with blood. Chen Mingwu's head had been severed from his body: his head was on the top of the house, but his body had been thrown to one side of the road. His face was red with recently-spilt blood. When he saw Hong Peizhu, he grinned and said: "My body has gone. There is only my head left."

Hong Peizhu smiled sadly and said: "I dreamed of him. I dreamed that he had his head cut off. His head kept smiling at me."

"Mingwu has not been killed," Xiyun said. "I got a good look at the head."

Hong Peizhu said: "But why did I dream that he was beheaded? Is he alive or dead?"

"Mingwu is not dead," Xiyun said firmly. "I know for a fact that he's not going to die."

Hong Peizhu didn't say any more, but she also did not go back to sleep. She recalled everything about Chen Mingwu. His excited speeches, his shy smiles, his gentle conversation, even his tactful refusal of her love, his subtle expressions and the bitter twist of his mouth – it all flooded into Hong Peizhu's memory together.

As she sat there in a daze, the sky brightened, and the sound of the guns started to die away, indicating that this round of the battle had come to an end. Hong Peizhu got out of bed and quickly put on her skirt. Xiyun followed; she seemed to have guessed what Hong Peizhu wanted to do. "You're going to go out," she said.

"Don't make a sound," Hong Peizhu ordered. "I'm going to the college to find Mingwu. If I don't find him, the worry will drive me mad."

"It isn't safe out," Xiyun said. "How can you go anywhere? At least let the major-domo go with you."

"Don't say a word to him," Hong Peizhu said, "because then I won't be able to go anywhere."

Xiyun thought for a moment and then said: "How about I go with you?"

Hong Peizhu looked at Xiyun and thought it would be better to have a companion given the violence going on outside.

"I have one condition," Xiyun said. "If we can't find Mingwu, we have to come straight back."

Hong Peizhu and Xiyun walked along the little side street and then turned out onto the main road. There were several people standing around the shop on the corner, which sold pickles. Xiyun came forward and took a good look, then she silently returned to where Hong Peizhu was standing.

"What is it?" Hong Peizhu asked.

"A man went to buy pickles," Xiyun said, "and before he left, he was killed by a stray bullet. Nobody seemed to know who he was. Everyone is helping to try and identify him."

Hong Peizhu felt her hair stand on end. She clutched Xiyun's hand tightly and walked on just as quickly as she could.

"That hurts," Xiyun said. "You're pinching me."

The main gate to the college was locked, and the side doors were blocked by sandbags. Hong Peizhu couldn't find a way in, and she was getting more and more flustered. She shouted at the top of her voice, but no one answered.

"I wonder if we can get over the wall somewhere," Xiyun said. Having said that, she dragged Hong Peizhu around the perimeter wall to find a good place. She saw that there was a big hole in the back wall. It was obvious that people had dug it on purpose. Hong Peizhu and Xiyun now squeezed through.

The elegant college grounds and buildings were no more. Everything had been wrecked, as if it had just been through an earthquake. The roof of the conference hall had been smashed to pieces, and the corners of the walls were broken. The walls of the washing facilities and canteen were riddled with holes, big and small, from the bullets. All the paths were covered with loose tiles, cinders and broken glass, but there was not a soul to be seen. Every now and then there was a sound overhead, as if a bullet had just flown past.

But Xiyun was not the least bit afraid; she was full of curiosity about the college. Looking around, she kept saying: "It's all so beautiful. I'm going to study here when I grow up."

"Great," Hong Peizhu said, "then you can stay at my house during the holidays."

Xiyun was really surprised: "Can I?"

"Sure," Hong Peizhu said. Somehow, Xiyun's cheerfulness unconsciously infected Hong Peizhu; the pain and fear in her heart started to dissipate, as if one strand of emotion after another were being pulled away.

Chen Mingwu's dormitory was unlocked, but there was nobody inside. The table was covered with books, and there was a teapot standing there, with biscuit crumbs all over the ground. "Mingwu must have been here these last couple of days," Xiyun said. Hong Peizhu asked why, and Xiyun explained: "If not, what are all these biscuit crumbs doing here? The college canteen must be closed, because otherwise Mingwu would not be so hungry he has to eat biscuits."

"You have a point," Hong Peizhu said, "but where is he now?"

"Do you think he has gone somewhere to hide?" Xiyun asked.

Hong Peizhu thought for a moment and then said: "Come with me!"

Hong Peizhu ran to the gymnasium with Xiyun. Sure enough, there were more than a dozen students from all departments seeking safety there. Hong Peizhu could not see Chen Mingwu anywhere, but she spotted Zhou Jincheng, who was talking angrily to several classmates. Hong Peizhu approached quietly and listened to him.

"The police headquarters sent people to enquire about the two men arrested at the foot of Snake Mountain yesterday," he said. "They wanted to know whether or not they were our students, because if so, we could get them out on bail. The college immediately wrote an official letter and got together a payment of three silver dollars, with Mrs Zhang making a special journey to deliver it in person. And what's the result? Mrs Zhang was held up on route by some grunt who robbed her of the money. What kind of a world is this? Soldiers are robbing people in broad daylight, out in the streets of the city!"

Zhou Jincheng's voice had just fallen, as his listeners burst out shouting and cursing. Hong Peizhu tugged on his sleeve. He turned to Hong Peizhu and asked in surprise: "What's the matter, miss?"

"We have met once before," Hong Peizhu said. "I'm a friend of Chen Mingwu. I was there once when you came looking for him."

"Oh, a friend of Mingwu's," Zhou Jincheng said happily. "That's great!"

"I want to know where he is," Hong Peizhu said. "I've been looking for him for days."

"Well, it's good you're here," Zhou Jincheng said. "Mingwu is in a bad state right now."

This was a disturbing thought for Hong Peizhu, and her voice was loud: "What's wrong with him?"

Zhou Jincheng looked at her in surprise and said: "I think he's suffering from shock. He's not eating or sleeping."

Hong Peizhu was now even more anxious and kept repeating: "Where is he? Where is he?"

Zhou Jincheng looked at Hong Peizhu in surprise and then said: "Follow me."

Hong Peizhu followed Zhou Jincheng, and Xiyun followed Hong Peizhu. They went to the music room, and Zhou Jincheng said: "He's inside."

Hong Peizhu looked in, somewhat confused: "Where?"

Zhou Jincheng walked straight over to the small stage and pointed underneath.

Not only was Hong Peizhu horrified, even Xiyun was deeply

shocked. Chen Mingwu's clothes were filthy and torn as he hid there, curled into a ball. He had shaved his head and seemed unaware of their arrival.

Xiyun screamed: "Mingwu!"

Hong Peizhu rushed over and cried: "Mingwu! Are you OK? What on earth has happened to you?"

Chen Mingwu ignored them completely and did not move. Hong Peizhu cried and shook him. She reached out and touched his face, but he did not respond. Zhou Jincheng pulled Hong Peizhu away and said: "Yesterday, he was still able to say a word or two to me. Today, he is in a much worse condition. He really needs to get to a hospital as soon as possible."

"What could have happened?" Hong Peizhu cried. "What kind of shock could do this to him?"

"They've burned his house down," Zhou Jincheng said, "his mother is missing, and he's heard the news that Wang Zizheng was shot."

"Wang Zizheng was shot?" Hong Peizhu exclaimed.

"Yes," Zhou Jincheng said, "it happened over by Pinghu Gate – his body was thrown into Ziyang Lake."

Hong Peizhu's heart almost stopped; she'd seen Wang Zizheng just a few days ago. She could see him standing in the doorway, talking to her. She sobbed: "That's dreadful! What happened to Wang Zizheng is so horrible, and so is what's happened to Mingwu."

Zhou Jincheng sighed and then said: "It is our misfortune to be born in troubled times. Sooner or later, each one of us will experience this kind of tragedy."

"You've got to help me," Hong Peizhu said. "Help me get Mingwu to my house. I'll make sure the doctor comes to see him."

Zhou Jincheng thought for a moment and then said: "That's a good idea. Let me go and find some classmates to help move him."

30

For several days in a row, Binyang Gate was the centre of the firestorm, and guns there fired constantly. They fought during the day, and they fought during the night; there was a constant state of high alert inside and outside the city. Ma Weifu had thought that the enemy would attack the city by stealth under cover of darkness, but in the daytime he often saw suicide squads rushing towards the city wall to try cradling the explosives they were carrying under a barrage of fierce firing.

The forces defending the walls were positioned high above them, so it was easy to concentrate fire during any attack of this kind. In the daytime, long before the enemy had got anywhere close to the city walls, the machine guns could pin them down, preventing both further advance and retreat. The soldiers who had charged forward were trapped, and few of them lived to return to their bases. At night, they gathered in groups, carried bamboo scaling ladders and attacked the walls in the dark; some brave people even took ladders to try and climb the battlements. Although they were not afraid of death, they were still human; either they were shot dead by the defenders, or they dropped from the ladders, or they fell to their deaths from the walls.

Colonel He could not understand what on earth they thought they were doing and said so to Ma Weifu: "They are crazy! Are they trying to get themselves killed?"

Ma Weifu was puzzled too and suggested: "Maybe they really don't mind dying like this?"

News came from headquarters that their defence of the city had significantly increased the prestige of the army, and the enemy's casualties were five times greater than their own. Major General Liu declared that when the battle was over, he would reward all his men generously. The defenders of the city cheered, and their morale soared.

However, as the last shouts of joy still lingered in the air, news came that shocked Ma Weifu to the core: Liu Zuolong,[1] who was stationed in Hanyang, had defected to the enemy with all his forces without a shot being fired: Hanyang was lost. Liu Zuolong's men then attacked Hankou with the Northern Expeditionary Army, and General Wu led his guards on foot to Jiang'an Station, where he boarded a train and fled to the north. Hankou was lost. Wuchang was now completely surrounded.

After Hanyang was taken, aeroplanes began to circle the skies over Wuchang every day, dropping leaflets and flying away. The leaflets proclaimed that the city had twenty-four hours in which to surrender. If it did not surrender, they would blow a hole in the walls with their artillery. Inside Wuchang, it was immediately rumoured that Deng Yanda[2] was the commander of the besieging forces and that the Revolutionary Army would be ordered to use artillery to attack Tongxiang Gate and blast a gap in the city wall there.

The area around Tongxiang Gate immediately descended into complete chaos. People living in that part of the city dragged their children off in the direction of Snake Mountain overnight. But every day there was an artillery barrage underway on Snake Mountain, and the guns would fire when you least expected it, with an earth-shattering, ear-splitting roar. People then poured down the hill because they found this was even more frightening than the prospect of staying around Tongxiang Gate, so they now ran back home as quickly as they could. With all this rushing back and forth, the inhabitants of the city looked like rats caught in a flood, and they threw the whole city of Wuchang into a tumult.

Ma Weifu hastened to headquarters at Jiangxi Guild Hall to see

Major General Liu Yuchun. At the entrance, he met several senior officers, and everyone's face was burning.

Ma Weifu grabbed Staff Officer Jiang, commanding the defence of Bao'an Gate (a man he knew well), and he asked in a low voice: "How is it going?"

Staff Officer Jiang shook his head: "The major general isn't here, but he's sent word that Cao Kun's former troops are coming down from the north, and will be here any day now. Sun Chuanfang's Five Provinces Coalition Army is also coming up in support of us to relieve the siege. We just need to hold firm here in Wuchang and defend the walls at all costs."

Ma Weifu thought for a moment and then asked: "Do you believe that?"

Staff Officer Jiang smiled: "How about you?"

Ma Weifu did not believe a word of it, but he could not say so. Liu Yuchun was known for his resolute obedience to orders, and his subordinates likewise.

Ma Weifu walked through the streets and alleyways on his way back to Binyang Gate. The streets and marketplaces were forlorn, with only the occasional pedestrian passing by with a tense, fearful face. Two or three of the guns on Snake Mountain had been turned and were now firing at Gui Mountain. Hankou and Hanyang had already fallen into the hands of the Northern Expeditionary Army, and standing on any elevation you could almost see the flags with their white suns on blue grounds fluttering along the banks of the Yangtze and the Han River.

Ma Weifu remembered that his cousin Hong Peizhu was ill, and he was also worried about the situation of the three members of the Yuan family. He decided to make a detour and headed for the Hong mansion.

When he got to the crossroads, a wealthy-looking old gentleman stopped Ma Weifu and asked: "Officer, are we going to open negotiations or not? I've heard that the Southern Army are bringing up many Russian-style guns. If they really start shelling the city every day, will there be any survivors in Wuchang at all?"

Ma Weifu said: "Sir, the enemy kill people without batting an eyelid – if we surrender, they will just massacre us."

"We could beg them not to kill us," the old gentleman said.

"Our commanders have ordered us to defend the city," Ma Weifu explained, "so that is what we are going to do."

Ma Weifu walked on, but the old man cried out in dismay: "You are talking about hundreds of thousands of civilian lives! Just think about it…"

That voice stabbed Ma Weifu right to the heart. If the Northern Expeditionary Army really did bring up Russian-style artillery, their shells could easily punch a hole in the city walls. Even if the soldiers on the watchtowers then fought to the last man, they would never be able to keep them out. Besides which, shells don't look where they have landed before they explode; more than half the inhabitants in the city could easily be blown to pieces in the process. With this in mind, he was so anxious that he couldn't think about his own personal affairs. He turned around and rushed back to Binyang Gate.

By the time he made it back to Binyang Gate, it was dark. Ma Weifu went into his room, but before he had even had time to get a drink of water, a soldier came to report that he had arrested a foreigner trying to get out of the city. Ma Weifu was surprised; since the beginning of the battle, the houses in the area over on Garden Hill where the foreigners all lived each had the national flag of their respective country hoisted up on the roof as a sign that they were to be protected. For the last couple of days, that was the safest place in Wuchang. Even if the Northern Expeditionary Army marched into the city, they weren't going to interfere in the slightest with any of them. Ma Weifu could not understand what this foreigner could be thinking. "Bring him here to see me," he said.

The person that the soldiers brought in was Mr Meng. He had been bound with a hemp rope, wound many times around his waist. Ma Weifu recognised him the moment he came in sight. "Mr Meng, what on earth do you think you are doing?" he asked.

"I knew you were guarding Binyang Gate," he replied. "Your uncle told me before he left. So I thought that would be the best place to get out of town because even if I was caught, I could explain what I wanted to achieve."

"So why do you want to go out of the city?" Ma Weifu asked.

"It's impossible to leave right now with the two armies fighting, and the enemy will shoot you dead if they spot you."

"I know it's difficult, but I have to go," Mr Meng explained. "I have to take the risk."

Ma Weifu indicated that he would like to hear more about his reasoning.

"I was going to beg them to stop the shelling," the foreigner said, "on behalf of the two hundred thousand innocent civilians inside the walls of Wuchang."

Ma Weifu was stunned; for a moment, he did not speak.

"Therefore," the foreigner continued, "I am asking you to let me leave."

"Are they going to listen to you?" Ma Weifu asked.

"Yes, I believe they will," the foreigner told him. "I am a neutral party. You have two armies fighting for different reasons. We have no right to interfere; and the civilian population has no power to stop you. But there is an old saying in China that he who wins the hearts and minds of the people wins the world. If they shell the city, tens of thousands of houses are going to be destroyed, and tens of thousands of people are going to be killed – their hearts will be completely lost, and international public opinion will condemn this as a massacre. If they prosecute the campaign like this, no matter how hard they try in the future, they will not win the hearts and minds of the people. That's what I'm going to tell them."

Ma Weifu revolved this idea through his mind. He thought that although Mr Meng's statements were completely reasonable, once battle was joined, was anyone willing to listen to reason? The soldiers of the Northern Expeditionary Army were also professionals. How could someone as insignificant as Mr Meng stop their attack on the walls?

The foreigner seemed to have guessed what he was thinking and said: "Do you think that I am just some ivory-tower intellectual? But it's better to have someone to go and talk to them rather than to have nobody say a word, right?"

Ma Weifu thought for a moment and said: "Yes, you're right."

Ma Weifu decided to help the foreigner leave the city. He called Colonel He over, and they talked for a few minutes, after which the colonel agreed too. But they could not simply open the gate. If something went wrong, nobody could possibly take responsibility for that. Besides, there were numerous sandbags heaped up behind the gate, and it would be very troublesome to move them. Ma Weifu took the foreigner some way away from where the fighting was going on and ordered the soldiers to tie a hemp rope around Mr Meng's waist and then lower him down from the top of the wall once they had found a discreet place to do so.

"I can't let you leave the city openly," Ma Weifu explained, "because the enemy might simply shoot you down like a dog. It'll be safer if we lower you down from here. Once you're on the ground, it'll all be a matter of luck."

Mr Meng looked completely calm. He said equably: "It's a mission of mercy, so God will be on my side."

Lowered into the endless darkness of the night, the foreigner landed safely and in silence. He stood at the foot of the wall, shook the rope to show his gratitude and then disappeared in the blackness.

Looking down just at the moment when Mr Meng turned around, Ma Weifu thought: Maybe he will be able to persuade them. It is not going to be easy to attack the city, and the Northern Expeditionary Army has already suffered heavy casualties. Maybe the foreigner will give them a graceful way to back out of their attack. That would be a blessing for everyone.

31

GRADUALLY, the people of Wuchang became accustomed to the deafening sound of gunfire. Even when the guns were going off with a sound like popcorn right in front of them, they went about their business as usual. If you wanted to survive, you had to leave your home. Pockmarked Liu, who made a living sharpening knives, was asleep in his bed when a shell landed on the roof of his house. The shell did not explode, but a beam collapsed under the weight, and he was crushed to death. After the city was closed, Shorty Zheng, the water-carrier, was rushing about outside from morning till night. A spent bullet pierced a hole in his hat but did not kill him. So if God wants you dead, there is nowhere to hide. If He doesn't want you dead, even if you spend all day wandering about in the streets, nothing at all is going to happen to you. This became a mantra of the inhabitants of Wuchang.

About ten days after the fiercest battle took place, the guns that had been firing all day stopped abruptly; only sporadic shots could be heard, coming from somewhere far away.

There were now more rumours in circulation than there were people on the streets. Some people said that the Revolutionary Army did not bombard the city with Russian artillery because Mr Meng, one of the foreigners living over on Garden Hill, went out of the city one night and risked his life to beg them not to injure civilians by mistake. The Revolutionary Army agreed to his request on the spot, so that was the reason why the shelling had stopped. They also said that when the foreigner returned to the city, he came in via Wusheng Gate. The Revolutionary Army asked the soldiers guarding Wusheng Gate to open it up for him, and they had promised that they would not seize the opportunity to attack the city. Mr Meng had swaggered back into the city from Wusheng Gate, the first person to enter Wuchang since the city had been closed.

The major-domo, Old Nuo, brought such rumours home from the street every day. Hong Peizhu had no interest in any of this because Chen Mingwu was still so ill. Xiyun's mother was helping Mrs Wu in the kitchen every day, and she was not interested either. But Xiyun and Xizi went rushing over the moment they caught sight of Old Nuo. Every day they stopped him because they wanted to listen to stories from the streets.

The German doctor had now visited Chen Mingwu twice, each time saying that this was a psychological problem and not something that medicine could cure; he would have to come to his senses of his own accord.

"How can he do that?" Hong Peizhu asked.

"It is hard to say," the German doctor said. "When something unexpected happens to stimulate him, he will come out of this catatonic state."

That morning, an aeroplane came droning over Wuchang and circled in the skies overhead. There was a scream in the street: "There's a plane up there! They are going to drop grenades on us!" For a time, the streets and alleys were in utter confusion. In the chaos, someone shouted: "It's no use running around aimlessly! If a grenade is dropped on you, you'll die wherever you are!" With this cry, the crowds running this way and that seemed to gain a new grasp of the situation, and the confusion was eased. The aeroplane circled in the air for a few moments and then flew away.

The next day, the aeroplane was back again. The people walking around in the streets seemed much more blasé, and they no longer rushed around like headless chickens. Then, without warning, the artillery batteries on Snake Mountain suddenly started to fire. The shells were aimed at the aeroplane, but the guns were much too far away, and they simply fell short. The aeroplane was still flying through the sky, dropping countless leaflets, before it departed in a leisurely fashion.

The shells raining down from the sky fell all over the city, exploding with an ear-splitting roar, spraying flesh and blood absolutely everywhere. Cries and screams rose up into the air. Dozens of people started cursing in the direction of Snake Mountain:

"You don't have any anti-aircraft guns, so what are you shooting for?"

"You haven't hit the plane even once, but you've killed plenty of your own people!"

An artillery shell landed on the defensive fortifications around Government Gate, blowing to bits the seven soldiers on guard there.

The troops who held Wuchang had been waiting patiently for reinforcements all this time. At headquarters, it was sometimes reported that Sun Chuanfang had dispatched six divisions to Wuchang; they were moving up from Jiangxi Province and would be there any day now. On other occasions, they said that Wang Weicheng was taking four divisions and three brigades, formerly commanded by Cao Kun, south by train. He was going to join Sun Chuanfang's Coalition Army at Huangshigang, and from there they would march on Wuhan to launch a major counter-offensive against the Revolutionary Army besieging Wuchang.

The leaflets that had fallen everywhere across the city carried a quite different message. According to them, Sun Chuanfang had sent a division to Wuchang to relieve the siege, but it had been stopped in its tracks by the main force of the Revolutionary Army. Cao Kun's divisions in Hebei were fighting back against Feng Yuxiang at Nankou, so they wouldn't be coming to help at all. They also said that Wu Peifu had been so terrified he'd fled all the way to Xiaogan before he stopped. He'd then been chased out through the Wusheng Pass by Xia Douyin's troops.

Some of this was true, and some of it was false, but it certainly served to trouble the minds of the soldiers defending the city. Everyone seemed to be worrying about whether they would hold Wuchang or not, and whether they themselves would make it out alive.

When Ma Weifu stepped through the main entrance into Hong Peizhu's house, nobody even noticed. It was not until he entered the living room that Xiyun caught sight of him and shouted happily: "Uncle Ma!"

The major-domo, Old Nuo, came out of the kitchen to greet him.

"Why don't you shut the front door?" Ma Weifu asked.

"I've just come back from buying some paper and soap outside," Old Nuo explained.

"In the future," Ma Weifu said, "you must bolt the door as soon as you come in. There are an awful lot of deserters in the city – even we aren't sure who they are when we try and reenlist them. They are completely out of control and do whatever they want. There are a lot of young women here, so you need to be careful."

"This is the Hong mansion," Old Nuo said, "so surely they wouldn't dare do anything to us?"

"What do you mean, they wouldn't dare?" Ma Weifu demanded. "In the minds of the Northern Army, they are conquerors. Wuchang is a city they have captured, and the people in this mansion are people under their control."

Old Nuo listened with alarm and said: "Yes indeed, young master, I will definitely remember your advice."

All this time, Ma Weifu had not seen Hong Peizhu emerge. "Where is Peizhu?" he asked.

"She's in Mingwu's room," Xizi said.

Ma Weifu was stunned and asked: "Mingwu?"

"I should explain," Xiyun said. "Well, Mingwu is sick and in a daze, so Peizhu brought him back to see a doctor."

"Is he in the guest room?" Ma Weifu asked.

"Yes," Old Nuo said, "in the east chamber."

Ma Weifu knew his way about the house and went straight to the east chamber. Whenever he'd visited his uncle, he'd stayed in this room. When he heard that Hong Peizhu had arranged for Chen Mingwu to stay there, it left a sour taste in his mouth.

He walked over to the bedside, and Hong Peizhu, who was giving Chen Mingwu some water to drink, looked at him. His face dark, he said: "Is this the man you made yourself sick over?"

"He is my classmate," Hong Peizhu said.

"What's wrong with him?" Ma Weifu asked.

"He's in shock," Hong Peizhu explained. "His mother disappeared, his house got burned to the ground, and his friend was killed by the military police. Within the space of just a couple of days, he has suffered one blow after another, and this is what has happened."

"What a weakling!" Ma Weifu said scornfully.

"Cousin," Hong Peizhu responded, "how about you stop talking about him like that?"

After she had finished giving him water to drink, Hong Peizhu cried: "Xizi, it's your turn!"

"Coming!" Xizi shouted. He came running in with a chamber pot in his hand. He inserted it under the quilt, listened for the sound of urination and then removed the chamber pot and ran out.

Ma Weifu watched all this with growing irritation. He pulled Hong Peizhu aside and said: "Get out of the way!"

Hong Peizhu did not understand, but she stepped aside and asked: "What do you want?"

Ma Weifu grabbed hold of Chen Mingwu's collar and said: "I'm going to cure this waste of space!" Then he slapped Chen Mingwu across the face a couple of times.

Hong Peizhu screamed, but Xiyun, from her position behind Ma Weifu, now spoke up and said: "Don't do that! Uncle Ma is going to cure Mingwu."

Hong Peizhu kept on screaming and turned on her: "What do you know about it?"

Hong Peizhu rushed to Chen Mingwu's bedside, reaching out to block Ma Weifu. "You bastard!" she shouted. "How many students have you killed? Do you want to kill them here now too?"

"I haven't killed any students," Ma Weifu said, "but I don't think much of this one. Who hasn't had problems in these turbulent times? Who hasn't had members of their family die? Xiyun and Xizi have been through much more terrible events than he has, and just look at how well this little girl has dealt with it all!"

"People are different," Hong Peizhu pointed out.

"Indeed they are," Ma Weifu said, "and the difference is that they deal with all the things that have happened to them, but he is crushed by them. The world is in such a dreadful state, and he is a grown man, but he can't be bothered to take care of women and children – he has you to give him sips of water to drink and this kid to help him pee – he might as well be dead!"

"If you say that again, I will be angry," Hong Peizhu said.

"I'm even angrier than you are," said Ma Weifu.

"Look!" Xiyun suddenly cried out. "Isn't Uncle Ma wonderful!"

Hong Peizhu turned around and realised that Chen Mingwu's eyes were slowly brightening. She was overjoyed and asked: "Mingwu, how are you?"

Chen Mingwu looked at Ma Weifu for several moments before he spoke. "He's right," Chen Mingwu said. "He's absolutely right."

"Are you conscious again?" Hong Peizhu asked in surprise.

Xiyun was also surprised: "Have you come to your senses?"

Hearing that Chen Mingwu was awake, the major-domo, Old Nuo, came running into the kitchen with Xiyun's mother and Mrs Wu. "Well," Old Nuo said, "I should have known. The young master is such a lucky person – the moment he arrives, everything sorts itself out."

Xiyun was circling happily around Ma Weifu, and when she heard Old Nuo say this she also chipped in: "I had a dream, and I dreamed of Dad – he looked just like Uncle Ma."

Xiyun's mother slapped her: "Don't be so silly!"

But Ma Weifu laughed: "OK, you'll be my daughter from now on!"

That evening, Ma Weifu ate his dinner at the Hong mansion. Although Chen Mingwu was still somewhat dispirited, his mind had obviously cleared.

During the meal, Chen Mingwu said to Ma Weifu: "You shouldn't look down on me as much as you do. I am a grown man – I have been chased by the military police and fought with local thugs."

Ma Weifu still despised him and said coldly: "I'm glad to hear it. If so, then it's time for you to take responsibility for all the people in this house. That's the only duty men who don't fight in wartime bear."

"Cousin, can I remind you that he's not well," Hong Peizhu said.

"In times of turmoil, men who are sick still have their duties to perform," Ma Weifu said.

"Peizhu, your cousin is right," Chen Mingwu said.

"Call me Staff Officer Ma," he snapped.

When it got dark, Ma Weifu had to go back to Binyang Gate. Seeing that Chen Mingwu was ensconced in the Hong mansion, his heart ached badly. When he was first rejected by Hong Peizhu, he didn't feel any particular pain. Now he knew Hong Peizhu had fallen in love with another man, his feelings were deeply confused. Ma Weifu thought to himself: I can't just give her up like this. He dragged her into her room and said: "Peizhu, you must look after yourself. If anything were to happen to you, how could I ever face my uncle?"

"I know," Hong Peizhu said. "You should also be careful. I've heard the really intense gunfire round Binyang Gate, and I've been so worried."

Ma Weifu felt his heart lurch and said: "Really? Are you worried about me, Peizhu?"

"Of course," she said.

"When I came here today, I was thinking that after I leave, I don't know whether I will ever see you again," Ma Weifu said. "Now that I know you have been worried, I will be more careful."

"Don't say such scary things," Hong Peizhu said with a smile.

"It's true," Ma Weifu said. "This time it's going to be really bad, so you have to be extra careful. Stay indoors, lock the door and don't go out unless you absolutely have to."

"I will," Hong Peizhu said.

"I don't like having your classmate living here, but for your safety I think it's better for him to stay," Ma Weifu said.

"He's homeless right now," she pointed out.

"Peizhu," Ma Weifu said, "after this battle, I am going to resign my commission – for your sake, I want to make some new choices."

"But I…"

Hong Peizhu started to speak, but Ma Weifu interrupted her: "Peizhu, you know how I feel. Don't say anything right now."

Hong Peizhu nodded and said nothing.

Ma Weifu thought that he might still have hope. When he reached the front gate, he stopped and turned back. Ma Weifu asked Xiyun to bring Chen Mingwu out to the backyard. He wanted to have a private word with him.

Chen Mingwu came into the backyard. His mental state was much improved, and when Ma Weifu saw his naïve yet open expression, he thought: He must be a clever young man; he certainly has strong ideals and great enthusiasm, plus a little weakness. There must be a reason that Peizhu loves him.

"Are you looking for me, Staff Officer Ma?" Chen Mingwu asked.

Ma Weifu nodded and stared at him, wondering what he should say.

"Whatever you want to say, just say it," Chen Mingwu said.

Ma Weifu decided to put it to him straight: "I know you support these anarchists."

Chen Mingwu's childish face showed his determination, and he said: "I do. What are you going to do about it?"

"I don't want to do anything about it," Ma Weifu said. "Peizhu loves you, but you don't seem to love her."

"That is between me and her," Chen Mingwu said. "It's none of your business."

"Good answer," Ma Weifu said. "Do you know? I love Peizhu, but of course Peizhu does not love me."

"That has nothing to do with me," Chen Mingwu said in dismay.

"Then let me talk about something that does concern you," Ma Weifu said. "The situation is now very critical. At any moment, the enemy could break through the walls, in which case there will be street-to-street fighting. Or maybe we will still be under siege for many days to come. But the city will not be safe whether it falls or we defend it. Do you understand? There are many deserters here, outside all control, and they are going to take advantage of the chaos inside the walls to engage in every kind of criminal activity. I hope you can take care of the adults and children here."

"Of course I will," Chen Mingwu said.

"I want to remind you," Ma Weifu said, "that when you were running for your life, Xiyun's family took a terrible risk to save you. When you got sick, Peizhu saved you regardless of herself. You must protect them now because that is how you pay them back."

Chen Mingwu stopped looking so aggressive because he clearly agreed with what the other man was saying.

"Peizhu is my cousin," Ma Weifu continued, "and the Yuan

family are my friend's closest relatives. Peizhu has no other family here besides me. Xiyun and Xizi's father has been killed in battle. I don't want them to suffer any more. I have a heavy responsibility to bear in guarding the city walls, and I can't help them myself. So I would like to entrust them to your care. I hope that you will not abandon them during this period and that you will do your utmost because you are a man. Besides which, Old Nuo and Mrs Wu will also be entrusted to your care." Ma Weifu had a solemn expression on his face.

"You can rest assured that I will do my best," Chen Mingwu said.

"In an emergency, you can say that they are all relatives of Major General Liu," Ma Weifu said. "Maybe it won't help, but perhaps it will be useful. If nothing else will save you, that's the final throw of the dice."

Chen Mingwu wanted to say something. He hesitated and swallowed his words.

"I have to go," Ma Weifu said. "I wonder if there will be an attack tonight. Anyway, I can't stay here any longer." As he spoke, he walked away, taking huge strides.

Chen Mingwu looked at him as he moved away, hesitated for a moment and then said aloud: "Since you have predicted that the city will be thrown into chaos and the people will suffer dreadfully, why not simply open Binyang Gate and let the Revolutionary Army in? Sooner or later they will come, and sooner or later they will put an end to all of this, so that the people of the city do not have to spend all day every day in fear and terror."

Ma Weifu stopped and turned back. "This is between me and Binyang Gate," he said. "It has nothing to do with you. You just keep your promise. And another thing. I didn't want to say it – if you touch Peizhu, I will forgive you, but I will shoot you dead first!"

"What do you mean?" Chen Mingwu asked.

"She's mine!" Ma Weifu said. Having said this, he left.

Once he had gone, Chen Mingwu cursed him angrily as the Beiyang warlords' little puppy dog.

32

THE WORST OF the fighting really seemed to be over, with only the occasional bullet whistling through the air. The Revolutionary Army had Wuchang under such tight siege that not even a mouse could get through; it seemed as if they were waiting for the city to fall of its own accord.

The ten gates were all closed. The terrible battle had ceased, but the idle soldiers now discovered that the prospect of not fighting was even more terrible. This feeling of sheer horror started at the dinner table. First, there were no fresh vegetables to be had. Then, rice began to run short. As they were eating, the soldiers would whisper to each other, and they had an awful lot to say on this subject. Gossip ran from dinner table to bedroom and back again, updated day by day.

The quartermasters sent people to place all the grain stores and rice shops in the city under seal; henceforth, they were not allowed to sell any grain, since everything was requisitioned by the military defending the walls. The reason given was that soldiers have to eat their fill in order to be able to fight, and they would be the ones protecting the whole city. Some brave inhabitants protested in front of one of the closed rice shops, shouting: "Who exactly are they protecting?"

The owner of the rice shop was crying and could not answer.

Then it began: the streets were full of people – both the rich and the poor – looking for food. As long as it was edible, someone would buy it. First, the made dishes on sale in little snack bars sold out; then the grocery stores were swept clean of their confectionery and pastries; then the pickled vegetable shops ran out of stock; and a few days later, the yams, jujubes and lotus seeds in the traditional Chinese medicine shops were all bought up to stave off hunger.

The first people to completely run out of food were the manual labourers. They make a living by selling their physical strength. They would work for a whole day, and when they got paid at the end of it they bought food: most such families had no reserves at all. Only three days after the siege began, poor families had run out of food. In the next few days, after earning money, labourers could still buy a little bit of this or that to eat. If they had no money, they could borrow some food. At first, people imagined that the city would be opened soon, so there were still those who were happy to lend food. Later, when they realised that the city would not fall any time soon, no one was prepared to do a good turn. Poor people now had to do their best to find food to survive. The lotus roots growing in Ziyang Lake were soon all dug up, and the wild herbs on the banks of Dusi Lake vanished in the space of a single day.[1] In the wilds out by the lake, you could see people wandering around with shovels every day. The sight of a purslane plant was as welcome as a nugget of gold; everyone would rush to grab it.

One day, the dog belonging to an important family living on Yanzhi Road ran out of the house and did not return at night. The family's nine-year-old child searched and searched for it and cried all the way. Someone told him that earlier that day, at Dusi Lake, they had heard a dog barking, and they were afraid that it had been butchered for meat. The child immediately ran to Dusi Lake and found the dog's tail and several pieces of its skin. The child was horrified, and by the time he got home he was running a high fever. Supposedly, the very next day he went completely insane.

People in the street sighed over how sad it was about this child and the dog, but suddenly they realised what this meant: small animals could be used for food. So, in a trice, all the wild dogs that roamed around beneath the walls of Wuchang disappeared, along with any cats. One day, an enticing aroma of barbecue was discovered to emanate from the home of the cobbler over on

Youtian Road, which attracted several passers-by to ask what he was eating. As the cobbler ate, he explained: "I used to think there were too many rats in my house, but now I find there are too few."

The major-domo, Old Nuo, went out every day, always trying to get something delicious to bring back, but each time he returned empty-handed. As soon as he got home, he would sigh and complain to Mrs Wu. There were no fresh vegetables in the house, and there was not much rice left. How on earth would they all survive if this went on much longer?

Xiyun's mother had taken to helping Mrs Wu in the kitchen. When the major-domo was lamenting over the situation with Mrs Wu, she stood to one side, shedding tears. When Old Nuo saw this, he made haste to explain: "The whole city has run out of food, not just our household."

Xiyun's mother said: "My family is making everything worse for you. If it weren't for us, you would have enough grain to eat until the city is open again."

"You can't say that," Old Nuo said.

"Your husband died for this country," Mrs Wu added, "so you're the widow of a martyr, and your children are the orphans of a martyr – it is entirely right and just that the Hong family should give you everything we have to eat."

Xiyun's mother was now crying even more sadly. Old Nuo turned around and scolded Mrs Wu: "If you want to talk about rice and vegetables, go right ahead, but you don't need to go on about martyrs and dying for the country!"

At noon, they had porridge and salted radishes to eat. It was difficult for Hong Peizhu to swallow so much as a mouthful. Mrs Wu wiped the tears from her eyes and said: "Why should Miss Peizhu have to suffer like this? If we had left the city one day earlier, we would not be in this awful situation."

Chen Mingwu knew that Hong Peizhu failed to leave the city because of him, and he felt really guilty about it. "This afternoon," he announced, "I will go out to get food."

"From where?" Old Nuo asked.

"Where there's a will there's a way," Chen Mingwu said.

"I can find us some wild herbs," Xiyun's mother said. "Most of the wild herbs that you see out in the fields can be eaten."

"You are quite right," Old Nuo said, "and some wild herbs would be better than no greens at all. Besides which, Mrs Wu is a good cook, so I'm sure she'll make us something delicious out of them."

Chen Mingwu thought for a moment and said: "In that case, this afternoon, I will go to look for rice while Mrs Wu and Madam Yuan go and hunt for herbs. Wild herbs in the south are different from those in the north, but Mrs Wu will know what to look for."

"That's right," she said.

"I want to go too," Xiyun announced.

"Yes," Chen Mingwu said, "Xiyun should go too. Old Nuo, Peizhu and Xizi should stay at home."

"You are all going out to work," Peizhu said. "Why should I stay at home?"

"You'd better stay at home," Chen Mingwu pointed out. "If anything happens to you, Staff Officer Ma will wring my neck."

When Chen Mingwu said this, everyone laughed.

"I can't stay at home," Old Nuo said. "I am a man, and I should also be going out to find food."

Xizi echoed him: "I am a man, and I should also be going out to find food!"

Chen Mingwu slapped him on the back of the head and said: "Your job is to take good care of Peizhu at home. This is a really important mission. If she gets sick, you will get a beating."

Xizi looked at Xiyun and asked: "Sis, is this really an important mission?"

"Absolutely!" Xiyun said. "Have you forgotten how Uncle Ma beat up Mingwu?"

Xizi did not dare to say another word when he remembered Ma Weifu's clenched fists.

Although they only had porridge to eat, the depression that had hung over them for days was now gone. Everyone was feeling brave and excited, as if they were about to go to the battlefield.

After dinner, Xiyun's mother and Mrs Wu went out, each carrying a bamboo basket, with Xiyun skipping along behind them.

"You need to keep your wits about you," Chen Mingwu instructed her, "and if you come across soldiers out on patrol and they try to bully you, you must give your father's name. You must say that you are all Major General Liu's relatives because then people would not dare to trouble you."

"But if I'm supposed to be a relative of Major General Liu," Xiyun pointed out, "what am I doing out picking wild herbs? I could go straight to him and demand some meat to eat."

Chen Mingwu laughed and said: "It's just to trick those brainless soldiers."

"It is true we do have a connection to him," Xiyun's mother said, "but with all that's happened, we do not want people to think we are encroaching."

"I only want you to do this," Chen Mingwu explained, "if it is absolutely necessary."

Chen Mingwu went out with Old Nuo. The major-domo said that he had a crony in the Jiulongjing District, where many officials lived, so he might be able to borrow a few kilograms of rice there. Chen Mingwu heard what Old Nuo said, and he remembered that his cousin Daying was also a long-standing resident of Wuchang and might be able to help them.

After Chen Mingwu and Old Nuo went their separate ways, he went straight to his cousin's house. To his surprise, the door of his cousin's house was closed. He knocked loudly, but no one answered. He was worried and asked around to find out where they could have gone. Their neighbour said that he had not heard them say they were going somewhere, but he had not seen any of them for the last couple of days. Chen Mingwu was now even more worried. He knew that this was the only place in the city his cousin had to live in. Where could they all have gone? While he was hesitating as to whether he should go away, or whether he should continue banging on the door, he suddenly heard the thump of someone falling over inside. Chen Mingwu raised his hand and thumped at the door, shouting: "Cousin! Daying! Cousin! It's me, Mingwu!"

After a long pause, the door slowly opened a small crack, but there was dead silence and no one was to be seen. Chen Mingwu did not understand the reason, so he reached out and pushed the door. The door was blocked by something. He looked down and saw his cousin lying on the ground, in the way of the door. "Cousin!" Chen Mingwu cried out. "What's the matter with you?"

He squeezed in through the door without too much difficulty and saw her lying on the ground, completely listless and with a skeletal face. He was horrified. He picked up his cousin and put her on the bed. Her husband was already lying there, barely conscious, and a shadow of his former self. Chen Mingwu was appalled and asked what had happened. His cousin's husband said in a weak voice: "Quick, help me find out if Xiaoshun is still alive." Xiaoshun was his cousin's youngest son. Chen Mingwu went to Xiaoshun's room, and the child was asleep in his bed, but it was almost impossible to recognise him. He touched him and realised that he was still alive.

He immediately rushed back to his cousin's room and said: "Xiaoshun is still alive. What's wrong with you all?"

"We haven't had anything to eat for five or six days," his cousin explained. "My husband's been without food for even longer."

Chen Mingwu was shocked: "Nothing to eat? Why not?"

"We've run out of food," his cousin's husband explained. "There's nothing in the house. I couldn't borrow anything either. For the last two days, I've only been drinking water. But then when I wanted to go out to find food again, I didn't have the energy to move."

"How could this happen?" Chen Mingwu exclaimed. He was in such a state that he walked round and round the room.

His cousin slowly pulled herself together and said to him: "Mingwu, I guess that you've been sent by God to save my family, right? Start by giving us some water, OK? And then get us something to eat. I am begging you, Mingwu. Get us something to eat. Even if you can't save the two of us, you must save Xiaoshun."

"Rest assured," Chen Mingwu said, "I will go right now and get you something. I won't let you die."

He put a large glass of water beside their bed and another glass of water at Xiaoshun's bedside. Xiaoshun had no light in his eyes; he just gazed at Chen Mingwu, without even the energy to speak.

Chen Mingwu ran back to the college as quickly as he could. The gate was still closed, so he climbed over the wall. He vaguely remembered that there were still some biscuits left in his dormitory.

When he stood at the door to his dormitory and looked in at his bed, his face turned white with fear. A shell had gone through the roof, landing straight on the bed, which had been smashed to bits. Fortunately, the shell did not explode; otherwise, the building would be in ruins. He did not dare to stay there another moment, as he was afraid the bomb might yet suddenly explode. He ran to the gym where some of his classmates were lying on the ground, chatting. When they caught sight of Chen Mingwu, one of them cried out; it was his roommate, Guo Wenjun. The bones in his square face stood out clear and sharp. Guo Wenjun was obviously very happy to see Chen Mingwu and asked: "Are you feeling better? I was so worried about you."

"What are you doing?" Chen Mingwu asked.

"Saving energy!" Guo Wenjun explained. "We eat only one meal a day, so we don't dare to do too much – we just try to stay alive. Did you see what happened to our dormitory? Think how dangerous!"

"I saw," Chen Mingwu said. "Were you there when it came down?"

"I had just gone out when I heard the noise," Guo Wenjun explained. "I was so scared that I couldn't move a step. What, are you thinking of coming back to the college?"

Chen Mingwu could not speak for a moment. He shook his head.

"What's wrong?" Guo Wenjun asked. "Whatever it is, just spit it out."

"I can hardly bear to talk about it," Chen Mingwu said.

"Do you need food?" Guo Wenjun asked.

Chen Mingwu nodded.

"From the looks of you," his classmate said, "you've been eating every day."

"It's not for me," Chen Mingwu said. "Just now, I went to my cousin's house – she and her husband and their kid haven't had a thing to eat for five or six days. They are lying there in their beds too weak to even get up. I... I'm afraid they'll starve to death. So I need to find something for them to eat."

Guo Wenjun sat up and said: "Well, I guess they must be poor people. Mingwu, I have a bag of barley flour here which I was going to eat over the next few days. You take it and go and save them."

"But… then what will you eat tomorrow?" Chen Mingwu asked.

"Never mind," his classmate said. "I'll think of something. Besides, I can go hungry for a few days, but your cousin and her family won't survive much longer. They'll be dead if we don't do something."

Chen Mingwu burst into tears and said: "My mother is missing, so my cousin is now the only relative I have left."

"Well, get back to her," Guo Wenjun said.

Some of the other students lying around said the same thing: "Go back to your cousin and look after her. There are lots of people here, so we'll be OK."

Chen Mingwu bowed to them and rushed off.

When he arrived back at Daying's house, Chen Mingwu divided the barley flour into five equal parts. He took one part and cooked it into a porridge, which he then fed to the three members of the family. "After being hungry for so long, you must be careful not to eat too much," he said. "Eat a little every day, just enough to stay alive. You will need more to eat, so I'll try and think of something. If I get anything, I'll bring it back for you."

His cousin had tears in her eyes as she said: "Mingwu, you have saved us!"

He looked at his cousin: "I want you to remember this – the person who saved your lives, he is called Guo Wenjun."

33

HUNGER NOW SPREAD through the city of Wuchang. But there was one thing more terrible even than the hunger, and that was the defeated soldiers and deserters who had fled and hidden themselves in every nook and cranny. The soldiery defending the city was composed of remnants of two defeated armies: from Tingsi Bridge and Hesheng Bridge. There were about ten thousand 'defenders', but only two thousand or so of them were under Liu Yuchun's direct command. Therefore, there were literally thousands of idle soldiers wandering around inside the city. Initially, they were indeed just walking about sightseeing. However, once they realised that food was running out and no reinforcements had arrived, morale and discipline simply collapsed.

The Northern Expeditionary Army dropped leaflets every day from aeroplanes. The leaflets proclaimed that the Hankou Chamber of Commerce was offering to put up three hundred thousand yuan to pay off the soldiers defending the city so the siege of Wuchang could be brought to an end as soon as possible; they also announced that a deal had been brokered with the Northern Expeditionary Army to offer safe conduct for the defenders as they withdrew. They said that Chen Jiamo[1] had agreed to negotiate, but that Liu Yuchun had categorically refused. The soldiers who made up the Northern Army were an ignorant lot; they were illiterate and stupid, and they did not read these leaflets, but the inhabitants of the city certainly did. They were all trying to talk to the soldiers about this offer: "They are going to give you money and send you back home, so where's the problem? What's the point of staying here hungry and suffering?"

Several soldiers listened to what they were saying and ran to ask Ma Weifu about it. "It's all lies," Ma Weifu said. "General Wu sent a telegram yesterday to tell Major General Liu to stand firm and wait for reinforcements. Sun Chuanfang's army will arrive at any moment – I guess that they'll be assembling at Huangshi."

The soldiers went away, not quite sure who to believe. Ma Weifu knew full well that he'd been lying to them, but if he hadn't how could he have talked them round? The defenders were angry because no reinforcements had come, so it was no wonder that there was such resentment.

One morning, notices were posted up all over the streets. The announcement read: "General Wu has telegraphed us to inform us of the following: The main army has already arrived at Xinyang, the army from Jiangsu is on its way back to Pingxiang, and the troops in Wuchang should hold firm and await reinforcements, since the food needed is being transported to them by the Juechuan warship."

It might have been thought that this announcement would cheer up the army. But both the military and the general public were by this time completely fed up with the whole situation. Food had run out, there was a shortage of clean drinking water, and they were trapped inside the city with no hope of rescue, so it was not surprising that the whole city was distressed. No matter what kind of propaganda they put out, it could not dispel the sense of deep desolation that pervaded the city.

Law and order had now broken down, so robbery had become a common practice. The first time he heard about soldiers robbing the city, Ma Weifu was so furious he pounded the table with his fist and immediately notified the headquarters, saying that they had to make an example of these people; otherwise, the consequences would be serious. But no one could stop this kind of thing from happening. Robberies spread like the plague. Once the infection took hold, there was no medicine that could cure it! Almost all the once-busy shops on Long Street had closed their doors, but almost all the closed doors had now been prised open again.

Ma Weifu was worried. If they had been defeated in battle, or if the city was captured by the Northern Expeditionary Army, the people would have forgiven them. But now, with idle soldiers robbing people for fun, even if the people were willing to live and let live, how could God forgive them? On one occasion, Ma Weifu had stopped soldiers carrying bundles of silk and said: "How can you go about robbing people in broad daylight?"

A soldier answered: "We are all going to die, so why shouldn't we have a bit of fun first?"

"You may be having fun, but what about the inhabitants of the city that you've stolen from? Aren't they going to be upset?" Ma Weifu asked.

Another soldier answered: "We'll be dead soon. These people may be unhappy now, but at least they've got a future to look forward to."

Another soldier put it even more cold-bloodedly: "The people here hate us, so they will be very happy when we die. What we are doing now is going to make them happier in the future."

Ma Weifu felt that there was nothing he could say to them.

When Chen Mingwu came to find Ma Weifu, he was standing lost in thought on the tower over Binyang Gate. A soldier led Chen Mingwu up. "How are Peizhu and the rest of them?" Ma Weifu asked.

"They are all doing fine," Chen Mingwu said, "except that there is no food."

Ma Weifu was shocked: "Have you eaten all the food in the house?"

"There wasn't much to begin with," Chen Mingwu explained.

"How long will you be able to hold out?" Ma Weifu asked.

"We only had porridge at lunch today. In the afternoon, the major-domo, Old Nuo, was able to buy a few kilograms of rice at a high price. Xiyun, Madam Yuan and Mrs Wu managed to dig up some banana roots. Mrs Wu cooked some and saved the rest, so we probably have enough to eat for two or three days."

Ma Weifu's heart ached at the thought: Peizhu was brought up as a little princess, and now here she is surviving on banana roots.

Chen Mingwu saw the gloom spread across Ma Weifu's face and said: "I heard that your army has a lot of grain, so I was wondering if you can get some for us."

"The army really doesn't have much food left," Ma Weifu said. "We are already reduced to eating only two meals a day, and we don't get a lot."

"That can't be right," Chen Mingwu said. "Today, the rice that Old Nuo had to pay so much for came from some lieutenant."

"Oh really?" Ma Weifu was surprised. "Is that the case? That's a death penalty offence!"

"There are so many death penalty offences with you people," Chen Mingwu pointed out, "that it's no wonder you haven't got round to this one. I just wanted to ask you if you can get some food for your family."

Ma Weifu shook his head and said: "I'm afraid not. I don't have the right."

Chen Mingwu sneered at him: "Xiyun's father died for nothing, didn't he? He gave his life for you lot, but his wife and children are left with no food to eat because you refuse to give them even the scraps from your table."

Ma Weifu's face turned white when Chen Mingwu mentioned Yuan Zongchun. He could almost feel Yuan Zongchun's gaze boring into his body.

"Madam Yuan and Major General Liu are some kind of relatives – doesn't that count for anything?" Chen Mingwu asked.

"You have a point there," Ma Weifu said. "I'll go and see Major General Liu and ask him to allocate them some rice."

"Great!" Chen Mingwu said. "I'll go back and wait for you to deliver it."

"Tell Peizhu and Madam Yuan not to go out," Ma Weifu instructed him. "If a soldier knocks, they must not open the door. You and Old Nuo must stay at home to protect them. The soldiers have now all gone mad with their thuggery."

Chen Mingwu was about to leave, but when he heard this he stopped and turned back to say: "So you know they are thugs? You know they've gone insane? In that case, why not just open the gates? You could let the people here live and let the soldiers leave. Of course, it's also important to leave yourself a way out."

"I know all of that," Ma Weifu said, "and I don't need you to tell me about it. Your job is to take care of those people, and that is not a trivial matter. You promised me."

Chen Mingwu did not speak. He just looked at Ma Weifu and then turned away.

Ma Weifu disliked Chen Mingwu's air of superiority and thought to himself: There you are still wet behind the ears, so how dare you carry on like this! However, as he meditated on what had just happened, he could not help thinking about things from Chen Mingwu's perspective.

It was very dark. Looking at the city of Wuchang from the tower above Binyang Gate, the whole place seemed dead, with a cold silence spread everywhere. Since lamps were lit in front of each house, you could see a string of lights running down each street, but because there was no one to be seen moving back and forth, or out and about talking to each other, walking along such roads was more frightening than walking in the dark.

Ma Weifu headed along a small but well-lit lane to the residence of Major General Liu. Less than one hundred metres from Liu's residence, he could hear someone murmuring. He approached to discover that the guards on a roadblock had arrested a junior officer and were taking him to the nearest lock-up. Ma Weifu asked one of the stragglers from this procession what had happened. The soldier answered that this man was a lieutenant in charge of logistics under the command of Yu Yinsen. Earlier that day he had stolen forty-eight kilograms of grain and sold them to civilians at sky-high prices, only to fall foul of one of the roadblocks. Headquarters ordered him to be shot tomorrow as a warning to others. Ma Weifu watched the group walk away and asked himself: Why do they shoot people who sell grain privately, while those who commit robbery get away scot-free?

Ma Weifu went to Liu Yuchun's office, where he was sitting, listening to the radio. As he walked through the door, Liu Yuchun turned off the radio.

"Major General, I have a request to make," Ma Weifu began.

"OK," Liu Yuchun said.

"Zongchun laid down his life for his country in the Battle of Tingsi Bridge," he continued.

"I know that," Liu Yuchun pointed out, "he worked for me for many years, and I was greatly saddened by his death."

"The day before the city was closed off," Ma Weifu said, "his wife came to find him with his son and daughter."

"Really?" Liu Yuchun was shocked. "Why didn't you tell me?"

"We were under constant attack," Ma Weifu explained, "so I did not dare to distract you with these minor matters. I arranged for them to stay at my uncle's house."

"That's good, well done," Liu Yuchun said. "We can't let a martyr's family suffer."

"However, with three more people staying in my uncle's house, they don't have enough food," Ma Weifu continued, "and I don't know…"

At this point, Liu Yuchun interrupted him and said: "I quite understand. Tell the quartermaster to allocate rations for three people to them and give them whatever canned food and milk I have left. Even if that means I don't get anything to eat or drink, I can't let Zongchun's wife and children go without."

There was a smile on Ma Weifu's face. He had followed Liu Yuchun for a number of years now and was very well-acquainted with his generous and straightforward spirit. Ma Weifu felt that the best thing about Liu Yuchun was his straightforwardness. Yes meant yes, no meant no; he wasn't the kind to twist and turn and say things that he didn't mean.

Ma Weifu thanked Liu Yuchun and made ready to leave. Suddenly, Liu Yuchun said: "What do you think of the current situation?"

"Do you want me to tell the truth?" Ma Weifu asked.

"There are just the two of us here," Liu Yuchun responded, "so you can tell me the truth."

"Our reinforcements haven't come," Ma Weifu said, "and morale is low – we are all going to die here."

"Are you certain of that?" Liu Yuchun asked.

"Oh, yes," Ma Weifu said. "In addition, lawlessness is spreading through the city, and the people are in a state of growing unrest about it – when the city falls, we are probably looking at a pretty grimy future."

Liu Yuchun was silent for a moment and then suddenly sighed.

Ma Weifu turned away quietly. He knew full well that this was a difficult moment for them both and that he ought to go.

Before he reached the door, Liu Yuchun said: "You have something more to say to me, don't you?"

Ma Weifu was shocked.

"Tell me everything," Liu Yuchun demanded.

Ma Weifu did not feel that there was anything else that he wanted to say, but since he was asked he thought about it and said: "Are the conditions they are offering at the negotiating table really so unacceptable?"

"They are totally unacceptable," Liu Yuchun said.

Then Ma Weifu asked: "Couldn't we throw open the gates in the name of saving the civilian population of Wuchang?"

"No, we can't," Liu Yuchun said.

"If we keep going like this," Ma Weifu said thoughtfully, "people will starve to death in their thousands."

"I know," said the major general. "But the military's duty is to obey, and since they have ordered us to defend the city at all costs we have to defend it right up to the last man."

"But we haven't been ordered to make the entire civilian population die with us," Ma Weifu pointed out. After he said this, he felt that he had said too much, but this is what he really thought, and he couldn't stop himself.

Liu Yuchun did not answer him directly or look at him but asked: "If you were me, what would you do?"

"I would abandon the siege," Ma Weifu said.

"Even at the risk of being court-martialled?" Liu Yuchun asked.

"Even if I was to spend the rest of my life branded as a coward or a traitor," Ma Weifu said, "I would choose to abandon the siege. Even supposing that people cursed me through the rest of eternity, at least I would have saved the lives of the civilians here. It may be a pity to ruin one's own reputation, but if that ruin can ensure the survival of countless innocent people it is worth it."

"I'm afraid no one would ever understand why you had done it," Liu Yuchun said.

"You don't do good deeds to show them off to other people," Ma Weifu retorted. "It doesn't matter whether anyone else understands

– what matters is that you can feel yourself that you have done the right thing."

"Feeling yourself that you have done the right thing?" Liu Yuchun said. "The most complicated thing in this world is the human heart. You may simply not be able to keep to your own sense of having done right."

"If you don't overthink things," Ma Weifu said, "I believe that you can maintain your own moral compass."

Liu Yuchun stared at Ma Weifu and said nothing, which made him feel nervous. Maybe I put it too strongly, he thought. After all, he is the major general in command of defending the city.

After a long pause, Liu Yuchun said: "You are right. But I want to tell you that I can only strictly abide by military orders. Such is my fate."

Ma Weifu thought about it for a long time and decided that leaving it in the hands of fate was a way to proceed. So he said: "You are right, sir. And as for myself, in spite of everything I have said, when it comes to the crunch I'm afraid I wouldn't actually be able to do it."

"Fine," Liu Yuchun said. "I've entrusted Binyang Gate to you – so no matter how much you care about the people, you also owe me a duty of loyalty. After all, you are a soldier."

Ma Weifu was struck dumb. He drew himself up to attention and shouted: "Yes, sir! You can rest assured I will do my duty."

34

THE MID-AUTUMN FESTIVAL now arrived in Wuchang, wrapped in tragedy.

The guns on Hong Mountain suddenly started firing again. As if trying to make a show of strength, the artillery on Gui Mountain roared as it pounded the opposite bank of the Yangtze River. It had now been a good few days since the last attempt to take the city by storm, but this time they began shelling each other, and every day they would fire from morning until night.

Looking down from mid-air, the three rises of Gui Mountain, Snake Mountain and Hong Mountain were almost on the same line. The artillery batteries inside Wuchang were located at Snake Mountain, which formed a long, steep ridge. Artillery was placed at both ends. One set of guns was aimed at Hong Mountain; the other at Gui Mountain. Fortunately, incoming shells fired from outside the city walls avoided the residential houses at the foot of the ridge, since they were aiming for Snake Mountain itself. For the first day or two, people were afraid to go out because of the firing of the guns. Eventually, they found that most of the incoming shells flew straight to Snake Mountain and did not fall on the civilian population, so they became bolder. People who liked to keep an eye on whatever was going on would take their stand in a corner and watch the cannons at work on both ends of Snake Mountain. When they finished bombarding Hong Mountain, they'd be firing in the direction of Gui Mountain.

Aeroplanes were also flying over Wuchang every day, circling around for a while, tossing out some leaflets and then leaving. Occasionally, a bomb or two were dropped. These bombs were not particularly big, but they could cause damage enough to whatever corner of the city they exploded in.

Early in the morning on the day of the Mid-Autumn Festival, Hong Peizhu had just finished breakfast when the major-domo, Old Nuo, brought back the news that since they had been deprived of access to the waters of the Yangtze River, people's drinking water had become unsanitary. Cholera and dysentery had begun to spread through the city. The hospitals were packed full of patients, and if disease spread through the city its consequences would be more terrible than any shelling. Hong Peizhu was horrified. Chen Mingwu thought that instead of sitting around at home waiting to die, he might as well see if there was anything he could do, so he decided to go back to the college, where at least he might find out more about what was happening.

Hong Peizhu wanted to go with Chen Mingwu, but he refused to allow her. While they were talking, someone knocked at the door. "That must be Uncle Ma!" Xiyun said. She ran to open the door, but she was wrong.

The visitor was Hong Peizhu's classmate Shuya. She had come to explain that she was going to get married this Mid-Autumn Festival, and she wanted Peizhu as a bridesmaid. Everyone in the room was stunned when they heard her say that she was getting married. Hong Peizhu simply couldn't believe her ears and asked why she would choose to get married at such a terrible time. Shuya took Hong Peizhu aside, and after stammering and stuttering over her story for a while she finally explained that she didn't have any other choice. She and her cousin had become lovers, and she was now three months pregnant. If she did not get married immediately, once she started showing, her life would be unbearable. The wedding was already planned before the siege of the city began. His family had not left because of the wedding. In such circumstances, no matter how dreadful the situation in which they found themselves, she had to get married; otherwise, how could she ever face her parents?

"Is your family planning to have a wedding banquet?" Hong Peizhu enquired.

Shuya shook her head with a bitter smile and said: "Of course not! We'll be giving our guests a bowl of porridge each."

Hong Peizhu saw how sad she was feeling and immediately promised to be her bridesmaid. When she told Chen Mingwu about it, he was very upset; to begin with, he felt really sorry for Shuya, but then he said that she'd forgotten Luo Yinan too quickly.

Luo Yinan was Shuya's ex-boyfriend, and the other students at the college thought they made a wonderful couple. But a few months earlier, they had split up.

"She's not to blame," Hong Peizhu said. "Luo Yinan can't give her a peaceful life, but that's what she really wants."

"She's made the right choice," Chen Mingwu agreed. "With Luo Yinan's family background, in the situation we see today, he really could not make her happy." As he said that, Chen Mingwu thought of his own position and became a little gloomy.

Hong Peizhu saw what he was thinking and said: "In fact, you are very lucky if you can marry the person you love."

Chen Mingwu smiled: "Yes, and you will be lucky in the future."

"But the person I love doesn't care about me," Hong Peizhu said, "so how can I ever be happy?"

Chen Mingwu knew what she meant, so he looked about him and then said: "Do you know why Guo Wenjun stayed behind at the college?" Then he felt ashamed of himself: How can I be so hard on poor Peizhu?

"Mingwu, I ask you, if things go wrong and I end up dead, what will you do?" Hong Peizhu asked.

"Don't talk nonsense," he said, "you won't die."

"But what if I do?" she persisted. "If I really were to die, can I die in your arms?"

Chen Mingwu was touched. He wanted to reach out and touch her face, but he held back. He could almost see Ma Weifu glaring at him. "No, you can't," he said.

Hong Peizhu burst into tears: "Why are you so cruel?"

"Because I know you won't die," he said, "and I don't want you to die either."

"I said if…" Hong Peizhu pointed out.

"If it comes right down to it, I will die first," he declared.

Hong Peizhu choked: "Then you will die in my arms."

When Chen Mingwu heard this, he very nearly hugged her. Nevertheless, he changed his mind at the last minute – it was best not to provoke someone like Ma Weifu. Hong Peizhu was a good woman, but he was utterly convinced that she could not possibly accustom herself to the poverty and hardships he had grown up with. He might find a girl from a rich family attractive, but he could never love her.

When Chen Mingwu left, Xiyun and Xizi were clamouring to go with him. They spent all day every day at home, and they were bored and depressed.

The major-domo said: "It's hard for little children being cooped up like this. It's safer these days, so why not take them out to play?"

Chen Mingwu thought carefully and said: "OK."

Xiyun's mother was washing some clothes and said: "We've run out of soap, so make sure you bring a piece back."

"I'll deal with that," Old Nuo said, "since I'm going out anyway to buy some candles."

When Ma Weifu arrived at the Hong mansion carrying two pounds of broad beans, Mrs Wu opened the door. The house was completely quiet, and Ma Weifu was not used to such silence. "Where is everyone?" he asked. Mrs Wu went into a long tale about where everyone had gone. Ma Weifu was somewhat sorry that he would not get to see Hong Peizhu.

Mrs Wu took hold of the broad beans and said happily: "This will provide breakfast for a good few days." After that, she asked how much they had cost. It was two strings and four hundred cash a pound. Mrs Wu gaped in amazement and said: "It used to be less than one string of cash a pound."

"What's the use of money now?" Ma Weifu asked. "You have to buy food no matter how much it costs. It was one of my men who got this from his relatives."

"That's very clever of you," Mrs Wu said. "We're lucky to have you around – otherwise, the whole family would be going hungry today, in which case none of us would have the strength to set foot outside the house, would we?"

Ma Weifu knew that if he got chatting with Mrs Wu, she would not stop talking for the rest of the day. He laughed and asked: "What about Madam Yuan?"

"Oh, she's hanging clothes out to dry round the back," Mrs Wu explained. "Women from the north are really terribly hardworking – without her help, with such a large household as we have here, I simply couldn't get everything done. When this is all over, it would be wonderful if you could talk to the master and persuade him to let them stay here."

"Her husband was an official," Ma Weifu pointed out, "so it's not likely she would want to work as a servant, is it?"

"You're right," Mrs Wu said. "She's not like us – we were born to be servants. But really, there she is with her husband dead, and she's been left to bring up two children all on her own. How on earth can she do it?"

Ma Weifu walked towards the backyard, as Mrs Wu's words struck him in the heart. He thought: Yes, how will she survive if she leaves the Hong mansion? What will happen to those two children? What will become of them? As he thought of this, Yuan Zongchun's eyes seemed to flash around him again, and his heart felt heavy.

The three buildings around the backyard provided housing for the servants. Hong Peizhu's mother's maid had accompanied her to Hankou, so Xiyun's mother took over her room and slept in there with Xizi. Originally, she'd been staying in the west wing of the mansion, but the other rooms there were empty, and Xiyun's mother was not accustomed to being all by herself like that. She wanted to live nearer to Mrs Wu, so that she would have someone to talk to, and she liked to be able to help her out. Ma Weifu knew that she was used to the work, coming from the countryside as she did, so he let her do what she wanted.

When he caught sight of Xiyun's mother, she was arranging a white shirt to dry in the sun. He recognised it: the shirt belonged to Chen Mingwu, so there was a little stab of jealousy in his heart. Why is everyone so nice to him? he wondered. Xiyun's mother noticed Ma Weifu's arrival and a smile spread across her face. "There you are, Staff Officer Ma," she said.

For the first time, Ma Weifu saw Xiyun's mother with a smile on her face. "Yes," he said happily, "I've come to see you all. Have Xiyun and Xizi gone out to play?"

"Yes," she said, "they demanded that Mr Chen take them out with him. Kids really can be relentless sometimes – they kept shouting at him, so poor Mr Chen felt he didn't have a choice, and he had to take them."

"It's not safe outside, so it's better for them to stay at home," Ma Weifu said.

"Those kids went through fire and water to get here with me," Xiyun's mother said, "so they are brave, and they've already been through a lot – they are not afraid of anything anymore."

Xiyun's mother was hanging clothes out to dry all the time she was talking. The sun shone on her face, so he could see that she was still very young, her skin pale and delicate. She raised her hands as she hung up the clothes, pushing back her sleeves automatically. For the first time in his life, Ma Weifu was watching closely as a woman went to work. Suddenly, his heart burst with tenderness.

"Do you want my help?" Ma Weifu asked.

Xiyun's mother smiled and said: "You're a big man, so there's nothing for you to do here. You helped me and the kids get a roof over our heads here at the Hong mansion, so really you've done enough for us already."

"Zongchun and I were as close as brothers," Ma Weifu said, "so that was the least I could do."

"With people dying all over the place, most people forget their obligations," Xiyun's mother said musingly. "You did what you did, you said what you said, and that shows you're a good person. There aren't too many of your kind around nowadays."

During their conversation, Xiyun's mother finished hanging out the laundry. Lifting up the basket, she said to Ma Weifu: "Come in and have something to drink." Ma Weifu followed her into her room.

Suddenly, there was a whistling sound overhead, which was so familiar that he almost felt his heart stop. Without a moment's thought, he launched himself at Xiyun's mother and hurled her into the corner. A shell scraped across the roof and landed next door. When it exploded, there was appalling screaming to be heard on all sides. The buildings in the backyard collapsed, the roof beams fell, and the sound of brick walls falling down lasted for several minutes.

Ma Weifu and Xiyun's mother were pinioned beneath a collapsed wall. Fortunately, the corner they were hiding in did not simply crumble. Xiyun's mother was pressed right up against Ma Weifu, trembling all over, so frightened that she did not dare to move. "Don't be scared," Ma Weifu shouted at her, "I am here! Someone will come to our rescue soon!"

Once all the sounds of collapse had come to an end, they realised their position: Xiyun's mother was in Ma Weifu's arms, and he was hugging her tightly. His heart was pounding, and his face was hot. He wanted to let go of her, but he could not move his arms. When he tried, he dislodged some broken bricks. Ma Weifu was embarrassed and said softly: "I'm sorry."

"How can you say that?" Xiyun's mother asked. "You just saved my life – otherwise, I would have been killed when the roof beam fell. I'm sorry, though. It's my fault you're buried in the rubble here."

"I was just doing my duty," Ma Weifu said.

"Not that again," Xiyun's mother said. "What about things that aren't part of your duties?"

Ma Weifu looked down to where he was holding her arm and asked: "What, like this?"

Xiyun's mother shook her head and said: "No, that's your duty too. It's all part of God's plan."

Ma Weifu did not understand what she meant.

Xiyun's mother, pressed close to Ma Weifu, now said: "Tell me something about Zongchun."

"What do you want to know?" Ma Weifu asked.

"I'd like to know if, in all these years away, he went to brothels?" Xiyun's mother asked.

Ma Weifu hesitated for a moment and said: "Yes, he did. We went together to a brothel in Luoyang. Sometimes it's really lonely, and we wanted someone to hold."

"That's OK," Xiyun's mother said, "I am happy for him to go with a whore because that way I know he didn't have some other woman."

"Oh, he didn't," Ma Weifu said. "He often spoke about how much he missed you and the children."

"That's good," Xiyun's mother said. "I wouldn't mind even if he visited a hundred brothels. That's what he should be doing. When a man has been away from home for a long time, what else can you expect?"

"You are a good woman," Ma Weifu said.

Xiyun's mother grinned bitterly: "What's the use of being good? No matter how good you are, life is hard."

Ma Weifu looked at her and suddenly felt a surge of emotion: "If I'm still alive after the siege is over, let me take care of you and your children in the future, OK?"

She didn't understand what he meant and said: "Aren't you taking care of us now?"

Ma Weifu started to stammer as he explained: "I mean... I want to say... I don't know if I'm the right person to take care of you all... as the children's stepfather?"

Xiyun's mother was shocked. She wanted to break away from his embrace, but bricks fell on them when she moved.

Ma Weifu grabbed her and whispered: "It's all part of God's plan."

"I know you're in love with Miss Peizhu," she said.

"But she doesn't care for me," Ma Weifu explained.

"And you don't care for me either," Xiyun's mother said.

"I am sure that I can grow to love you," Ma Weifu said, "and in fact I've already begun."

When he said this, Xiyun's mother glued her lips to his and gave him a hard kiss. Then she said: "This is your reward. By the time the siege is over, I'm afraid I'll be dead."

"No, you won't," Ma Weifu said firmly. "With me here, nobody is going to die."

Xiyun's mother was not convinced: "I have a feeling that this is all this is ever going to amount to."

All of a sudden, they could hear Mrs Wu's cries of terror. Ma Weifu called out to her: "Mrs Wu! Hurry up and get us out of here, we're under here!"

Mrs Wu screamed for assistance, but it still took nearly an hour to remove the roof beam and broken bricks. By the time Ma Weifu and Xiyun's mother were extracted, their hands and feet were completely numb. Mrs Wu squatted on the ground, kneading Ma Weifu's legs vigorously. She kept saying over and over again: "You're very lucky, young master. Four people got killed just next door! What a disaster! The building has completely collapsed, so where are we going to live?"

"Mrs Wu," Ma Weifu said, "you and Madam Yuan, as well as Old Nuo, had better all move into the west wing."

"We couldn't possibly do that," Mrs Wu said. "The master would have a fit!"

"There's a battle raging," Ma Weifu pointed out. "Do you really think he's going to come over from Hankou just to have a fit?"

As he said this, Mrs Wu started to laugh.

Before dinner, Chen Mingwu came back with Xiyun and Xizi. When he heard about the shell exploding, his face turned white. "Today, several shells were dropped near Snake Mountain," he said. "I don't know whether that was intentional or not."

"I have to pick up Peizhu," Ma Weifu cut in. "I can't let her walk back alone."

"Let me go," Chen Mingwu said.

Ma Weifu was just saying something about how it was nothing to do with him, when he caught sight of Xiyun's mother glancing at him. His heart gave a lurch, and he changed his mind. "Well, you'd better go," he said. "I'll wait here until Peizhu comes back."

Xiyun and Xizi were very excited and kept chattering about their visit to the college. "The staff hid ten bushels of rice, which they were going to cook for the students," Xiyun explained, "but then soldiers came and found it. The students are now eating buns made from rice bran and banana roots."

"Those soldiers are really bad," Xizi said.

Xiyun's mother scolded Xizi for that.

"But they are!" Xiyun said. "When we were on the way back, we saw soldiers searching a house and robbing a granny of her last bits of rice. The granny just sat on her step and cried."

"I told you to shut up, and you just keep talking," Xiyun's mother complained. While she was scolding Xiyun, she looked at Ma Weifu, who had a very ugly expression on his face. "They are just little kids, and they don't know any better," Xiyun's mother said. "Don't listen to them."

Ma Weifu had imagined that when Chen Mingwu took the two children to his college, he would have instilled them with a lot of idiotic propaganda. But now he found he couldn't blame the children because what they were saying was the truth. Little kids believe what they see, not what adults try to tell them. Hearing Xiyun's mother yelling at the kids and giving her glib explanation, Ma Weifu said: "They are right. I've seen soldiers stealing things too."

Xizi immediately cheered up and said: "I said Uncle Ma wouldn't be angry, and I was right, wasn't I?"

"Who said I would be angry?" Ma Weifu asked.

"Mingwu said we shouldn't complain about the soldiers in front of Uncle Ma," Xiyun explained. "Then Xizi said Uncle Ma was a good soldier and wouldn't be angry."

"I am not a soldier," Ma Weifu said, "I'm an official."

Xiyun pulled Ma Weifu aside and said: "Mingwu was talking for ages to someone named Zhou. He said that it was only by opening the city gates and letting the Revolutionary Army come in that we can save the people."

"Oh, really?" Ma Weifu said. "And did they say anything about how they were going to open the gates?"

"They said they were going to persuade the soldiers," Xiyun explained. "Uncle Ma, can you order the soldiers to open Binyang Gate?"

"I can't," Ma Weifu said.

"Why not?" Xiyun asked. "Aren't you an official?"

"It is my duty to guard Binyang Gate," Ma Weifu explained. "If I open it, they will cut my head off."

Xiyun was horrified and said: "That's not right at all! Uncle Ma, no matter what Mingwu says, you must not open Binyang Gate! Tell them to open the other city gates."

Ma Weifu grinned bitterly and said nothing.

Suddenly there was a burst of gunfire out on the street. It seemed to be somewhere quite close, and a scream went up all around immediately: "They are fighting in the streets! The city has fallen!" Ma Weifu leapt to his feet, and his hand went to his waist to feel his gun.

Xizi was so terrified he jumped into his mother's arms. Xiyun ran over to Ma Weifu and held his hand tightly. Xiyun's mother had turned as pale as a corpse; she was hugging Xizi and trembling all over.

Ma Weifu cocked his head, listening. Then he said: "It doesn't sound like gunfire. Stay indoors and don't move. I'll go out and have a look."

"No!" Xiyun said. "I don't want Uncle Ma to go."

"I'm just going out to see what's going on," he said. "Don't be afraid. You take care of your mother and little brother. I'll be back in a minute."

Ma Weifu hurried to the gate, and just as he was opening it Hong Peizhu and Chen Mingwu burst in. Hong Peizhu had her hand on her chest, and she was gasping for breath. She kept repeating: "Goodness that was scary! That was scary!"

"What happened?" Ma Weifu asked.

"A couple of soldiers broke into a firecracker shop, only to discover that there was nothing inside but firecrackers," Chen Mingwu said. "They were angry, so they took all the firecrackers out of the shop and let them off in the street."

"I thought they were shooting at us," Hong Peizhu said. "Then I saw the sparks flashing, and I knew it was firecrackers."

Ma Weifu couldn't help cursing: "What were those motherfuckers thinking!"

It was getting dark, but the major-domo, Old Nuo, still hadn't come home.

35

EARLY THE NEXT MORNING, the major-domo's body was found in a small street at the foot of Snake Mountain.

Old Nuo lay by the side of the road, and a nasty little piece of shrapnel was stuck in one side of his neck: that little piece had been enough to kill him. There was blood on the ground, forming a lake around him. An old man walking down the street said that the blood simply poured out when he was hit. He'd tried to speak even as he collapsed, but before he could say a word he was dead.

Hong Peizhu cried her eyes out. The major-domo, who was a relative on her mother's side of the family, had worked for them for many years. Hong Peizhu had known him almost all her life and always regarded Old Nuo as part of her own family. Ma Weifu came rushing back the moment he got the news; after all, Old Nuo was family to him too. When he saw his mangled neck, Ma Weifu also started to cry.

Chen Mingwu whispered in his ear: "How are we going to bury him? All the coffins have sold out."

Ma Weifu didn't respond; he just grunted.

"There are too many people dead in the city," Chen Mingwu continued, "and there are no coffins left."

"I don't care," Hong Peizhu cried. "Old Nuo has to be buried properly in a coffin!"

"Peizhu, you can rest assured that I will get it done," Ma Weifu said.

Ma Weifu took several soldiers and went from house to house looking for a coffin. After walking up and down several streets, he finally found one in an old rich gentleman's house in the Xinhualin district. The rich old gentleman and his family had fled Hankou, leaving only the gatekeeper in the house. The gatekeeper begged them to leave: "You can't have it! The master paid a lot of money for this, and it's for himself. What shall I tell him when he comes back?"

Ma Weifu put down a large sum of money and said: "Give him this and tell him his coffin was taken by the soldiers defending the city. I reckon that will show it was not your fault."

Ma Weifu took several people off, and they buried the majordomo at the foot of a secluded part of the city wall. There were large numbers of new graves under the wall, and the white funeral banners were pale in the sunshine.

On his return, as he walked down Long Street, a number of soldiers came rushing past carrying various pots and jars in their arms. One of his men suggested that they must have been robbing the soy-sauce makers over the other end of Long Street. Ma Weifu didn't even feel angry; he was so numbed that he could feel the stiffness in his legs even when he was walking.

When he got to Dacheng Road, there were many people clustered around in front of one of the houses there. There were also people standing in twos and threes by the side of the road, either openly crying or silently wiping away their tears.

Ma Weifu asked one of the passers-by what had happened. The passer-by answered: "The people here had nothing to eat, so the entire family hanged themselves – nine of them all told." Ma Weifu listened to the news with a thumping heart. "What's the point of trying to defend this city when it is already completely surrounded?" the man asked. "Is this to protect us, or to protect yourselves?" Ma Weifu was speechless. The man was now shouting: "The mandate of heaven has passed to another. What mortal man can thwart the will of heaven?"

Ma Weifu ran down the main street as if he were fleeing for his life and made his way back to Binyang Gate. There was no fighting going on outside the gate, and the sound of gunfire seemed almost unrelated to anything happening there. In the evening, Colonel He came to see Ma Weifu. They both smoked cigarettes and sighed over the situation. "We are pretty much out of food," Colonel He said. "This afternoon, the soldiers guarding Bao'an Gate could not withstand their hunger any longer and opened the gate to go and steal some rice from the people outside the walls. Half of them were killed, and they were only able to steal about enough rice for a single meal."

"What do the men here think?" Ma Weifu asked.

"If I tell you," Colonel He said, "you are not to shout at me."

"Go ahead," Ma Weifu said.

"They know the city is going to fall," the colonel said, "and they've been talking about robbing a few rich families and then escaping with other civilians in the chaos. After all these years of fighting, even if they did not get promoted to some official position, they don't want to go home with nothing – they've got to have something to show their parents and fellow villagers."

Ma Weifu grinned bitterly and said: "So that's how they're going to do it, is it? What about you? Are you going to do the same?"

"I don't see any other way out," Colonel He told him. "Look, is there anyone who hasn't prepared an ordinary suit to change into? What's the difference between any of us and the civilian population once we take off our uniforms? You need to wise up. With all of these defeats, none of us officers can expect to be promoted, but at least we might make a bit of money."

"I don't agree," said Ma Weifu. "I don't know if I will be alive or dead once the siege is over. If I'm dead, what will it matter to me how much money I have?"

Colonel He smiled, but his smile was a little cold. Then he said: "If you die, that's a matter of luck – the problem is what happens if you are not killed? How are you going to live?"

"That's quite enough of that," Ma Weifu said.

Soon after Colonel He had left, a soldier came to report that a man who claimed to be his cousin wanted to talk to Ma Weifu. He thought it might be Chen Mingwu, who had come to find him because something had happened at home, so he invited him in.

The young man who entered was a complete stranger. Although his cheeks sagged with hunger, he still looked highly intelligent and focused. Ma Weifu knew at a glance that he was a young man with great ambitions.

"Who are you?" Ma Weifu asked. "How dare you impersonate my cousin?"

"I am one of Hong Peizhu's classmates," the young man explained, "and she told me to say this."

Ma Weifu's tone eased when he mentioned her name. "What is the matter?" he enquired.

"My name is Zhou Jincheng," the young man said. "I want to talk to you about something important."

"What's the big deal?" Ma Weifu asked. "Is there anything more important right now than defending the city?"

"There is," Zhou Jincheng said categorically.

"There is?" Ma Weifu said. "Then how about you tell me what it is."

"I want you to open the gate," Zhou Jincheng said.

"Did the Revolutionary Army send you to talk me into a mutiny?" Ma Weifu enquired.

"Oh, no," Zhou Jincheng said, "I sent myself. I'm not asking you to carry out a mutiny – I am begging you to save the city."

"That's a pretty tall order," Ma Weifu said.

"I heard that you are Peizhu's cousin," Zhou Jincheng said, "so I came here to ask you to save the people of Wuchang. You must have seen that the people of Wuchang are suffering terribly, and there are hundreds of deaths every day. On my way here today, a mother died in the corner of the road. The baby in her arms lay on her body and continued to suck at her breast. I stood beside her and asked myself, what can I do for her?"

Ma Weifu smiled indifferently and said: "You could have picked up the baby and taken it to another mother and asked her to adopt it."

Zhou Jincheng, learning from Ma Weifu, also smiled indifferently and said: "But what if that mother dies in another corner?"

"Then you keep on going," Ma Weifu said.

"No," Zhou Jincheng said firmly, "such deaths cannot continue. I'm not cold-blooded – I think I can do something to help them. I can lay down my dignity and come here to beg you. Please save these mothers and their children." As he said that, Zhou Jincheng fell to his knees and prostrated himself on the ground.

Ma Weifu frowned. He shouted: "Can I have some help here!" A soldier came running in response to his call. His face wooden, Ma Weifu gave his orders: "Get him to his feet. I want to talk to him standing up."

The soldier came forward and tugged at Zhou Jincheng. He snapped: "Stand up! Officers don't like to talk to people on their knees." Zhou Jincheng stayed down for as long as he could, but he could not stop the soldier's strong hands pulling him to his feet.

When the soldier went out, Ma Weifu said: "I don't like to talk to people who don't do anything to preserve their dignity. Because I want to be respected myself."

"In that case," Zhou Jincheng remarked, "you'd better go and talk to that dead mother."

"Are you studying humanities by any chance?" Ma Weifu asked.

"No," Zhou Jincheng said, "I'm studying physics."

"If you are studying physics," Ma Weifu said, "you must first learn to be objective, to understand that the simple surface of an object may conceal great complexity behind it. The world lies far beyond the control of any one individual."

"And in studying physics," Zhou Jincheng said, "we also learn that objects with complex surfaces are often simple underneath."

"I'm not here to talk to you about physics," Ma Weifu snapped. "The simplest thing to do right now would be to shoot you, but the problem is that it would upset Peizhu. Please go back and tell her that she shouldn't let herself be used by any more of her classmates."

Zhou Jincheng was stunned, and the spirit in his eyes diminished. He looked at Ma Weifu and did not speak for a moment.

Ma Weifu thought coldly: You are nothing but a kid in college, and you come here wanting to be a hero.

"No wonder Chen Mingwu said that you wouldn't be persuaded," Zhou Jincheng said.

"Well, he understands that about me," Ma Weifu remarked.

"Now I know some more about you too," Zhou Jincheng said. "Before I came, I wanted to ask you to save the people of Wuchang.

Now, I know that you need to save yourself more than the people. Because you are suffering more from your conscience than the civilian population is here when they risk their lives."

Ma Weifu pulled the pistol out of his belt and slapped it down hard on the table. The moonlight pierced the window and shone on the handle of the gun. Far in the distance, they seemed to hear the sound of gunfire coming from the direction of Hong Mountain. "Get the hell out of here!" Ma Weifu roared.

On that night, the moon was bright and round. The moon on the sixteenth is fuller than on the fifteenth. But in this dark night sky, the brighter the moon was, the lonelier it seemed.

Ma Weifu found it very difficult to fall asleep that night. Zhou Jincheng's words disturbed his rest. He tried to imagine the mother's dead body slumped by the roadside and the baby tugging at her nipple. He felt heartsick, but he also felt helpless. It was only when the sky began to brighten that he slipped into a dream. Someone in his dream was shouting: "The mandate of heaven has passed to another. What mortal man can thwart the will of heaven?"

36

THERE WERE MORE and more dead people in the streets. Everything had been eaten: the domestic dogs and wild dogs in the city, snakes and mice, lake frogs and pet cats, leather shoes and suitcases, the sparrows and the rats. Every day, people walked to the banks of Ziyang Lake, stood there for a moment and jumped in. At first, some people tried to pull the bodies out, but then there were too many such jumpers, and the people trying to save them got tired of it all. It seemed better to let them lie at the bottom of the lake than to haul them ashore again because there was now nowhere to bury all the dead. The living even began to regret that they did not die earlier. Those who died at the beginning of the siege could still be properly buried; but those who died later ended up in heaps at the foot of the city walls, exposed to the sun and the rain, gradually rotting into a disgusting pile of filth and putrefaction. Who could face dying like this? If you can't live and yet also cannot face dying, the only way out is madness.

One day, there were three children walking around Government Gate with strands of hay tucked in by their necks. A woman was shouting in a weak voice: "Good people of this city, take my children away! If you have money then give me some. If you have no money, at least give my children a chance to survive!"

A passer-by asked: "Are you selling all three children?"

"Of course," the woman said. "Two of them are the children of my neighbour – one of their parents starved to death, and the other threw themselves into the lake. The other is mine – my husband was shot by a stray bullet, and he died. I am selling them to save them. Please do your best for them!"

The passers-by were all muttering, but nobody would buy any of the children.

There was an epidemic of crime. Just one shop in Long Street was visited by three gangs of thieves in the space of one morning, and the place was completely cleaned out.

Mrs Wu went out to look for some wild herbs. Just as she turned into a road near Pinghu Gate, the tall man who was walking in front of her suddenly fell at her feet. Mrs Wu was going to ask him if he was OK, but then she saw that his eyes were closed. His nostrils fluttered a few times, and then he died. Mrs Wu screamed in horror. She did not dare carry on her search anymore, so she took a few tottering paces back and then turned and ran for home.

Chen Mingwu did not know how his cousin Daying was faring, so he decided to go back and see. Hong Peizhu told him to take them some food, but he refused.

"We have more ways to get something to eat than they do," Hong Peizhu pointed out, "and if we run out of all other options, I can go to Garden Hill to borrow some food from the foreigner, Mr Meng. I know the Catholic Church still has grain reserves."

"I don't want your Staff Officer Ma to come here and put a gun against my head," Chen Mingwu said. "Besides which, there is not much food here."

"He knows I care about you," said Hong Peizhu, "so he wouldn't dare."

"But he loves you," Chen Mingwu pointed out. "There is nothing he would not dare for the woman he loves."

Hong Peizhu looked at Chen Mingwu and asked: "Are you jealous?"

Chen Mingwu wanted to say no, but, when he saw Hong Peizhu's expectant expression, he said: "What if I am?"

Hong Peizhu's face immediately burst into a brilliant smile.

"What are you so pleased about?" Chen Mingwu asked.

"I like to see you jealous," Hong Peizhu said.

Chen Mingwu walked around several streets and eventually

discovered a small shop that still had food to sell. He bought a bunch of lotus stems for six hundred yuan; then having turned out his pockets he found another two hundred yuan, with which he bought four bran cakes and three lotus roots. Chen Mingwu was a little excited, thinking that with these things, Daying and her family could survive for a few more days.

Every now and then he came across dead people, their corpses laid out by the side of the road; nobody was shocked at the sight anymore. None of the pedestrians walking along moved at all quickly: they came slowly, and they left slowly. If they said a word to one another, it was almost in a whisper. If you said more, you would be short of breath. Chen Mingwu felt agony in his heart: what was the difference between this and hell?

Arriving at the entrance of Juxian Hotel, he suddenly spotted his classmate Lan sitting in the middle of the hall with her unbrushed hair loose down her back. Chen Mingwu, a little shocked at this sight, went in and called her name. Lan's eyes were glassy, and she didn't appear to even hear him. Someone inside heard him and came out; Chen Mingwu recognised him as Lan's uncle.

"I am one of her classmates," Chen Mingwu said. "What's wrong with her?"

Lan's uncle burst into tears and said: "Those bastards! They insisted that she was a member of the Revolutionary Party, and she was arrested a few days ago. If you want to chop off her head, go right ahead! At least that way she would have stayed pure... but now... She was gang-raped by seven or eight men at a time every day for days! Now she's gone insane, so they've sent her home to us. This... now... What on earth will happen to her?"

Chen Mingwu could hardly breathe. He didn't know how to help Lan, nor how to comfort her uncle. He walked out of Juxian Hotel in a trance, feeling that everything was dark and colourless.

Daying's family was still struggling to survive. Every day, they got just a few mouthfuls of water and a little barley flour to keep them alive, but they didn't even have enough energy to go out and search for food. In the meantime, Chen Mingwu had brought them wild herbs several times, and coarse rice, a little at a time. His cousin would divide it into several parts, enough to keep them going for a few days.

"Grandma Zhang and her son next door are lying dead in bed," Daying said. "Today, I heard her daughter-in-law crying over the bodies, so I was wondering if we could give her a bran cake?"

Chen Mingwu's heart was thumping as he said: "You can't worry about other people right now, cousin, you have to put your own family's lives first."

Daying became hysterical: "Why should this happen to me? I wish they would either attack the city, or if there is not going to be any fighting, why don't they just open the gates? We've been under siege for a month now – how is anybody supposed to survive if they carry on like this? We'll all be better off dead."

"Don't say that," Chen Mingwu said. "In a few days, the city will be opened. The soldiers on the walls can't keep it up much longer. Believe me, it'll be easy for the Southern Army to get rid of them."

Once he got out of his cousin's house, Chen Mingwu thought to himself: Why should Daying believe a word that you say? He was held captive there inside the besieged city, just like a fish in a waterhole in a river that had otherwise run dry – he could only struggle in vain. If the siege of Wuchang continued for another ten days or two weeks, how many survivors would there be? Even if you didn't starve to death, wouldn't you have gone insane? And for himself, how much longer could he carry on struggling? Chen Mingwu's mood was suddenly so bad that he was about to collapse again. He was desperate to find a hole to hide in, where he wouldn't have to see anybody or do anything for the rest of his life.

Peace talks had been going on all this time, but the conditions proposed for resolving the situation had often proved unacceptable to one side or the other. The words 'corpses' and 'rampant criminality' were regularly mentioned by the negotiators. Liu Yuchun seemed to be in a state of panic, and finally he agreed that just the city gates facing towards the Yangtze River were to be opened for a set period of time to allow refugees out of the city to get food.

The sadness of these dark days was suddenly illuminated by this good news. People could see a glimmer of a bright future again, and the hope that they might yet survive also began to spread.

A notice was posted on the wall beside Government Gate. The announcement said that the Hankou Chamber of Commerce was informed that the civilian population in Wuchang did not have food to eat, so they had launched a rescue campaign for them. In consultation with the forces defending the city, various charities in Hankou jointly demanded that a city gate be opened to allow women and children out of the city to get food. An agreement had been reached to this effect.

When Chen Mingwu saw the announcement, he quickly went home and discussed with Hong Peizhu whether she should leave the city or not.

"Are they just going to open the gate for one day?" Hong Peizhu asked.

"No," Chen Mingwu said, "the gate is going to be open from eight in the morning to three in the afternoon every day. It will be open like this for a few days. Both sides have agreed to stop the shelling, but they are only going to open Wenchang Gate."

Ma Weifu heard the news and rushed over. "Since they've agreed to open the gate for seven or eight hours a day for several days, it would be a good idea not to rush out on the first day," he said. "It would be best to see what the situation outside the walls actually is. What if they change their minds and suddenly attack?"

"Why would they?" Chen Mingwu asked. "The Southern Army is very trustworthy."

Ma Weifu's face was stiff and wooden: "I know better than you what war is and what the army is."

Hong Peizhu agreed with Chen Mingwu's point of view, but she also felt that since Ma Weifu had been in the army for many years he had more experience of these things. She thought for a moment and then said: "Let's wait and see…"

On the eve of the opening of the gate, rumours spread throughout the city. Wuchang had seemed to be on its last legs, but now it had been pricked into action, and everyone was full of excitement. The bloodless faces of the starving population were flushed with this excitement. It was said that two steamers would be sent from Hankou every day to tow barges of refugees across the river. Every boat would be equipped with a small white flag, and the service personnel would all be wearing Red Cross armbands. The refugees would board at Baishazhou, and they would be transported by barge to Parrot Island in Hanyang. Any number of large pots would be waiting for them on the shore to serve porridge, together with storekeepers with stalls to sell white flour, steamed buns and noodles. At the same time, there would be one thousand bushels of rice distributed to the needy every day, and five hundred coffins would also be sent across daily to allow the corpses by the sides of the roads to be collected.

As long as there was food to eat, the people didn't care anymore whether the Northern Army opened the gates or whether the Southern Army attacked the city. Neighbours clapped their hands and celebrated together: "We'll be getting out of here alive!"

That day, Long Street was full of hurrying people before it even got light. The roads and alleyways around Wenchang Gate were full of people. It looked like a hundred rivers were racing to meet the sea, as if the entire population of the city were determined to leave all on the same day.

Chen Mingwu was chatting with Hong Peizhu at home and told her about what had happened to Lan. Hong Peizhu's face turned pale with fear, and it was a very long time before she recovered. She wanted to go and see Lan, but she was afraid to face up to her tragedy.

"When I saw her," Chen Mingwu said, "I really felt that she had suffered a fate worse than death. I don't know how Liang Wenqi will be able to cope."

"Why did Liang Wenqi have to go to Guangzhou?" Hong Peizhu asked. "If he had stayed at home, Lan would never have ended up in this dreadful state."

"When Liang Wenqi got that letter from his cousin, he could think of nothing but joining the Northern Expedition," Chen Mingwu explained.

"It's your fault too," Hong Peizhu said. "You went on and on about calling him Young Master Liang. It's not his fault he comes from a rich family."

"You're right!" Chen Mingwu sighed. "When I saw Lan in such a state, I really did blame myself. If I hadn't always been making fun of Liang Wenqi as a rich playboy, he might not have been in such a hurry to join the army. Now I don't know where he is – maybe he's just outside the city."

"Do you think Lan can be happy in the future?" Hong Peizhu asked.

"No," Chen Mingwu said. "She will always live in hell – not a hell on earth, but a hell in her own heart."

"Why?" Hong Peizhu asked.

"Her life is ruined by the disgusting things that were done to her," Chen Mingwu said, "because nobody will be prepared to turn a blind eye to them."

"When you say 'nobody', who do you mean?" Hong Peizhu asked.

"Men, women, but most of all herself," Chen Mingwu said.

"I don't think she should be blamed for what happened to her," Hong Peizhu said. "Do you?"

"Oh, yes," Chen Mingwu said. "Because I am a man."

Hong Peizhu looked at him without saying a word.

Zhou Jincheng came in while they were still talking. "This is a critical moment in the history of the city of Wuchang," he said, "and we cannot wait a moment longer – we must induce the guards at each of the city gates to mutiny, one after the other. I am sure that by this time their morale has collapsed, so we must awaken the conscience of the Northern Army soldiery, make them understand the seriousness of the situation, make them raise the flag of righteousness and throw open the gates to welcome the Northern Expeditionary Army into the city."

Zhou Jincheng's words fired Chen Mingwu's enthusiasm. He thought: Yes! That's right! Wuchang is sitting in the eye of the storm, and I am just relaxing here chatting with a young lady! What kind of man am I? I should go out and fight with my comrades!

Chen Mingwu decided to go with Zhou Jincheng. Hong Peizhu wanted to go too, but Chen Mingwu said: "You should stay at home – it's safer. It's chaos outside. I don't want to have to take responsibility if anything happens to you."

Hong Peizhu laughed: "Are you afraid of my cousin or of something happening to me?"

"I'm afraid of both," Chen Mingwu said.

"You know, my cousin is a really good person," Hong Peizhu said.

"If he was a good person," Chen Mingwu retorted, "he would

have opened the gates to the city and saved people from all of these horrors."

"He's a soldier," Hong Peizhu pointed out, "and it's his duty to carry out his orders."

"Soldiers also have a duty to protect the people," Zhou Jincheng said.

"Well, whatever, I don't want you to blame him," Hong Peizhu said. "He knows that both of you are involved with the Revolutionary Party, but he didn't betray you."

"That's because he loves you," Chen Mingwu said.

"You are quite wrong," she retorted. "He didn't betray you because he knows you are in the right."

"Really?" Chen Mingwu said. "So it seems you love him too?"

"I only love one person in the world, and you know perfectly well who he is," Hong Peizhu said.

"Let's not talk about this right now, OK?" Chen Mingwu returned.

"But I want to talk about it," Hong Peizhu said.

"Mingwu, I'll be waiting for you outside," Zhou Jincheng broke in quickly.

As soon as Zhou Jincheng had gone out, Chen Mingwu said: "Peizhu, don't be angry – let's talk about it when we get back."

"What are you running away from?" she asked.

"Nothing," Chen Mingwu said.

"No," she continued, "you must have a reason for all of this. Is it because you're afraid of my cousin?"

"No," Chen Mingwu said. "I am the son of a poor family, and I hope to devote my entire life to the cause of the revolution. It would be hard for me and a rich young lady like you to be together. You can see that from what just happened to poor Luo Yinan."

"But aren't we together now?" Hong Peizhu asked.

"This is a special situation," Chen Mingwu told her.

"Is that the only reason?" she pressed him.

"I think so," Chen Mingwu said.

"So you don't love me at all?" Hong Peizhu asked.

Chen Mingwu found that difficult to answer. He hesitated for a moment and then said: "I do, but not that much."

Hong Peizhu was overwhelmed by an intense feeling of sadness that seemed to well up from the bottom of her heart until it engulfed her. In an instant, her eyes were full of tears. She did not understand why the man in front of her was unwilling to love her. She did not know what was wrong with her, why he was so determined to keep away from her. Was this really just because her family was rich or was there something else?

Chen Mingwu saw how her smiling face had been swallowed up by misery, and he felt a certain degree of pain. He thought that she was too nice to him and he really didn't deserve her. He wanted to comfort her, or even leave some room for her to hope, but the thought of Ma Weifu's sharp eyes stopped him short. Chen Mingwu did not want to die at Ma Weifu's hands. He knew that it would be only too easy for Ma Weifu to kill him. "Peizhu," he said, "I'm sorry." Then he turned around and walked out.

Hong Peizhu watched Chen Mingwu go and then sat down by the side of her bed. Her mind was completely blank. It was a long time before she came back to her senses.

Xiyun's mother wanted to take her little girl out and came to tell Hong Peizhu so. "We'll go and see what is happening outside the walls," she said. "I've heard they are handing out white flour and steamed buns. Xizi hasn't had noodles to eat for the longest time. I don't know whether I can find some noodles to bring back for him..." When she finished, she repeated it all over again because Hong Peizhu was just staring at her blankly.

With a start, Hong Peizhu came to her senses: "Don't go, just put up with things for another two days."

"I'll have Xiyun with me," her mother said, "and we'll keep an eye on things. If we can go out safely, we will, but if not we'll come straight back. Xizi will stay at home if you don't mind taking care of him."

"That's OK," Hong Peizhu said. "If it's too dangerous outside, come back as soon as you can."

"I will," Xiyun's mother said. "We experienced all kinds of dreadful things on our travels from Hebei Province."

The room was quiet all of a sudden, only broken by the sound of Mrs Wu washing the dishes in the kitchen.

Xizi was playing in the backyard for a while, and then he came to find Hong Peizhu. She was sad and bored. In order to relieve her bad mood, she decided to teach Xizi to read. When the banging on the front door started, Xizi had just learned the word 'hand'.

Hearing the knocking on the door, Xizi shouted happily: "Mum and Sis are back!" He jumped up and ran out of the room. Mrs Wu also emerged from the kitchen to open the door. Xizi shouted: "It must be Mum and Sis!" He ran round Mrs Wu and headed straight to the front door, swinging the latch open with a bang.

A group of soldiers burst through the door, frightening Xizi so much that he staggered back, before falling to the ground on his bottom.

"What are you doing?" Mrs Wu shrieked. "This is the Hong mansion, Mr Hong's home!"

"Why should we care who the hell he is?" a soldier asked. "We're searching for members of the Revolutionary Party. We've heard there is a Revolutionary Party member hiding here."

"What on earth are you talking about?" Mrs Wu screamed. "There are only old people and children here."

Hearing the noise outside, Hong Peizhu came out of the room: "What's wrong, Mrs Wu?" As soon as she appeared, the soldiers' eyes all turned to her. They exchanged glances and started moving towards her. "What do you think you are doing?" Hong Peizhu demanded.

"We want to know if you belong to the Revolutionary Party," one of the soldiers said.

"I do not," she retorted. "Please leave immediately."

"And why do we have to do what you say?" another of the soldiers asked rhetorically.

The soldiers were now inching towards her. Hong Peizhu's mind turned to the image of Lan, which made her feel weak all over, and she began retreating towards the house. The soldiers followed her into the room, and over the course of the next few minutes sounds of screaming and salacious laughter could be heard from inside. Mrs Wu, her face white, decided that nothing mattered any more: she rushed into the kitchen, grabbed a knife, and burst into Hong Peizhu's room. "How dare you touch our young lady!" Mrs Wu cried. Some of the soldiers were startled to see Mrs Wu in such a state. One of the soldiers laughed and then hit her hand with the butt of his rifle. The knife immediately fell to the ground. Mrs

Wu hurled herself at the soldiers, scratching, kicking and biting them. "Run, Miss Peizhu!" she shouted. Hong Peizhu pulled herself together and managed to fight her way out of the room in the midst of all this confusion. Her hair had come down, her clothes had been torn, and one shoe had fallen off and was lying under the bed.

Hong Peizhu had no idea where she was going. Instead of making for the front door, she ran towards the backyard. Before she had even made her way out there, three soldiers came running after her. The first thing Hong Peizhu saw was the wellhead in the backyard. She rushed towards it, shouting: "Don't come any closer! If you come any closer, I'll jump!"

The three soldiers seemed to be brought up short by her words. They stood still and looked at each other as if they were debating something.

The wellhead lay open like a huge gaping mouth, as if just waiting to swallow up a fresh life. Cold air from the well touched her arm, as if pulling her towards it, and she suddenly felt an overwhelming sense of despair. Am I really going to die today? she thought. Is this really the end? If so, let me die here and now, let me suffer no more.

When one of the soldiers saw Hong Peizhu standing still on the edge of the well, he cried: "How can you give up your life like this, miss? Your family is so rich. You've been so happy. Are you going to give that all up? All you need to do is give us a little bit of your happiness and let us be happy too. That's all we want. Why do you have to die?"

Am I just giving up? Hong Peizhu thought to herself. Have I been happy? Yes, it is true that I don't want to die. It is true that I used to be very happy. But from today on, I can never be happy again. Because Mingwu said that Lan's life would be ruined by the disgusting things that were done to her. It is not up to me to say that these things aren't disgusting. It is not up to me to decide how the man I love will feel about them. If I have to live like that, I might as well be dead! As she pondered her future, tears rolled down her cheeks, pouring down her face, and then falling quietly down her front.

Hong Peizhu, who had always been a simple and straightforward character, now felt her mind was as blank as a sheet of white paper. White paper with nothing written on it. She felt a sense of intense relief. All of a sudden, her body relaxed from having been as tightly wound as a spring.

One of the soldiers was watching her closely; he thought that Hong Peizhu had decided to let them have their way with her and was walking towards her, grinning from ear to ear. When he got close to Hong Peizhu, so close that he could touch her with his hand, Hong Peizhu kicked the other shoe off her foot and jumped into the well.

After a muffled thud, everything was quiet again. The three soldiers in the backyard were struck dumb.

37

XIYUN and her mother got quite close to Pinghu Gate and then found they could go no further. There were people everywhere, foul-smelling and badly behaved. Xiyun wanted to turn back, but there were too many people packed in behind them. There were hordes of people pressing in and crushing them, and there was no way out at all. News from the front, like running water, was conveyed towards the back. First of all, anyone who wanted to leave had to have a city exit permit before they would be allowed out. Then they were told it was possible to force your way out beyond the walls, but then you had to be checked by the Southern Army at Baishazhou. Later on, it was said that there were too many sandbags packed round the gate, and only one half had been opened. The people in front could not move, but those behind them kept surging forward, and many were trampled to death. All kinds of rumours broke over them, like waves. Xiyun's mother was feeling frightened. She hugged Xiyun tightly for fear of losing her in the crowd.

Hours later, more news came that the gate had now been closed, so anyone wanting to leave would have to wait until tomorrow. They were also told that they would have to stay by the river; no boats would be running. Finally, the people packed in behind them began to move away. Knowing that they would not be able to get out of the city today, the crowds started to disperse.

Xiyun and her mother walked back wearily to the Hong mansion. They did not have enough to eat at the best of times, and having missed their meal today they were so hungry that they found it difficult to walk and their sight was blurred.

The front door was sitting half open. Xiyun was a little worried and asked: "Why is the door open?"

"Maybe Uncle Ma has just arrived," Xiyun's mother said, "and they haven't closed it again yet."

"No," Xiyun said, "Uncle Ma shuts the door tightly every time." She ran on ahead, stepped through the door and shouted: "Peizhu! Xizi! We're back!"

There was no response inside the house. Xiyun's mother followed her in, echoing her call: "Xizi! Mrs Wu, we're back!"

Mrs Wu came out of Hong Peizhu's room, moaning softly. Her jacket was torn to pieces, her breasts were exposed, she was naked from the waist down, and blood flowed down her thighs. Xiyun and her mother stood rooted in place for a moment, motionless. Mrs Wu was howling like a madwoman, but she seemed beyond speech. She raised her hand, like an automaton, and pointed towards the backyard.

Xiyun pulled herself together. She ran as quickly as she could towards the backyard. She was shouting: "Peizhu! Xizi! Xizi! Peizhu!"

The backyard was empty, and no one answered. Xiyun saw the shoe lying beside the well. She knew it was Hong Peizhu's shoe, and she understood that something terrible must have happened. Xiyun rushed over to the well head and looked in, screaming wildly: "Peizhu! Peizhu!"

Xiyun's mother, who had followed her, also climbed up on the edge of the well. She could see a garment floating in the water. She did not say a word, but fainted dead away, right there beside the well.

Ma Weifu spent the whole afternoon up in the tower over Binyang Gate. It was quiet outside the city, though occasionally the sound of gunfire could be heard going from Hong Mountain towards the top of Snake Mountain. After each of the shells exploded deafeningly, it was very quiet and somewhat gloomy.

His ears were already well-accustomed to such loud bangs. In fact, if a whole day went past without such a sound, he would feel that things were not quite right. However, for all that the sound of gunfire rent the sky, it had nothing to do with the tower over Binyang Gate, and because it had nothing to do with them the soldiers were bored and restless. Ma Weifu missed the time when they had been fighting in the first few days after the siege began. As long as he was fighting, it did not really matter whether he won or lost: there was something to do. Now, with a ceasefire in operation, they were neither fighting nor withdrawing – it was a stalemate. Day after day of deadlock was stressful and exhausting for everyone. The soldiers guarding the walls and the towers were no longer interested in standing guard, and they no longer kept an eye out for the enemy; in fact, they didn't even salute anymore. They sat around in little groups of twos or threes, basking in the autumn sunshine, listlessly smoking and chatting to each other. Bending over the walls, you could see the soldiers of the other side off in the distance, talking and laughing. Suddenly a shout would go up, friendly in tone, but with ulterior motives. The loudest cries the defenders could hear were: "Brothers, are you getting enough to eat over there?"

It was normally a perfectly innocuous question, but here it was like a sharp knife whirling through the air. It was a more lethal weapon than any gun, and the burden of this refrain was: You have lost.

The soldiers up on the walls were annoyed by any mention of food, so they shouted back, cursing them: "Eat, eat, eat... That's all those motherfuckers ever want to talk about!" The soldiers from the north were vulgar, loud-mouthed men, and they would have been happy to curse them roundly, but after days of not having enough food they could not make their voices heard. As a result, they were subjected to such assaults on their morale every day.

Ma Weifu took a little turn around the city. The shops on Long Street had been closed for many days, but a good number of them had now reopened. The astonishingly high prices had also begun to fall. One reason was that soldiers were eager to cash in on what they had stolen and had started auctioning their ill-gotten gains. Secondly, the shopkeepers were afraid of being robbed again, so they were trying to get rid of anything they had left to anyone who would pay something for it. Thirdly, the inhabitants of the city were now leaving one after another. It was estimated that half the city would be empty in two or three days' time, and demand would inevitably drop in consequence. Ma Weifu actually bought a Parker pen in one small shop that only cost him a few hundred strings of cash. Two days earlier, the same sum would only have been enough to buy a bran cake to eat. Ma Weifu sighed at this, and the shopkeeper told him that it was a soldier who had just brought the pen in and asked him to sell it on his behalf. Then he added that you sell stolen goods for whatever you can get. Ma Weifu was going to give this pen to Xiyun. He thought that since Xiyun was still a child and she was obviously so clever, she really ought to go to school.

Ma Weifu wanted to go to Hong mansion because there he could relax. He got quite close and then turned around again. He felt it might be awkward for him to be confronted with Hong Peizhu and Xiyun's mother together. One was the woman he loved but who did not love him; the other was the woman he did not love but wanted to take care of. He wanted both of them but knew that his desires would only make both of them miserable. Besides, it might be the case that neither of them wanted him. He decided that if he was dead by the time the siege was lifted, this web of desires was all completely pointless.

When he returned, Ma Weifu saw the coffins were sitting under the walls, next to where the bodies had been spread out by the side of the road. The bodies were all being put into the coffins. They said that they would sit below the city wall until the peace talks were over, and then they would all be buried at the same time.

The situation inside the city was suddenly a great deal more positive. They were planning that the defenders of Wuchang would leave the city unarmed and be amalgamated into the troops commanded by Liu Zuolong over in Hanyang. Ma Weifu felt that if a peaceful settlement of this kind could be reached, it would be good for both sides. But he didn't quite believe these rumours because he knew Liu Yuchun. How could someone as hard as Liu Yuchun agree to let his soldiers put down their weapons? How could he put his men under the command of a traitor like Liu Zuolong?

CHAPTER 37 | 331

Returning to Binyang Gate, he bumped into Colonel He. The colonel asked him how the negotiations were going, and Ma Weifu said he had no idea. Colonel He then informed him that the negotiations had broken down. Major General Liu insisted that his troops leave the city with their weapons, but the other side refused to allow this. The next step would be to fight another battle.

"Then let's fight," Ma Weifu said. "Anything's better than this."

"How can we possibly fight?" Colonel He asked. "A group of people so hungry that they can't even hold up their own guns, fighting against a group of well-fed, well-trained victorious troops? We couldn't even fight Ye Ting's crew when we had enough to eat – now we are so hungry, how can we possibly defeat them?"

"Even if we are going to lose, we still have to fight them," Ma Weifu said, "because we don't have any other choice."

"So you don't care about the lives of your men?" Colonel He asked.

"Fighting is the only way to put an end to this," Ma Weifu said. "Otherwise, pretty much all the civilians left in Wuchang are going to die."

"There is still a way to settle this without fighting," Colonel He suggested.

Ma Weifu stared at him and said: "You and I have followed Major General Liu for many years. Please don't do this to me."

Colonel He clearly felt a little guilty and hung his head. He spoke in a voice so low that Ma Weifu could only just hear him: "I will do as you say."

An aeroplane flew across the sky again: the final challenge. Leaflets were dropped, and grenades were thrown. The grenades landed on the hill, while the leaflets were blown through the streets by the wind. Ma Weifu climbed up the tower and stared out into the distance, looking around him in perplexity. Have I made the right choice? Should I join with Colonel He in his betrayal, when such a treason would mean saving the lives of the people of Wuchang? But at the same time, this betrayal would result in destruction, since it will ruin us. Any act of treachery, big or small, would ruin our lives because we would lose what we need to survive: a good reputation, a strong character and dignity. Can I afford such a thing? Ma Weifu wondered.

The wind was up, and the branches of the trees waved about, while the sky looked as if it might rain. Ma Weifu felt confused. Just then, he heard Xiyun's piercing voice. The sound came from under the tower, shocking, horrifying and sharp enough to make him feel that the whole building might collapse. Ma Weifu came out in a cold sweat. He rushed down the tower.

When Xiyun caught sight of Ma Weifu, her legs buckled underneath her, and she sat down in a heap on the ground. "What's happened?" Ma Weifu demanded. "Tell me!"

Xiyun said: "Peizhu... Peizhu... And Xizi..." and then she could not get another word out.

Ma Weifu knew that the worst must have happened.

38

CHEN MINGWU WAS CRYING when Ma Weifu arrived at the Hong mansion with two of his men and Xiyun.

Chen Mingwu had gone to Bao'an Gate to encourage them to revolt; a lieutenant there was an acquaintance of his cousin Daying. The lieutenant said that if there was an uprising, he would support it, but he himself was in no position to take the lead. Chen Mingwu felt pretty good to have got the man to say as much.

When he emerged, he encountered two soldiers out on the street, secretly selling rice. Chen Mingwu bought a small bag and went around to his cousin's house. Her whole family was now in good enough condition to be able to get out of bed and walk slowly, but there was absolutely no food left in their house. Chen Mingwu's rice arrived just in the nick of time. His cousin was overjoyed; she decided to make porridge with this rice the following morning so they could all eat a full meal and then leave the city.

"Mingwu," she said, "we're family, and I know you'll say I don't need to thank you, but you've saved our lives. I feel I ought to repay you."

"OK," Chen Mingwu said, "once the siege is over, I'll come to your house every day for dinner and eat until I'm full." His cousin smiled at this, and Chen Mingwu also smiled. Neither of them had been in such a good mood for a long, long time.

Chen Mingwu arrived back at the Hong mansion ten minutes before Ma Weifu did. Just at that moment, Xiyun's mother came round after her faint, and the missing Xizi had been located among the bushes in the backyard. He was too frightened to look at anyone and just snuggled up in his mother's arms, shivering. The neighbours had helped to pull Hong Peizhu out of the well. Xiyun's mother told Mrs Wu to wipe her face clean with a towel and put her down on her own bed. Hong Peizhu, whose clothes were torn, was pale and her eyes were slightly open. She seemed very calm, as if she had not suffered at all.

Chen Mingwu had no idea what had happened. When he saw Hong Peizhu, it was a bolt from the blue. He fell to the ground beside her, calling her name. He reached out to take her hand, only to find that her body was stone cold – she'd been dead for a long time. Chen Mingwu was dumbstruck; then after a long pause, he began to wail. "Peizhu!" he cried, "what's the matter with you? What on earth has happened?"

Ma Weifu rushed in like a whirlwind. He did not even look at Chen Mingwu but grabbed hold of him with one hand and threw him against the wall. Then he turned around and looked at Hong Peizhu, but with that one glance his heart broke. He had loved his cousin so much, he had loved everything about her, and now her stiff corpse was lying there, cold, painless and joyless. His tears poured down his cheeks, and he shouted to her over and over again: "Peizhu! Peizhu! Why did it have to be you?"

Then he pulled out his gun and fired several shots into the sky. The neighbours were startled, and a good few of them rushed in through the front door. "Who did it?" Ma Weifu cried. "Who is responsible for this?"

Mrs Wu came over and knelt on the ground, crying: "Young master, why don't you kill me? Five soldiers came in – I couldn't stop them… I couldn't protect Miss Peizhu. Young master, Miss Peizhu was afraid they would rape her, so she jumped into the well! Just kill me, young master! How am I supposed to show my face here ever again! Five of them took turns… they took turns… I… How am I supposed to live with the shame of what they did to me?" Mrs Wu cried until she was completely out of breath.

Ma Weifu gave a start. He looked straight at Mrs Wu and said: "Tell me exactly what happened."

Mrs Wu explained all over again. This time, Chen Mingwu also understood clearly what had happened here during his absence. In Mrs Wu's crying, he felt his own heart break.

Ma Weifu, like a maddened animal, leapt around the room, screaming and roaring. He shouted at the two men who had come with him: "Find out who did this! I'm going to kill them! There were five of them, and I'm going to kill them all!"

As he spoke, Ma Weifu's eyes fell on Chen Mingwu. He went over, reached out his left hand, grabbed his collar and pulled out his gun with his right hand. Ma Weifu put the muzzle of his gun right up against Chen Mingwu's temple and said sharply: "You too! What did you promise me? I told you to protect them – is this how you do it? Why didn't you stay with her? You swore you'd look after her, didn't you?"

Chen Mingwu knew that this time, there was no escape. No matter how much he regretted his actions, it was too late to save Peizhu. Henceforth, Hong Peizhu's sad gaze would be a heavy cross to bear, but it was a burden he would have to bear; he would have to carry it for the rest of his life. He had abandoned her just when she most needed his protection. Chen Mingwu's tears fell on the back of Ma Weifu's hand. "Kill me!" he said. "I would like to show my regret by dying. With Peizhu dying like this, I will never be happy again. Kill me, because I want to die. Peizhu always wanted to be with me. When she was alive, I always refused. Now, I agree. Just bury me with her."

Ma Weifu's hand was shaking. He really wanted to kill this useless man. It was for his sake that Peizhu had refused to leave the city, but he had wandered off by himself just at the moment when Peizhu needed him the most. What would be the point of leaving such an irresponsible person alive? Kill him! Ma Weifu said to himself. It's his fault Peizhu is dead! He really was almost at the point where he was ready to pull the trigger.

Suddenly a small voice, a very small, soft voice said: "Uncle Ma, you mustn't do this. None of this is Mingwu's fault." Ma Weifu realised that it was Xiyun's voice. It was as tiny as the sound of a mosquito or a buzzing fly, but it was quite clear to Ma Weifu. The powerful tremor in her voice forced him to think about her distress.

Ma Weifu lowered his hand and pushed the gun back into its holster. He felt a sigh of relief from the people around him. He walked over to Hong Peizhu and reached out to close her half-open eyes. He thought that if he killed Chen Mingwu, from wherever she was in the underworld, Peizhu would never forgive him. "It is for Peizhu's sake that I have left you alive," he said.

Chen Mingwu choked: "I feel that I might as well be dead. I really hoped that you would kill me."

Ma Weifu did not say another word. He sat down beside Hong Peizhu's body. Xiyun slid alongside him like a cat and whispered: "Uncle Ma, let me go out with Mingwu to find a coffin. Otherwise, Peizhu won't have one."

Ma Weifu nodded his head slightly. Xiyun took Chen Mingwu's hand and led him out of the door.

Xiyun's mother's sobbing reminded Ma Weifu of her presence. He looked over towards her and saw Xizi's terrorised little face, his body curled up as small as it would go. His heart skipped a beat, and he said: "What's wrong with Xizi?"

"I'm afraid he's suffering from shock," Xiyun's mother said. "He won't say a word."

"Did he see her… jump?" Ma Weifu asked.

"I am afraid so," Xiyun's mother said.

When Ma Weifu wanted to ask further questions, he saw huge tears rolling from Xizi's eyes. "There's nothing to be afraid of," Ma Weifu said. "It's all over. I promise no one will hurt you anymore. Tomorrow I will take all of you out of the city."

Ma Weifu stopped speaking. The room was quiet. Xiyun's mother and Mrs Wu did not say a word, so they sat quietly until dark.

When Chen Mingwu and Xiyun came back with the coffin, the sky was already quite black. "Shall we put her in it immediately?" Chen Mingwu asked Ma Weifu.

"No," he said, "I want to watch over her tonight."

"OK," Chen Mingwu said.

That night, nobody ate a thing. Xizi fell asleep in his mother's arms. Xiyun sat next to Ma Weifu. When she became really sleepy,

CHAPTER 38 | 337

she climbed onto his lap and went to sleep. Chen Mingwu sat at the table, his mind in a state of complete confusion. He had an appointment that evening to go to Tongxiang Gate with Zhou Jincheng and talk to a certain Major Liu there, but now he couldn't get away, nor could he even get a message to his friend.

In the middle of the night, there was silence all around, and the only thing that could be heard inside the room was the soft sound of breathing. Ma Weifu looked at Hong Peizhu, and countless thoughts passed through his mind. In the silence, he made up his mind about a few things; he knew that these were things he was determined to do whatever the cost to himself.

Now he spoke to Chen Mingwu: "Tomorrow morning, I want you to take the three of them out of the city." He gestured to Xiyun and her mother as he spoke.

"I don't know if we'll be able to leave," Chen Mingwu pointed out.

"I will escort you out of the gate myself," Ma Weifu said, "and once you are out of the city, you must protect them. There may be more fighting, or it may be all over. Whether the battle is over or not, I don't feel happy about leaving them here in the city. Where is your hometown?"

Chen Mingwu hesitated for a moment and then said: "In Hanchuan."

"After you leave the city," Ma Weifu instructed him, "you must go straight back to Hanchuan. Don't stay in Hankou. It'll be safer in the countryside. You can't afford to make any more mistakes. As soon as the siege is over, I'll go there to find you. You'll only have to take care of the three of them for a short time, and I'll give you enough money to live on. Later on, I'll be taking care of them, and you can go back to college."

Chen Mingwu nodded and said: "Will you be able to find us?"

"Oh, sure," Ma Weifu said. "If there is any problem and I can't find you, then next Mid-Autumn Festival we will meet at Binyang Gate. That's the deal."

"OK," Chen Mingwu said, "we'll be there."

"And if I don't turn up," Ma Weifu said, "it'll be because I've died."

Xiyun woke up at this point and said: "Uncle Ma, don't die."

Ma Weifu patted her on the head and continued talking to Chen Mingwu: "If I don't make it, please take care of them for me. Peizhu was very kind to you, and you never paid her back. Xiyun and her family have also been good to you. Now, if you pay the two of them back at the same time, I'm sure Peizhu will be pleased. Didn't you say that you regretted what happened? Well, this is the only way you can make sure she rests in peace."

Chen Mingwu was deeply moved. He decided that this horrible man did have his good points after all. "I assure you that I will do my best," he said. "You should also take care of yourself, for the sake of the children and Madam Yuan if nothing else." After Chen Mingwu said this, he put out his hand. Ma Weifu hesitated for a moment and then took it. The two of them shook hands.

39

Before dawn, Ma Weifu escorted Chen Mingwu and Xiyun's family out of Wenchang Gate. The inhabitants of the city who wanted to leave had already formed an immense, snaking queue. Two of Ma Weifu's men raised their guns to open up the road ahead. Ma Weifu carried Xizi on his back, while Xiyun and her mother were sandwiched in the middle. Chen Mingwu followed close behind them and served as a rearguard. As a group, they forced their way down the road until they got to the tower by Wenchang Gate. Behind them, there was a dreadful sound of shouting and swearing, which made the skin on the back of Chen Mingwu's neck prickle with cold.

The defenders at Wenchang Gate recognised Ma Weifu, and when they heard that he was escorting the family of Staff Officer Yuan, they immediately proclaimed that they would be the first to leave when the gates were opened. Ma Weifu did not dare to say anything more, so he stayed with them at Wenchang Gate, waiting for the sun to rise.

At dawn, the people in front of Wenchang Gate were seething. People who had been hungry for more than a month, who had been reduced to yellowed skin and bone, were using the last strength they had to wait here. When the clock struck eight, two soldiers came out and opened the gate. Other soldiers raised their guns to keep order. The gate opened, and all kinds of voices could be heard behind them, but taken all together these weak and feeble voices sounded like a low whistle.

Since they were under Ma Weifu's protection, Chen Mingwu and his party made their way out of the city gate without the slightest hitch. Standing at the gate, Ma Weifu spoke to Chen Mingwu: "You and I have never had anything in common, not even the same ideas. But today we have been brought together to achieve a single aim – to protect that family. I guess this was meant to be. Hopefully this time, you really will keep your promise. This promise will give you something to live for."

"I will do my very best," Chen Mingwu said. "But I hope you can find something to live for too. We both need the same thing. My classmate Zhou Jincheng can help you, and he should be coming to find you very soon." Having said that, and without waiting for Ma Weifu to reply, Chen Mingwu lifted Xizi onto his back and turned away.

Xiyun's mother moved back, and Ma Weifu said to her: "You can forget what I said to you. I don't know if I will ever be able to take care of you and Zongchun's children because I have no idea whether or not God will let me live."

Xiyun's mother just bowed her head, but her eyes were wet and her throat was tight.

"Uncle Ma," Xiyun shouted, "we'll be waiting for you to come."

"Xiyun," Ma Weifu told her, "you've got to help Mingwu to look after your mother and little brother. Oh, yes…" Ma Weifu suddenly remembered the Parker pen he had bought for her. He took it out of his pocket and gave it to Xiyun. "You must go to school and study and become a useful person in the future."

"Uncle Ma, I will be waiting for you to take me to school," Xiyun replied.

Chen Mingwu and his party were disappearing from Ma Weifu's sight. It may well be, Ma Weifu thought, that having said goodbye today, I will never see them again.

Ma Weifu returned to the Hong mansion. He had hired some men to help him bury Hong Peizhu temporarily in the backyard. There were corpses everywhere by the foot of the city walls or in any wasteland or bit of overgrown land. The people who died on the streets, although they were being placed in coffins, were not being buried. They were being piled up at the foot of Snake Mountain or around the city wall in areas away from human habitation. Ma Weifu didn't want Hong Peizhu to be thrown in among the others, and he didn't want her to be buried in some cheap and nasty coffin. When it was all over, the Hong family would be coming back, and at the very least they could invite Daoist priests from Changchun Monastery to hold a funeral ceremony for her so that her soul could rest in peace. Ma Weifu made his arrangements and told Mrs Wu why he had done this. He gave Mrs Wu a sum of money and asked her to look after the Hong mansion.

"Surely it will still be quite a long time before the master comes back?" Mrs Wu asked.

"A few more days," Ma Weifu said. "The city is pretty much on its last legs."

After doing all this, Ma Weifu felt extremely sleepy. He said he wanted to sleep in Hong Peizhu's bed, so Mrs Wu quickly made the bed for him with fresh bedclothes. Ma Weifu lay down on his cousin's bed, smelling the familiar smells, and he could not help grieving all over again. He wondered: How could such a gentle girl as Peizhu have turned out to be so strong? He thought that if she had not been as angry and unhappy as it was possible for her to be, she would never have thrown herself into that well. He decided that it was no wonder that she hated soldiers like him. He realised that it was soldiers like him who had forced Peizhu to commit suicide. He thought that only by avenging her could he fully express his love for her. Thinking about it, Ma Weifu couldn't sleep. He got up and left the Hong mansion.

The once-bustling city of Wuchang was now barely recognisable. There were fortifications at each intersection, and some remote places were now defended with trenches placed at right angles to each other. The doors of shops and houses facing towards the street had mostly been dismantled, and the soldiers of the Northern Army who fled into the city were using them to sleep on. Ma Weifu knew full well that for every day this raggle-taggle army had been in the city, they had been destroying the place. Now that civilians were beginning to leave the city, they had wrapped up the proceeds of their crimes and made their way outside the walls mixed in among the other inhabitants – the number of soldiers swaggering through the streets was already clearly being reduced.

Passing by Hong Peizhu's college, Ma Weifu could not help thinking about her again. Standing by the gate, he remembered that in the past, when it was late, he had often been sent by his uncle to pick her up. She would come out of the gate in a pretty dress, smiling, with a light footstep... he could almost see her before his very eyes. Ma Weifu's heart felt as if it were being painfully seared. On the spur of the moment, an idea came into his mind.

Ma Weifu went into the college and asked one of the students there about Zhou Jincheng.

"Are you looking for him?" the student asked. "I'm afraid he's dead."

Ma Weifu was shocked: "When did this happen?"

"Just today," the student said. "This morning, when all the artillery was firing, he and a classmate were watching from up on the third floor, and he was hit in the head by a stray bullet. They took him to the Tongren Hospital, but it was just packed with the wounded, and they simply could not treat him. They were going to take him somewhere else, but before they even got out of the door to the Tongren Hospital he died. Dreadful, really!"

Ma Weifu hesitated for a while and then walked away. All the way to the tower by Binyang Gate, he thought about the brilliant, lively young man. What was it that he'd said? *Now, I know that you need to save yourself more than the people. Because you are suffering more from your conscience than the civilian population is here when they risk their lives.*

That night, it rained and the wind blew. The weather covered everything; it seemed that the whole world was nothing but wind and rain. Ma Weifu sat all night in the guardroom in the gate tower, looking out at Changchun Monastery, half-hidden in the darkness, and the grey shadow of the pagoda that topped Hong Mountain. You were wrong, young man, he thought to himself. No matter what I do, I can't save myself. This is my destiny. I came into this world and walked this road. Whatever choice I made, the end result would have been the same: destruction.

It was a long night.

40

CHEN MINGWU's night was even longer than Ma Weifu's.

Once they got out of the city gate, they walked along the river. Chen Mingwu was thrilled to see the waves of the Yangtze River rising and falling. Finally, they had escaped and could put the horrors of the last month behind them. On his back, he was carrying Xizi, who had been sleeping the whole time. He decided that the first thing to do when they got to Hankou was not to continue to flee but to take Xizi to a doctor. He mentioned this to Xiyun's mother, who agreed.

Even when they were still a long way away from Baishazhou, there seemed to be a lot of people about – more and more of them in fact. When they arrived at Baishazhou, the crowds were enormous. Xiyun was amazed and said: "We were the first to get out of the city today, so how come there are so many people here?" Chen Mingwu did not understand either. On enquiry, he was told that too many people had left the city the day before, added to which there were many refugees outside the walls anyway. The people in Hankou had underestimated the number to be transported and had not sent enough boats over, so thousands of people had waited by the river the whole night.

They were now being joined by more and more people streaming out of the city. The barges could only take very few people away at a time, and even when they got on board the inspection by the military police was extremely slow. People crowded around, and there was shouting, cursing and crying. A child had become separated from his family and was crying himself hoarse when he was nearly trampled to death. Chen Mingwu was shocked by the sight and immediately grabbed hold of Xiyun and her mother. "There are too many people coming out of the city," he said, "and at this speed we will still all be here when it gets dark."

"Will they sail in the dark?" Xiyun's mother asked.

"I don't know," Chen Mingwu told her. "But there are too many people here, so Xiyun must hold your hand, and we must keep close together. If we should be separated, you must not go aboard any of the boats. Walk upstream until you find a place where there aren't so many people, and we can find each other there. Xiyun, can you remember that?"

"Oh, yes," Xiyun said.

The sky was becoming darker and darker, and it looked like it was going to start raining at any moment. People's patience had now reached its limit, but the barges were still only allowing them on one at a time, until it seemed that these wretched panicking refugees were all going to be stuck on that riverbank until doomsday. Chen Mingwu was worried that Xiyun's mother would not be able to stand much longer and asked them if they wanted to find a place to rest. "It doesn't matter," Xiyun's mother said, "I'll hold on even if it kills me – it will all be worth it if I can get on the boat."

The people escaping from the city were still pouring down to the river. There was some pushing and shoving near the closest of the barges, and then someone started shouting: "He's been crushed to death! Stop it – you are crushing him!" The situation was chaotic enough to begin with, but this shouting created an even greater panic. The hordes pushed this way and that; nobody could control their own movements; you just had to move with the flow of people. Chen Mingwu was worried that someone might indeed have been killed, and he told Xiyun and her mother to stick close and follow him out of the crowd. "If this is allowed to carry on, there really will be trouble!" he shouted. "Let's wait here tonight, and we'll leave tomorrow morning."

Chen Mingwu led them out of the crowd and found a place where there weren't so many people. Suddenly, he caught sight of an old lady in ragged clothes, holding a bundle in her arms, struggling along. She looked just like his mother. His heart leapt and started thumping; he couldn't stop himself from running after her and shouting: "Mum! Mum!" He kept shouting until he was completely hoarse. However, when he finally caught up with the old lady and saw her face, he discovered that he had made a mistake. The old lady looked at Chen Mingwu with tears in her eyes. Chen Mingwu stood there with tears in his eyes. They nodded to each other and then went their separate ways.

When Chen Mingwu recovered from this blow, he realised that Xiyun and her mother were nowhere to be seen. He knew that he had done something very wrong; his impulsiveness had resulted in him leaving them behind. Xizi was still fast asleep on Chen Mingwu's back, lying there without moving. Chen Mingwu held fast to him with one hand as he anxiously pushed his way through the crowds, shouting: "Xiyun! Madam Yuan!" Chen Mingwu used all his strength to shout, but in such a noisy crowd no one could hear him.

It rained during the night, and Xizi began to run a temperature. Chen Mingwu, who was almost insane with worry, ran several miles and finally succeeded in locating a pharmacy out in the countryside. He told his story to the old man behind the counter, and when he had finished he fell to his knees. He begged him to take care of Xizi for the time being. He took out all the money Ma Weifu had given him and put it into the hands of the old man before returning to the riverbank to continue his search. Why do I make a mess of everything I do? Chen Mingwu thought bitterly.

As soon as it got dark, the boats stopped running. The river was as black as ink, and only the small steamer Wanwu, moored beside the barges, had its lamps lit. These bright lights swayed up and down with the movement of the waves. The rain was getting heavier and heavier, sometimes coming down in gusts and sometimes as sheets, together with an icy cold wind. People stranded on the riverbank had nowhere to take shelter, but they could not bear to be out in the wind and rain and began to make their way towards the barge. The barge was soon dreadfully overcrowded, so some people crossed the guardrail onto the steamer Wanwu and went on board to shelter from the rain. Once one person had gone, they were joined by countless more. The more people went on board, the more violently the ship swayed in the wind and rain. The crew realised that something was terribly wrong, but it was too late. They shouted: "Get off the boat! The boat is going to sink!" But the wind and the noise drowned out their voices. The people on the shore, caught in the heavy rain, continued to pour on board the small steamer.

Eventually, amidst piercing and terrifying screams, the small steamer sank. It went down so fast that people just dropped into the water. The crowds on the shore stood there stunned for a few seconds; then some rushed to the rescue, while others turned and fled. As they ran, those who slipped and fell to the ground were trampled by those behind them, and their screams and cries resounded along the dark and desolate riverside.

In just a few minutes, the small steamer was swallowed up by the river, leaving no trace behind it; it was as if it had never even existed. Grabbing lamps from the barge, staring at the impassive surface of the river, hundreds of people were calling out to any survivors. Their helpless cries, mixed with the rise and fall of the waves and the whistling wind and rain, flowed out into the depths of the night.

When the sky began to brighten, the cries turned into sobbing. Originally, they had thought that they were fleeing for their lives, but now countless families had lost one or more of their members. Chen Mingwu's eyes were bloodshot, and his voice was hoarse. His heart was numb, and he had no idea what to do next – his mind was completely empty.

As he walked upstream, he saw fewer and fewer people. Chen Mingwu really had no expectation that he would ever see Xiyun or her mother again. Suddenly, he heard a familiar voice that lifted his spirits immeasurably. He raised his head and caught sight of Xiyun standing beside a clump of reeds by the riverbank. She was soaked from head to foot and looked deeply traumatised.

Chen Mingwu ran over to Xiyun as fast as he could, picked her up and wept for sheer joy. "That's wonderful!" he said. "You're still alive. That's wonderful!"

CHAPTER 40 | 347

Xiyun struggled out of Chen Mingwu's arms and screamed with an angry shrill voice: "What about Xizi? Where's my brother?"

"He's perfectly safe," Chen Mingwu said, "but he's sick. I left him at the doctor's house. I'll go and get him now." Xiyun sat on the ground in a boneless heap. "Where's your mother?" Chen Mingwu asked. "Is she out looking for us? Which direction did she go in? You stay where you are. I'll go and find her."

Xiyun pointed to the Yangtze River and said: "Mum... yesterday... shelter from rain... the ship sank. Mum pushed me... but she drowned." Xiyun seemed incapable of coherent speech.

"What are you talking about?" Chen Mingwu asked in a loud voice.

Xiyun was too feeble to do more than just point to the river: "Mum is over there."

"How can that be?" Chen Mingwu shouted frantically. "How can that possibly be?"

Xiyun did not say another word, and no matter how Chen Mingwu questioned her about what had happened she did not speak. Chen Mingwu fell at her feet. He didn't know what to do. Looking out at the muddy yellow waters of the river, he wanted to cry but found he had no tears. His tears seem to be held back in his blood, solidified at the bottom of his heart, precipitated into hatred and sadness. He hated this murderous world and mourned the human lives cut short as if they meant no more than a weed. He felt that he simply could not bear this pain a moment longer; he just was not strong enough to cope. He wanted to find a dark corner and hide himself away.

After a long pause, Xiyun said: "Let's go. I want Xizi." Chen Mingwu did not move. Xiyun now continued: "Mum told me to look after Xizi, then she drowned. I want Xizi." Chen Mingwu still did not move. Xiyun stood up and stared at his face, and he looked back at her indifferently. Xiyun suddenly raised her hand and slapped him across the face. "What do you think you are doing?" she asked sharply. "What did you promise Uncle Ma? Do you need Uncle Ma to slap you around before you can behave like a man?"

Chen Mingwu sighed deeply, and then he spat out a mouthful of blood, which sprayed all over Xiyun's wet skirt. She just gaped at him, open-mouthed.

Chen Mingwu stood up slowly. He wiped his mouth and said: "Let's go."

At noon that day, Chen Mingwu finally boarded a small steamer for Hankou, carrying Xizi on his back and holding Xiyun by the hand. The steamer landed them at Parrot Island where they were greeted by the Southern Army on the shore. From time to time, people handed in leaflets that were entitled *Letters to the People of Wuchang*. They apologised and consoled the people of Wuchang for the hardships they had suffered as a result of the siege. Chen Mingwu took the leaflet and thought: What does any of this matter when so many thousands have died?

Parrot Island was strung with the banners of the Hankou Red Cross and other charitable organisations and churches. After the rain, the sun had come out, and everything looked really cheerful. There was a huge queue in front of the stalls selling hot food. From time to time, students would take up positions by the roadside and warn the refugees loudly that even if they were starving, they shouldn't eat too much for fear of tearing their stomachs.

Chen Mingwu sat down at a small stall with Xiyun and Xizi, and they each had a bowl of porridge. Xizi's fever had gone down, but he was too tired to speak. Xiyun finished her own porridge and then fed her little brother. Chen Mingwu looked at the two children and felt a surge of love in his heart. They are only little, they have lost their father and their mother one after the other, and they have been through such terrible times. How will that affect them for the rest of their lives?

After finishing his porridge, Chen Mingwu said: "We must get to Hankou before it gets dark."

"We will do whatever you say," Xiyun told him. So they set out, along with many other refugees, walking round Gui Mountain, past Hanyang and across the Han River, to arrive at Hankou at dusk. With the bells of Jianghan Pass ringing in their ears, Chen Mingwu was at last reassured that they had managed to escape this disaster with their lives.

When the street lights came on, Chen Mingwu led Xiyun and Xizi to find a small inn in Wan'an Lane in Hankou. As they entered their room, the lamplight shone on their faces. The two children were already absolutely exhausted. Chen Mingwu saw the panic and uneasiness in their eyes, hugged them impulsively and said with tears in his eyes: "In the future, I'll be father and mother to you. Whatever happens, you can count on me."

41

NONE of the five soldiers who had broken into the Hong mansion were ever found. Investigations revealed that they were members of a local militia under the command of Sun Jianye. After robbing more than a dozen households that day, they had changed into plain clothes and left the city with whatever gold, silver and cash they had been able to steal. They were thought to have returned to their homes.

Ma Weifu would never be able to get his revenge. He shut himself up for a whole day without ever setting foot out of doors. He was full of hatred but with nowhere to vent it.

In the evening, Colonel He arrived with wine and a few snacks. "One drink can relieve a thousand sorrows," the colonel remarked conversationally.

"Where did you get that?" Ma Weifu asked.

Colonel He explained that it had come from the Southern Army. "They hoisted this up in a basket over by Bao'an Gate. It was a present from someone from the same village as me."

As Colonel He said this, he looked straight at Ma Weifu, but the latter did not say anything. He just swept the clutter off the table and said: "Pour it out."

As they were drinking, Colonel He said that although the negotiations had not advanced, morale among the troops had already hit rock bottom. There was nothing to eat, there was nothing to drink, and half the population of the city had already run away. "I don't know what Major General Liu is thinking. Is he still waiting for General Wu to give the order?"

Ma Weifu grinned bitterly: "General Wu has forgotten all about us, hasn't he? We've run out of food, and there's no hope we'll be reinforced, so even if we wanted to defend the city, how can we possibly do so? Major General Liu just wants to preserve his military strength and make his way back to Henan."

"But will they let him get away with it?" Colonel He enquired. "If you fight and the other side wins, are they just going to let you walk away?"

"Exactly," Ma Weifu said. "Tang Shengzhi has absolutely set his face against it. He says that the only thing on the table is to throw open the gates and surrender, in which case he guarantees good treatment for the prisoners."

"So there are still decisions to be made," Colonel He said.

"What do you think they should do?" Ma Weifu asked.

"You know exactly what I think," Colonel He said, "but I will listen to you."

Ma Weifu raised his glass and tried to say something; but after a short pause he put it down again.

"A hero is someone who can see the bigger picture," Colonel He said. "Hankou and Hanyang have both fallen to the Revolutionary Army. Wuchang is isolated and under siege, and there is no point in trying to defend it any longer. You can't stop their northward march. Look at how much the ordinary people in Wuchang have suffered – look at the suffering of your men! This last month… it would be unbearable even if you had a heart of stone."

Ma Weifu remembered his cousin's pale face, and the pain immediately overwhelmed him.

"And with what happened to your poor cousin…" Colonel He continued.

Ma Weifu interrupted him: "I don't want you to talk about her."

"Well," the colonel said, "I've been a soldier for more than a decade, and this is the worst it's ever got. When it is all over, I'm not going to stay in uniform any longer. I'm heading back home and taking up growing corn again."

In the end, Ma Weifu drew a long breath, raised his glass, tapped

Colonel He on the arm and said: "How about opening the gate at ten o'clock tonight?"

The colonel immediately drained his glass of wine in a state of high excitement. Before Ma Weifu had even touched his own wine, he leaned forward to say: "I knew you would make the right decision. Last time that student came to you, I knew that he would persuade you. I'm going to get ready right away. The Revolutionary Army is waiting for our reply."

After the colonel left, Ma Weifu drank up all the rest of the wine.

At ten o'clock that night, the moon shone like water. It was quiet in the city, and many of the street lights had been put out of action by the heavy rain the previous day, leaving few, if any, lit up. Colonel He led a few of his men to open Binyang Gate, which had been closed now for forty days. At last, with a shriek from the hinges, the gate swung open. The leaves were pushed flush against the wall with a dull crashing sound, like a giant breathing heavily.

The Revolutionary Army, which was waiting outside, armed to the teeth, came running through the gate in single file. As the two armies swapped over, the Revolutionary Army started to pour into the city, dividing into different units as they went, running as fast as they could in the directions of the other gates.

Ma Weifu stayed in his room the whole time, listening to the movements outside. A soldier in the Revolutionary Army poked his head in at the door of his room and announced: "If you want to go, hurry up!" Then he left.

"It's all over," Ma Weifu thought to himself.

It was 9 October 1926.

Colonel He came in, dressed in plain clothes and carrying a heavy bundle. When he saw Ma Weifu sitting there motionless, he tried to get him to move: "Let's get out of here. If you're still here when the main army turns up, I'm afraid you'll be looking at a pretty nasty future."

Ma Weifu sighed. Colonel He handed him a piece of paper. Ma Weifu took it and read what it said. *This man played a key role in lifting the siege of the city. He must be treated according to the letter of the law and is not to be harassed.* It was signed by Tang Shengzhi.

"I know you've lived pretty much your whole life in Wuchang, and I was afraid you wouldn't want to leave," said Colonel He. "I got this specially for you." As he said this, he undid his bundle, took out an ordinary suit and handed it to Ma Weifu. "However, for now you're going to be better off out of here," he said, "because that way you can stay out of trouble. You need to get out of here before daybreak." Then he turned around and walked out. When he got to the door, he looked back and said: "Goodbye and good luck."

"Indeed," Ma Weifu said, "goodbye and good luck."

The uproar in the city started like a series of small waves, rolling up one after another from a distance, until they rolled right in front of you, climbing into the sky as a tidal wave. As soon as it was light, the whole city was engulfed in the most appalling noise. Guns were going off, but you could hear that they were firing into the air in a show of force. After the shooting, there was shouting: "Put down your weapons!" "Hands up!" "Surrender or die!"

Ma Weifu, who had changed into plain clothes, slipped quietly through the streets to the Hong mansion. The Hong mansion was quiet and peaceful. He rapped on the knocker, but no one answered the door, then he climbed over the wall and made his way in. He knew that since all the buildings in the backyard had collapsed into rubble, Mrs Wu had been living in the west wing. Ma Weifu tried to find her, but she was nowhere to be seen. He went through to the backyard, where he was brought up short by the sight of Mrs Wu hanging dead from an osmanthus tree. The osmanthus tree was covered with fragrant blooms, and a few pale yellow petals had been caught in her unbound hair.

Ma Weifu cut Mrs Wu's body down and thought to himself: Maybe this was the only way for her to find any peace. He laid her down under the tree and searched the collapsed buildings to find a mat, which he placed over her face. Then he sat by the side of the well.

At the foot of Snake Mountain, there was intense gunfire: it sounded like a battle was raging over there. Ma Weifu realised that the Northern Army was making its final stand, and he felt a little ashamed. But at the same time, he knew full well that it was all over, so what was the point of trying to fight back?

The sun rose. As the light hit the edge of the well, it glittered and floated on the surface of the water, but he could not imagine how far down it was to the bottom. Ma Weifu did not dare to look down, because if he so much as glanced at it he would feel the cold and darkness coming up from inside. For him, this was an abyss – an abyss that sank right down to the centre of the earth.

The sound of gunfire faded away, and the racket ebbed away. Ma Weifu understood that life in Wuchang had now returned to its original track. His uncle would soon be back, and he would be reunited with his other cousins. But when they came through the door all happy and cheerful, how could he explain what had happened here? When he thought of this, he was terrified – so frightened that he broke out in a sweat, as if they were standing in front of him at that very moment. I have to get out of here, Ma Weifu thought. Otherwise, I will have to tell them everything, and I really think that would kill me.

He hopped back over the wall. As he jumped down, a neighbour passed by and gave him a curious look.

The streets were filled with signs saying *Welcome to the Revolutionary Army*. There were students everywhere in a fever of excitement, as well as signs telling the people to stay calm, not to mention propaganda teams giving speeches. Although Wuchang had fallen and the city was lying in ruins, every street and lane was filled with joy. In spite of everything, they had managed to survive; in spite of everything, they were going to have a future.

Scattered through the lanes and alleyways, the Northern Army could hear the gunshots. They imagined that the Southern Army had succeeded in attacking one of the gates and that street-to-street fighting was about to begin, so they made their way to the fortifications one after another, ready to resist the enemy. When they actually saw the Southern Army with their own eyes, they were all frightened to death. Those with guns immediately indicated that they were only too happy to put them down; those without guns fell to their knees and begged to be spared. There were a few people guilty of exceptionally evil deeds who were immediately pointed out by the local inhabitants; the Revolutionary Army did not bother with too many questions but just lined them up at the foot of the wall and executed them by firing squad on the spot. Others, who had merely been following orders from the Northern Army, now tore off their uniforms and went round to the former provincial governor's office and Chuwang Tower in the hope of being re-enlisted into the Revolutionary Army.

That afternoon, Ma Weifu went into a little eatery and asked for a bowl of noodles. There were plenty of people in the eatery, and it was many days since they had last been able to get a bowl of noodles. They were all very excited at the mere sight. The owner kept saying, over and over again: "Don't eat too much. Just have half a bowl at a time. We are all lucky to survive – none of us have starved to death, so don't die of overeating now. This morning, a man who had eaten two bowls of noodles managed to explode his stomach and had to be rushed to hospital. I have no idea whether he's alive or dead now. Ladies and gentlemen, please bear with it. Please take it slowly, one day at a time."

While they were eating, someone came in and reported excitedly that crowds were massing on Long Street. They had captured Liu Yuchun at one of the foreigner's houses over on Garden Hill, and now they were going to parade him down Long Street. The man also said that Liu Yuchun had taken a thousand men out that morning, and they'd all fought to the death under Snake Mountain, but in the end they'd lost to the Southern Army and the survivors were all completely exhausted. Liu Yuchun was dragged off by his staff to hide in the house of one of the foreigners, Mr Meng, but the Chinese servants had tipped the wink to the Southern Army. They'd rushed over there and captured him alive.

The people in the little eatery applauded happily when they heard that. Then they all put down their bowls and ran out onto the street. Ma Weifu was so horrified by this news that he managed to tip half a bowl of noodles down his front.

Long Street was absolutely packed with people. Liu Yuchun was tied up and paraded around on the back of a car. The car was covered with white banners on both sides, on which there was written in huge black letters: *Liu Yuchun has been captured alive, Chen Jiamo is also our prisoner!* The people of the city were pressed close around the car, in front and behind, to left and right, and they were all screaming curses at Liu Yuchun, spitting at him and shaking their fists. The Revolutionary Army was standing by with guns, constantly forcing back those who were pressing too close. People were shouting in voices that suggested they were half-crazed: "Shoot him! Stab him to death!"

Ma Weifu managed to squeeze in close enough that he could actually see him in the car. In his ropes and chains, he kept his head lowered and closed his eyes; his face was expressionless. His attitude was one that Ma Weifu knew well. It told him that Liu Yuchun would accept defeat, but he would not admit that he had made a mistake. That was because he was a soldier and it was his duty to carry out his orders. Ma Weifu suddenly felt terribly ashamed.

When he walked away from Long Street, he was feeling deeply pained, and without even thinking about it he turned his footsteps towards Binyang Gate. The flags above the city gates had now all changed, and so had the soldiers defending the walls. Ma Weifu stood at the entrance to Binyang Gate, looking up at the tower above the walls, with a thousand emotions pressing on his heart.

One of the soldiers came up to Ma Weifu and said: "What are you doing sneaking around here like this?"

"Nothing," Ma Weifu said, "I just came to have a look."

Now another of the defenders came over, and this one looked like an officer in the Revolutionary Army. He looked Ma Weifu up and down and said: "I'm afraid it's not just a matter of curiosity, is it? What are you up to?"

Worried that they might just drag him off and shoot him on the spot, Ma Weifu took the note Colonel He had given him out of his pocket. The Revolutionary Army officer read it through a few times and then returned it to him, saying: "Why are you still here?"

Ma Weifu could not explain. He thought about it and said: "I thought I'd come and take a look, and then tomorrow I would go and visit Mr Tang Shengzhi."

The officer just sneered at him: "Do you really think that you've achieved something by opening the gate? Do you imagine that we're going to reward you?"

Ma Weifu had always been an arrogant man, and when he heard this his face changed colour.

"Get the hell out of here," the officer shouted at him. "Get out of Wuchang as quickly as you can. Don't let me see you again!"

CHAPTER 41 | 357

Ma Weifu had never suffered such humiliation. His first reaction was to try and pull out his gun, but when he put his hand to his waist he discovered that he didn't have a gun on his person. Ever since the dawn of time, you're a king if you win and dead meat if you don't – that's the truth, and it always has been. He calmed his rage and finally realised that he had no choice but to turn around and leave in peace. As he walked away, he heard the silly jumped-up little officer tell the other soldiers on guard: "I absolutely cannot stand people like that – we can't reenlist him. Who knows when someone like that will betray their senior officers again? Next time it might be us he turns against!"

Every word of this sentence was like coals of fire, falling one by one into Ma Weifu's heart, burning him unbearably. Ma Weifu felt that he was on the brink of collapse. He thought: Now, even the worst and most shameless people in the world can mock and abuse me at will. Zhou Jincheng was nothing but a fool! Tell me, exactly how did I save myself? I may have acted according to my conscience, but it came at the cost of destroying everything else I have ever held dear.

Before Ma Weifu decided to open the gate to the city, he knew that the future would be hard to bear, but he did not anticipate that he would not be able to cope. What was it that Liu Yuchun had said? The most complicated thing in this world is the human heart. You may simply not be able to keep to your own sense of having done right. Now he understood why Liu Yuchun had been so stubborn about just obeying orders.

That evening, while the Southern Army was busy drinking wine and eating meat to celebrate their victory, he quietly made his way up to the top of the city walls. The autumn vistas beyond, glowing in the sunset, were absolutely beautiful. The smoke rising above Changchun Monastery curled through the air. Some people were having a ceremony performed; Daoist priests were there intoning, accompanied by drums and zithers, and the sound floated out on the breeze along with the smoke.

What a dreadful world. What a terrible life.

Ma Weifu sat down in a corner of the walls. It was getting dark, but he didn't mind. He thought: Once you set out, there is no way to turn back. Even when what lies before you is an abyss, you have to jump in. Because if you look back, there will be an even deeper and darker hell waiting for you.

The cold that night pierced to the very marrow of his bones, and even his pain seemed to freeze. Ma Weifu's heart was so calm that it might as well have been frozen too; he felt all his enthusiasm and passion had gone as cold and as hard as ice. That ice was so hard that nothing could break it, nothing could melt it. What a failure I have made of my life! As a friend, he had been unable to save Yuan Zongchun when he was wounded on the field of battle; as a lover, he had seen the woman he loved with his whole heart turn away from him to a weak and incompetent fool; as a relative, he had neither been able to protect his beloved cousin, nor even to avenge her; as a soldier, he had betrayed his commanding officer who had always trusted him. He wanted friendship, love and loyalty; these were things that he had always valued highly, but in the end he had no choice. The only choice he could make was to run counter to what he most wanted. Perhaps this is not the worst thing that could happen in this world, but in his heart he felt he was guilty of an unforgivable evil. What was the point of even being alive?

The moon was waning. It was already late autumn. Ma Weifu stood up and walked over to the tower. Without hesitation, he jumped. The wind whistled past his ears. Below him was Binyang Gate.

42

CHEN MINGWU FLED from Hankou to the countryside with Xiyun and her little brother. He had no money and no means to keep the three of them alive. On the day of their departure, Hankou was celebrating. All day they were singing and dancing in the streets, waving red flags, and during the night you could hear music and drumming, and all the lamps were lit. Everyone seemed to have gone mad with joy. But Xizi was still very sick; he did not speak, nor did he raise his eyes to look at people. He was completely listless, and his face was wan and wasted. This worried Chen Mingwu so much that he could not really enjoy the atmosphere in Hankou.

Chen Mingwu had explained to Xiyun that his grandfather was a doctor specialising in Chinese traditional medicine. He lived out in the countryside, so they should take Xizi there where he could be looked after properly. "If it can help my brother," Xiyun said, "I'm happy to go anywhere."

In this way, Chen Mingwu took Xiyun and her brother back to the countryside to live.

They spent a whole year there. In order to support them all, Chen Mingwu set up a little primary school for children from rich families in the neighbouring villages. He made sure that Xiyun was able to attend too. He remembered that Ma Weifu had said that Xiyun ought to learn to read and write.

Ma Weifu never came to look for them. After Xizi had spent six months taking various herbal remedies, his condition was much improved, and he started to have some colour in his face. Xiyun took him out into the fields to play, where he could watch the animals and the flying insects, and then he would smile. Occasionally, he would say a few words, but only in a low voice, as if he was afraid of something. Xiyun was anxious that he would always be like this after he grew up. However, Chen Mingwu's grandfather reassured her: "He will be fine. He just needs to take things slowly."

Mid-Autumn Festival would soon be here. Sitting in the courtyard, watching the moon gradually getting rounder and rounder overhead, Xiyun told Chen Mingwu: "We ought to go and find Uncle Ma."

"Yes," he agreed. "We should leave three days ahead of our appointment."

"I hope Uncle Ma is OK," Xiyun said.

"Your Uncle Ma is a very competent man," Chen Mingwu said, "and I am sure he is doing just fine. But as a soldier, he may not be able to choose where he gets sent."

"I don't remember Dad at all," Xiyun remarked. "Now, whenever I think of Dad, he has Uncle Ma's face."

"He will be a good father to you and Xizi," Chen Mingwu said.

On the day of their departure, Chen Mingwu hired a horse and carriage for them. With all the stops and starts they had to make, the journey took two days. When they got to Hankou, they took a small steamer over the river to Wuchang, and by the time they arrived it was dark. They entered the city via Hanyang Gate, and they saw that the moat outside the city had been pretty much filled in. Chen Mingwu was amazed to see that the city wall seemed to have collapsed in many places. Did that mean that more battles had been fought here after they all left?

Chen Mingwu went straight to his cousin Daying's house. She was very surprised to see them and dragged them straight in. Then she started to get a room ready for them while also cooking them a hot meal. After Xizi and Xiyun had fallen asleep, Chen Mingwu, his cousin and her husband spent most of the rest of the night talking. They told each other who was dead and who had survived. The memories of that painful past, covered up and smoothed over by time, now appeared again before their eyes. Every event was like a sharp knife; speaking about them pierced the heart. When he mentioned the Hong mansion, his cousin said that after the family came back, they had cried bitterly for many days. Miss Hong was buried on Snake Mountain, and her grave was supposed to be in a very fine location. His cousin knew full well that it was Miss Hong who had saved Chen Mingwu, so on the day of the Qingming Festival she had gone there to pray that she might rest in peace. Chen Mingwu was sobbing when he heard her say that. Daying also burst into tears and said: "Let's not talk about that – it's too sad."

Chen Mingwu sobbed and repeated what she had said: "Let's not talk about that, it's too sad."

Early the next morning, Chen Mingwu and Xiyun went over to Binyang Gate. Half of Binyang Gate had already been demolished, and the city walls on either side had huge gaps in them. Chen Mingwu was puzzled and asked the passers-by why they had torn down the walls. One passer-by said that the senior officials had decided that they were an obstacle to progress, so they had ordered the demolition as part of their plan for redevelopment.

Binyang Gate no longer seemed familiar to them. Outside the city gate, it proved impossible to find any trace of where Chen Mingwu's house had once been; there was a completely new street plan, and he could only recognise one or two of the names on the shop-signs. In the space of just one year, everything that had once been well-known had become utterly alien.

They sat down on a pile of fallen bricks and waited a whole day, but Ma Weifu never came. As it started to get dark, the moon shone high in the sky with a clean and clear light, and it was beautifully round. The pain and suffering of the previous year had been blown away on the wind. The streets were all illuminated with colourful lights, as each and every family celebrated the Mid-Autumn Festival. The children were laughing and scurrying around with lanterns in their hands. Xizi suddenly seemed to cheer up and said: "Sis, I want a lantern too!"

"Xizi is better," Xiyun said happily. "He knows that Uncle Ma is coming, so he's got better."

But where was Uncle Ma?

Chen Mingwu speculated that some of the residents nearby might know what had become of Ma Weifu, so they went to enquire. At the third house they visited, an old man said that one night after the siege ended, a man had jumped from the tower over Binyang Gate in the middle of the night. He had landed right by the main gate, smashing himself to smithereens. Supposedly, he was one of the officers who'd been on guard there. "I don't know if he's the one you've been waiting for," he said

Chen Mingwu was appalled. He was sure that it was Ma Weifu.

Xiyun turned around and ran back to Binyang Gate. She stood where the barbican had once been and shouted in her sharp voice: "Uncle Ma! Where are you? Why don't you want me and Xizi?" As she shouted, her voice broke into a scream. This was the first time Chen Mingwu had ever heard Xiyun cry, a bitter and tragic wail. It shocked Chen Mingwu to the core, just like the explosion he heard when he woke up from his afternoon nap just over a year before.

Under the moonlight, the broken and battered walls lay there like a dying tiger, chopped to pieces. There were gaps everywhere; you could just walk into the city any time you chose. Chen Mingwu thought that maybe everything would have been different if it had been open like this one year earlier.

It was the autumn of 1927.

The walls of Wuchang were gone.

APPENDIX I

THE HISTORY OF THE WUCHANG CITY WALLS

IN AD223, Sun Quan of the Eastern Wu dynasty built a military fortification on the northern side of Huanghu Mountain (now known as Snake Mountain) near his capital city, Wuchang (today known as Echeng). It faced towards the Yangtze River, backing onto Snake Mountain, and was located opposite the mouth of the Xia River (now known as the Han River), from which it took its name: Xiakou. The famous Yellow Crane Tower was a military observation platform overlooking the city of Xiakou. This saw the beginning of the development of the modern city of Wuchang.

During the Eastern Jin dynasty (317-420), there was endless warfare. Xiakou occupied an important strategic position at this time. During the Southern dynasties (420-589), the province of Yingzhou was established, and Xiakou was the administrative capital. Therefore, Xiakou was also known as the city of 'Ying'. At this time, Xiakou occupied such an important position in the government administration that the city walls had to be expanded and repaired. The vestiges of the ancient Yingzhou walls are today the oldest remaining parts of the walls of Wuchang. The only surviving sections are located behind the Yellow Crane Tower.

After the Sui dynasty unified the whole country in 589, Yingzhou was renamed Ezhou. Two walled cities were recognised: Jiangxia (today known as Wuchang) and Hanyang. Because Jiangxia was the administrative centre for Ezhou, some people also called this city by the name Ezhou.

During the Baoli reign era (825-827) of the Tang dynasty, the military governor of Wuchang, Niu Sengru, undertook a major rebuilding of the walls of Ezhou. Before this point, the walls of Wuchang were built of pisé. However, in times of flooding, the whole city would fill up with mud, which was extremely inconvenient for the residents. Niu Sengrun had the original wall rebuilt with one made from bricks and tiles. This was the first major renovation since the founding of the city of Xiakou and its expansion as the capital of Yingzhou. At this time, Huanghu

Mountain had gradually evolved into a tourist attraction. The military post standing there in the Three Kingdoms period had become the Yellow Crane Tower, which was one of the three great sights of the Yangtze River. Countless travellers were invited to attend banquets and see off travellers there, whereupon they would quaff wine and recite poems.

Merchant ships flocked to this region in the Song dynasty (960-1279), and Ezhou was one of the centres for water transport up and down the Yangtze River. During the Yuan dynasty (1279-1368), the government established provinces across China, and the administrative centre of the newly-created Hubei Province was transferred from Jingzhou to Ezhou (now known as Wuchang). During the Dade reign era (1297-1307) of the Yuan dynasty, the original Ezhou Route Command was first renamed the Wuchang Route Command, and then Wuchang prefecture. The name 'Wuchang' was henceforth officially associated with the place still known as Wuchang today.

After the Ming dynasty put an end to the Yuan dynasty, Zhu Zheng, the sixth son of the first Ming emperor, Zhu Yuanzhang (r. 1368-1398), was installed in Wuchang as the King of Chu. Subsequently, the kings of Chu ruled in Wuchang for 262 years, from the beginning of the Ming dynasty to its end (1368-1644). During the reign of Zhu Yuanzhang, the Marquis of Jiangxia, Zhou Dexing, who had been honoured for the key role he played in the founding of the Ming dynasty, greatly expanded the old city of Ezhou from its original dimensions during the Song and Yuan dynasties to encompass both sides of Snake Mountain, and he renovated and expanded the walls of Wuchang again. The whole wall was constructed using bricks, and it was made extremely high: the northern and western walls were thirteen metres tall; the southern and eastern walls were seven metres tall. Outside the walls, there was a huge moat, more than nine kilometres long, more than six metres deep and just over eight and a half metres wide. To the west of the city was the Yangtze River, which formed a natural boundary. There were nine gates in the wall, namely Dadong Gate, Xiaodong Gate, Zhupai Gate, Pinghu Gate, Hanyang Gate, Xinnan Gate, Bao'an Gate, Wangshan Gate and Caobu Gate. In the fourteenth year of the reign of the Jiajing Emperor (1535), the Censor Gu Lin changed the name of Dadong Gate to Binyang Gate, while Xiaodong Gate became Zhongxiao Gate, Xinnan Gate became Zhonghe Gate, Caobu Gate became Wusheng Gate, and Zhupai Gate became Wenchang Gate.

Now the walls of Wuchang City had basically reached their final proportions.

At the end of the Qing dynasty, construction of the Guangdong-Wuhan Railway reached Hunan Province. Zhang Zhidong, the Governor of Huguang, ordered the construction of a new gate located between Binyang Gate and Zhonghe Gate, which was named Tongxiang Gate. The railway station was located outside the gate, and it was called Tongxiang Gate Station. As a result, there were now ten gates in the walls of Wuchang. At this point in time, the walls were about ten metres high, twenty-one metres thick at the bottom, seventeen metres wide at the top and more than eleven kilometres long. The distances between the gates were as follows: just over seven hundred metres separated Binyang Gate and Zhongxiao Gate; then it was one and a half kilometres from Zhongxiao Gate to Wusheng Gate; it was one kilometre and two hundred metres from Wusheng Gate to Hanyang Gate; five hundred metres from Hanyang Gate to Pinghu Gate; just over seven hundred metres from Pinghu Gate to Wenchang Gate; again just over seven hundred metres from Wenchang Gate to Wangshan Gate; and half a kilometre from Wangshan Gate to Bao'an Gate; while from Bao'an Gate to Zhonghe Gate was just over five hundred metres; from Zhonghe Gate to Tongxiang Gate it was seven hundred and fifty metres; and from Tongxiang Gate to Binyang Gate it was another seven hundred and fifty metres. The city walls were three kilometres north to south; and two and a half kilometres east to west.

The city of Wuchang is situated on the west bank of the Yangtze River. It had two water gates and three land gates – Hanyang Gate, Pinghu Gate and Wenchang Gate – facing in that direction. In addition, Wusheng Gate faced north; Tongxiang Gate, Binyang Gate and Zhongxiao Gate faced east; and Wangshan Gate, Bao'an Gate and Zhonghe Gate faced south. The moat outside the walls encompassed the northern, eastern and southern sides of the city.

At this time, it was about six metres deep, eight and a half metres wide and just over eleven kilometres long.

After the 1911 Uprising, Zhonghe Gate was renamed Qiyi Gate.

In 1926, the Northern Expeditionary Army marched north, winning every battle that they found. Wu Peifu of the Beiyang Army was defeated in the battles of Tingsi Bridge and Hesheng Bridge. He fled to the city of Wuchang and gave orders that it was to be defended at all costs. On 1 September, the soldiers of the Northern Expeditionary Army approached the city and Wuchang was closed. The subsequent confrontation endured for forty days until the city fell on 10 October. During this period, the Northern Expeditionary Army carried out a series of fierce attacks on the walls, resulting in many deaths. Furthermore, the civilian population of Wuchang suffered terrible hunger and violence, which also caused numerous casualties. There have been many sieges and battles in the history of Wuchang, but this was the cruellest one.

In 1927, in order to redevelop the city and expand the urban area, and in view of the fact that the Northern Expeditionary Army had discovered the high walls to be a serious obstruction, the authorities decided to demolish all the walls and towers around Wuchang except for Qiyi Gate. Deng Yanda presided over this demolition.

The walls of Wuchang were gone.

APPENDIX II

Map Showing the Plan of Campaign During the Attack and Defence of Wuchang

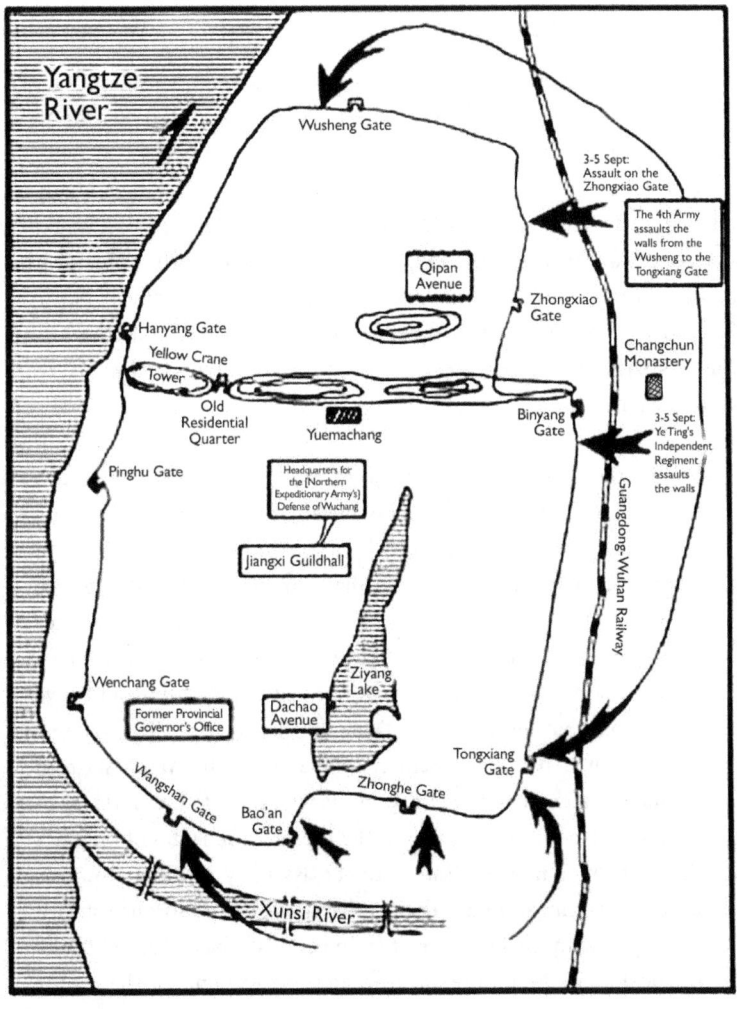

APPENDIX III

THE NORTHERN EXPEDITION AND THE THREE GREAT BATTLES OF THE E (HUBEI) REGION

1. THE NORTHERN EXPEDITION

SUN YAT-SEN DIED in Beijing on 12 March 1925. On 1 July 1925, the Kuomintang established their Nationalist Government in Guangzhou. On 4 July 1926, in order to fulfil Premier Sun Yat-sen's dying wishes, the Kuomintang Central Committee in Guangzhou convened an interim plenary meeting at which the 'Declaration Concerning the Northern Expedition of the National Revolutionary Army' was agreed. This proclaimed that the aim of the Northern Expedition was to overthrow the Beiyang government:

> We in the Kuomintang have consistently advocated building a unified government by peaceful means, for we believe that the government of the Republic of China should be in the hands of the Chinese people; and we believe that our people should live free from the scourge of civil strife. Therefore, when the late premier went north, he earnestly called on the whole country to convene a national assembly to resolve the current situation. Who could have anticipated that the villainous Duan Qirui would publicly support the idea of a national assembly, while trying to wreck it from behind the scenes; and the imperialists would incite the warlords to commit further atrocities. Up to the present moment, not only has the idea of a non-partisan national assembly working towards peaceful reunification not been realised, but the traitorous warlord Wu Peifu, with the help of British imperialists, has returned to the political scene in an attempt to follow the example of the traitor Yuan Shikai. He intends to borrow vast sums from overseas and use this funding to destroy any movement for freedom and independence. The imperialists are offering the usual bait of profits from tariff increases, as well as aid in the form of money and arms.

They are openly helping the traitorous warlord Wu Peifu to block the Chinese National Revolution; but indirectly they are seeking permanent control over tariffs in order to stifle China's economic development. The villainous Wu Peifu is aware that the forces of the National Revolution are expanding day by day and that his opportunities to betray his country and feather his own nest are running out. Hence, on the one hand, he has spared no effort in attacking the base areas of the National Revolution, sending bandits and desperados to cause trouble in Guangdong; while at the same time he has assembled his henchmen to invade Hunan and assault members of our party there. This situation is completely unacceptable, so we feel we have no choice but to launch a military expedition against him.

At this time, Duan Qirui's government had collapsed, and the Beiyang government had come under the control of the Fengtian warlord clique headed by Zhang Zuolin (1875-1928). Wu Peifu, a warlord associated with the Zhili clique, occupied Hubei, Hunan, Henan, Hebei and Shaanxi Provinces and controlled the Beijing-Wuhan Railway. The five southeastern provinces were held by Sun Chuanfang (1885-1935), a warlord who had split off from the Zhili clique and built up his own power base.

Chiang Kai-shek (1887-1975), generalissimo of the National Revolutionary Army, took command of the forces in Guangzhou on 9 July 1926. This was the beginning of the Northern Expedition.

The Military Commission of the Guangzhou Revolutionary Government presided over a root-and-branch reorganisation of the various armies in Guangdong and abolished all the local militias. All units were given designations within the National Revolutionary Army.

The First Army consisted of the Whampoa Student Army and part of the Cantonese Army; it was commanded by He Yingqin.

The Second Army was composed of the Hunan Army under the command of Tan Yankai.

The Third Army was composed of the Yunnan Army under the command of Zhu Peide.

The Fourth Army was composed of the Cantonese Army, led by Li Jishen.

The Sixth Army was composed of the Hunan Army, led by Cheng Qian.

The Seventh Army was composed of the Guangxi Army, led by Li Zongren and Huang Shaohong. Li Jishen took command of this reorganised force.

The Eighth Army consisted of Tang Shengzhi's troops, and this was reorganised by the Guangdong National Government, though Tang Shengzhi retained command.

Deng Yanda became director of the Department of Political Affairs, and Guo Moruo was appointed as the deputy director.

The core units of the Revolutionary Army consisted of approximately one hundred thousand men, but the Beiyang Army was much bigger. Wu Peifu was far from being the strongest of the warlords, but he still commanded around two hundred thousand men. Sun Chuanfang occupied five provinces, and he claimed to have an army of two hundred thousand elite soldiers. Zhang Zuolin was even better equipped than either Wu or Sun, with an army of around three hundred and fifty thousand elite troops. Adding their forces together with those of other warlords, big and small, the Beiyang Army totalled somewhere in the region of one million men. Because of the great disparity in strength between the two sides, if the Northern Expeditionary Army wanted to do away with these warlords and unify the whole country, it would have to resort to extraordinary tactics and take them by surprise. Therefore, the Northern Expeditionary Army made use of the following slogan: "Overthrow Wu Peifu, make a deal with Sun Chuanfang and ignore Zhang Zuolin."

Following this basic plan, the Revolutionary Army marched first on Hunan and Hubei, both provinces where Wu Peifu was in control. They were able to advance northwards, sweeping away any resistance, winning one battle after another, until on 1 September they found themselves beneath the walls of Wuchang. This forced Wu Peifu, who had hitherto occupied Wuhan, to flee. At the same time, the Northern Expeditionary Army units marching on Jiangxi Province, after much arduous fighting, were able to take Jiujiang and Nanchang that November, wiping out the main force of the warlord Sun Chuanfang in the process. At the same time, troops of the National Revolutionary Army under the command of Feng

Yuxiang (1882-1948) also seized control of the northwest and prepared to go east through the Tong Pass in order to meet up with the Northern Expeditionary Army. The great victory won by the Northern Expeditionary Army caused warlords in Fujian, Zhejiang and other provinces of China to join them. In less than one year of the Northern Expedition being launched, the National Revolutionary Army basically wiped out the armies of the warlords Wu Peifu and Sun Chuanfang, seriously damaged the forces under the command of Zhang Zuolin and inflicted severe damage on the Beiyang government, accelerating the Chinese revolution significantly.

In December 1926, the Guangzhou National Revolutionary Government moved to Wuhan.

In April 1927, Chiang Kai-shek established the Nanjing National Government in opposition to the Wuhan National Government.

In April 1927, the Wuhan Government appointed Tang Shengzhi as commander-in-chief of the Northern Expeditionary Army, and a further Northern Expedition began on 19 April.

On 1 May 1927, the Nanjing government also issued an order, dividing their army into three to continue the Northern Expedition.

In September 1927, the Nanjing National Government merged with the Wuhan National Government. The Wuhan National Government moved their seat to Nanjing.

In March 1928, Chiang Kai-shek led his troops across the Yangtze River, and the second Northern Expedition began, with the aim of eliminating the remaining forces under the command of the warlords Zhang Zuolin and Sun Chuanfang and their Fengtian clique.

On 29 December 1928, Zhang Xueliang (1901-2001), the son of the late Zhang Zuolin, announced by telegram that he was changing sides, proclaiming his loyalty to the central government in Nanjing. The Northern Expedition was hence declared to be a resounding success.

2. THE BATTLE OF TINGSI BRIDGE

Tingsi Bridge, located within the boundaries of the city of Xianning in Hubei Province, is the first gateway to Wuhan, as you approach from the south. The terrain is dangerous, easy to defend and difficult to attack, and this area has always been heavily fortified since it represents a key strategic position. In August 1926, the Northern Expeditionary Army invaded Hubei. The warlord in command there, Wu Peifu, urgently deployed large numbers of troops to guard Tingsi Bridge in an attempt to prevent the Northern Expeditionary Army from proceeding further north. On 26 August, the Northern Expeditionary Army launched an attack on Tingsi Bridge. They were met with stubborn resistance by the enemy, and this halted their advance. The local peasant forces led the Thirty-sixth Regiment of the Twelfth Division, the Twenty-eighth Regiment of the Tenth Division and the Twenty-ninth Regiment of the Fourth Army along back roads during the night so that they were able to make their way right in front of the enemy's positions. They then proceeded to launch a series of surprise raids under cover of darkness and took control of several key points along the front line. The next morning, when the general offensive began, the Thirty-fifth Regiment decoyed the enemy towards the railway bridge. The Thirtieth Regiment and one battalion from Ye Ting's Independent Regiment joined the attack. The Beiyang Army failed to hold the line and began to move towards Xianning. Ye Ting's Independent Regiment, led by local peasants, climbed over rugged mountain roads and bypassed Gutangjiao to launch an unexpected assault on the Beiyang Army as they retreated, following the railway line. This resulted in a total collapse of the Beiyang Army, with their troops panicking and fleeing towards Xianning. The Northern Expeditionary Army then took control of Tingsi Bridge.

3. THE BATTLE OF HESHENG BRIDGE

After the Battle of Tingsi Bridge, Wu Peifu retreated to Hesheng Bridge, another important military pass south of Wuhan. There, he regrouped his forces and prepared to defend vigorously. On 27

August, Ye Ting's Independent Regiment captured Xianning and then followed up on their earlier victory with an attack on Hesheng Bridge. Wu Peifu personally took command of the main force at the Battle of Hesheng. At dawn on 30 August, Ye Ting's Independent Regiment launched a sudden assault on Wu Peifu's position at Yanglintang and then turned to attack Taolinpu. The battle was fierce, and the two sides fought hand-to-hand. The Independent Regiment soon broke through the enemy's defensive line, penetrating deep into their territory. Wu Peifu's First Brigade counter-attacked from positions out on the wing, attempting to encircle Ye Ting's Independent Regiment, which was attacked by enemy artillery fire on three sides, causing heavy casualties. The Twenty-eighth Regiment of the Tenth Division and the Thirty-sixth Regiment of the Twelfth Division provided reinforcements just in the nick of time and joined forces to fight against the enemy, breaking through the enemy lines at Taolinpu and launching an attack on Hesheng Bridge. After the Seventh Army occupied the high ground, it immediately attacked South Bridge on the east side of Hesheng Bridge. By this time, not only had Wu Pei's main force been defeated but they were now coming under attack by the enemy from the sides and behind, causing the whole defensive line to collapse. Wu Peifu's inspection team executed a number of officers holding the rank of colonel or above, but this did nothing to avert his defeat. Finally, the Fourth Army launched a frontal assault and captured Wu Peifu's command position. Hotly pursued by the Northern Expeditionary Army, Wu Peifu fled to Wuchang by special train. His army retreated as best they could. Some crossed the Yangtze River, while others entered the city of Wuchang. By the morning of 30 August, the Battle of Hesheng Bridge was over.

4. THE BATTLE OF WUCHANG

After the defeat at Hesheng Bridge, some of the defeated soldiers from the Beiyang Army fled to the city of Wuchang. The defending forces closed the ten gates on 1 September 1926. On their arrival beneath the city walls, Tang Shengzhi, Li Zongren, Chen Keyu and other senior officers held a series of meetings in which they decided to attack Wuchang with the Fourth Army, the First Brigade of the Seventh Army and the Second Division of the First Army. Meanwhile, the Eighth Army attacked Hankou and Hanyang to prevent the enemy from reinforcing Wuchang. Li Zongren was the commander of the siege, and Chen Keyu was the deputy commander. In the early morning of 3 September, the troops began to attack the city, and fierce battles commenced outside the gates. Wu Peifu's army launched a fierce defence with heavy artillery and machine guns firing from the city walls, Snake Mountain and Phoenix Mountain, and the warships moored on the Yangtze River also counter-attacked strongly. By 6.00am, the besieging forces had to return to their original positions, and their first attack failed. On the evening of 3 September, Chiang Kai-shek, Bai Chongxi, and other senior commanders arrived at Yujiawan Train Station in Wuchang. On 4 September, a conference was held to discuss the capture of the city, and the attackers were ordered to take Wuchang within forty-eight hours. At the same time, rewards were offered for anyone reaching the top of the walls. In the early morning of 5 September, the Fourth Army and the Seventh Army launched another general offensive against Wuchang. By noon of that day, the offensive had to be halted because of the heavy casualties. On 6 September, Liu Zuolong, the commander of the Hanyang garrison, changed sides. On 7 September, the Second Division of the Eighth Army crossed the Han River and captured Hankou. As a result, two of the three cities in the Wuhan conurbation had been captured. Wu Peifu fled to Xinyang in Henan Province, leaving more than twenty thousand troops behind to defend Wuchang. Since the fighting in Jiangxi Province had reached a critical juncture, the main bulk of the forces prosecuting the Wuchang siege was transferred to Jiangxi, leaving the Fourth Army behind to maintain the siege of Wuchang. Chen Keyu now took command of the campaign. After two weeks of siege, the Beiyang Army troops trapped inside the city were desperate for food, and the civilian population was starving to death in really large numbers. In addition, there was periodic shelling, and defeated soldiers systematically robbed the city. During the forty days of siege, the people of Wuchang suffered intensely. By the end of September, through appeals and mediation on the part of the Hankou Chamber of Commerce and other charitable organisations, it was agreed that

APPENDIX III | 375

the city gates would be opened for three days to let the old, the sick, women and children to go out in search of food. One Colonel He, serving with the Third Division of the Beiyang Army, secretly made contact with the Northern Expeditionary Army and agreed to surrender. On the evening of 9 October, he opened Binyang Gate (other accounts state it was Bao'an Gate) to allow the Revolutionary Army to enter the city. The forty-day siege of Wuchang came to an end on 10 October. Liu Yuchun, commanding the defence of the city, withdrew to Snake Mountain where he fought his last stand, and he was eventually captured alive. Another senior commander, Chen Jiamo, the military governor of Hubei Province, was arrested when he attempted to flee through Hanyang Gate along with other refugees. This was the end of the Battle of Wuchang.

APPENDIX IV

Important Historical Figures in the Wuchang Campaign

CAO YUAN (1900-1926), original name Cao Xinkuan, also styled Puquan, from Shou County in Anhui Province. A student in the first graduating class of the Whampoa Military Academy. He was admitted to Wuhu Anhui Public Vocational College in the autumn of 1921 and was elected president of the student union. In the autumn of 1922, he dropped out of college and went to Shanghai where he audited classes at Shanghai University. He was admitted to Whampoa Military Academy in the spring of 1924 in the third group of the first graduating class; in the same year, he joined the Chinese Communist Party. After graduation, he was appointed as commander of a regiment of students from the Whampoa Military Academy and Party representative, with the rank of lieutenant. He participated in the First Eastern Expedition, the Second Eastern Expedition and the pacification of the Yang Liu rebellion. In August 1925, he was appointed as lieutenant colonel commanding the First Battalion of the Ninth Regiment of the Third Division of the First National Revolutionary Army. At this time, he was stationed in the Chaoshan region. During the Northern Expedition of 1926, he was commander of the First Battalion of Ye Ting's Independent Regiment of the Fourth Army of the National Revolutionary Army and participated in the Battles of Tingsi Bridge and Hesheng Bridge. On 5 September of the same year, he headed the attack team assaulting the city walls in the Battle of Wuchang, where he was killed in action.

CHEN Dingyi (1905-1926), also known as Chen Xuehao, a native of Yijiadun, Qiaokou, in the city of Wuhan. In the autumn of 1923, he entered the Provincial No. 1 Normal College and at the same time joined the Association of Progressive Students. He also became a member of the Hubei People's Association, a progressive student group in the college. He later became one of the leaders of the association and joined the Kuomintang in the same year. He also participated in the formation of a group to organise reform of the corrupt educational system, for which he was expelled. Later, in the face of public anger, the college was forced to restore his student status, and Chen and his classmates took advantage of the situation to mobilise students to remove the reactionary dean. In the autumn of 1924, he was appointed as chairman of the Hubei Students' Federation. When a warrant for his arrest was issued by the warlord Xiao Yaonan (1877-1926), he was hidden from the police by other progressive teachers and students. He adopted the name of Chen Dingyi at this time; since the real Chen Dingyi was a student who had dropped out of college. Following the Shanghai Massacre in 1925, he joined the Chinese Communist Party. In June, the Hubei provincial division of the Kuomintang was established, and he was elected as a member of the Supervisory Committee. In August, as a representative of the Hubei Students' Federation, he went to Beijing to attend the Congress of the National Students' Association. Subsequently, he played a leading role in the anti-Wu Peifu demonstration in Wuhan that took place on 25 November 1925. On 27 December, he was elected the first executive member of the Hankou Special Municipality branch of the Kuomintang, and he was also placed in charge of party organisation. In January of the following year, he attended the Hanyang Workers' Congress and was arrested because a blackleg informed against him. He was released in February because he refused to confess, in spite of being tortured. In May, he organised strikes at the Anglo-American Cigarette Factory in Qiaokou and spinning works in Tai'an and Shenxin. In July, the National Revolutionary Army launched their Northern Expedition. Chen Dingyi was ordered to join Ding Juequn (1899-1978) in a mission to instigate a rebellion among the warlords' forces. On 13 August, he was betrayed and arrested, which led to his execution in Wuchang.

CHEN Jiamo (dates unknown), styled Xianting. A native of the city of Renqiu in Hebei Province. He was married to the niece of Feng Guozhang (1859-1919), the founder of the Zhili clique. After graduating from the Baoding Military Academy, he served under Cao Kun (1862-1938), a situation caused by discord between husband and wife. During the Wuchang Campaign, he was the governor of Hubei Province and major general in command of the Twenty-fifth Division. After the city of Wuchang fell, he was captured alive. He was released in 1928 and died in Tianjin during the Anti-Japanese War.

DENG Yanda (1895-1931), styled Zesheng. A native of Yonghu Township, Huiyang County, Guangdong Province. He entered the Guangdong Military Primary School in 1909 and participated in the 1911 Revolution. Later, he studied military science at the Guangdong Military School, the Second Wuchang Military Preparatory School and the Baoding Military Academy. He became interested in the study of economics, as well as political and social sciences. In 1920, Sun Yat-sen ordered Deng Keng to establish the First Division of the Cantonese Army. Deng Yanda was appointed as the division's staff officer and head of the Independent Infantry Battalion, and he became an active follower of Sun Yat-sen. In 1925, he was appointed as director of the Centre for General Education at the Whampoa Military Academy. In January 1926, he was elected as an executive member at the Second National Congress of the Kuomintang. In July of the same year, he was appointed director of the Department of Political Affairs of the National Revolutionary Army and participated in the Northern Expedition, directing the attack on Wuchang. He was elected by the Third Plenary Session of the Second Central Committee of the Kuomintang as an executive member of the Central Committee, a member of the Political Committee of the Central Committee, a member of the Central Military Commission and as minister of the Ministry of Peasant Affairs. After the 12 April split between the Communist Party and the Kuomintang (hitherto a single political bloc), he strongly supported the Eastern Expedition against Chiang Kai-shek. In 1927, he went into exile in Europe. On 1 November, following a meeting in Moscow with Song Qingling (1893-1981, Sun Yat-sen's widow) and others, they jointly issued the Declaration on the Revolutionary People of China and the World, declaring that they had inherited the legacy of Sun Yat-sen and would continue the struggle against imperialism and feudalism.

Deng Yanda returned to China in May 1930. In August, the Chinese Revolutionary Party, which had been established in 1927, was reorganised as the Provisional Action Committee of the Chinese Nationalist Party, whereupon he served as the director-general of the Central Committee in an attempt to establish a third political party. On 1 September, he founded a new journal, *Revolutionary Action*, of which he was also the chief editor; this advocated the establishment of a democratic government focusing on improving the lives of peasants and workers in China, and it held to an anti-imperialist, anti-feudalism and anti-Chiang Kai-shek line. In November, he established the Whampoa Revolutionary Students' Association in Shanghai, which made contact with former students and tried to instigate a mutiny to oust Chiang Kai-shek from power. While actively planning operations to remove Chiang Kai-shek, he was betrayed and arrested on 19 August 1931. On 29 November of that year, he was secretly killed on the orders of Chiang Kai-shek at Shazigang outside Qilin Gate to the city of Nanjing.

GUO Moruo (1892-1978), originally known as Guo Kaizhen, styled Dingtang, with the baby name Wenbao, and entitled Shangwu. A native of Shawan Hamlet, Guan'e Township, Leshan City, Sichuan Province. During the course of his career, he wrote under various pen names: Guo Moruo, Mai Ke'ang, Guo Dingtang, Shi Tuo, Gao Ruhong, Yang Yizhi and so on. He was a famous modern Chinese writer, poet, playwright, archaeologist, philosopher, philologist, historian, calligrapher and scholar, not to mention a renowned revolutionary and social activist, with a towering reputation at home and abroad. In 1926, Guo Moruo participated in the Northern Expedition and became deputy director of the Department of Political Affairs of the National Revolutionary Army. After Chiang Kai-shek purged the communist members of the Kuomintang in 1927, he participated in the Nanchang Uprising led by the Chinese Communist Party. In February 1928, he was declared a wanted man by the Kuomintang government and went into exile in Japan, devoting himself to the study of ancient Chinese history. After the outbreak of the Anti-Japanese War in 1937, he returned to China as the third director of the Department of Political Affairs of the Military Commission and later became the director of the Cultural Work Committee, uniting progressive cultural elements to engage in anti-Japanese campaigns and the national salvation movement. After 1946, he stood at the forefront of the movement for democracy in China and formed a revolutionary vanguard in cultural circles within Kuomintang-held areas. After the founding of the People's Republic of China, he was elected chairman of the All-China Federation of Literature and Art Circles, vice premier of the State Council, director of the Committee on Culture and Education, president of the Chinese Academy of Sciences, vice chairman of the Standing Committee of the National People's Congress, and a member of the Ninth, Tenth and Eleventh Central Committees of the Chinese Communist Party. On 12 June 1978, he died in Beijing at the age of eighty-six.

JI Defu (dates unknown), an interpreter and communist who worked for a Russian adviser to the Department of Political Affairs of the Northern Expeditionary Army. He was about twenty-six years old at the time of his death. Other circumstances of his life are unknown.

LIU Yuchun (d. 1932), styled Tieshan. A native of Yutian County in Hebei Province. Towards the end of the reign of the Guangxu Emperor (r. 1875-1908), he joined the army. His unit enabled him to study at the Jiangwu School in Manchuria. After graduation, he was assigned to the Eighth Division of the Beiyang Army. He rose from corporal to lieutenant colonel and then brigadier general in the Eighth Division of the Beiyang Army. During the Battle of Wuchang, he was in overall command of the defence of the city. On 10 October 1926, he was captured at Garden Hill in Wuchang. He was court-martialled for the crimes committed during the siege but was found not guilty because it was impossible to prove personal responsibility. Later, he settled in Tianjin, where he died in May 1932.

. . .

LIU Zuolong (1874-1936), entitled Hansan. Also known as Liu Wanqing. A native of Tianmen County, Hubei Province. After the abolition of the imperial examination system in the late Qing dynasty, he joined the New Army, where he served under Li Yuanhong (1864-1928). He received a scholarship to study at the Military High School and the Jiangbian College, and after graduation he returned to serve under Li Yuanhong. After the Wuchang Uprising in the Xinhai Revolution of 1911, he was promoted to the rank of brigadier general commanding the Fourth Brigade of the Hubei Army. For many years he was stationed with the garrison in Yangxia. Later, he was appointed governor of Hubei Province and commanded the forces defending Hanyang. During the Northern Expedition, the Revolutionary Party brought about a mutiny in Hanyang, which led to a general uprising. Liu Zuolong was arrested for illegally executing Geng Dan, his deputy. After his release, he resided in rented accommodation within the Japanese Concession at Hankou.

WU Peifu (1874-1939), styled Ziyu. He was born in Wujia Village, Beigou Township, Penglai County, Shandong Province, though his family traced their ancestry back to the city of Changzhou in Jiangsu Province (Yanling County). He graduated from the Baoding Army Academy, and he joined the Huai Army in 1898. In 1906, he was appointed as captain in the division of the Beiyang Army commanded by Cao Kun, who came to value him highly. Later, he was promoted to brigadier general. When protests began over Yuan Shikai's attempts to establish himself as emperor, he led a battalion into Sichuan to block the Yunnan Protection Army led by Cai E (1882-1916). In July 1917, he led the vanguard of the western branch of the Anti-Imperial Army and participated in the campaign against Zhang Xun's (1854-1923) attempted restoration of the Qing dynasty. In the same year, Sun Yat-sen formed a military government. In December 1919, the warlord Feng Guozhang, founder of the Zhili clique, died of illness. Together with Cao Kun, Wu Peifu succeeded him as a Zhili clique warlord. In July 1926, the National Revolutionary Army appointed Chiang Kai-shek as generalissimo and swore an oath to undertake the Northern

Expedition. Wu Peifu, occupying the provinces of Hunan and Hubei, became the prime target of the Northern Expeditionary Army. After the battles of Tingsi Bridge, Hesheng Bridge and Wuchang, he lost control of Hunan and Hubei and fled to Sichuan. It was not until the spring of 1931 that Chiang Kai-shek allowed him to leave Sichuan. In the autumn of the same year, he settled in Peiping, occupying a large mansion in the Shijinhuayuan hutong presented to him by Zhang Xueliang. He also received a four thousand yuan monthly stipend from Zhang Xueliang. In 1939, due to a dental infection, he was running a high fever. In December, at the age of sixty-five, he was murdered by a Japanese dentist. The Kuomintang government posthumously appointed him to the rank of field marshal.

YE Ting (1896-1946), originally named Ye Xun, was a native of Heshui Township under the administration of the city of Xingning in Guangdong Province, though he was actually born in Zhoutian Village, Huiyang County, Guangdong Province. He was educated at the Guangdong Army Primary School, the Second Preparatory School of the Wuchang Army and the Baoding Military Officer School. In 1919, he served as an officer cadet in the Guangdong Army and joined the Kuomintang in the same year. In 1921, he was appointed lieutenant colonel, commanding the Second Battalion of the Guard Regiment serving Sun Yat-sen, grand marshal of the Army and Navy. In 1924, he went to the Soviet Union to study at the Communist University of the Toilers of the East in Moscow and the Chinese class at the Red Army Academy. In the same year, he joined the Chinese Communist Party and moved away from the Three Principles of the People to become a staunch believer in communism. After returning to China in 1925, he was appointed as colonel commanding the Thirty-sixth Regiment of the Twelfth Division of the Fourth National Revolutionary Army, and he took command of his Independent Regiment. He followed Major General Zhang Fakui (1896-1980), the commander of the Twelfth Division of the Fourth Army, on the march into Hubei Province and participated in the battles of Tingsi Bridge, Hesheng Bridge and Wuchang. He was proclaimed "a famous general of the

Northern Expedition", and the Fourth Army became known as the Iron Army. After the Northern Expeditionary Army occupied Wuhan, the army expanded on a large scale, and Ye Ting was promoted to the rank of major general commanding the Twenty-fourth Division of the Eleventh Army. After the Nanchang Uprising began, he served as general commanding the Eleventh Army, composed from former enemy units. In December 1927, he sneaked into Guangzhou and played a leading role in the Guangzhou Uprising, where he acted as commander-in-chief of the Red Guard of the Soviet of Workers, Soldiers and Peasants. After the uprising was crushed, he was severely criticised by the Comintern, broke away from the Party and went into exile in Europe, before travelling to Macao, where he lived in seclusion. In 1934, he joined the Chinese People's Anti-Japanese Revolutionary Alliance, organised by Li Jishen (1885-1959) and Chen Mingshu (1889-1965). After the outbreak of the War of Resistance, Ye Ting was appointed as general, in command of the New Fourth Army. In January 1941, during the Southern Anhui Incident, when the Kuomintang turned on their communist allies, to the shock of both China and foreign countries, he led his troops to break through the siege. They fought for eight days and nights, suffering appalling casualties. He was arrested when he went to negotiate with the Kuomintang Army. He was imprisoned first at Shangrao in Jiangxi Province, then at Enshi in Hubei Province, and then at Guilin in Guangxi Province, before he was finally moved to the concentration camp maintained by the Sino-American Special Technical Cooperative Organisation in Chongqing. On 4 March 1946, following representations from various quarters, Ye Ting was released from captivity. On 8 April, the plane carrying Ye Ting from Chongqing to Yan'an crashed in mysterious circumstances near Heicha Mountain in Xingxian County, Shanxi Province, and he was killed instantly.

APPENDIX V

Battle Hymn of the Northern Expeditionary Army

Hail to our warriors! Listen to my prayer! The people are in pain, they are suffering.
Bandits and warlords torment them, imperialism ruins them.
To save the nation and the people, our army is rising.
Our founder's dying wish shines like the sun.
We will free the people from these warlords, stop the murderous chieftains' killing,
We will restore equality and reassert our freedoms.
Hail to our warriors! Advance for the people! Loyalty to the country will keep us going.
Implementing our doctrines, sacrificing our individuality,
Our heart and blood, our revolutionary spirit we will be devoting.
Hail to our warriors! United as one! No humiliation, no hardship will turn us back,
Do not begrudge your death, no life is more deserving,
Better to die as a hero than live as a slave.
Hail to our warriors! Let us defend this country. Hail to our warriors! People need protecting.
Keep disciplined, obey orders, for only with discipline and order can we win.
Your survival is a private matter, but discipline is your public doing,
Your survival does not matter, but obeying orders is crucial.
Hail to our warriors! Unite your spirits, from beginning to end, to each other be loving.

Don't be afraid of strong enemies, don't
  underestimate fools,
Let us all join together, as if in the same boat
  we are sailing.
If we don't kill the thieves, will they ever be
  willing to stop?
We cannot coexist, and they do not believe in
  reforming.
If I do not make this sacrifice, the country will
  be destroyed,
If I do not shed my blood, the people will ever
  need pacifying.
If my country is ruined, how can my family
  survive?
If the people go unpacified, how can I carry on
  living?
Hail to our warriors! You are loyal to the Three
  Principles, to the soul of revolution.
Hail to our warriors! If the revolution fails, to
  our warriors this will be shaming.
Hail to our warriors! We are as brothers, living
  together and dying together.
Life and death will be decided now. Military
  law is impartial, for those who now are
  failing.

APPENDIX VI

Soldiers of the National Revolutionary Army (Fourth Army) Killed in Action in the Wuchang Campaign

This list of casualties from the Fourth Army in the Wuchang Campaign is taken from the website of the Whampoa Military Academy. It is quite horrifying. Only some of those killed in battle are recorded here, but if all of them were named how many would it be?! I can't describe how I felt when I saw this list. It is quite possible that my decision to write the 'Attacking the Walls' section of *The Walls of Wuchang* was based on reading this list. However, I suspect that the names of those killed on 4 September were in fact killed on 3 September. This is because in the historical books and memoirs that survive, there is no mention of any fighting taking place on the fourth. The two biggest battles in the attack on Wuchang, in which countless people were killed, took place on 3 and 5 September. On 1 October, most of the dead came from the fighting when the enemy broke the siege at Tongxiang Gate and destroyed the tunnels dug by the Northern Expeditionary Army.

During the Northern Expedition of 1926, soldiers from the Second Division of the First Army, the Fourth Army, the Seventh Army and the Eighth Army are known to have participated in the attack on the city of Wuchang. However, since casualty lists are very incomplete, the vast majority of the dead listed below are those from the Fourth Army.

KILLED IN ACTION ON 3 SEPTEMBER 1926

- WANG Zhen from Daye in Hubei Province. Soldier in the First Army.

KILLED IN ACTION ON 4 SEPTEMBER 1926

- AN Huanzhang from Guangdong Province. Lance corporal in the Fourth Army.

- CHEN Chunxiong from Hunan Province. Corporal in the Fourth Army.
- CHEN Defa from Jianghua County in Hunan Province. Private first class in the Fourth Army.
- CHEN Desheng from Hunan Province.
- CHEN Jianxun from Guangxi Province.
- CHEN Wenping from Guangxi Province.
- CHEN Yunfeng from Xingning in Guangdong Province. Captain in the Fourth Army.
- DONG Chengyou from Guangdong Province. Private first class in the Fourth Army.
- DUAN Jumao from Chaling County in Hunan Province.
- FAN Deqing from Yongzhou in Hunan Province. Private second class in the Fourth Army.
- FAN Desheng from Wuling County in Hunan Province. Military nurse holding the rank of corporal in the Fourth Army.
- GAO Guilin from Wuling County in Hunan Province. Private first class in the Fourth Army.
- GU Teyuan from Chaling County in Hunan Province. Private second class in the Fourth Army.
- HAN Shengchu from Qinzhou in Guangdong Province.
- HE Debiao from Guangxi Province.
- HUANG Chunshan from Hubei Province. Lance corporal in the Fourth Army.
- HUANG Ruiyuan from Guangdong Province. Corporal in the Fourth Army.
- HUANG Sicheng from Guangdong Province. Corporal in the Fourth Army.
- HUANG Shunting from Guangxi Province. Private first class in the Fourth Army.
- HUANG Zhirong from Guangxi Province. Private first class in the Fourth Army.
- JIANG Baoqing from Wuling County in Hunan Province. Private first class in the Fourth Army.
- JIANG Ying from Guangdong Province. Corporal in the Fourth Army.
- JIANG Yisheng from Jiangxi Province.

- JIANG Zhilan from Hunan Province. Private first class in the Fourth Army.
- LI Binghu from Hengshan County in Hunan Province. Lance corporal in the Fourth Army.
- LI Hongchun from Wuling County in Hunan Province. Private first class in the Fourth Army.
- LI Shunhua from Jianghua County in Hunan Province. Private second class in the Fourth Army.
- LI Wenliang from Hunan Province. Private second class in the Fourth Army.
- LI Xiangxi from Guangdong Province. Corporal in the Fourth Army.
- LI Xiong from Hunan Province.
- LI Zhangkui from Chuzhou in Anhui Province. Private first class in the Fourth Army.
- LI Zhengcai from Guangxi Province. Private first class in the Fourth Army.
- LI Zhengshan from Guangxi Province.
- LI Zhiguang from Hunan Province. Corporal in the Fourth Army.
- LIANG Guifu from Hunan Province.
- LIANG Quansheng from Guangdong Province. Lance corporal in the Fourth Army.
- LIN Hongsheng from Guangxi Province.
- LIU Desheng from Guangdong Province.
- LIU Yonghe from Hunan Province.
- LU Shengbiao from Guangxi Province. Lance corporal in the Fourth Army.
- LU Wenhua from Xinghua in Jiangsu Province. Private second class in the Fourth Army.
- LU Xin from Guangdong Province. Corporal in the Fourth Army.
- LUO Sheng from Guangdong Province. Private first class in the Fourth Army.
- LUO Yudong from Jiangxi Province. Lieutenant in the Fourth Army.
- LUO Yunsong from Guangxi Province. Private first class in the Fourth Army.

- LUO Zuqi from Wuling County in Hunan Province. Private second class in the Fourth Army.
- MO Biao from Guangdong Province.
- MO Deguang from Guiping in Guangxi Province. Private first class in the Fourth Army.
- MO Zhenting from Guangxi Province. Lance corporal in the Fourth Army.
- PAN Zhensheng from Guangxi Province. Private second class in the Fourth Army.
- PEI Hanhua from Jiangxi Province.
- PEI Zhenchu from Wuling County in Hunan Province. Military nurse holding the rank of corporal in the Fourth Army.
- QIN Long from Guangdong Province. Corporal in the Fourth Army.
- QIN Tai from Guangxi Province.
- QUAN Gouxin from Guangxi Province. Private first class in the Fourth Army.
- RUAN Lifu from Guangxi Province.
- SHEN Mingqing from Hunan Province. Private first class in the Fourth Army.
- SHEN Yifa from Chaling County in Hunan Province. Private first class in the Fourth Army.
- SHENG Zikun from Guangxi Province. Corporal in the Fourth Army.
- SONG Jiasheng from Guangdong Province.
- SU Quanwu from Guangxi Province. Sergeant in the Fourth Army.
- SUN Li from Hunan Province.
- SUN Youfa. Soldier in the Fourth Army.
- TANG Fengbiao from Guangxi Province.
- TANG Zhunan from Hunan Province. Private second class in the Fourth Army.
- TU Deyu from Hunan Province. Private first class in the Fourth Army.
- WANG Yingbiao from Xinfeng County in Jiangxi Province. Lance corporal in the Fourth Army.

- WANG Zitong from Pingxiang in Jiangxi Province. Private second class in the Fourth Army.
- WEI Ruilin from Guangxi Province.
- WU Gui from Guangdong Province. Quartermaster with the Fourth Army.
- WU Shengcai from Guangdong Province. Military nurse serving with the Fourth Army.
- XIAO Guibin from Hunan Province. Private second class in the Fourth Army.
- XIE Baolin from Hunan. Soldier in the Fourth Army.
- XIONG Degui from Hunan Province. Private second class in the Fourth Army.
- XU Jinbiao from Hunan Province. Private second class in the Fourth Army.
- XUE Deli from Guangxi Province. Corporal in the Fourth Army.
- YANG Desheng from Qingjiang in Jiangsu Province. Private first class in the Fourth Army.
- YANG Duanting from Hunan Province.
- YANG Yuqing from Jiangxi Province.
- YI Nan from Guangdong Province.
- YU Huiyuan from Hunan Province. Private second class in the Fourth Army.
- ZENG Jisheng from Hunan Province.
- ZHANG Qingyuan from Guangdong Province. Bugler holding the rank of corporal in the Fourth Army.
- ZHANG Weiying from Guangxi Province. Lance corporal in the Fourth Army.
- ZHANG Wensong from Guangdong Province. Private first class in the Fourth Army.
- ZHANG Xiuyun from Wuling County in Hunan Province. Military nurse holding the rank of corporal in the Fourth Army.
- ZHENG Guiying from Guangxi Province.
- ZHENG Hongyuan from Guangdong Province.
- ZHENG Ting from Hunan Province. Lance corporal in the Fourth Army.

APPENDIX VI | 391

- ZHONG Zhengqin from Guangdong Province. Private first class in the Fourth Army.
- ZHOU Xingyuan from Hunan Province.
- ZHOU Zhenting from Guangdong Province. Private first class in the Fourth Army.
- ZHU Guilin from Hunan Province. Bugler in the Fourth Army.

KILLED IN ACTION ON 5 SEPTEMBER 1926

- CAI Wenduo from Xiangshan County in Guangdong Province. Maintenance worker with the Independent Regiment of the Fourth Army.
- CAO Yuan from Shou County in Anhui Province. Battalion commander in the Independent Regiment of the Fourth Army.
- CHEN Gui from Yunfu in Guangdong Province. Soldier in the Independent Regiment of the Fourth Army.
- CHEN Shengjie from Shunde County in Guangdong Province. Soldier in the Independent Regiment of the Fourth Army.
- CHEN Siguo. Soldier in the Independent Regiment of the Fourth Army.
- CHEN Zihe from Lipu County in Guangxi Province. Soldier in the Independent Regiment of the Fourth Army.
- DAI Zhishun from Mengshan County in Guangxi Province. Soldier in the Independent Regiment of the Fourth Army.
- DENG Fangzhong from Maoming in Guangdong Province. Adjutant in the Fourth Army.
- FENG Nengzhe. Soldier in the Independent Regiment of the Fourth Army.
- FU Ba from Nanfeng County in Hunan Province. Squad leader in the Independent Regiment of the Fourth Army.
- GAO Chao from Xishui County in Hubei Province. Company commander in the Independent Regiment of

- the Fourth Army.
- GUO Changsheng from Xiaogang in Hunan Province. Private second class in the Independent Regiment of the Fourth Army.
- HE Changhua. Soldier in the Independent Regiment of the Fourth Army.
- HE Ruibo from Wuzhou in Guangxi Province. Private second class in the Fourth Army.
- HE Shuguang from Deqing County in Guangdong Province. Platoon commander in the Independent Regiment of the Fourth Army.
- HONG Quhuo. Soldier in the Independent Regiment of the Fourth Army.
- HU Guibiao from Ningyuan County in Hunan Province. Private first class in the Fourth Army.
- HUANG Zhenxiang. Soldier in the Independent Regiment of the Fourth Army.
- JIA Deqing from Yongzhou in Hunan Province. Squad leader in the Independent Regiment of the Fourth Army.
- JIANG Wanli. Soldier in the Independent Regiment of the Fourth Army.
- JIANG Yiqing from Xing'an County in Guangxi Province. Mess cook with the Independent Regiment of the Fourth Army.
- JIANG Zhongsheng. Soldier in the Independent Regiment of the Fourth Army.
- LAI Shengchu from Jiangxi Province. Captain of the Fourth Army stretcher bearers.
- LI Daqian. Soldier in the Independent Regiment of the Fourth Army.
- LI Darong. Soldier in the Independent Regiment of the Fourth Army.
- LI Dongjie from Yongxing County in Hunan Province. Soldier in the Independent Regiment of the Fourth Army.
- LI Donglin from Ningxiang County in Hunan Province. Private second class in the Independent Regiment of the Fourth Army.

- LI Guiqing. Soldier in the Independent Regiment of the Fourth Army.
- LI Jishan from Hunan Province. Section commander in the Independent Regiment of the Fourth Army.
- LI Liangsheng from Qingzhou in Hunan Province. Soldier in the Independent Regiment of the Fourth Army.
- LI Qiming. Squad leader in the Independent Regiment of the Fourth Army.
- LI Shengbiao from Pingnan County in Guangxi Province. Private second class in the Independent Regiment of the Fourth Army.
- LI Youming. Soldier in the Independent Regiment of the Fourth Army.
- LI Yukai from Longzhou County in Guangxi Province. Soldier in the Independent Regiment of the Fourth Army.
- LI Yunbiao from Shaozhou in Guangdong Province. Platoon commander in the Independent Regiment of the Fourth Army.
- LI Zhongshi from Xinning County in Hunan Province. Squad leader in the Independent Regiment of the Fourth Army.
- LI Zhougui from Qingzhou in Hunan Province. Soldier in the Independent Regiment of the Fourth Army.
- LIU Hanqing from Yongzhou in Hunan Province. Squad leader in the Independent Regiment of the Fourth Army.
- LIU Zhaozhang from Guilin in Guangxi Province. Private first class in the Independent Regiment of the Fourth Army.
- LIU Zhengbao. Bugler in the Independent Regiment of the Fourth Army.
- LIU Zhijia from Guangdong Province. Military nurse with the Independent Regiment of the Fourth Army.
- LONG Hu. Soldier in the Independent Regiment of the Fourth Army.
- LUO Guangjie. Soldier in the Independent Regiment of the Fourth Army.

- MIN Guiting from Xinghua in Hunan Province. Soldier in the Independent Regiment of the Fourth Army.
- MO Qibiao from Yunan County in Guangdong Province. Company commander in the Independent Regiment of the Fourth Army.
- MO Ruwu. Soldier in the Independent Regiment of the Fourth Army.
- MO Zhida. Soldier in the Independent Regiment of the Fourth Army.
- OU Guiting from Guilin in Guangxi Province. Private second class in the Independent Regiment of the Fourth Army.
- OU Yang from Wuzhou in Guangxi Province. Deputy platoon commander in the Independent Regiment of the Fourth Army.
- OUYANG Wei. Soldier in the Independent Regiment of the Fourth Army.
- PENG Dongsheng. Soldier in the Independent Regiment of the Fourth Army.
- PENG Bowen from Qiyang County in Hunan Province. Private second class in the Fourth Army.
- QIN Hanqi from Rong County in Guangxi Province. Platoon commander in the Independent Regiment of the Fourth Army.
- SU Yiyang from Quanzhou County in Guangxi Province. Soldier in the Independent Regiment of the Fourth Army.
- TAN Mingcai from Heng County in Guangxi Province. Soldier in the Independent Regiment of the Fourth Army.
- TAN Sheng. Soldier in the Independent Regiment of the Fourth Army.
- TAN Yunsheng. Soldier in the Independent Regiment of the Fourth Army.
- TANG Laiqiao from Yongzhou in Hunan Province. Private second class in the Independent Regiment of the Fourth Army.

APPENDIX VI | 395

- TAO Gouwan. Soldier in the Independent Regiment of the Fourth Army.
- TU Yimin. Soldier in the Independent Regiment of the Fourth Army.
- WANG Jianfei from Quanzhou County in Hunan Province. Soldier in the Independent Regiment of the Fourth Army.
- WANG Junguo. Private second class in the Independent Regiment of the Fourth Army.
- WANG Xianlu from Leping in Guangxi Province. Soldier in the Independent Regiment of the Fourth Army.
- WANG Zhongquan from Yangshuo County in Guangxi Province. Soldier in the Independent Regiment of the Fourth Army.
- WEI Shubin from Guiping in Guangxi Province. Soldier in the Independent Regiment of the Fourth Army.
- WEI Zhenming. Soldier in the Independent Regiment of the Fourth Army.
- WU Tonglu from Quanzhou County in Guangxi Province. Corporal in the Fourth Army.
- WU Zhengfang. Soldier in the Independent Regiment of the Fourth Army.
- WU Zongzuo from Hepu County in Guangdong Province. Lieutenant in the Fourth Army.
- XIONG Kengquan from Wanzai County in Jiangxi Province. Private second class in the Fourth Army.
- XIONG Yide. Soldier in the Independent Regiment of the Fourth Army.
- XU Yungui from Quanzhou County in Guangxi Province. Soldier in the Independent Regiment of the Fourth Army.
- XUE Huirong from Yulin in Guangxi Province. Private first class in the Fourth Army.
- YANG Debiao from Longteng County in Guangxi Province. Soldier in the Independent Regiment of the Fourth Army.
- YANG Disheng. Soldier in the Independent Regiment of the Fourth Army.

- YANG Yonghe. Soldier in the Independent Regiment of the Fourth Army.
- YE Sheng. Soldier in the Independent Regiment of the Fourth Army.
- YI Xiguo. Soldier in the Independent Regiment of the Fourth Army.
- ZENG Xiangfeng from Qiyang County in Hunan Province. Soldier in the Independent Regiment of the Fourth Army.
- ZENG Xiebin. Soldier in the Independent Regiment of the Fourth Army.
- ZHAN Shuping. Soldier in the Independent Regiment of the Fourth Army.
- ZHANG Zhongde from Xing'an County in Guangxi Province. Soldier in the Independent Regiment of the Fourth Army.
- ZHAO Xiang. Soldier in the Independent Regiment of the Fourth Army.
- ZHENG Shisheng from Yangshuo County in Guangxi Province. Soldier in the Independent Regiment of the Fourth Army.
- ZHOU Laiqing. Soldier in the Independent Regiment of the Fourth Army.
- ZHOU Sen from Kaiping County in Guangdong Province. Soldier in the Independent Regiment of the Fourth Army.

KILLED IN ACTION ON 1 OCTOBER 1926

- AI Yulin. Soldier in the Independent Regiment of the Fourth Army.
- BEI Yunsheng. Soldier in the Independent Regiment of the Fourth Army.
- CAO Xuewu. Soldier in the Independent Regiment of the Fourth Army.
- CHEN Changcai from Liling in Hunan Province. Deputy commander of the reconnaissance unit in the

APPENDIX VI | 397

Independent Regiment of the Fourth Army.
- CHEN Fangyuan. Soldier in the Independent Regiment of the Fourth Army.
- CHEN Fenggui. Sergeant in the Independent Regiment of the Fourth Army.
- CHEN Fuzhi. Soldier in the Independent Regiment of the Fourth Army.
- CHEN Hanqing. Soldier in the Independent Regiment of the Fourth Army.
- CHEN Kuihu from Xiangxiang in Hunan Province. Company commander in the Independent Regiment of the Fourth Army.
- CHEN Songfu. Bugler in the Independent Regiment of the Fourth Army.
- CHEN Xin. Soldier in the Independent Regiment of the Fourth Army.
- CHEN Ziqing. Runner for the Independent Regiment of the Fourth Army.
- CHENG Jinguo. Soldier in the Independent Regiment of the Fourth Army.
- CUI Haibo. Soldier in the Independent Regiment of the Fourth Army.
- DENG Xinsan. Soldier in the Independent Regiment of the Fourth Army.
- DENG Yongsheng. Private first class in the Independent Regiment of the Fourth Army.
- GUO Fei. Soldier in the Independent Regiment of the Fourth Army.
- HU Yucheng. Soldier in the Independent Regiment of the Fourth Army.
- HUANG Desheng from Liuyang in Hunan Province. Soldier in the Independent Regiment of the Fourth Army.
- JIANG Biaoyuan from Chaozhou in Guangdong Province. Platoon commander in the Independent Regiment of the Fourth Army.
- JIANG Bin from Qiyang County in Hunan Province. Squad leader in the Independent Regiment of the Fourth

Army.
- LAI Yuanliang from Ba County in Sichuan Province. Deputy battalion commander in the Independent Regiment of the Fourth Army.
- LI Dehua. Soldier in the Independent Regiment of the Fourth Army.
- LI Fuliang. Soldier in the Independent Regiment of the Fourth Army.
- LI Guichu from Liuyang in Hunan Province. Soldier in the Independent Regiment of the Fourth Army.
- LI Haiqing from Xiangyin County in Hunan Province. Company commander in the Independent Regiment of the Fourth Army.
- LI Jimin. Soldier in the Independent Regiment of the Fourth Army.
- LIANG Haiguo. Soldier in the Independent Regiment of the Fourth Army.
- LING Daode from Liuyang in Hunan Province. Soldier in the Independent Regiment of the Fourth Army.
- LIU Longsheng. Soldier in the Independent Regiment of the Fourth Army.
- LIU Manzai. Soldier in the Independent Regiment of the Fourth Army.
- LIU Ruichu. Soldier in the Independent Regiment of the Fourth Army.
- LIU Youxuan. Soldier in the Independent Regiment of the Fourth Army.
- LU Boxian. Soldier in the Independent Regiment of the Fourth Army.
- LUO Jinliang. Soldier in the Independent Regiment of the Fourth Army.
- LUO Qingbiao. Soldier in the Independent Regiment of the Fourth Army.
- LU Ceguo. Soldier in the Independent Regiment of the Fourth Army.
- MAO Aitang from Xiangtan in Hunan Province. Squad leader in the Independent Regiment of the Fourth Army.

- MAO Fuguo. Soldier in the Independent Regiment of the Fourth Army.
- MENG Wenbiao. Soldier in the Independent Regiment of the Fourth Army.
- OU Guangguo. Soldier in the Independent Regiment of the Fourth Army.
- OUYANG Long. Soldier in the Independent Regiment of the Fourth Army.
- QIU Changsheng. Soldier in the Independent Regiment of the Fourth Army.
- SUN Weizhong. Soldier in the Independent Regiment of the Fourth Army.
- SHI Yaoqing. Soldier in the Independent Regiment of the Fourth Army.
- SUN Youqing. Soldier in the Independent Regiment of the Fourth Army.
- TAN Feiting. Soldier in the Independent Regiment of the Fourth Army.
- TAN Haozhen. Soldier in the Independent Regiment of the Fourth Army.
- TAN Yousheng from Liling in Hunan Province. Soldier in the Independent Regiment of the Fourth Army.
- TANG Ganlin from Yongzhou County in Hunan Province. Captain in charge of the communications division in the Independent Regiment of the Fourth Army.
- TANG Guixing. Soldier in the Independent Regiment of the Fourth Army.
- TAO Jiunan from Liuyang in Hunan Province. Soldier in the Independent Regiment of the Fourth Army.
- TIAN Yubiao. Soldier in the Independent Regiment of the Fourth Army.
- TIAN Yulin. Soldier in the Independent Regiment of the Fourth Army.
- WANG Deqing. Soldier in the Independent Regiment of the Fourth Army.
- WANG Peihuang from Jiangxi Province. Officer cadet in the Independent Regiment of the Fourth Army.

- WANG Pengguo. Runner for the Independent Regiment of the Fourth Army.
- WANG Qisan. Soldier in the Independent Regiment of the Fourth Army.
- WANG Shoucheng. Soldier in the Independent Regiment of the Fourth Army.
- WANG Yunan. Soldier in the Independent Regiment of the Fourth Army.
- WEI Debiao. Soldier in the Independent Regiment of the Fourth Army.
- WEN Liangcheng. Soldier in the Independent Regiment of the Fourth Army.
- WEN Yubiao. Private first class in the Independent Regiment of the Fourth Army.
- WEN Zhaozheng. Soldier in the Independent Regiment of the Fourth Army.
- XIANG Zezhou. Soldier in the Independent Regiment of the Fourth Army.
- XIE Dongcai. Soldier in the Independent Regiment of the Fourth Army.
- XIONG Guangbi from Guangxi Province. Platoon commander in the Independent Regiment of the Fourth Army.
- XU Benwan. Soldier in the Independent Regiment of the Fourth Army.
- XU Zhao from Changsha in Hunan Province. Platoon commander in the Independent Regiment of the Fourth Army.
- YANG Delin. Soldier in the Independent Regiment of the Fourth Army.
- YANG Laowu. Soldier in the Independent Regiment of the Fourth Army.
- YE Hongrong from Guangdong Province. Platoon commander in the Independent Regiment of the Fourth Army.
- YE Xingsheng. Soldier in the Independent Regiment of the Fourth Army.

- YIN Xiangnan. Soldier in the Independent Regiment of the Fourth Army.
- YOU Desheng. Soldier in the Independent Regiment of the Fourth Army.
- YOU Zhongsheng. Soldier in the Independent Regiment of the Fourth Army.
- YU Dingguo. Soldier in the Independent Regiment of the Fourth Army.
- YU Quce. Soldier in the Independent Regiment of the Fourth Army.
- YUAN Zichun from Ningxiang County in Hunan Province. Supernumerary officer in the Special Brigade of the Independent Regiment of the Fourth Army.
- ZHANG Deliang. Soldier in the Independent Regiment of the Fourth Army.
- ZHANG Yuzhen. Soldier in the Independent Regiment of the Fourth Army.
- ZHAO Guiguo. Soldier in the Independent Regiment of the Fourth Army.
- ZHAO Rongguang. Soldier in the Independent Regiment of the Fourth Army.
- ZENG Yongnian. Soldier in the Independent Regiment of the Fourth Army.
- ZHOU Guiqing. Soldier in the Independent Regiment of the Fourth Army.
- ZHOU Haiqing from Yongzhou County in Hunan Province. Platoon commander in the Independent Regiment of the Fourth Army.
- ZHOU Tiancheng. Soldier in the Independent Regiment of the Fourth Army.
- ZHOU Wenqing. Squad leader in the Independent Regiment of the Fourth Army.
- ZHOU Zhengguo from Liuyang in Hunan Province. Company commander in charge of logistics support for the Independent Regiment of the Fourth Army.
- ZUO Dechang. Soldier in the Independent Regiment of the Fourth Army.

AFTERWORD

Wuchang used to have a wall. This was something I did not know for the longest time.

I have lived in Wuhan for more than half a century. When I was a teenager, I lived in Hankou, on the north bank of the Yangtze River. I was in my thirties when I moved to the south bank, to Wuchang. I walked all over Wuchang, up and down the streets, over the mountains and down to the river, and gradually came to know it like the back of my hand. I sat on the bus and looked out at Hong Mountain and Snake Mountain, and I rode my bike through the old quarter of the city, along Yanzhi Road and out to visit the old church in Garden Hill. But I never so much as wondered whether Wuchang had ever been a walled city.

Then one day, my classmate Xia Wuquan invited me to visit some of the old buildings in the Tanhualin District of the city. Xia Wuquan is the deputy editor of *Changjiang Daily News*, and we were in the same class together in the Chinese Department of Wuhan University. After graduation, we stayed in contact because we work in related fields. They were going to do a piece about the preservation of old buildings in the city, and they wanted me to say a few words. I felt I had to respond to such an invitation. Standing in the rear courtyard of the former residence of Shi Ying (1879-1943, patriot and revolutionary), I got to see a little surviving bit of the walls of Wuchang for the first time in my life. The historian who had joined us, Mr Feng Tianyu, explained that the bricks came from the old city wall. I was a little surprised, even a little shocked. Touching those ancient bricks, I felt very emotional. It was wonderful to know that Wuchang had once been a walled city.

After that, I began to pay attention.

For quite a long time, I had been reading materials in libraries and archives and travelling through the streets and alleys of Wuhan in preparation for writing three books: *A Visit to the Old Villas of Lushan*, *The Vicissitudes of Hankou* and *The Hankou Foreign Concession*. On one occasion, I even drove out to run the entire length of Zhang Zhidong's (1837-1909) levee from end to end.

After so much reading and rushing around, my understanding of the city of Wuhan deepened. I discovered that the city I had lived in for many years has a rich and complicated history and was the scene of many thrilling events. Time has buried all this. People today live only on the surface, and they always seem to be so busy; they know nothing at all about the fascinating past of the place in which they live. That includes the siege of Wuchang in the autumn of 1926.

I have asked many people: "Do you know about the siege of Wuchang?" The answer always seems to be the same: "No." One day, I stood at Dadong Gate, looking towards Snake Mountain and the roofs of Changchun Monastery, thinking: You know everything. You witnessed those terrible scenes, and you were soaked in the blood of the dead and the dying. But you just keep silent.

I decided to write *The Walls of Wuchang* in 2006. While reading memoirs about the Battle of Wuchang, I started to write. That year was the eightieth anniversary of the end of the campaign. In October, pretty much on the anniversary of the fall of the city, I completed the first half: 'Attacking the Walls'. This was published in the magazine *Zhongshan*. Because it was too long to reprint, not many people read it at that time. This is something I regret very much.

Shortly after it was published, my second brother, who is a professor at Northeastern University, came to Wuhan for a conference and stayed with me for a few days after it was over. My brother is a keen reader. When he was a teenager, as an "educated youth" sent down to the countryside during the Cultural Revolution, he wrote novels and short comic dialogues. In those days, he was regarded as a very talented amateur writer in Hubei Province. We often joke that if he had chosen the Chinese Department in the college entrance examination, he might have made it really big in the 1980s. But my brother wanted to be a scientist, and he chose to study engineering and became an expert in his field. Although he no longer writes himself, my brother loves to read. He has read all of Gao Yang's historical novels once, and my complete set of Eryue He's novels seems to have migrated onto his bookshelves. His wife is also Wang Anyi's most devoted fan. During the two days he stayed with me, my second brother read *The Walls of Wuchang*. He said: "You write very well. I like it very much. But why didn't you write it as a full-length novel?"

In fact, from the very beginning, I had thought of this project as culminating in a novella. I was afraid I didn't know enough about the historical context, that I wouldn't be able to get the battle scenes right, and I had never really considered writing a whole novel. But my brother's suggestion was very tempting. Yeah, I thought, this would make a good novel. I can write it in my own way: I can use the context as I understand it and write the battle scenes as I imagine them. After all, fiction is not the faithful reporting of the original events; it is much more important that the author should be able to write what they imagine to have happened.

So I went back to the beginning, and reread the material again. All sorts of information about the Battle of Wuchang that I had ignored in the first instance now came floating up to the surface. Meanwhile, I began to use the internet to find more interesting details and thus discovered many things I had not previously known. While searching one database, I found a casualty list recording the names of some of the people who died in the Battle of Wuchang. This list stunned me. Looking at so many names, I decided that, come what may, I had to write this book. I wanted people to know that there were mass graves all around Dadong Gate and Xiaodong Gate, which we pass by without thinking. This land was drenched with their blood. We need to remember them, and we need to think about why they died. Our peaceful lives today were made possible by their sacrifices.

So, in 2010, I started to rewrite *The Walls of Wuchang*. This time, I decided to show the war in two independent halves. In 'Attacking the Walls' and 'Defending the Walls', you have two different perspectives, and each half offers its own view on things and records the two sides' pain and sorrow.

War exposes the good and evil in human nature. I believe that of the soldiers who enlisted in either the National Revolutionary Army or the Beiyang Army, some did it in order to eat, some wanted to fight against oppression, some were aggressive, while others were simply helpless. There were also idealists. They hoped that China would have a bright future and devoted their lives to the cause of bringing peace to this country. Their ideals might be the same, but their choices were totally different.

We should all remember these people.

In order to give readers a more thorough understanding of the Battle of Wuchang, I compiled various appendices which include supplementary historical background to the novel. After all, this happened a long time ago.

In the spring after I finished writing the novella entitled *The Ant on the Blade*, I began to work full-time on *The Walls of Wuchang*. However, things kept happening to interrupt my writing. So with all these stops and starts, I did not finish my manuscript until Chinese New Year.

I would like to thank my editor, Yang Liu, for her patience. She edited my first novel, *The Chronicle of Wuni Lake*, and she had to wait more than ten years for me to finish it. I have a great appreciation of her seriousness and professionalism. Since we first met in Lanzhou in 1983, nearly thirty years have gone by, so we really are old friends. All this time, she kept on asking me to write another full-length novel. As the years went by, nothing seemed to change for either of us: she carried on working as an editor, and I wrote fiction. In the beginning, we were young, but now we are on the verge of old age. Sometimes I feel that it is only in peacetime that it becomes possible to do the same thing in the same place all one's life and never change. Thinking about this, I would really like to thank those who laid down their lives so that we might enjoy peace and tranquillity today.

When I handed the manuscript of *The Walls of Wuchang* to Yang Liu, I said to her: "If you like it, I'm glad."

Fang Fang
Wuchang, in the spring of 2011

NOTES

CHAPTER 1

1. Chen Dingyi, also known as Chen Xuehao, was born in Hankou in 1906. He went on to study at the first teacher training college in Hubei Province. In 1924, he was chosen to be the chairman of the Hubei Provincial Student Union. Since the local warlord issued a warrant for his arrest, he changed his name to Chen Dingyi. During the Northern Expedition, he was arrested and executed by the Beiyang warlords at Huo Alley in Wuchang

CHAPTER 3

1. Cao Yuan, a native of Shou County in Anhui Province, served as a battalion commander in the Independent Regiment of the Northern Expeditionary Army. He was killed in action during the attack on Wuchang
2. The Northern Army was the term applied by the local people to the Beiyang Army. They called the Northern Expeditionary Army the Southern Army (because it came from the south) or the Revolutionary Army
3. Liu Yuchun, from Yutian in Hebei Province, was the commander of the defence of Wuchang for the Beiyang warlords

CHAPTER 4

1. CY was a contemporary acronym for members of the Communist Youth League; CPs were members of the Communist Party

CHAPTER 5

1. Long Street was the busiest commercial road in Wuchang. Today this is Liberation Avenue

CHAPTER 8

1. Ji Defu was one of the interpreters provided by the Northern Expeditionary Army for their Russian military advisers. He was shot dead within the precincts of Changchun Monastery during the Wuchang campaign

CHAPTER 19

1. Wang Zizheng was a revolutionary from Huangpi in Hubei Province. He was killed during the siege of Wuchang

CHAPTER 30

1. Liu Zuolong was a major-general in the Beiyang Army who commanded the defence of Hanyang. He defected to the Northern Expeditionary Army
2. Deng Yanda was the director of the Department of Political Affairs of the Northern Expeditionary Army

CHAPTER 32

1. Both Ziyang Lake and Dusi Lake are located inside the city of Wuchang

CHAPTER 33

1. Chen Jiamo, a native of Renqiu County in Hebei Province, was the military governor of Hubei Province at this time. During the Northern Expedition, he commanded the defence of Wuchang with Liu Yuchun

ABOUT THE AUTHOR

Fang Fang was born in Nanjing in 1955, and grew up in the city of Wuhan. She is the author of a number of novels including *The Chronicle of Wuni Lake* and *Soft Burial*. Fang Fang's novels have won numerous literary awards in China, including the National Award for Excellence in Fiction, and the Lu Xun Literary Prize. She is currently a distinguished professor at the Huazhong University of Science and Technology, and director of the Centre for Research in Contemporary Writings.

ABOUT THE TRANSLATOR

Olivia Milburn is professor of Chinese language and literature at Seoul National University. She completed her first degree in Chinese at St Hilda's College, University of Oxford, a master's in Oriental studies at Downing College, University of Cambridge, and a doctorate in classical Chinese at the School of Oriental and African Studies, University of London. She has authored several books including *Cherishing Antiquity: The Cultural Construction of an Ancient Chinese Kingdom*, *The Spring and Autumn Annals of Master Yan* and *Urbanization in Early and Medieval China: Gazetteers for the City of Suzhou*. In collaboration with Christopher Payne, she has translated two spy novels by Mai Jia, including the bestselling *Decoded*, from Chinese to English. In 2018, Milburn's translation work was recognised by the Chinese government with a Special Book Award of China, which honours contributions to bridging cultures and fostering understanding.

About **Sino**ist Books

We hope you enjoyed this story about the 1926 siege of Wuchang.

SINOIST BOOKS brings the best of Chinese fiction to English-speaking readers. We aim to create a greater understanding of Chinese culture and society, and provide an outlet for the ideas and creativity of the country's most talented authors.

To let us know what you thought of this book, or to learn more about the diverse range of exciting Chinese fiction in translation we publish, find us online. If you're as passionate about Chinese literature as we are, then we'd love to hear your thoughts!

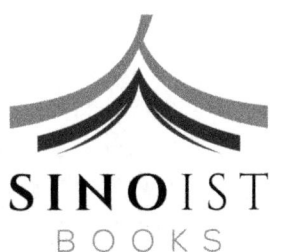

sinoistbooks.com
@sinoistbooks